PRAISE FOR *IN THE UNS*

Thomas Davis's novel *In the U..........* .....y a black fisherman community on Washington Island (near Milwaukee) in the 1850s, does what fine writing and thinking always do, blurring our trusted and assumed categories. Where is the line between imaginative fiction and historical fact? Where between prose and poetry? Whose story is this: theirs or ours?

~**J.D. Whitney**, author of *Grandma*, *Cousins*, and other books of poetry.

While putting my thoughts together to write this review, I came across a quote by Mahatma Gandhi I immediately felt encapsulated the journey and destination of Thomas Davis' compelling new novel: *The moment the slave resolves that he will no longer be a slave, his fetters fall.*

In the Unsettled Homeland of Dreams, its title taken from a Pablo Neruda poem, begins painfully, cruelly, despairingly, throwing the reader into the brutality plantation slaves were regularly subjected to. Yet, from the first encounter with fourteen-year-old Joshua, his shirt and flesh cut through, his stubbornness and resentment riled, his resilience tested from a particularly vicious whipping, we also meet the central theme of the novel: slavery might seem to succeed in owning the bodies of men, women, and children, but only because it unconscionably misjudges the power of resistance in their hearts, minds, and souls, and the risk they are willing to take for freedom and life as it is meant to be lived.

This meticulously researched historical fiction is set before the Civil War, based on actual people and events. Originally, as is noted at the back end of the novel, it was a sonnet sequence. Thankfully, as Mr. Davis is a master of poetic language and form, a sonnet, whether Shakespearean, Miltonian, Spenserian, Italian, French, or *Terza Rima*, heads each chapter. In contrast, his prose is appropriately and effectively folksy, clearly conveying the perspective, experiences, and emotions of the story's characters, especially the young Joshua, who travels both literal and metaphoric miles in his odyssey from rebellious, enslaved child to responsible, unfettered adult.

The story follows a group of Missouri slaves that includes families, some reunited after years of separation, the elderly, young children, and adolescents like Joshua. They are led by an imposing, determined, paternal preacher in their escape to the slave-free but not altogether safe north via the Underground Railway. Mr. Davis' gripping narrative portrays the fear, hardship, starvation, exhaustion, and relief of these desperate travelers making their way for hundreds of miles on foot off the beaten path through thick woods, mud, and otherwise rough terrain, or hidden in wagons, suffocating and cramped, here and there recuperating in safe houses and the kindness of abolitionists. Their flight is under constant threat due to Fugitive Slave Acts that makes capturing runaway slaves a lucrative business. Through Mr. Davis' empathetic writing, the anxiety of knowing that in a moment their flight to freedom could be ended—their lives turned back to estrangement from those they love and enslavement by those who "care" for them only as chattel—is also the reader's unsettling experience.

Fannie Barrie Williams, the author of *Black Women in Nineteenth Century American Life* wrote that the most savage thing about slavery was "its attempted destruction of the family instinct of the Negro race in America." *In the Unsettled Homeland of Dreams* gives this travesty real lives the reader becomes deeply invested in. This important and moving story of a black fishing community of West Harbor, Washington Island, Wisconsin, insists that the savagery of slavery can be—must be—obstructed. Mr. Davis speaks to the need for all human beings to live freely, individually, uniquely while forming families, friendships, and community; to be at liberty to compete and cooperate, to feel love returned and even unrequited, to know how life is naturally given and taken, to enjoy the refuge of home, to have work *and* leisure and an education, to make plans and pursue hopes and dreams.

~**Diane Denton**, author of *Without the Veil Between, Anne Bronte: A Fine and Subtle Spirit, To a Strange Somewhere Fled, A House Near Luccoli, A Friendship with Flowers,* and more.

Thomas Davis has told a story of racism, survival, and self-determination in the mid-19th century. Inside *In the Unsettled Homeland of Dreams* is a fascinating story of "Negros" escaping slavery. The novel is a work of historical fiction and conveys a true history of the routes taken by slaves. Moreover, Davis's novel illuminates how and why there continues to be mistrust among races today. As an American Indian from Wisconsin, now living in the south, I still find many whites "Afraid of the Dark."

~**Dana Grams**, College English and Communications Instructor and Videographer

In the Unsettled Homeland of Dreams

Thomas Davis

In the Unsettled Homeland of Dreams
Copyright © 2019 by Thomas Davis

This is a work of fiction based on historical fact. While certain individuals named did exist, the circumstances of their lives is entirely the product of the author's imagination.

ISBN: 978-1-7327237-8-8
Library of Congress Control Number: 2019945294

To Ethel, for getting me to finish
In the Unsettled Homeland of Dreams
and Deb Wayman who got me to
start writing it

Acknowledgments

A lot of research has gone into this book, on Washington Island, on the period just before passage of the Fugitive Slave Act of 1850, and especially on the Underground Railroad as it operated between the southern states and Wisconsin. I was writing a sequence of sonnets about the black fisher community on Washington Island when my nephew Grant Wells and I visited Faire Isle Books. Deb Wayman, while we were in the store, convinced me that I wanted to write a book rather than just a sonnet sequence. I am indebted to the slave narratives developed by the WPA during the Great Depression even though they are deeply flawed as historical documents, and other narratives written by famous and not so famous escaped slaves. Some of these came from the archives of the Wisconsin Historical Society. I have also dipped into the scholarship of the pre-Civil War era in writing this novel and spent time in the archives on Washington Island, at the Sturgeon Bay, Wisconsin library, and in the archives at the University of Wisconsin—Green Bay. There is also a considerable literature on the history of Washington Island and Door County that has been valuable.

PREFACE

In the Unsettled Homeland of Dreams is a historical novel, although some of the stories and events depicted in it actually happened. People such as Preacher Bennett, the black families that formed the fisherman's community on Washington Island, Wisconsin, Jesse Miner, Henry Miner and his wife, Joel Westbrook and his son, and others, were real people.

This is, of course, a work of fiction. There are hints in the historical record about what Preacher Bennett was like, but those hints do not make a character that lives and breathes on the page. Joel Westbrook and his son were arrested for certain crimes, and there are suggestions that his character was not as upstanding as an officer of law's ought to be. There is no evidence that he was involved in all the events in this story.

It is hoped that what is recounted here, this effort to tell the story of a black community of fisherman and their families on Washington Island, becomes part of a conversation about the complexity of the American experience, especially as it relates to race. There are a lot of strands to that conversation; this novel explores one strand with numerous branches extending out into multiple races and through the arrow of time as that concept is understood by contemporary physics.

The purpose of conversation, of course, is to provoke thought and cause more conversation and storytelling. Hopefully, that is where healing and health can be found.

Then, at night,
your small
closing
window
opens up from the other end, like a tunnel
to the unsettled homeland of dreams.

~From Pablo Neruda's poem, "Ode to the Eye"

BOOK ONE

IN THE UNDERGROUND RAILROAD

Routes of the Underground Railroad

Chapter 1
Inflamed Imagining

Inside the swamp beside a cypress tree
(White herons in the water, bullfrog croaks
A symphony as dusk, as stealthily
As cat's feet stalking small, shy birds, evokes
The coming night) the preacher slowly stokes
The fire blazed in his heart and starts to sing
Songs powerful enough to loosen yokes
White masters forged through endless menacing.

The words he used burned deep; he felt their sting
And saw his spirit fire alive in eyes
Awake to dreams, inflamed imagining
Of days spent free beneath glad years of skies.

The darkness deepened underneath the tree.
He'd preach, he thought, then, later on, they'd flee.

Joshua did not want to go with his mother when she came down after dark from Master Bulrush's big house where she was the Mistresses' servant. He'd gone through another miserable day. His stubbornness, born out of unfocused resentment, was always getting him in trouble. He couldn't seem to want to protect himself.

The Overseer, an aging black man called Silver Coats, who had terrorized Bulrush plantation slaves for years, had struck out with his whip and cut a shirt already threadbare twice that day. The last time the whip's cord had touched *him*, leaving a long, red welt crusted with blood on his skin. The painful cuts were made on purpose. The Overseer was an expert at gauging how deep his whip would bite flesh.

Joshua, small for his age, mostly didn't cry when the big black man, gray haired, light skinned, with a mean streak and perpetually snarling face, whipped him. He was fourteen years old and had long ago decided he was not going to cry every time the Overseer or Master brought out one of the whips hung in a small lean-to shed attached to the plantation's red barn.

Crying did not elicit sympathy in the quarters. Everyone was whipped off and on no matter how hard they tried to follow directions the Overseer, or the disdainful, blue-eyed Master Bulrush, gave them. But this time the force behind the whipping had been too great. The pain had burned, searing into his back, and made him feel faint. Silver Coats had never slashed him that angrily before. Tears had come to his eyes even though he had tried to force them away. He had almost collapsed.

He'd worked hard all day, too. In the morning he'd pulled weeds in the two-acre garden by the house in hot sun. Sweat had made him blink. Then, in spite of how undersized he was, he had struggled to carry bunches of pitchforked hay from the back of the barn to the horses' stalls.

What had gotten him into trouble was when the Overseer followed him into the barn. The sun was lengthening shadows beneath trees as Joshua had looked sullenly at the old man, his resentment boiling up, and then looked away. He hadn't said anything, but Coats, already angry, had grabbed his arm, making him drop the forkful of hay he was carrying.

"You think you're better than the rest of us?" the burly man had sneered. Then, before Joshua could think of what to say, he had been dragged out of the barn toward the Overseer's favorite whipping spot in front of the shed where the whips were kept.

Joshua had no energy left to go with his mother into Mingo Swamp that night, not after that whipping. He felt dizzy and was barely able to walk from the pain. His stomach was queasy. He could not imagine following her down the dirt road into the blackness that loomed where the swamp tracked into wilderness. He was exhausted.

He knew he should go with her. He knew she didn't like to go alone to the preacher's place beneath the big cypress a quarter mile past where water seeped out of the ground to the surface. The dark didn't bother her, she said, but the aloneness in the swamp did.

She was rarely able to slip out of the big house to see him. He had long ago been banned from going to see her there. The Master and Mistress ruled the house with iron wills that seldom let her escape to the quarters to either see her son or visit the preacher.

He was a troublemaker, according to both the Master and Mistress. The frail looking white woman with her watery blue eyes and elegant dresses, usually made by Joshua's mother, had never liked his boundless energy. He knew his mother sometimes got into trouble when she did come to see him. But, given his mood, his tiredness, and the whip cuts on his back, he just could not see going with her no matter how important it was to her that he come.

When he objected, however, she looked at him the way Old Simpson had the night he died. The old man had been Joshua's best friend and protector ever since he'd been moved from the big house to the ramshackle quarters row strung out below the garden a little removed from the plantation's largest cotton fields.

After the Overseer had lost control and whipped the old man too long for complaining about not feeling good one too many times, he'd laid on the gunnysacks they used as beds in his drafty cabin in the middle of winter and asked to see Joshua. Joshua had been in the barn feeding the brown Jersey milk cows. When he'd come into the cabin, scared and feeling like he was still a baby, the old man had not said anything, but looked at him in a strange, lost way, and gasped his last breath as he'd died.

"What are you looking like that at me for?" he asked his mother, who stared at him unblinking. The truth was that she was scaring him.

His mother was a strong woman who carried herself with pride. She was also better fed than most of the other slaves since she did a lot of the cooking for the Master and his family even though she worked under another slave called Cook. He knew even the Master thought she was an "extraordinary looking woman." He'd heard him say so to his own son in the barn one evening. She had a dusky face dominated by large, expressive, chocolate-colored eyes not quite brown or black. When he had lived in the master's house, Joshua had hated the way the white man with the beefy, red face had looked at his mother with a hunger that would not have boded well for any slave.

"You've got to come," she said in her soft voice as she turned toward the door of the shack where Old Simpson had breathed his last.

He looked around for Sammy, the man he lived with, but saw no way around his mother's determination. It didn't matter. Sammy wouldn't have protected him from his mother. He had once confided that she scared him with her proud and "uppity" ways.

Sighing, Joshua got off the gunnysacks and gingerly struggled to his feet and followed her out the door. The death look she had given him had shivered through his body.

***

It didn't take long to reach the swamp. His mother walked in front in a tremendous hurry. As tired as he was, Joshua forced himself to keep up. Every step he took jolted through him.

The first time he had gone with her to listen to Preacher Bennett, the strange black man who delivered sermons beneath a massive cypress tree beside a stretch of clear water, she had talked to him the whole way. She had told him how important it was to accept Jesus Christ as his savior since Jesus could remove him from the torment he was placed in and lead him to freedom.

He hadn't understood much of what she had been trying to tell him.

He'd heard talk about Jesus in the quarters but hadn't paid attention. Without his mother to guide him he was more concentrated on what he felt than on what the quarters' talk was one way or another. He remembered he'd felt good that she had gotten out of the house and was taking him to the meeting with her. When they sat with a dozen other slaves from neighboring plantations and listened to the preacher's powerful voice that rose and fell in a cadence filled with powerful emotions, Joshua was puzzled.

Here they were, slaves, and all the preacher could talk about was New Jerusalem and freedom. Joshua didn't even know what freedom was. He'd never heard of New Jerusalem. He knew a slave would be whipped almost to death if he tried to escape the plantation. The Overseer and people in the quarters all agreed on that. He'd heard Master Bulrush once tell Sammy, who had looked desperately around for help after he'd realized he was in for a whipping, that he would never live if he tried to run.

What Joshua did know was the Overseer's meanness whenever Joshua got a little stubborn and refused to jump to the man's bidding quickly enough. The Overseer was a slave who hated slaves. What good was a preacher in a swamp underneath an old cypress tree? The preacher looked ordinary enough with his long black beard streaked gray and his thin face that danced when he talked. What did he really offer other than words?

Nobody seemed to know where he'd come from, either. When Joshua had asked his mother about the man on the way back from the first meeting he'd attended, she'd shaken her head and said, "None of the people at the meetings know. I think he came south from up north somewhere. He might even be a freed man, but I don't know." What she did know was that he didn't belong to the local plantations.

The preacher remained more puzzle than answer. He spewed out a mysterious hope that could not lead to anything but more whippings. Why did so many slaves keep coming to hear his sermons when they did no good for any of them? Jesus talk was fine. A lot of the slaves talked about Jesus. Even Old Simpson had believed in the white savior. But Joshua had yet to see pleas to the good Lord stop how the Overseer's black whip felt as it slashed into flesh.

As soon as they entered the swamp, his mother motioned to him. She'd veered off the faint path that let them avoid getting wet with strong smelling swamp water while they made their way to the cypress tree. She went to a willow thicket and buttonbush and knelt down. The ground smelled rotten.

Joshua felt uncomfortable in the near dark and had since the day his mother had been forced to move him to the quarters when he was eleven years old. He'd heard her pleading with the mistress to let him stay. He'd heard and understood what she was pleading for even though he hadn't entirely understood what was happening.

He had sassed the white Mistress after she had told him for what seemed like the thousandth time he was a worthless boy. He hadn't thought about what he was going to say before he said it. His mother had always praised him and told him to learn to "hold in to yourself" when white people said bad things to him. He had sassed the old woman before and only gotten a light whipping for his untamed tongue. He hadn't been afraid of her. She wasn't very strong.

This time had been different. The Mistress had flown into a rage. Spittle had flung out of her mouth as she screamed at him. She'd looked like she might collapse under the weight of her anger.

Master Bulrush, red faced, had rushed out of the parlor and roared for Joshua's mother. Joshua hadn't even known she was in the house. He'd thought she had gone to the cellar on an errand for Cook. Then the Master had screamed at Joshua that he was banned from the house and would never be allowed to see his mother again.

Joshua's mother had come rushing into the room just as the Master spat out his judgment in a voice that rung with a finality that terrified the boy. Joshua's mother had looked at her son and then at the Master, her eyes filled with panic

"You can't do that Master," she'd pleaded. "Please."

It was common knowledge that Master Bulrush had a heart of stone when it came to slaves, especially young slaves. They were his property, property that needed to be invisible, getting their work done and adding to his wealth, but not bothering his consciousness. White children were enough trouble. Black children were insufferable.

The Master had stared at Joshua's mother, the usual look of hunger on his face absent. She had hesitated, but then took Joshua's hand. Shaking her head and crying, she had kept saying, "Please, Jesus," softly over and over again. Then she had taken him to Old Simpson's cabin. Joshua had cried, too, although afterward he had decided he never would again. It certainly hadn't done his mother any good.

That first night in the quarters, so different from the tiny room he shared with his mother in the big house's dank basement, he had been up all night while Old Simpson, supposedly his mother's father's cousin, had tried to comfort him. The next day Silver Coats, who he'd hardly known up until then, had rousted him off his gunnysack and forced him into the fields, laughing at his confusion and eyes red from lack of sleep.

At the willow thicket his mother spoke, jarring him from his reverie. "Come on, hurry."

He moved cautiously to where she was kneeling. Frogs and crickets and endless other sounds were making the swamp alive. Strong odors oozed on every side of them even though they were just on the edge of land, thick vegetation, and stagnant water that went for miles into tangled wilderness.

His mother pulled out three big gunnysacks from the brush. *How had they gotten there?* They seemed too stuffed to be forced into the hollow where his mother dragged them from into the open.

"What's going on?"

"This is a special night," she said, not looking at him. "A special night. You'll have to help carry these."

He grabbed the end of one of the sacks and grunted. It was heavy. His back burned from his blood-crusted wounds. *How is she going to carry two sacks? She's strong, but the sacks are stuffed full. How can I carry even one the way I feel?* The familiar stubbornness that always got him into trouble stirred.

"What's in these?"

His mother looked at him at last, tears in her eyes. He could just make them out in the darkness.

She stood and forced one of the sacks onto her shoulders. "Food," she grunted. She looked at him. "You're strong enough." Her voice sounded dull, dead. "I know you were whipped today."

Stubbornness leached out of him. He bent down, grabbed the sack by its neck where it had been tied shut with twine, and gasped at the pain that shot through his back and down his legs as he stood. The sack was really heavy.

His mother grabbed the other sack and dragged it behind her toward the path that led to the cypress tree. Joshua had a cold feeling in his stomach. He felt the same fear as when he'd walked into Old Simpson's shack to say goodbye.

His suspicion stunned him. She'd stolen food from the cellar at the house. They would notice. There was no hiding the fact that food had gone missing. With a sack over his shoulder he would be judged guilty of theft, too.

He had no idea how—or why—she had hidden the sacks in the swamp without anyone in the Master's house knowing. Cook would have been overjoyed to find her out. The other house slaves would have told on her. There was no love between house slaves always trying to get the better of each other in the Master and Mistresses' eyes.

Old Simpson had been whipped to death. Joshua had not known it at the time— Old Simpson had been sick—but Sammy told him later that the Overseer had lost control of himself. That could easily happen to his mother and him when they returned to the plantation. Everyone would know what she'd done. Slaves who were thieves received no mercy.

They hadn't gone far when a big black man Joshua had never seen before stepped from behind a cypress where the path curved around an inlet. Moonlight splashed on dark water. Joshua jumped when the man suddenly appeared.

"Jason," his mother exclaimed, her voice still soft. "Thank God." She turned to Joshua, smiling. "This is Jason, Joshua." She gestured toward the big man. "Your father."

Joshua's head spun. The world had tilted and was careening out of control. He tried to get himself to understand what his mother meant. *I have a father?* He had dreamed of it but had never been told about one. He had assumed his father was dead like Old Simpson. Only a few of the slave children living in the quarters had fathers. Some didn't even have mothers. They all had to have had fathers, of course, but that didn't mean they'd ever know where their missing fathers—or mothers—were, especially if any of them had been sold off the plantation.

The man was huge. He lifted up the sack Joshua's mother was dragging and picked up the other sack as if they were of no consequence. He looked at Joshua and smiled. Joshua felt tiny next to him. *Do I want a father? What does having a father mean? How can I be so small for his age if my father's so big?*

His mother looked at him, still smiling. She's nervous, Joshua thought. Nervous and excited.

"Can you handle that sack?" the big man asked.

"I'm fourteen years old and used to work," Joshua said, irritation in his voice.

His mother opened her mouth, then closed it. "He doesn't know about you," she told the big man.

Jason, even darker than the night, laughed, a rich, powerful laugh that seemed out of place in the swamp. The swamp was rich with life and dark, not a joyous place.

"He knows now." His voice sounded powerfully confident. He turned and walked down the faint path. He acted as if everything were normal; as if he met a son he'd never met before every day.

Joshua couldn't even make out the path in the darkness.

His mother hesitated, but then followed Jason, leaving Joshua to struggle behind them, wincing every time the sack rubbed against his wounds. *If I have a father, why did my mother always avoid my questions on the subject?* He told himself not to think about it now. He'd figure out what was happening later. He thought about the Overseer, his tiny black eyes and how they could fix on you and make you shudder even though you were desperately looking away from them.

***

He heard the crowd by the cypress before they came out of the swamp. They were trying to talk softly, but their sounds rose above the natural sounds of frogs, insects, and birds.

He kept stumbling over roots in the path in the dark. A couple of times his mother dropped back from the man she was trying to keep up with and asked Joshua if he wanted her to take the gunnysack for him. Both times he shook his head emphatically. The big man did not look back at them, but kept moving effortlessly.

As the sounds around the cypress grew louder, Joshua started saying silently, "I have a father, I have a father" over and over again. He was not sure what that meant, but the more time he spent in his thoughts, the more important the meaning of what he was saying to himself grew. As he reached the clearing, he wondered what his father, if he really *was* his father, was like. *Will I like him? Why hadn't she ever mentioned him?* Not even when he had gotten mad because she wouldn't tell him anything. *What's he doing in the swamp?* He was clearly not from any of the neighboring plantations. The tiredness Joshua had felt in the quarters was mostly gone.

Eventually, it became clear to him that something he had never dared dream of was in process. He not only had a father, but the preacher was going to try to help them all escape the plantation and slavery.

He had heard rumors of a conductor on the Underground Railroad whispered late at night in the quarters. Once his best friend, Jamie Bullock, had avowed that if he ever had the chance, he would ride the railroad right off the plantation. But Joshua had thought the conductor was supposedly a woman, not a preacher. He'd never asked anybody about the rumors. He suspected now that he not only had not understood what they meant, but that he had thought they were dreams people dreamed after they had been brutalized once too often by the Overseer.

Willie Bullock, Jamie's father, broke from the group by the cypress tree the minute Joshua walked into the clearing. Joshua was surprised to see someone from the quarters already there. He'd known Willie and his wife Massie and their two sons, Jamie and Jeremiah, had been going to listen to the preacher. They'd been at one of the meetings he had attended with his mother. But he hadn't known the Bullocks were crazy enough to try to run away.

Willie was light-colored and supposedly had white blood from a master-father who'd sold his son to the Bulrush plantation. He was the kindest slave in the quarters, always trying to help others by repairing torn clothes with thread he'd somehow gotten or giving them part of his meager meals if the Overseer had punished them by shorting them on food. Massie was a robust, dark woman who went about her work, never causing trouble and always looking out for her two sons, the best friends

Joshua had.

Joshua flinched when Willie came and took the gunnysack off his shoulders.

"Here," Willie said. "You shouldn't carry that. You've had a bad day, and we're going long tonight."

Willie smiled at Jason as if he knew him, but did not otherwise greet him. He did not seem surprised the big man was there. He nodded to Joshua's mother.

Before Joshua could mumble thank you, letting Willie shoulder the sack, the preacher pointed to him.

"Come young Joshua," he said. "We're organizing."

His mother, standing by his unexpected father, left his father's side and walked over to Joshua, holding out her hand. She seemed to be shining like she had when his father had come out of the dark behind the cypress tree.

"We're escaping tonight," she told him excitedly, looking at him as if she were wondering what he was going to make of what she was saying. "With your father. That's why you had to come. I knew about your day, but I couldn't leave you behind."

Her eyes searched his face, trying to ferret out what he was feeling. He glanced at his father and tried to make sense of his situation. A father? he asked himself again. Alive and standing near me? Escape?

Joshua let his mother pull him into the half circle around the preacher, wondering how he could run in the shape he was in. He quickly counted seventeen or eighteen people in the circle; there may have been more. He, Jamie, and Jeremiah weren't the only young people. There were several couples with children standing next to them, most of them girls. One looked to be no more than five years old.

He recognized some of the adults, too. Besides Willie Bullock and his family, there were men and women he'd seen from nearby plantations. He was amazed that so many were willing to face the inevitable consequences if they were caught.

The wounds on his back felt wet. He wondered what was going to happen to him. He didn't have any concept of what freedom was. It was just an idea he'd heard slaves long for in whispers when no master or tool of the master was around.

The preacher's coal black eyes were wild with a crazy power. His voice had a deep timbre and rang with authority that did not allow for stubbornness.

"It's going to be a tough journey," he said.

Joshua stared at him so hard he blocked out the swamp, his mother, his supposed father, and even the painful cuts on his back.

"Sister Mary has brought us sacks of food she will pay dearly for if the masters or their slavers catch us." The preacher motioned toward Joshua's mother. "That means once we start movin', we're not going to stop until dawn. Chas, freed by his master a long time ago, has scouted out our path. We must follow him without question. I don't have to tell you what you will face if we are caught leaving this place." He paused. "Brother Chas."

A man who looked vaguely like his brother, Willie Bullock, but whose skin was lighter, stepped over to stand beside the preacher. He looked stronger and better fed than his brother, with high cheekbones and short-cut hair that shaded from dark brown to black. Joshua got the sense from the way Chas held his lean, wiry body that he had never met an obstacle he hadn't overcome.

"First we'll divide the food into bags I've brought," he said. "We'll all need to move fast. Even though Jason Billings can carry a wagon around on his back we need everybody to carry their share." His smile was grim.

He looked at the people gathered around him. "We're going through the swamp," he told them. "Sometimes only one person at a time will be able to be on the path. The swamp's dangerous. We have to especially be on the lookout for snakes. That means you need to rest while you're waiting to get through the tight places.

"We don't know when your masters will discover you've run, but they *will* know, and they *will* come after us. You've got to keep up, even the young ones. All of us are going to get wet. You'll dry while you're walking. The swamp will mask our scent from dogs they'll use, but we need to be a long way from here before dawn."

Looking at Willie Bullock's surprise brother, Joshua felt irritated he had not known about him, either. Neither Jamie nor Jeremiah had told him they had a freed uncle. It seemed his whole life was surrounded by secrets.

The preacher bowed his head.

"May God protect us all," he said. "May all of us reach the shores of New Jerusalem and freedom's paradise." He touched Chas's right shoulder. "Let's go," he said.

The adults began grabbing gunnysacks piled by the big cypress tree whose branches twisted into the night sky above the pond's dark waters. Chas did not wait for the quick division of the food Joshua's mother had stolen for them and started walking west along the pond's edge. Jason handed out the sacks as each adult walked up to him. Within seconds all of them were moving.

Joshua, however, hesitated. He could not believe what was happening. When Joshua failed to move, his mother looked at him in despair. Along the water's edge, Jamie hesitated and looked back, but then moved with the rest of his family when Willie reached out and touched his arm. Although he was bigger than Joshua, he looked small in shadows lengthening into the intensity of huge trees, vines, and profuse vegetation.

His father appeared out of nowhere, looking down at Joshua with a troubled expression.

"Can I call you son?"

Joshua had the sense the man had been thinking a lot about the question he'd just asked. His voice did not sound confident, but, rather, hesitant. It was a crazy question to ask just before they were getting ready to run for their lives.

Joshua felt his mother's eyes without looking at her. They really were running away. His mother had brought him to an attempted escape.

Silver Coats glared at Joshua, his eyes filmy and dull, a malicious, black whip in his hand. How many bad whippings could a boy take and walk away alive?

"Joshua?" his mother asked, her voice soft.

Master Bulrush was laughing. "Send him to the quarters," he roared, his face flushed and ugly. Joshua's mother came into the kitchen.

"Joshua?"

Cook was standing over him, hands on her giant hips, her face filled with excitement. "You heard the Master," she said in her meanest voice.

"If you don't want me to, I won't," the big man said. In spite of rumbling his voice was gentle.

"We're escaping," his mother said. "You, your father, all of us." She paused. "I never thought this day would come."

She looked toward the people strung out and walking swiftly along the pond's edge. They were all trying to be quiet, but the rustle of so many people moving was loud to her ears. They were putting distance between them and the cypress tree.

Joshua knew he would not escape another whipping by going back to the plantation. Not if people from the quarters had escaped. He'd have to report his mother, too, if he didn't want to get a whipping as bad as what Old Simpson had endured.

"You can call me son," he said in a small voice.

He could ignore the fire on his back and being tired, he decided. He could ignore shock and fear pounding in his ears.

"Good," his father said, relief in his voice. "I'd like you to call me Pappy. That's who I am."

"Freedom," his mother said, her eyes fastened on Joshua. "We've got our family and freedom. I'll never be pawed by a white man again." She inserted herself between the two of them and put her arms around them as they started walking hurriedly to the water's edge. "New Jerusalem and paradise," she whispered fervently. "Freedom."

Pappy started running with the two of them behind him.

Chapter 2
Freedom's First Night, Before Dawn

The white man, with his wide brimmed hat and face
Stunned pale inside a night that breathed with sounds
From woods they'd passed through in their frantic race
Against the coming dawn, turned back around
To look toward the barn that loomed ahead
Of where six families hid in heavy brush.
He sighed as if he couldn't flee the dread
He felt in dark before dawn's first red blush.

"I made a space to hide you runaways,"
He said. He turned again and looked at eyes
That looked at him, cold fear a noxious glaze
Infecting even how the dreaded sun would rise.

"Six families can't escape at once," he said.
"I've got my family too. They're still in bed."

The preacher looked into the man.
His eyes looked past white outer flesh
Into the place his soul began.
The white man turned again, the mesh

Of eyes surrounding him afraid
To move, to dream, to think they'd leave
This place before their master flayed
Their bodies. It made their spirits grieve.

As night wore on, the dread and excitement Joshua had felt by the cypress tree was replaced by numbness disassociating mind and body from the nightmare they were walking through. The man who wanted to be called Pappy — *why Pappy?* — seemed to be everywhere. Whenever they stacked up at a place where swamp and strong smelling, black muck forced them into a single, long line in the darkness between stretches of water, he was at the back of the line, making sure no one was left behind. Then he would be splashing through water and thick, black mud as they got moving more rapidly again, asking in his deep, rich voice if everyone was okay.

Sometimes they could hardly see when the swamp's canopy blocked off even starlight. Then they'd come out into a clearing where the moon reflected white on a pool's black surface.

At first the cloud of mosquitos that tormented every inch of exposed skin made all of them miserable. Even the buzzing sounds seemed unbearable, part of the toxic mix of fear, clammy clothes that plastered uncomfortably to skin, and unknown *things* slapping or crawling on them in the darkness. They felt increasingly filthy, too, with swamp mud clinging to their flimsy shoes and hands and even their hair. They had all been hot, dirty, and miserable in the fields most of their lives, but this was different, as if the swamp's dark smells got into who they were and stained bodies and spirits as they ran and slipped and stumbled and ran.

After a while, the buzzing bloodsuckers became more fact than nuisance. Welts on skin stopped itching even though they could still be felt. When someone slipped in the smelly mud or thought they saw—or felt—a snake they couldn't make out in the dark, they cursed, forcing the sound to be so soft it became part of the endless swamp sounds croaking, buzzing, crying, and squawking eerily around them.

Joshua's threadbare pants were soaked to his hips. His mother walked silently beside him as if she could not bear to be away from his side. Inside his numbness he thought that it was good to be walking by his mother.

When they finally came to the swamp's western edge, Chas Bullock gathered them in a clump in front of a big cotton field. He seemed calm, competent.

"We have to move quietly and quickly," he said with the preacher beside him. "Beyond this field there are woods that go for a while. We'll be okay in there, but here we can be seen if somebody from the Jensen's quarters can't sleep and is where they're not supposed to be."

"Do we keep moving in daylight?" the old man Joshua had seen when he had been at the preacher's meeting the first time asked.

The preacher looked at the man who kept glancing at the old woman with him. She looked fragile and tired in the darkness.

"Maybe they've jumped the broom," Joshua thought, although he wasn't sure why that idea had jumped into his head. Jumping the broom was unusual on the Bulrush plantation.

And then only if done in secret.

Slave couples were, in his experience, hardly ever allowed to claim to be a man and wife even when they lived together as a family. Instead, like the Bullocks, they denied the obvious, at least when they were where they could be overheard by either slaves or the master, producing more property for the master as children were born. Property did not have rights or the illusion that they could live by conventions, like marriage, of the white race. Joshua had heard quarters' women talk about how marriage happened with the approval of masters on other plantations, but not on Bulrush lands.

The old couple looked like they belonged together.

He looked at his mother. She was staring at the ground as she picked her way, following indentations left in the muck by those ahead of them. He wondered if she and Pappy had jumped the broom.

"We've made arrangements," Preacher said to the old man, but didn't explain.

Chas moved into the field without looking back.

Joshua's mother smiled at him. "You okay?"

He glanced at her but kept quiet. He did not feel okay, not really. He was tired. His back burned. Sometimes he felt like he was walking through a nightmare and was distant from where he really was. He was unsure about the idea of having a father. He had not had one or even imagined he had one, and now a man he had never met was Pappy.

None of it made sense. Escaping through the swamp the wrong way, west rather than north, made no sense. The idea the Overseer would beat his mother, him, Jamie and Jeremiah Bullock, and their parents, Willie and Massie, to death when they were caught made sense. It would come true if they were caught, and they would likely be caught. The Master had horses and dogs. Nobody could outrun horses or dogs.

Since leaving the cypress tree, he had been more stunned than afraid. His reluctance to follow his mother to the preacher's meeting had been knocked out of him when his mother had told him he had a father and introduced a giant of a man to him. Seeing Willie and Massie and then Jamie and Jeremiah and realizing they were all going to try to escape the only place he knew anything about seared into his exhaustion.

What are we doing? Have we lost our minds?

Instead of looking at his mother, he moved into the field. His father went to the old man and woman. He took the old woman's arm and led the two of them toward the middle of the group.

"Quiet," he heard his father whisper.

***

Joshua was amazed at how little sound so many people were making. Even the little girl, carried on her father or mother's back off and on, hardly made a noise. The four girls with their mother and father were just as silent. *We're scared. I'm scared. There's no telling what people can do when they're scared.*

16

The field they were running through was vast. They moved through rows of planted cotton without hesitating. Joshua wondered how much night was left as he struggled to ignore his back. He was vaguely aware that they had stopped moving west and were now moving north, but he drifted in and out of strange dreams.

Once he woke with a start. He had heard dogs. His heart was beating. But there were no dogs. The only noise was the soft sound of running feet. If the masters who owned them had figured out they were gone, they had not yet found where they were.

Not long after he made out woods ahead of them. His father joined him and his mother, moving up the strung-out line from where he had been helping the old couple.

"We have to move faster," he told them. "We're doing good, but we have a ways to go before we get to where we need to be at dawn."

His mother touched Jason's hand and smiled. "We'll make it," she said.

Then his father was falling back again, urging everyone to move faster. At one point he took the little girl from her mother and hoisted her to his shoulders, moving along as if she had no weight at all.

Once they passed the tree line at the field's edge and were deep enough to be hidden by thick brush, Preacher stopped and waited until everyone was gathered together again.

"Praise God, we're doing good," he told them once the old couple and Joshua's father had joined them. Chas Bullock was missing. "Freedom's a long ways away, but it's coming, it's coming," he said in his cadenced voice. "We make it through these woods, and Chas will be waiting for us. We need to get under cover before sunrise. We're going to rest during the day and then go on." He smiled, the whiteness of his teeth bright in the darkness. "Ready?"

Without waiting for an answer, he turned and moved down a faint deer trail. He seemed to know where he was going. Joshua wondered if he had been there before.

As Joshua got to his feet, his big father loomed over him. "You okay?"

Joshua wondered how he felt about having a father yet again. As he tried to understand what he was missing when he thought about his feelings, he discovered he was not surprised his mother had not mentioned his father before. She'd always told him he shouldn't think about things he could do nothing about. She'd said that was what it meant to be a slave. You accepted things. You didn't have to like them, but rebelling only brought trouble.

He knew his mother hadn't always lived on the Bulrush plantation and worked in the Master's house. She never mentioned it, but Old Simpson had told him she'd given birth to him less than a month after she'd been sold from her previous place and moved into the quarters. He said she'd been moved into the Master's house after she'd caught his eye. Whenever Joshua asked his mother about her life before the Bulrush plantation, she'd just shrugged.

"That's past," she'd say. "Let the past be past."

He'd thought about where she'd been before being bought by Master Bulrush. He'd even talked to his best friend Jamie about it when they had managed to spend a few hours away from quarters at the pond south of the garden where they could catch catfish the women would cook over an outdoor fire. But in the end, he had done what his mother had made clear she wanted him to do. He'd passed by and never thought about her life before the Bulrushes. Now, as they moved further from the plantation than he had ever been, Pappy, the man his mother said was his father, kept checking on him, asking if he was okay.

He was thinking that it felt strange to feel so looked after when a branch whipped his face. He gave a small, involuntary cry.

"Hush!" one of the women running by his mother whispered harshly. He did not look toward her, but stared at trees in front of him.

His mother, while he moved, grabbed his arm and looked at him as they continued running. He could not fully make out her face, but he could tell she was worried. He shook his head and sped toward the front of the line. They were no longer moving as fast as they had when setting out. *How long can we keep going?* He remembered hearing dogs in his dream and moved even faster, passing others running as fast as they dared in a dark, unknown wood. He felt ashamed he had made a sound. He was not a baby. The branch had startled, not hurt him. It was time to start acting like a man, not a little boy.

***

He stopped thinking. He forced the dream that kept tugging at him away so he could pay attention to where he was walking. He could hear heavy breathing all around. Then, long hours after they had left the clearing dominated by the old cypress, Preacher slowed the pace. The two men and one woman in front of Joshua slowed, too. Suddenly the preacher stopped, held up his hand, and motioned them to gather around him again.

Joshua realized he could see a little better. Dawn hadn't come, but the sun was creeping toward it.

"This is where we're meeting Chas," Preacher said. "We're close to a farm, so we have to be extra quiet. We'll wait here. Sit on the ground and rest."

Preacher sat, gracefully crossing his legs with no more effort than if he were a child.

They hadn't been waiting long before Chas Bullock appeared like a ghost out of the woods. He nodded to Preacher and then looked at the rest of them.

"There's a white man waiting for us," he said.

Joshua's eyes, along with others', opened wide.

"He's a good man, but nervous. We have to be real respectful. We need to hide in his barn during the day. There's too much chance we might be seen. Just act calm and respectful. Okay?"

Joshua felt an old bitterness inside. No white person could be trusted. Not ever.

Preacher rose to his feet. "We'll be okay," he said. "We're in God's good hands."

Joshua didn't move for a long moment. He didn't want to move. He wanted to stretch out right where he was and forget about the pain in his back and sleep, avoiding Preacher, white men, and his father. The idea of a white man waiting for them terrified him.

A few minutes later, they were standing on the woods' edge. Across an orderly yard with a woodpile, axes, and a couple of wagons, a small gray barn stood. An older, sallow faced white man was waiting behind Chas as they came in sight of the farm. Joshua could make out the man's troubled expression in the morning's gray light.

"I didn't expect so many of you," he said, his voice shockingly loud.

Joshua looked at his mother. She looked frightened, eyes narrow with distrust.

"You didn't tell me there would be so many," the white man said to Chas.

"Mister Jemmie," Chas said, keeping his voice soft. "I didn't expect so many. But they're here, and we've got to keep them from the slavers."

The man sighed and shook his head. "Up in Illinois they burned a Quaker out of his house that was helping negras," he said, his voice still too loud. "I have a family to think of."

"We'll be gone at dusk," Chas said. "You're a good man. You won't let slavers find these people." There was a stern tone to his voice.

The man looked at exhausted faces around him and shook his head again. "I said I'd do this," he said. "I will, but I didn't make a place for so many. I don't know if all of you will fit in the loft."

Preacher stepped out of the crowd to stand by Chas. "We're tired," he said. "We've run all night. We'll be quiet and sleep. We don't mind crowding."

"I put the dogs in the house," their reluctant host said. "After we close the barn door, I'll let them out. If the dogs start fussing, you'll know to go out the back door and run. I made a hidey-hole in the loft, but it's too small. I didn't expect so many."

He abruptly turned and walked toward the barn. Joshua wondered what good running would do if someone stirred up the dogs. Some might get away, he supposed, at least for a while. But the slavers would have horses and most likely dogs. Most of them would be caught, and maybe the white man would have his farm burned down. He wondered how Chas and Preacher could trust the whiney old man. No white man could afford to help escaped slaves even if, as the result of miracle, they might want to. Even white men could be whipped.

No one said anything, but his mother took his arm and walked resolutely to the barn. The rest followed. Joshua felt like he was walking around naked and exposed in the early morning light.

***

Once in the small loft, Joshua had trouble getting to sleep. He had been so tired, so desperate to rest. The minute he fit himself by Pappy with Willie and his family squeezed in beside them, he had closed his eyes. Events ran through his thoughts over and over again: the whipping, his mother coming to quarters, the sudden appearance of Pappy as he and his mother carried gunnysacks she had stolen from the plantation, his realization that he and his mother were going to try to escape, the mind numbing running and waiting as they wound through the big swamp, the recurring dream of barking dogs, and now the unreliable white man.

No one had said anything crawling into the loft up a wooden ladder. The family with the four girls had crawled on hands and knees to the far wall. One by one, exhausted slaves filled up the small, dark space until, finally, Preacher and Chas crawled up and the small trap door was put into place.

Pretty soon Joshua was sure he was the only one awake. His back hurt, making his whole body hurt, his arms, legs, and head. Finally, after what seemed forever, he, too, slept.

***

A large hand touched Joshua's shoulder. He opened his eyes and saw his father kneeling next to him with his finger on his lips. People were quietly moving.

"Mr. Jemmie's moving us," Pappy whispered. He climbed down the ladder.

Joshua was confused. The loft was full of dim sunlight and uncomfortably hot. He had thought they were going to wait until dark to start running again. Moving in day seemed unacceptably risky. Had the white man betrayed them after all? No dogs were barking. They had to have been put back in the house.

Joshua felt better than he had when they had climbed the rickety wooden ladder to the loft. The loft floor was more comfortable than where he slept in the quarters. At home the floorboards had rotted and poked him whenever he shifted his body. The loft floor was sound and not only had a covering of straw but was smooth and didn't poke him.

His mother hovered over him in the loft's dim light as she crawled toward the ladder. "You okay?" she asked softly, hesitating for a moment before turning her body backwards to descend. Joshua looked blankly at her, trying to shake fog out of his head. "This is a lot to take on when you didn't expect it, I know" she whispered.

"You could have hinted," he said at last, trying to keep accusation out of his voice.

She looked away from him as Massie crawled around her to the trap door and backed down the ladder. Jamie and Jeremiah both smiled at Joshua as they disappeared into the barn.

Joshua looked at his mother's tired face. The determination he'd encountered when she'd come to get him to go to the preacher's meeting was back in her eyes. "I couldn't have," she said, her voice so soft he could barely make out her words.

She backed to the ladder and quickly climbed out of the loft.

In the barn, the white man, wearing a funny square hat, had harnessed a team of large brown horses that looked muscular and had arched backs. As the quiet slaves surrounded him, he looked uncomfortable, as if he didn't like what he was doing. Pappy stood at the two horses' heads, holding the traces.

When everyone was out of the attic, Mr. Jemmie cleared his throat.

"I know I said you could spend the night here," he said nervously. "But my family is worried. I wasn't going to tell them about you, but I didn't think there would be so many. What I'm going to do instead is cover you with straw. A couple of you are going to have to risk following through the fields on foot. I've got two wagons. One's pretty old and used up, but I put some boards down. It won't be comfortable, but it'll work. Not every farmer has four horses, but I do." There was a hint of pride in his voice.

"What we're going to do is load into the wagons. I'll drive one and be in front. Mr. Woodruff will drive the other one. Mr. Bullock and Mr. Bennett have told me they're walking. They feel like they're the ones that can move the fastest on foot. We're going to go out through the back of my property and pick up the road Winston Rogers put in to get to the sawmill he built five years ago and then gave up on. The road isn't in good shape, but it goes into the woods several miles, passing only one squatter cabin. The Baileys like to be left alone. Those on foot will be able to avoid the cabin. It'll be getting toward dark by the end of the road. At that point you'll get out of the wagon beds and go on your way. I'll have done my duty both by you and God."

He paused and looked at Chas standing directly in front of him. Chas looked at Preacher. What was the use of asking questions? Joshua asked himself.

"We'll be all right. God is looking after us," Preacher said, looking shaken. "I will strengthen thee; yea, I will help thee; yea," he said in his deep voice.

They had barely started, and their plans were already not working out. Joshua wasn't surprised.

"It'll be a little out of the way," Chas said somberly, but then walked toward the barn door. "God knows how we get everybody together down the road," he muttered as he went out into the sunshine.

The white man didn't respond to Chas's muttering, but climbed up on the wagon's seat and stared toward the open doors. Preacher and Pappy started dividing them up, pointing smaller people, including Joshua and the old woman, outside to the older wagon.

Jamie, Jeremiah, and the oldest girl from the family with four girls drifted with Joshua out of the barn behind the horses.

"My uncle's not happy," Jamie said in close to his normal voice. He did not try to whisper.

Joshua looked at him. He was taller and, like his father, darker than Joshua, though his hair was not quite as black. Around the quarters the two of them, often with Jeremiah in tow, were a constant presence. The only teenagers around, they were allies in a world mostly against them.

"You didn't tell me you had a freed uncle," Joshua said, the irritation he'd felt with his mother as she climbed down the ladder from the loft adding sharpness to his voice. He stopped and looked at Jamie. "You didn't tell me your family was going to try to escape."

"Boys," Willie, who was just in front of them, said, turning around to look at them.

"We didn't know we were escaping or that we had a freed uncle," Jeremiah said, ignoring the shocked look on Jamie's face.

"Are you two friends?" the girl asked. She sounded doubtful. About Joshua and Jamie's age, maybe a year younger, she had long black hair and thick lips, and a face that seemed as it had been carved from an ideal of what a girl's face should look like. Not used to girls his own age, Joshua thought she was prettier than any girl he'd ever seen. He was shocked she'd turned away from her family and come up to them without hesitating. "My name's Esta May," she added. "Esta May

Woodruff."

"Boys, Esta May," Willie said again, holding his finger over his lips and looking exasperated.

"Glad to meet you," Joshua muttered without trying to make himself heard. "Good Lord," he thought. He was escaping with these people, putting his and his mother's life in their hands, and he didn't even know them.

In the big space outside the barn Chas and Joshua's father, using wooden pitchforks, threw straw over the top of the seven people who had crowded over rough boards thrown into the old wagon's bottom. The two brown horses hitched to the wagon looked old, too, but Joshua didn't pay them much mind. At his father's signal, he climbed up with Jamie, Jeremiah, and Esta May into the wagon from the barn and tried to get comfortable. The road was rough, the white man had said.

The thing was, though, he told himself, by traveling this way—if they weren't caught—they'd be a long way from the farm by nightfall. If they could keep moving all night again maybe they'd have a chance. He hadn't thought about the possibility that they might actually escape. He had just moved with his mother, assuming, he suddenly realized, that they would be caught and brought back to the Bulrush plantation. For the first time he wondered what freedom, talked about in whispers so often in the quarters, might be like.

Then the wagons were rolling. Joshua felt as if he had been put in a closed sack like Old Simpson had been put in for burying after he had died. He was sweating from afternoon heat and the bodies crammed next to him. He didn't know how he was going to stay still while horses plodded over rough roads for however many miles they would be going. He could wander in his thoughts, he decided, and maybe sleep, no matter how rough the road was, as long as he didn't have to go back to the Bulrush plantation.

The realization that he didn't want to go back, even if all punishment were suspended, surprised him. The quarters were what he had known all his life, the quarters and the Master's big white house. He had not expected to run away. He had not expected a father. He was exhausted. The run through the swamp had been a nightmare.

He closed his eyes. Keeping them open was hard beneath the straw. He wondered if he, his mother, and Pappy were on the Underground Railroad he'd heard quarter slaves whisper about. He wondered ....

Chapter 3
Like Moses in the Wilderness

Like Moses fleeing from the Pharaoh's wrath
Before the miracle of waters parting,
The preacher blazed a trail on freedom's path
As fear accompanied their endless fleeing.

What was that man or woman really seeing
As they snuck past and tried so hard to hide?
What accident of fate would send them running
As slavers found them tired and terrified?

The preacher prayed away grim miles and tried
To make their spirits testify that dreams
Are greater than the fear that crucified
Their faith that they could get across the streams
And past the towns that blocked their way and threatened
To let the slavers pounce and leave them bludgeoned.

When Joshua crawled out of the straw he felt better. The wagon ride had been jarring and made his bones ache, but he'd managed to sleep most of the way. No one was allowed to talk, or even groan, so sleeping had been the best thing to do. It seemed the older people crammed in beside them had not fared as well. They groaned as they climbed out of the dimness.

Looking around, Joshua realized a young white boy, no older than he, was now sitting on the newer wagon's seat. When Joshua looked up at the boy, the boy smiled shyly and tipped his head in greeting. Joshua instinctively looked away. Even white children could be dangerous to a slave. Joshua's father and Willie were already encouraging people, who had not been able to move for too long and were stiff, away from the wagons into the road.

"We're going to wait here," Pappy told the slaves. "It's going to take a while for Preacher and Chas to get here." He looked up at the white man and his son. "We appreciate this, sir," he said. "I know how risky this is for you. Not every man would do it, not for a bunch of slaves."

"I hate slavery," the man said without getting off the wagon. "It's an abomination in God's eyes. A man should not put another man in chains. I don't hold to those who see you as less than men." He looked at his son. "Eli," he said.

Eli did not acknowledge his father, but climbed down from his wagon seat and climbed up on the other wagon as Willie gave up the reins.

Joshua realized his mouth had dropped open and snapped it shut. A white man who hated slavery? The Master and Overseer said that God had made white men naturally superior to negras. Blacks needed the white man to make sure they followed the right ways in life.

White people were masters, people who told black people what to do. He had heard the Bulrush plantation was harsher than others. In the quarters at night people talked endlessly about other masters they'd known and about how some were better than others, but he had never imagined white people could actually be human beings. The white man in the funny hat had shaken Chas Bullock's hand as if he was not a master, and Chas was his equal, not a slave. The world seemed to hold surprises Joshua had not dreamed could be true.

Still, the whole idea of Mr. Jemmie didn't sit right, not really. He wondered yet again if Chas and Preacher were right in placing their trust in him. In the end, white men were white. They were not human the way slaves were. They couldn't be. Mr. Jemmie didn't act like other white people, but that did not mean he could be trusted. Not ever. He had to be treated carefully and with respect that did not really mean respect, but a quiet obedience .

His father touched his arm. "Joshua?"

Joshua turned and saw his mother where the road ended at the edge of the woods. She was waiting for him. The look on her face told him she would forgive no dawdling.

Joshua sighed and followed her as Mr. Jemmie and his son turned the wagons around in the tight cleared space at the road's end.

"I'll pick up the other two if I see them and bring them back here," Mr. Jemmie said. "I probably won't see them, but if I do, they'll get here faster."

Pappy, holding the lead horse's reins to help the wagon turn the tight circle, nodded his thanks.

In the woods, the band of travelers settled in a spot where basswood with grayish trunks stood and undergrowth was sparse to wait for Pappy and Willie, unsure about what to do. The older couple, the youngest girl, and the other two men sat on the ground and put their backs up against tree trunks. When Pappy and Willie arrived, the men quickly jumped to their feet again. Jamie, Jeremiah, Esta May, and Esta May's younger sister Ella had all drifted over to stand by Joshua.

"Relax," Pappy told them. "We're going to rest for a while. None of us know where we're going. Chas is the one who has the best idea. Maybe having Chas and Preacher as the walkers was a bad decision." He paused. "But I don't know all of you, and you don't know me. We've already spent hours together, so we should maybe use this time putting names to faces."

Willie sat up and put his arms around his knees. "I'll start," said the medium-sized man with a face made for smiling, even though it didn't get to that often. "I'm Willie Bullock, Chas's brother, though I hadn't seen him for a long while before last week." He motioned to Massie. "Massie's my wife, though on Bulrush's folks who weren't married weren't allowed to jump the broom. The Overseer was a slave, and he didn't countenance any humanity at all." The women, including Joshua's mother, smiled. Willie pointed at Jamie and Jeremiah. "The boys are Jamie and Jeremiah, our sons. Most of you know us from meetings."

"We're Harrison and Junebug Stimson," the old man said, looking from one to the other of them with a direct gaze. Both he and Junebug's foreheads had wrinkles furrowing the skin above black eyebrows. Junebug looked steadily at her husband as he talked, even though Joshua thought she looked slight enough to blow away in a stiff wind. "We come from the Billard plantation and been coming to meetings ever since Tom Bennett met me in town while the Master was off drinking his whiskey on a hot day."

Both he and Junebug, whose hair looked more blue-black than either black or gray, smiled. Her face retained a youthful sweetness, even though it was really old. She even looked a little bit sassy despite what had to have been almost impossible exertion as they had fled the cypress tree. "We're too old for this and prob'ly shouldn't have tried," she said. "But we've waited and looked for a chance like this for so long. Freedom sounds so good. If we become too much of a burden we'll drop behind, avoid capture as long as we can, and fend for ourselves." She looked to her husband, who nodded his agreement.

Jamie touched Joshua's shoulders and motioned when Joshua looked at him. "Come on," he said.

The tall, thin man with the little girl and a wife a foot shorter than he was said, "We're Woodruffs from the Greason plantation. We don't know everybody. I'm Franklin. This is Zelda and Abbie." He kept glancing at the ground as he talked. He pointed to the man standing next to him. "Bill's my older brother." He looked up from the ground at Pappy as if to see if he had said what had been asked of him.

"I don't know everybody," Joshua said quietly to Jamie, irritation in his voice. "Seems like we should," he continued. "We're depending on them."

"We already know everybody," Jeremiah announced. "Except the big man and our uncle."

The last man to speak, who ran like a stork with jerky, long, almost uncoordinated strides, squatted on his heels. "I'm Bill Woodruff," he said. He bit his words off as if he was more used to silence than talking. "Franklin's older brother. Our household has Beulah and our daughter Ertha, the young one there." He pointed. "Then Ella, Eunice, and the oldest, over there by the boys." He smiled. "Esta May."

Jamie touched Joshua's shoulder again. Joshua looked at his mother. She did not look happy with him.

"Come on," Jamie said.

"I'm Jason Billings," Pappy said. "This is Mary Simpson." He gestured grandly toward Joshua's mother. "You all know her." Pappy hesitated and then pointed to Joshua. "That's Joshua, our son."

Joshua nodded at the group of adults before turning abruptly and following Jamie. Ella, with Ertha tagging along, walked gracefully away from her mother and father and toward Esta May. Esta May and Jeremiah followed Jamie and Joshua.

The minute they were out of sight of the adults, Jamie stopped beside a lone sycamore growing amidst the basswood. He turned and confronted Joshua, a stubborn look on his face.

"What are you all high and mighty about?" he asked as the younger kids caught up to them.

Joshua looked back at him as stubbornly as he always did whenever he was challenged. "You didn't let me know what was going on," he said. "You're supposedly my best friend and didn't breathe a word about your freed uncle or running away or anything. You were going away and didn't even say boo."

He looked at Jeremiah who had started, in his usual way, to say something even if he wasn't being addressed. Smaller than Jamie, he still usually put himself forward as if he were the older one. "You neither," Joshua added aggressively.

Jamie stared at him. "We couldn't say anything," he said defensively. "Paw and Maw warned us. They said just your knowing would make it harder on you after Silver Coats and the master figured out we'd run."

"I was coming with you," Joshua countered. "I'm here, aren't I? I just didn't know it. You could have warned me."

"Paw said you weren't," Jeremiah popped up, unable to control himself any longer. "He said your Maw wouldn't come."

Joshua glared at him. Jeremiah, suddenly frightened, looked at Jamie.

I wasn't supposed to come? My mother hadn't planned on coming? He shook his head.

Esta May impulsively put her hand on his shoulder. He glanced at her and then looked away. "But ...."

"I wanted to tell you," Jamie said. "I just couldn't. If I'd known you were coming, we could have talked and got ready together."

"It doesn't matter," Esta May said. "We got enough to worry about. We got to keep from getting caught. If we're caught, we'll get whipped, and I've never been whipped before."

The boys looked at her in amazement. At the Bulrush's all slaves were whipped. It was part of everyday life. Sometimes the whipping was just more serious.

"Knowing you were running or not knowing ahead of time won't mean anything if we're caught," she continued.

Ella stared at her sister with wide eyes, but did not say anything. She was a slight girl and slender. Her face was plain, unlike her older sister's, and she seemed even younger than she probably was.

"Joshua was whipped bad just before we left the quarters," Jeremiah said. "We thought maybe the Overseer wouldn't let us go to the meeting the way he usually did."

"He didn't cry," Jamie added. "He never cries." He'd always been amazed by Joshua's self-control.

The two girls looked shocked, as if they had never known a boy could be whipped the way Joshua had been over and over again. Esta May took her hand off his shoulder as if he'd burned her.

Joshua sighed. Darkness was gathering. He wondered if they'd run any further or if they'd have to wait all night for Preacher and Chas. The fact his mother had told Willie and Massie that they weren't going to join the others running away troubled him. She and the Bullock adults must have talked about the escape. In the woods Chas had told Mr. Jemmie he hadn't expected so many. He wondered if he and his mother were the ones not expected. But at the cypress tree Chas had seemed to know Pappy, his father. He suspected the reason they had joined the others was his father's presence. The whole thing was a puzzle.

"I don't want us to be caught," Eunice, the smallest girl who had joined them, said. Eunice's voice was softer than Esta May's or Ella's.

"They won't catch us," Jeremiah said cockily. "Nobody catches a bunch of wild crows once they get away." He laughed.

Jamie looked disgusted. "May the Lord keep and protect us," he said.

The look in the Overseer's eyes popping into his mind made Joshua shudder. "Esta May's right," he said. He held his hand out solemnly to Jamie. "Our job is to escape. Really."

Jamie smiled and took Joshua's hand and shook it. Esta May smiled, too.

Beulah Woodruff, a robust woman who was clearly the one in the family that Esta May most resembled, came around brush hiding them from the adults. She walked slowly to where they were by the sycamore.

"Esta May?"

"Yes, Maw," Esta May said, and she and Ella started walking to where the adults were gathered. The three boys and Eunice followed.

Pappy and Joshua's mother were on the ground beside each other, their backs against a large basswood's trunk. They'd been talking, but when they saw Joshua they looked up at him. His mother smiled.

"We can rest now," she said. "Preacher and Chas won't be here for hours."

"Sitting still doesn't seem right," Pappy said. He sounded nervous. "Seems like if we're running, we should keep running."

Joshua looked intently at the two of them without sitting. His mother, like everyone else, was a lot smaller than Pappy. He had to admit they seemed close to each other, as if they really did belong together.

"Jamie says we weren't going to escape with the preacher," he told his mother, his voice sounding angry even to him.

Pappy looked at Mary Simpson's face before sitting up straight, away from the tree trunk. She looked startled and pained.

"We need to rest," Pappy said sternly.

"I didn't know your father would be with the Preacher for sure," his mother said. "When I was told that by Massie, we had to come."

"But you stole the food in the gunnysacks," Joshua protested. "You knew they'd know who did that. The Overseer would have ...." He imagined the strength and viciousness Silver Coats would have put into blows aimed at his mother. Joshua could not count the number of times he'd been told that his mother "put on too many airs" for a "negra" woman.

Her face grew hard. "The Master shouldn't always get his way," she said, her voice harsh.

Joshua stared at her in disbelief. *What is she saying? What is she thinking?*

His father got to his feet and put his big hands on Joshua's shoulders. The man's strength was incredible even though he was being gentle.

"Rest," Pappy commanded. "Hold your peace for now and rest."

Joshua stood against the shoulder pressure for a moment, fighting his father's authority. *Why do you have any right to tell me what to do? You haven't been around my entire life.*

Joshua yielded and sat beside his mother.

After a few minutes of uncomfortable silence, his father cleared his throat. "I'll be right back." He turned and walked toward the road.

***

Most of them were asleep when Preacher found them. Jason had been waiting by the road and led the exhausted man to the rest of them in the woods. Then he went around gently waking people.

After they were awake, Preacher, feeling tired and old, got them together. Even his voice had lost some of its vitality.

"Chas tells me we're off the course we were meant to be on," he said. "He's gone to find out how we get back to where we need to be. We're blessed to be this far away from where we started, but we need to keep moving. There's not much night left, but I think we ought to get as far as we can and rest when morning comes. Chas has help waiting for us in the hills up ahead, but we can't be late getting to where we need to be." He paused, massaging his chin with his hand as if that would ease his exhaustion. "Let's say a prayer to ourselves as we move," he finished. "Then keep moving."

He looked at each of them, trying to see even into the young people's eyes. After a brief moment with his head bowed, he started walking north.

There could not be much left to the night, Joshua thought, but he also felt, like Pappy had hinted at earlier, relieved to be moving again. The further they were from the Overseer and Master Bulrush, the better.

***

Chas did not show up for two days. In the dark before morning they walked steadily, but slowly, trying to avoid brush, roots sticking out of the ground, and overhanging branches. The woods were dry, so they did not get wet the way they had running through the swamp, but they were unfamiliar and difficult to navigate. The preacher never hesitated. He was pushing himself almost beyond his endurance, but he kept walking with his body leaning forward.

Joshua's mother kept close to her son as they moved. Nobody talked much. They had managed to sleep waiting for the preacher, but now fear made them bite words off if they discovered they had something to say. The general sense was that only if they were silent, even if they were in wilderness, could their escape become real.

Dawn was not long in coming. Pappy seemed to have inexhaustible energy. As far as Joshua knew, he had not slept with the rest of them, but had waited by the road watching most of the night. He made sure the old people kept up, and sometimes carried Abbie, or even Ertha, on his shoulders. The little girls still did not complain. Abbie wore a determined, stubborn look on her small face that reminded Joshua of how he often felt inside his head.

Watching his father, Joshua thought about how his mother had acted when Jason had come out from behind the tree in the swamp. She hadn't fussed over him as if she hadn't seen him for a long time. Joshua wondered if she and his father had been in contact in some way. How that could happen since his mother was seldom allowed out of the big house to even come see him, her only son, was a mystery. It didn't seem possible, but the more he thought about it, the more he became convinced they had been seeing each other. They had kept it secret so that it could not get out the way secrets almost always got out in the quarters. They had not even let him know.

When first light turned the night sky a dirty gray, Preacher called a halt. Joshua and his mother were almost always in sight of Preacher since his father had determined that they belonged close to the front of those picking their way through tree trunks and the tangle of heavy brush.

Chas had not yet made an appearance, so they were on their own without the guidance on which Preacher and Pappy relied. After they had all gathered, Preacher had them bow their heads. He said another prayer thanking the Lord and Jesus Christ for their first days of freedom out of slavery. Then he talked about an island in a great lake in a wilderness called New Jerusalem. Jesus Christ had supposedly lived a long time ago, Joshua thought, and Jerusalem, if it still existed, was a long way away. When Preacher had finished the prayer, Joshua wondered why he kept talking about New Jerusalem, but then was told to find a place to sleep.

"We're free, thank the Lord we're free," his mother whispered as they found a small opening in the heavy brush where they could lay down.

***

The next morning, the routine that would define their flight began. Joshua woke while the sun was high in the sky. He was caught up on sleep, but hungry. The food they'd brought with them was dwindling. It was hot. Even though he'd slept on the ground, he was sweating. His mother was still sleeping, although his father had left them and was already checking to make sure everyone was okay.

Joshua looked around at the other young people. Nobody had wandered very far from where they'd spent the night. Esta May joined him when he squatted on his heels to watch his big father. She pointed to Abbie, who was still sleeping between her parents.

"Abbie's your cousin," she said. "She came from the same plantation your," she hesitated, "father came from."

Joshua looked closely at the little girl and then at her parents. One surprise after another, it seemed. The little girl was plucky. She kept up the best way she could and did not complain. Her father, mother, and

Pappy had carried her off and on, but she seemed determined even though she was too little to keep up.

The idea of having relatives seemed strange, almost as strange as having a father.

"Franklin Woodruff's my Pappy's brother?" He squinted at Esta May who had squatted down beside him.

"Paw says Zelda's his half-sister," she said. "They had the same mother."

The implications of having the "same mother" sank into the silence that followed Esta May's revelation. Joshua did not say anything, but continued to stare at his sleeping cousin. He glanced at Pappy's half-sister. She looked nothing like him. She was not overly large. She didn't seem delicate, but she wasn't much bigger than Joshua was. None of the women with them had the refined aura his mother did. Zelda was lighter than Pappy or the other women. It was hard for him to see the two of them as brother and sister.

As Joshua thought about the Franklin Woodruffs, he also started thinking again about New Jerusalem. Preacher kept talking about it as if it were a place in the remote wilderness on an even remoter island. *What is it really?*

"How do you know about my father?" he asked Esta May.

Jamie was stretching, waking up Jeremiah.

"My Paw was sold off their plantation when they were all young," Esta May said. "He said that master was always buying and selling slaves."

Joshua glanced at his mother. Preacher had woken and was on his feet.

"Pretty confusing," Joshua said. "All these slaves all over the place. Some even related."

"South Carolina's a long way away, too," Esta May commented.

Joshua looked at her sharply. "South Carolina? Pappy's from South Carolina?"

Mystery was piling on top of mystery, and neither his mother nor Pappy was telling him anything. *How could Pappy have made it to Missouri from South Carolina as an escaped slave?* Pappy was one of the most remarkable looking men Joshua had ever seen. *How could he have come so far without being noticed? How far away was South Carolina from Missouri? How had he known where we were? How had he even found us? Chas Woodruff had said he knew Pappy. How had that happened? And how had the two of them discovered Preacher?*

"I think we can move during the day in these woods," Preacher announced. Everyone was awake and on their feet now. Most had gone off into the woods for morning necessities. "There's no use milling around. That can attract as much attention as us walking. We might as well get going."

People started moving toward Preacher, expecting a prayer, but Preacher seemed to have forgotten his usual pattern. He moved north again without looking at anybody or saying anything. Jamie joined Esta May and Joshua away from their parents.

As afternoon gave way to evening and evening to night, they hardly stopped to devour the small portions of food Franklin Woodruff carefully handed out. When night finally gave way to dawn, they were still deep in the woods with no sign of other people. Joshua, like the rest of them, had settled into a daze. Most of the time he was not aware of thinking at all. Their ceaseless movement kept him going through and around, carefully watching the ground for things that could not be seen clearly in the dark. They sometimes heard deer in the brush, or a hawk or other bird as dawn neared, but mostly they were alone.

***

After another day of sleeping until darkness fell, they had been walking for hours when Chas appeared. Joshua's father was checking on the old couple when Preacher, always in front of the rest of them, stopped. Chas was then standing beside him, waiting for the others.

"These woods go on longer than I thought," he said. Joshua was surprised to hear him using a normal voice rather than a whisper. They all had gotten used to whispering when they had to talk. "We ought to be safe in here for another day. We're not far from where we need to be, but after tomorrow we'll be in hills, and we can't avoid crossing roads."

"Are the roads isolated?" Preacher asked. "Can we avoid being seen?"

Chas was silent as he looked around at the group. "There's one spot," he said. "A bridge. I couldn't find a way across. I think it's the St Francis River, but I'm not sure. I can't find a place where it can be waded. It's running pretty high. There are houses by the bridge—and dogs.

"Just beyond, if we can get to him, a preacher's willing to put us in wagons and haul us north for fifty or sixty miles. But we've got to figure out a way to cross the river."

"We're getting down to the last food," Willie Bullock said.

His brother looked at him. "I know," he said, his voice sober. "Mary risked a lot for what she could gather, but we need help. And there's no help except beyond that bridge. There's not enough anti-slavery belief in this area. Further north …."

"We've been hungry before," Joshua's father said. He was standing beside Mary. "Going hungry for a while in exchange for freedom's a pretty good trade."

Preacher smiled at him. "God will take care of us," he said, pressing his hands together as if he were praying.

"One step at a time makes a journey," Massie Bullock said.

"One step at a time," Preacher repeated. Then he followed Chas.

The conversation had left Joshua feeling queasy. He did *not* like the thought of a bridge they would have to cross where dogs and white people lived. Dogs on the plantation had always been friendly enough to him and the other kids, but they had barked ferociously whenever a strange person, white or slave, came near the Master's house or quarters. Somebody, no matter how late it was, always came out to see who had come.

His back had healed pretty well, but as his mother impulsively grabbed his hand as they followed Preacher and Chas, he felt the pain of the whip cutting into his flesh.

"Slaves really didn't escape," he thought, although they had managed to come a long way. They were always caught. Old Simpson's face in the dark cabin always walked with him.

He wondered if Preacher and the God he kept bringing up every time he spoke were powerful enough to really let them get away without facing hell.

Chapter 4
The Bridge that was a Wall

The bridge, inside the night, was like a wall,
Small, wooden, unassuming, houses dark
Beside a path that seemed to be a call
To all who needed passage to embark
Upon a journey to the river's other side.

They hid in brush, mouths dry, dread strong enough
To make them sick, and, silently, wide-eyed,
Saw spectres armed with whips and iron cuffs
Stand gleaming where they'd have to cross the bridge
Without disturbing dogs or waking up
The people in the houses as the ridge
Beyond the river beckoned past the interrupt
Between their anxious, fear-filled dreams and where
Their breaths would feel God's freedom in the air.

    The next day and night were much like the previous day and night.
Sometimes they saw faint signs of people, a trail horses had been on, or
faint smoke from a cooking fire, but Chas kept them in deep forest.

    The sun was descending toward the canopy of branches and leaves
they were walking under, but it was early, rather than late, evening. Chas
had already left, leaving Joshua to wonder if the man ever slept.

    Joshua's father went around stirring everyone to their feet. They were
given a dried apple and a few nuts to eat, along with the information that
this would be their last meal for a while. They had to get out of the
woods to the next place Chas had talked about before they would eat
again. Preacher was the first one ready to go. As the rest of them stirred,
he stood—like Joshua imagined an ancient prophet would have—beneath
a big black walnut tree, hands at his side, and wild eyes looking north as
if he saw beyond the woods to the New Jerusalem he was always going
on about.

    After they had gathered, little Abbie Woodruff for once started
complaining she was tired, but Jason picked her up and hoisted her to his
shoulders. They started walking, Franklin and Zelda beside Pappy and
their daughter. After they had started, Preacher turned around, walking

backwards through a small clearing.

"Chas said we can get further if we walk in the light today," he said. "He said we haven't been near a cabin since early yesterday afternoon. We'll have to go on all night, though. Remember, every step is another step toward freedom."

He turned and strode determinedly through the rest of the clearing into the brush lining the other side.

As walking became more difficult after the sun had set with a golden glow, Joshua noticed they were not moving as frantically as they had been. Pappy had even stopped checking on him so obsessively and was paying more attention to Mary instead. Joshua, Jamie, Jeremiah, and Esta May tended to stick together, sometimes joined by Esta May's younger sisters. Having girls around so often seemed a little strange to Joshua, but, then, the experience they were having was not like a day on the plantation.

They were steadily going north, but the panic driving them had been dulled by routine. After dark had deepened under the wood's canopy, people stumbled more often than they had during their first two nights of fleeing.

Abbie started complaining more often, too. She's too young for this, Joshua thought, even as his irritation at her voice grew. *Will she be able to be quiet if we're facing danger?* She had been unnaturally silent in the barn and moving through the swamp, but Joshua was starting to be a little afraid of her. Her mother was always quick to shush her. She followed her mother's commands, but the longer they kept running, the more normal she became. She was just a young child.

Late in the night, they came to the first road they'd seen since leaving Mr. Jemmie's wagons. It was deserted, so they quickly scrambled across and kept going.

Toward dawn, they passed another road. This one was obviously better traveled than the first one, but it was as empty, so they crossed it quickly, too.

Joshua had been dreaming as he walked, imagining an island in the middle of a large lake restless with big waves, so he was startled when he suddenly became aware that he was in the open beneath a slender silver moon. He, like all of them, he supposed, was beyond tired and hungry, but they could not stop. They had to keep pushing forward.

At dawn, Chas showed up and had them stop on top of a ridge beneath a small hill's crown. He appeared like he always did, so quietly no one had warning before he was suddenly there.

"We'll sleep here today," he said loudly.

They were all hungry. Breakfast had not been much. But no one, not even Abbie, complained. They spread out and made beds of old leaves.

Joshua didn't even look toward Jamie. He walked over to where his mother was kneeling on a bed of oak leaves Pappy had piled up. He was asleep almost before he put his head down.

When the day had mostly passed, Joshua's father and Chas got people up and moving again. After everyone had made their trip into the bushes, Preacher waited while they gathered around him. He started out with his morning prayer about the promise of New Jerusalem and their need for God's protection during their effort to escape the terror of lives lived on plantations.

"Chas tells me this is going to end up being a dangerous day," he said after the prayer. "He estimates that about midnight we're going to be coming to more populated territory. There'll be busier roads than those we crossed yesterday. Then, tomorrow night, we're going to have to cross that bridge he told you about." He paused. "I don't have to tell any of you how dangerous this is. But we have no choice." He glanced at Joshua and then at Franklin Woodruff. "We won't have anything to eat before we get to the bridge, so this is going to be hard, but if everyone can follow what Chas says, we're going to be all right. God is with us in our need."

"I'm going to stay with you now," Chas announced after Preacher had finished. "After the bridge and another six miles we'll be able to get food and rest. We just need to hold ourselves together until then."

***

After a restless day when no one seemed to be able sleep, only partly because of how hungry they were, evening came, with Chas keeping them from going forward.

"We're coming to settled territory again," he said. "We don't want to get near the bridge before dark."

Waiting to travel onward again, Joshua sat talking with Jamie and Jeremiah. They kept their voices so low that no one, other than the three of them, could have possibly heard them.

"I'm a little scared," Joshua admitted.

"That bridge sounds beyond scary," Jeremiah said in an almost inaudible voice. "It sounds like we could get caught there."

"We got to go over it," Jamie said matter-of-factly. "Uncle Chas said we don't have a choice."

Joshua looked intensely at Jamie. "How come he's your uncle and a freedman?" he asked. "You and your parents are slaves. Back in the quarters you never said anything about your freedman uncle."

"Maw and Paw told us not to after they found out he was with the preacher," Jeremiah answered. "They said we had enough troubles without folks knowing about our uncle. They hardly talked about him when we were little. I wasn't even sure he was real until he showed up at the Sunday meeting in the swamp when the preacher started talking about running. They didn't let Jeremiah and me hear anything about their plans, but we guessed. He just surprised us that night."

Joshua sighed. "I didn't know my father existed," he admitted. "My mother didn't say a word about him to me ever. I'm still not sure about what having a father is all about, especially one I never met before."

"The quarters was filled with secrets," Jamie said. "Master Bulrush is a bad master. That's what Paw has always said. Being scared all the time makes people close up. Saying anything can turn into a rumor that reaches the Master's ears and makes bad things happen."

Joshua was silent while thinking about what Jamie was saying. *Was that why my mother never told me about my father? Had she been afraid that if I knew he was on another plantation that the knowledge could create a problem for either me or my father?* He tried to penetrate the fog that always seemed to be in his head whenever he thought of the big man his mother was obviously so attached to. Pappy was always helping everybody, so he was a good man, but Joshua still hadn't come to terms with his existence.

He glanced up and saw Pappy moving around with his mother talking to different people in their what? Camp? How could it be a camp without food or any kind of shelter? Being a slave, he reckoned, meant that none of them had anything.

"We're going," Jamie announced.

Joshua looked from his mother and father to Preacher and Chas. Preacher was motioning to them. Jamie and Joshua got to their feet, but Jeremiah stayed on the ground looking up at them.

"I wonder what not being a slave would be like?" he asked.

Joshua looked sharply at him, but neither he nor Jamie said anything. They moved to where Preacher was getting ready to start the day with their New Jerusalem prayer.

***

Chas disappeared for a half hour or so and then reappeared out of the dark to walk beside Preacher. Jamie, walking by Joshua, pointed at his uncle.

"He's back," he said.

Jamie and Joshua had been walking together since they had started up again. Joshua was thinking about how he had been short with Pappy. The big man had gotten up after hearing Chas say "It's time," and come over to Joshua, a smile on his face. For some reason the smile had gotten under Joshua's skin. Nervous, he had been anxious to move again. He knew he had to listen to Chas and knew the man had a better sense than he did about what to do, but he also felt dogs sniffing their trail, always getting closer. When Pappy had come over to where he was sitting under a sycamore tree, he'd said, out loud, "What do you want?" as if he didn't know. His mother had looked at him, alarmed.

Pappy was always looking after everybody, including him. How could he always seem so calm and in control? Over his mother's objection, Joshua had gotten up from the ground and walked off ahead of everyone. Jamie, seeing him, had hurried and caught up. The truth was that the combination of hunger and the journey's length was making everyone irritable. Plagued by unanswered questions and a sense the Overseer was just ahead or behind them with his whip, Joshua could hardly get himself to believe they might escape. Slaves never escaped. They were always taken to the whipping yard.

"I wonder what Uncle Chas is looking for when he disappears?" Jamie asked.

The two of them had wandered away from the group without realizing it. Chas had noticed and was suddenly beside them. He looked stern in the late afternoon light.

"We can't separate," he said. "I want you boys to make sure you don't wander. You're young and have a lot of energy. The Stimsons are old and can't do what you guys can do, and the little girls are little. We have to keep our wits about us. Okay?"

Then he had turned, sniffing, and looked at the sky. Joshua and Jamie stared. A faint smudge of smoke was just west of where they were heading.

"It's okay," Chas mumbled more to himself than the two of them. He looked at his nephew. "Bunch up," he ordered and made them wait for Preacher before running into the woods toward the smoke.

Joshua thought Preacher might make them stop. Smoke obviously meant that people were nearby. But instead Preacher and Pappy hurried everybody up.

Joshua and Jamie's mothers made a beeline toward their sons as soon as Chas had disappeared.

"I don't think we're ever going to feel clean again," his mother was telling Massie as the two of them came up to the two boys.

"You two can't go off on your own," Massie told them. "Jason says we're coming to places where people are. We can't afford to be careless."

When Jeremiah, who had been talking to Esta May, Ella, Ertha, and Eunice, saw his mother going toward Joshua and Jamie, he broke off from the girls and trotted to his brother's side.

"We understand," Joshua said. Jamie nodded in agreement. They should have been more careful.

Preacher, seeing Pappy walking with the Stimsons and three Franklin Woodruffs, lengthened his stride and started moving even faster.

"Just be careful, that's all," Massie said, pleading in her voice.

Jamie nodded and followed Joshua, who had started matching Preacher's long strides.

The rest of the night fulfilled Chas's prediction. They had not gone far before they came to the first road. Nerves were on edge when Chas motioned to them to stay hidden a bit longer. A horseman passed, going west, just before they came out of the woods. The men, seeing Chas's signal, put their arms out as if they were holding the rest of them back. They crouched behind bushes and tree trunks, hardly daring to breathe. When Chas and Preacher stood up and signaled to cross open space bristling with danger, they all scurried across as fast as they could. They ran like they had run the first night through the swamp.

Not long after the road, they came on the first fields they'd seen since leaving Mr. Jemmie. At first, they were able to keep to the field's edges, hiding in woods, but then they came to where cotton plants stretched out in every direction. Chas did not hesitate, but led them into the field. They were again moving like they had the first night. Being in the open was unnerving. Joshua felt eyes watching every step he took. His mother ran beside him as his father dropped back to the Stimsons.

"The good Lord save us," his mother whispered when they first stepped out in the open.

After the field they crossed another road into a small woodlot that a plantation was using to harvest wood for stoves and fireplaces. They passed areas where there were only the stumps of trees and even saw an axe sticking out of a stump. Out of that woods, they ran through more fields into another wood and then another and then another road. Once they made out slave quarters to the east of where they were running. Later on they saw the master's house of a plantation. A constant fear ran with them.

They were entering another wooded stretch with a high canopy when Joshua realized that the sky had clouded up and a stiff wind was starting to blow. "Oh no," he thought. "It's going to rain." They hadn't had to deal with a storm since starting on their trek to freedom. None of them had spare clothes, of course.

The first drops began to fall just as Chas signaled they were to stop. They clustered together as Chas and Preacher stood waiting. A faint, distant thunder rumbled in western skies.

"We're near the riverbank," Chas said when they were all there. "What we're going to do is go through the willows and brush toward the bridge. When we're near the bridge, but too far away to set the dogs at the houses off, we'll stop before making a run for it. Tom Bennett and I've been talking. We've decided we'll all cross as quickly as we can, all at once. There's no way we won't set the dogs to barking no matter how we do this. If we're lucky, the people in the houses will be asleep, and we'll be out of sight before the dogs get them out of bed to look. Willie?" he asked, pointing at his brother. "You'll carry Abbie." Willie nodded. "Jason," he said, pointing at Joshua's father, "you'll be behind everybody, making sure nobody stumbles."

He paused. Preacher had his head bowed in prayer. "We're not going to talk after this," Chas said at last. "We're sticking together until the bridge. When I stop, you stop." He looked into each one of their eyes, taking his time. "Understood?" he asked at last.

Nobody said a word.

***

In the dark, the river seemed huge. Water flowed swiftly and gurgled and murmured as it rushed past. A raindrop splashed on his head. In the Bulrush fields they worked during rainstorms, but, after the day was done, they could dry out. Here, they'd have to sleep in the storm.

They moved east along a small ridge above the river. The darkness became denser and more thunder rumbled in the sky.

Chas and Preacher stopped. Chas put his arm up in the air and crouched down. Joshua tried to see what the man was looking at, but brush was in his line of sight. Chas looked back at them. Joshua could hear his own heartbeat pounding in his ears. His mouth was dry. A sense of endlessness made the night and storm malevolent, beyond frightening.

"Don't stop," Chas whispered. "No matter what, keep running."

He was whispering, but his voice seemed louder than the peel of thunder accentuating his words. His face hardened, he turned, and they were running. More thunder. Rain fell cold inside a picking-up wind. The three houses were east of the bridge. They were not large, the houses of masters, and they were dark.

Once they broke from the willows and brush, the ground was bare.

Joshua took a quick look around. His mother was beside him, running as fast and as effortlessly as if she had been running like this her whole life. He could not hear dogs. Thunder rolled again. The rain came down harder in wind-driven sheets. The sound the storm was making might have hidden their running sounds. Then Joshua heard them, but the houses stayed dark and still. No one was yet awake to see what was happening at the bridge.

Then they were on the bridge, then on the other side of the bridge. Joshua looked back. The Stimsons, as usual, were bringing up the rear with his father. He could not make out faces in the storm, but they seemed graceful and ghostly as they moved. A forking flash of blue lightning lit the sky. They all turned right, following Chas and Preacher, and were finally in the relative safety of woods again.

Joshua could still not make out lantern light at the houses across the river. He and the others were breathing hard. Esta May was on her knees retching up the nothing in her stomach. Her mother was beside her. "It's okay, Esta," she said over and over again. "We made it. We're over the bridge."

Preacher, looking nervous, put his hand on Chas's shoulder. "Wait," he said.

"We've got to get moving. We can't stay here," Chas answered, impatience in his voice. Joshua thought he could hear a hint of the fear that was making him feel slightly ill in Chas's voice as well.

The rain had turned into a deluge. Wind whistled through the canopy. Preacher bent down beside Esta May.

"Esta May?" he asked.

Beulah took her eyes off her daughter and looked at Preacher. "We'll keep up," she said.

Bill took his daughter's arm. Esta May got control of her stomach and shakily got to her feet. Joshua's father knelt on one knee. "Crawl on my back," he told the girl. Bill started to object, but looked toward his wife and daughter and stopped whatever he was going to say. Esta May hesitated—*I'm too old to be carried like Abbie*—but then put her arms around Pappy's neck. He rose and immediately they were walking again as the rain fell, wind blew, thunder rumbled, and lightning flashed over and over again.

They were past the bridge.

Chapter 5
Miracle Inside a Storm from Hell

Their misery growing as they splashed through streams,
They felt huge clouds above the battered trees
That flung down branches as the sorceries
Of wind and hunger roused a storm of screams
Into their fears, their hatred, useless dreams
The preacher had asserted with an ease
That wasn't true, not when the miseries
Of hell danced in the storm's wild, fierce extremes.

And then, as if inside a miracle,
They reached a lonely church, the raging storm
So fell they quailed inside its crucible,
And knew the light of God, their spirits warm,
The dreams the preacher preached so lyrical
It made them feel, inside their hell, reborn.

The storm intensified. Rain plastered Joshua's threadbare shirt and pants against his skin. At first the ground was only wet, but as gusts of wind shook the canopy, streamlets rushed down hillsides as they climbed. When they crested the hill north and east of the river, they followed a downhill slope into a stream's rushing wildness that made Joshua pause before he reluctantly crossed it. Black water pounded his legs. Halfway across, he looked up from the water and saw an exhausted-looking Franklin carrying Abbie across the torrent. Joshua wondered, before forcing himself forward again, how Abbie, or even Eunice, could keep going day after day. They were so young and so small.

On the stream's other side, back under oak and walnut trees, several people were kneeling in the mud. Joshua felt faint-headed. None of them had eaten for far too long. Preacher was going from one individual to the next, touching arms and heads with his large hands.

"We'll rest before dawn," he said over and over again. "And we'll be safe before too many more miles."

In the open, as they crossed the stream, rain hit them with such force it stung their skin. Too many eyes stared at Preacher as though they could not understand what he was telling them. Thunder rolled a long roar above their heads. Lightning, smelling like ozone, lit blue-white traceries in a black sky.

Joshua's father got them going again. He still had Esta May on his shoulders. Joshua marveled that he could carry someone her size so far in such conditions. When Jason got to where the rest of them had stopped, eyes vacant as they let the storm's fierceness pound them, he put Esta May on the ground and looked at her.

"Can you walk now?" he asked, stretching his shoulders. Esta May nodded and took his hand as he lurched from where he was standing up the next hill's slope. "Come on then," he said, looking around. "We've got to move. Preacher's right. We've got to get to where we can get food and rest."

Preacher stopped trying to comfort everyone and walked calmly to the front, taking the lead for the first time since they had left the swamp. Chas went to Junebug and Harrison and gave the old woman his hand to help her to her feet. Joshua, Mary, Jamie, and Jeremiah followed Jason, while the others trailed behind Chas and the Stimsons.

The next few hours were nightmare. Just when it seemed the thunder had rolled to a stop, it began again, driving lightning wild as it peaked toward a crescendo. Rain fell and fell, driven by winds that swirled and blew into their faces even beneath the trees. Nobody fell behind, though. As they got to the crest of the second hill, Jason dropped back behind everyone again and helped whoever stumbled or looked on the verge of collapse. Chas and Preacher started downhill and kept going over hill after hill.

They had come off the slope of a particularly big hill into a flat stretch of land when Chas stopped. He looked at Preacher. Preacher smiled. "Thank God Almighty," he said.

"You need to wait here," Chas said as loud as he could to make sure his voice carried over the wind. The thunder increased, then paused again. Joshua stopped and looked about. For a minute, no one else stopped. Then several people walked to a wet tree trunk and used their hands to help them sit on soaked ground. The night was not cold, but he was shivering. Chas disappeared into a copse of brush.

"We're almost saved," Preacher announced. Then he, like everyone else, was silent. He half collapsed to wet ground.

Joshua's mother followed the example of the other adults, went to a tree and leaned on the trunk as she slowly lowered herself to the ground. She looked at Joshua after she was sitting with her back to the tree.

"I knew this would be hard," she said. "I couldn't bear to leave without you." He thought she might be crying, but it was difficult to tell because of rain running down her face.

Joshua didn't sit even though he was exhausted. He looked up at scuttling clouds he could sense, but not see in the darkness. The night had to be close to being over. Rain forced him to close his eyes.

"If we make freedom," he said. "I'll thank you for making me come every day the rest of my life."

She looked so exhausted he wasn't certain she'd understood his words, but, after a long moment, she smiled.

Joshua had just sat beside his mother when Chas came out of darkness again, looking significantly more energized than when he'd gone off. He went straight to Abbie and picked her up from where she was leaning on her mother's shoulder.

"Let's go!" he said loudly. "They're waiting for us."

Abbie stared blankly into his face. "'They're?'" Joshua thought. "Who's 'they're?'"

Zelda, Abbie's mother, quickly got to her feet. She was not going to let her daughter out of her sight. The thunder rolled again, covering groans as almost everyone objected to moving even though where they were on the ground was miserable. Joshua's father and Preacher helped the Stimsons and women and girls to their feet. Jamie and Jeremiah, standing beside their father and mother, looked expectant, as if they thought the energy in Chas's voice might mean something important. Esta May, just a few feet from Jamie and Jeremiah, got to her feet and helped her youngest sister, Ertha, stand. The rest of the Woodruffs followed the two of them.

A few minutes later they were on their way again. They had not gone far, however, when they stopped. A tall, stooped man was walking toward them through the storm. They had only met two people, the white farmer and his son, since they had left the swamp.

Joshua felt his heart pounding in his ears again. His mouth was dry in the way it had been in the brush before the bridge. He hated white people. Even if Mr. Jemmie had helped them. Uneasy feelings assaulted him the minute he saw one. Master Bulrush seemed to stare out of their white man's eyes, diminishing who Joshua was or could ever be with his hate-filled stare.

"Reverend!" Chas said. Abbie buried her head in his shoulder. Preacher came forward, too.

The man was pasty white in the darkness. Joshua held back, staying close to his mother, who had put her hand on his arm.

"Welcome," the white man said. He wore a long cloak that was repelling the rain. "We've got a little food. Come."

Food. Joshua's stomach rumbled. Hearing the promise in the man's voice, all of them stepped forward almost at once.

A few minutes later, they were in a clearing around a white church with a wooden steeple and actual windows facing the woods. The church stood at the end of a road. A small white house was beside it. Lantern light lit both the house and the front of the church.

As they climbed wooden steps to the church, the door opened and spilled light from inside into the storm's darkness. Joshua did not hesitate, but scaled the steps, following his mother. Chas, Abbie, Preacher, and the Woodruffs were already inside. It felt odd to finally be out of the rain. He and the others were dripping all over the stone floor in a small room with a door to the chapel. An elderly white woman greeted each of them as they came inside.

"Welcome," she said. "Welcome. We're glad you're here."

The man closed the door when everyone was out of the storm, then hurried to a bushel basket in the corner of the room. The woman turned and started handing out small apples. When Joshua got his apple, he didn't hesitate. He bit into it and finished it so fast he could hardly believe it was gone. It tasted so sweet it made him feel more alive than he had ever been in his life. The white man handed him another apple, and he ate that. Then the bushel basket was empty. A willow basket appeared, and the woman started handing out biscuits. Real biscuits! Better biscuits than any that Joshua had ever eaten in his life.

When the biscuits were gone Joshua was even hungrier than he had been before. He looked around for more food and noticed that Preacher was looking at the mess they'd made on the floor. Muddy puddles were everywhere. The white woman, seeing Preacher's look of dismay, shook her head.

"Don't worry about that none," she said. "It'll clean."

"It's been a long trail," Preacher said. He looked at the man Chas had called Reverend in the woods. "We owe you, Reverend Hale," he said. "You and Mrs. Hale both. Fugitive slaves don't have many places of safety in this old world."

Reverend Hale looked grim. "It's safe tonight," he said. "But not too safe. We're prepared, though. We've got the attic ready with blankets so you can sleep. We'll have a better breakfast tomorrow morning. Then Mr. Benson will come over, and he and I will hide you under canvas and start getting you north to the next stop. I know you're tired, but Wisconsin is a long way away."

"Isn't there any more to eat?" Abbie asked.

Her mother bent down and hugged her. "Hush," she said. The white woman smiled at the little girl. "Not now," she said. "We've learned. Not too much or you'll get sick. Tomorrow. You'll be able to hold more tomorrow."

Joshua felt lost at the woman's words. They were hungry. They needed food. He felt desperate, but kept silent.

Reverend Hale had gone back to the corner where he'd gotten the

46

apples and biscuits from and grabbed a rope Joshua hadn't noticed dangling from the ceiling. He tugged it, and a trap door opened. A rope ladder was on a hook attached to the door's lid. He lifted the ladder off the hook and set it so that it led into the attic's dark.

"It'll be warm up there," he said. "You won't have a light. We leave the light on down here a lot, so people won't wonder if they see it at night. This is God's house and is always lit by the light of God. But having one in the attic would be risky." He glanced at his wife. "You'll say your prayers tonight. We'll come with breakfast in the morning, and then you'll leave. Mr. Woodruff," he continued, pointing at Chas, "said you got steered off course, but now you're back on a known road."

Chas went over to the man and held out his hand. "Thank you," he said. He had held out his hand to Mr. Jemmie, too, and he had shaken it. Joshua was amazed to see that happen a second time. Masters don't shake a black man's hand. They give him an order. Reverend Hale smiled. Mrs. Hale bent over and hugged Abbie. "Sleep good, dear," she said.

Abbie instinctively shrunk away from the white lady. Then, one at a time, they climbed into attic. Preacher went first and handed each one a blanket.

***

Joshua had a strangely vivid dream in the attic. He, Jamie, and Jeremiah were home at the plantation. Somehow they had escaped the notice of the Overseer, the Master, and his son, and were walking toward the meandering stream, Fisher Creek, flowing out of Mingo Swamp. Old Simpson had carved each of the three boys hooks out of rabbit bone. They were on their way to try to catch supper in the stream's large, stagnant pools. A blue heron flew above them getting ready to land. Joshua wasn't hungry, nor tired, and he felt pretty good just being a boy on his way to a fishing hole. He felt better than he had felt for a long, long time.

Then, suddenly, he was awake in the attic. Pappy was shaking him gently. The attic was crowded, but bigger than the Jemmie barn's loft. A dim light let everybody see everybody else. The faces around Joshua were becoming increasingly familiar even if he had hardly talked to some of the adults. They all had dark circles under their eyes and looked tired. Their clothes had dried during the night.

Joshua felt disoriented. He felt like he'd just gone to sleep. He wondered why they were getting up so early, although he had no idea why he thought it was early. His father was staring at him as if trying to memorize his face.

"This is going to be a different day," Pappy whispered.

Other people were whispering, too. Joshua looked for Jamie and Jeremiah. They were sitting up not far from where Esta May and her family were. He felt relieved. The dream had felt more real than the attic. He'd been afraid they were still on the plantation. *We've escaped the Overseer.* He looked into his father's long face. A question welled out of his confusion. "Who are you?" he asked silently. "How did you get to the swamp from South Carolina?"

"How come I didn't know about you?" he asked instead. He'd asked the question before, he knew, but hadn't gotten a clear answer. He looked from Pappy to his mother. They were on the run and could be caught and were hiding in a church with a white preacher. Pappy, startled, looked at Mary and then back to Joshua. His mother looked afraid—like she had the last time he'd asked that same question.

"I'm your father. I'm just glad to finally get to know you. I've known about you for a long time, but your master is not the best master in the world, and my master didn't trust me. I've got too rebellious a spirit. For slaves, separation is part of life."

"He's stubborn like you, Jason," Mary said. "It gets him into trouble."

Jason's face lit up with a huge smile. Everything about the man seemed big.

Joshua heard voices below the attic. He cocked his head. "It seems like we should be sleeping," he complained.

Pappy looked expectantly at the trap door. "We'll have time for sleeping later," he said.

The trap door opened, and Preacher stuck his head into the attic. Joshua had not noticed he wasn't among them.

"Come on down," he said. "Reverend and Mrs. Hale have breakfast."

No one hesitated. They filed to the trap door and climbed to the foyer below. When Joshua's turn came, he followed his mother. He had just put his foot on the stone floor when Mrs. Hale, smiling, handed him two biscuits and a slab of salt pork. Without thinking, he wolfed it down. Manners, learned when he had been living with his mother in the master's house, were beyond him and everyone else getting their handful of food.

When everyone had eaten, Reverend Hale smiled. "Let us pray," he said. Everyone bent their heads, including Mrs. Hale. "Please protect these souls fleeing their terrible persecution, especially since, like Ezekiel in Babylon after the Jerusalem temple's destruction, Preacher Bennett—" he gestured toward Preacher without lifting his head—"has seen a vision of a New Jerusalem, a place where mistreated slaves can gain dignity in wilderness on an island in a distant inland sea and be freed forever from their bonds. We pray you protect those who will help them over the next two days flee north toward Wisconsin. Confuse the eyes of slavers amongst us.

"For God sees injustice and, in His own time, prepares to deliver justice to those who do not treat each human being with the righteousness commanded by our Lord and savior, Jesus Christ. May Preacher Bennett's vision of New Jerusalem be realized. May we all pray for safety in Jesus holy name." He paused. "Amen."

In almost one voice the rest of them repeated "Amen," a few of the adults, including Joshua's mother, loudly. Junebug Harrison looked at the white preacher with a smile almost too big for her face.

Reverend Hale turned to Preacher. "Do you have anything you want to add, Preacher Bennett?" he asked.

Preacher looked at him. "Only this," he said. "We thank the Lord for our safe journey so far, and we ask his blessing on the good people who have helped us and those who will help us in days to come. Slavery is blight upon this land. If one soul escapes the whip and chain, then God's grace has been given to those that have helped that soul along his way. As it says in Galatians, 'Stand fast therefore in the liberty wherewith Christ hath made us free and be not entangled again with the yoke of bondage.' I would only say that."

Reverend Hale smiled and said softly, "You are an extraordinary man, Tom Bennett." Preacher, hearing his words, looked at the ground.

Then all of them, except Chas, Preacher, and the Hales, flinched and reflexively moved away from the door. Horses were coming up to the church outside. Reverend Hale held up his arms.

"Don't worry folks," he said. "That's the Braxton twins and their oldest brother, Sam. They're your ride north. They've made special wagons to help people escaping hide beneath what looks like a load of lumber. They're clever, good men. They haven't lost a single individual to slavers yet."

Moments later the church door opened, and three young white men came inside. They were smiling. They went around the room shaking everyone's hands, including Joshua's. The fugitives all looked bewildered at how eagerly the white men looked into their eyes.

"I'm Sam," the one wearing overalls said. They were small men. The two twins looked really alike. "You won't be able to tell," Sam continued. "But that's Carl, and that's Cal." He pointed at one and then the other twin. Joshua could not tell the difference. All three had brown hair and brown eyes, and energy telegraphed through short, quick movements. When they were done shaking hands, even with Abbie and Ertha, who cringed back against their mothers, Sam stood by the door with Carl and Cal behind him.

"What we're gonna do," Sam said. "Is move a load of cut lumber north. We've built a false floor to hide you all in a compartment beneath each wagon." He paused, looking at them. "We haven't moved a group this big before," he continued. "So even with three wagons it's going to be tight. We've never used all three wagons before, either. We're nervous about if that might attract attention. The main thing is for all of you to be quiet when we need you to be quiet. Chas?" Even though Chas was not as tall as the preacher, he was still a head taller than the white man. "You're the leader of this group?"

Chas shook his head. "No," he said. "Preacher's the leader. I've been following him since our days on Lake Erie with the Navy. He's helping me get my brother and his family and these other folks free."

Sam glanced toward where Preacher was standing with Reverend Hale.

"Well, I know you," Sam said to Chas. "You and the preacher are going to have to manage your folks really well. You're going to be uncomfortable, and we're only gonna stop after the horses get too tired to go on. We'll take two short breaks a day for all of you to do your business, but we'll only do that when there are woods you can hide in off the roads. We'll feed the horses then, too, and water them if there's water near. Other than that we're going to keep moving until we're out of Missouri and into Illinois. In Illinois, Chas has another group to keep you moving north." He paused, looking each one of them in the eyes. At last he nodded. "Any questions?"

"These men will be careful and take good care of you," Reverend Hale said. "We've put dried pork, biscuits, potatoes, beets, rutabagas, and carrots in the wagons beneath the buckboards. It's not much, but it'll keep in this heat, and it will keep you alive."

"We're ready," Preacher said. "Every slave's been ready for freedom for a long time."

Sam nodded. His brothers, with quick, decisive movements, turned and went outside. The rest followed.

The three wagons in the churchyard were oversized compared to the wagons they had squeezed into at Mr. Jemmie's. The back gates were down and Joshua could see the crawl space where they'd hide beneath the lumber. He glanced at Pappy. He didn't see how his father would fit into the small space with his big frame. Quicker than he would have thought possible, though, they were all beneath the false floor. Pappy couldn't lie on his side, but looked up at the wagon bed above his head.

Inside the gray light, once the horses had lurched forward and started the wagons rolling, Pappy, lying beside Joshua and Mary, said, "May God have mercy on us."

Joshua closed his eyes. He was tired. He was on his back, too, and the wagon's movement made him restless. He was amazed at how many white people were helping them.

White people, even white children, could not be trusted. He knew that. He'd been taught that by their meanness all his life. But maybe it was different for freedmen. Maybe freedmen didn't have to distrust every white person they met. He tried to get back the dream where he, Jamie, and Jeremiah were fishing. He imagined Esta May was with them, looking pretty, and smiling and laughing at them. He tried to imagine putting worms they had dug by the stream's banks on their bone hooks.

The whole time at the church already seemed more dream than reality. He couldn't even picture clearly the white preacher and his wife. He could remember the biscuits and salt pork. He could even taste the salt pork. He could remember the sharpness of hunger while they made their way through the dark woods, but the preacher and his wife were like ghosts in his head.

The whole escape didn't make much sense. White people seemed ready, prepared to help them. They seemed to all know Chas, yet, Chas had said that they'd gotten off the planned track at Mr. Jemmie's.

Joshua strained to look around and saw Jeremiah beside Willie and Massie. He couldn't see Jamie. Esta May and her sisters were in the other wagon. The space was too close to allow hardly any movement. Jeremiah, his eyes wide, looked at Joshua.

Joshua turned off his back onto his right side toward the compartment's side. He stared at rough-cut pine boards as the wagon swayed.

Chapter 6
Inside the Turning of Time

Inside the rhythm of the wagon's wheels,
The preacher, with his people crammed beside
Him underneath a false floorboard, untied
His consciousness from who he was, ordeals
He'd faced for years now in the past, and reels
Of rainbow light exploded, amplified
A vision where he felt Ezekiel's tide
Of prophecies burn like a fire that heals.

He saw his Promised Land, boats filled with fish,
A land of gardens lush as men could wish,

And in the garden of his vision, black
As midnight skies, a shining Adam spoke
A chant so sibilant with grace the almanac
Of hours turned like the wagon wheel's spokes.

The hours dragged by. At first, worn out from the storm and short night at the church, Joshua slept. The hard boards swaying in rhythm to horses' hooves was uncomfortable, but he was worn out. Escaping to freedom was not easy. But then, he reminded himself, he had assumed it was in fact impossible.

When he woke up, he was disoriented. The days and nights since the swamp were a jumble of wild images in his head.

He squirmed, waking his mother, and looked at Jeremiah. Jeremiah's eyes opened the second he felt Joshua looking at him. Joshua had barely paid attention to who was in the space beneath the wagon's false floor when he had crawled into the hole. They had been pushed by the Braxtons, his father, and Preacher to get out of sight as quickly as possible. He had felt exposed and vulnerable in the daylight anyway, so he had moved quickly. He had noticed that Chas had a horse and was mounted, but, like the whole experience, he hadn't thought about what that meant.

"You okay?" he whispered to Jeremiah.

"Sure," Jamie answered. He was lying against the front board by his parent's feet. They were packed so close no one had room to move. Joshua was startled that Jamie was as close as he was.

"Shush," Willie said from the other side of the wagon. "We don't know if it's safe to talk."

Joshua strained his head around to look at Pappy. He decided he had liked the straw Mr. Jemmie had put over them better. It had been softer, and after a while he'd gotten used to breathing with straw covering his head. Although they'd even had less space in those wagons, he had been grateful to not be walking. Seven people were in the space they were packed in now, three of them kids. They had a little room to move around, but not much.

There was no way to see where they were going or guess at how much time was passing. After a while, Joshua started trying to think about Preacher's New Jerusalem, the place they were running towards. Supposedly it was an island. He had seen islands in the swamp, small clumps of trees and brush that stuck up out of the water, and had even waded or swum over to them.

New Jerusalem couldn't be like the islands he knew. It had to be big if they were all going to live on it. He wondered how they were going to get enough to eat. Swamp islands had plenty of birds in the trees and brush as well as rabbits and other small mammals, and snakes, frogs, and fish that somebody could catch if they were skilled and quick enough. He and his friends had done their share of catching back at the plantation. It was a good way to supplement their thin rations. Seemed like living only on what you could catch would be risky.

His thoughts shifted to the intensity in Preacher's voice and eyes. Preacher was not as big as Pappy—no one was as big as Pappy—but he somehow seemed larger because of the fire burning through almost every word he spoke.

Joshua wondered why the Overseer had ever let any of the quarter's slaves go to the preacher's meetings. Master Bulrush would have never let that happen, especially if he'd known about the power in the preacher's voice, although Master's not knowing made sense, since he never came to the quarters after dark. Not even Silver Coats had seemed to wonder what was going on in the swamp on Sundays. Good thing, because had any of them met Preacher, they would have marked him as a dangerous man, what with his prayers and visions.

The Bulrush's had built a small chapel in the big house. The slaves were encouraged to be Christians, although they were discouraged from going into the chapel for any reason other than cleaning. The Mistress often remarked that "Jesus would not like that" when she was displeased with someone's behavior. But the Bulrush's Christianity was nothing like Preacher's fiery Christianity with its sermons about New Jerusalem, paradise, and freedom.

When he heard a horseman pass by in the road, his attention snapped back to the present abruptly. His body tensed. He suddenly understood they were not in the same situation that they had been with Mr. Jemmie and his son. They were driving down a road where white men with whips and guns traveled. They could be discovered.

The horseman passed. He heard the driver of the wagon he was entombed in say hello. The horseman said hello in return. Suddenly Joshua was not thinking about what might be in front of him, but he could almost feel the Overseer whip's anger as it raised welts, then blood as vicious strokes struck him over and over again.

He realized he had been frightened, but free from the plantation for days. He never wanted to see the Overseer's narrowed black eyes again or hear his deep voice. He'd never thought about freedom even when Willie, old Simpson, and the others had whispered about it. Now, scared as he was, it was, at least in a sense, surrounding him in the wagon's closed space. He stilled himself into a silence that he hoped would make him invisible.

Not long after the horseman had gone past, a wagon passed them and then another horseman. Joshua tried not to think. His body was so rigid it ached.

After hours of lying tense, he was surprised when the wagon turned slightly and stopped. His fear spiked to even greater heights

The wagon's gate opened, making him blink at afternoon light.

"You can get out now," one of the twins said in a conversational voice. "You need to get in the woods quick. I don't think anybody'll be along, but you can't tell. Stretch a little, then get together and come back. We don't need delay. I'll have salt pork and a raw potato for everybody. My brothers are behind us. We're safer a little apart during stops."

Out of the wagon and in the woods, Joshua felt a large freedom. Below the wagon's false floor he felt imprisoned, but the great oak trees surrounding him with early summer blue sky overhead made him feel like running into the woods and never stopping. The fear that had nagged him in the wagon disappeared.

Then Pappy was beside him, his father's big body small beside large oak trunks. He smiled. "Feels good," he said softly. His voice sounded like deep music rumbling out of his chest.

Joshua nodded. Other fugitives were coming into the woods and finding their own trees and brush. Joshua looked out at the road. It looked dry already. The rain they had run through had not left evidence of its ferocity in the road's dirt.

"Where's my mother?" he asked as they walked back to the wagon.

Jason was watching the Braxton twin as he pulled raw potatoes and slices of salt pork out of the box beneath the wagon's seat. "She's going to ride in the first wagon," he said, "with Preacher. I told her to. Preacher'll calm her down. I thought she was going to have a heart attack when that rider passed."

The Braxton twin driving their wagon looked toward the woods. Jason put his hand on Joshua's shoulder. "Let's go," he said.

Harrison and Junebug Stimson, who looked better than they had the night before, heard Jason and quickly ran toward the wagon, too. Esta May, looking small and vulnerable, came out of the brush in front of them. Jamie followed her out of the woods. A minute later they were underneath the false floor as the Braxton twin flicked black leather reins and said, "Gah!" and the horses started off again.

The rest of the day passed without incident. Other horsemen and wagons passed them, but the sound of horses and wheels and the half-light of the space they were in let Joshua drift in and out of sleep. He thought about the people he and his mother had joined, and about his father, Jason, and about Preacher's intensity and Chas's scouting. They all kept quiet. The risk of making a noise at the wrong moment was just too great.

After dark, the wagon pulled off. When they crawled into the night's darkness, all three wagons were parked behind a cornfield where they couldn't be seen from the road. There was more salt pork and apples, but Sam Braxton told them they were safer if they hid in the cornfield for the night.

"If we dared, we'd have you by the fire," he said. "You've had a hard time and could use a fire, but I don't think we ought to risk it."

The next day started before dawn. A bare smudge of gray light was on the eastern horizon when Sam Braxton came into the cornfield and talked quietly to Preacher. Chas, with his horse, had joined them in the night. Joshua was amazed he could ride so boldly on a road during daylight without worrying about being taken into chains as a fugitive.

"We'll be at the next station after dark," he said, talking to Preacher. "We got to keep moving. You'll be in Illinois late this afternoon."

"A long way yet," Preacher said.

Chas nodded, but didn't say anything. Instead he went over to where the Braxtons were standing by the lead wagon. "Thanks," he said. "I'll see you tonight. I'm scouting out the next leg."

"Be careful," one of the twins said.

He got on his horse as the rest of them crawled into their spaces. Joshua's mother had slept next to him in the cornfield that night. Now she grabbed his arm as he started toward the wagon he had ridden in the day before. "I want you with me," she said. "I don't feel comfortable not having you close. You were taken from me for a long enough time."

Joshua didn't object. Pappy was making sure everyone was in the wagons before he crawled into the wagon he and Joshua had ridden in the day before. "He's always trying to make sure nobody's left behind," Joshua thought. He slipped into the wagon with Bill and Beulah Woodruff and their girls. Esta May was against the eastern sideboard while he was on the western one. Franklin, Zelda, and Abbie had taken their places in the wagon his father climbed into after everyone was loaded.

Mary sighed as they turned back toward the road.

The entire day was a mirror of the day before. The horses kept pulling the wagons. They stopped once to visit the woods and have their meager meal. Then they went on again. Horses and wagons passed them, but their caravan didn't seem to raise any suspicion.

Joshua's thoughts turned to his mother. For a long time after he'd been forced to move to the quarters, he'd been angry with her, as if his loneliness had been her fault.

It wasn't until after hours of talk in the discomfort of Old Simpson's cabin with its rickety floorboards and moldy smell that he had finally understood. He was a slave. He'd always known that, but what he'd not known was that both boys and girls who were slaves were often separated from parents the day they were able to work the fields. Often they were sold to another master on another plantation.

"You'd better accept what you are," Old Simpson had told him over and over again. "If you don't the Overseer's going to go crazy one of these days. This old man, for one, will grieve about what he does to you."

***

Just before dark, the wagon stopped. "Whoa! Whoa!" Sam Braxton, driving the wagon he and his mother were in, shouted.

"Run! Get them out and running," a voice screamed, coming out of a cotton field onto the road. "Sherriff Branson's up ahead with a bunch of men!" Her voice was hysterical.

Joshua, heart pounding, wondered what was happening. Were they going to be caught after coming so far? His mother was the first out of the wagon. The other wagons had pulled off the road behind their wagon. Preacher was beside a young white girl standing on the side of the road crying.

"What's wrong, child?" he asked, his voice calm.

They were out of the woods. Fields of cotton surrounded them. The entire universe seemed out in the open and exposed.

"Paw said they're going to catch you!" she said. "You've got to run. Paw's bothering them to give you time!"

"We got to move north," Pappy said in his big voice. "Now!" He walked over and touched his wife's arm and pointed toward the cotton field. "There, Mary," he said. "I'll get everyone moving."

Joshua, without waiting to see what the others were doing, ran toward where his father had pointed. His mouth was dry again, and he felt stiff from riding in cramped space all day.

"Do they have dogs?" Preacher asked, urgency in his voice. He sounded panicked.

"I don't think so," the girl answered. "Just horses."

In the panic, no one thought about grabbing food. They ran.

"Turn the wagons around." Joshua heard Sam order. "No wagons to see, no hidden slave fugitives to find."

Joshua thought he could make out woods a long, long way across the field. He was vaguely aware of his mother and others beside him. "Maybe the dark will help," he thought. He didn't want any of them to be caught. He didn't want to hear the sound of horses or dogs pursuing them. Light was fading, but not fast enough. *Anybody could see us from the road. Please Lord, don't let them catch us. Dear Jesus, don't let them catch us.* He wondered if the Braxtons had turned the wagons and were gone.

They were still running when it got too dark to see the plants under their feet. Joshua felt the woods in front of them more than he saw them. He glanced at his mother, who was keeping up with him, running with an apparent ease he did not feel.

When Joshua reached the woods, he stopped and bent over, breathing hard. He felt sick to his stomach. His mother and the Bullocks were right behind him. Others crashed through brush one and two at a time. He looked at the field they had run across. Small clouds blocked out the moon's light and then let it shine again. He could see his father still running behind the Stimsons. His hearing was so sharp he could hear them running and gasping for breath. Then the field was empty.

Everyone instinctively gathered around Preacher. Harrison knelt down, gasping, although Junebug seemed both calmer and stronger in spite of how frail she looked. Joshua's father was not even breathing hard.

"We're separated from Chas," Preacher said.

"What does that mean?" Bill Woodruff asked.

Preacher looked at him. "Chas and I know people who'll help us," he said. "But Chas has scouted out the route and made the contacts we need."

"We go north," Pappy said. "I can always tell where north is. I been pointed toward freedom ever since I learned there was such a thing." He paused. "But I didn't think of food. We shouldn't have been so panicked we didn't get any food from the wagons."

"My brother will find us," Willie Bullock said. "He won't let any of us go back to our plantations."

"I saw a vision in the wagons," Preacher said, his voice angry sounding. "I saw the prophet Ezekiel in Babylon. He was talking about New Jerusalem. I saw how it was going to be there with more food than a belly could want and more freedom than a soul can count on." He looked out at the empty field. "Chas and I hid a boat we built not far from the big lake in a warehouse. We've been planning this for a long, long time."

He abruptly turned and started walking through the woods, no one noting the strange news that he had built and stored a boat in a warehouse.

"Don't worry, Chas will find us," Willie told Massie. "He always has, even when I thought I'd never see him again."

"Come on," Pappy said, bending over to help Harrison and then Zelda, who was kneeling on the ground next to Harrison.

"Thank you," Zelda whispered. She bent over, holding her stomach as if she was in pain. "I knew this was going to be hard."

Joshua and his mother followed Preacher. An owl hooted. Wings whooshed through air in front of them. Joshua wondered if Sherriff Branson would find where they had gone into the field. The Sherriff and his men had horses. "They probably have dogs. too," he thought. The young white girl had likely been mistaken about that. White men looking for slaves always had dogs.

All the escapees had was desperation and their legs. They'd have to run all night again. They had rested in the wagons, but now they'd have to run.

Chapter 7
A Force Inside the Dream of God

Their stomachs ached; they felt ice cold, their eyes
Sunk back into their sockets. Still, worn out,
They kept on moving, moving. When the skies
Were dark enough, they got up, brushed the flies,
Mosquitos off, shoved fear and gnawing doubt
Into their belly's emptiness, and ran, their route
Through hills and fields, past roads, an exercise
In dreams that live on while the body dies.

But as they moved, the preacher was a force
Inside the dream of God, a man possessed.
He would not fade. His tongue, without remorse,
Whipped legs too tired to move to movement, stressed
Them all until a blessed miracle
Made life and dreams again seem possible.

Chas found them in a swale near a road three days later. They had
walked hard through fields at night, crossed road after road, and passed
close to houses as they kept moving mostly north. At some of the houses,
dogs were set to barking as they picked up their pace and ran. They had
dry mouths, were endlessly thirsty and hungry.

Once they had to go east and then northwest to circle a town. They'd
felt a pulse-pounding terror as they looked at the cluster of buildings.
Then they faded back into the cover of darkness. The little town had
seemed alive and bristling, even though it was silent.

They had not eaten in so long their stomachs ached even though
sharp hunger pains had disappeared. Sometimes they felt faint, as if legs
were about to give out. But they did not stop, or complain, or talk about
giving up. Even Abbie and Ertha and old Harrison and Junebug did not
falter, although Abbie's eyes sunk into her skull and had purplish-black
rings around them.

In the darkness, Preacher led while Jason helped people from behind.
Joshua's father time and again almost picked people up by putting his
arms around them as they faltered, too tired to go any further. His
strength seemed endless. He was especially careful of the youngsters,

helping whenever they seemed to be wearing out or becoming discouraged.

"We got to keep moving," he said over and over again. "Just think how freedom will fill our bellies and souls. This will all seem like a dream past."

Every few minutes, Preacher would say, "We'll make it. We'll make it. Keep them moving, Jason, Willie, Bill, Franklin. Keep them moving. New Jerusalem's ahead of us."

When Preacher stopped , Willie and Bill, who kept their families close to them, would stop, too, causing the rest to pause. The women tended to children and the Stimsons. Then they pressed on, following Preacher, his body more shadow than substance, as they avoided a house or slave quarters or a field he didn't trust. Sometimes, crossing a stream, they got on their knees and drank water that either tasted good or brackish, depending upon whether it was running downhill or not.

Chas startled all of them when he appeared on the crest of a swale that dipped down in a field of tobacco plants. No woods were close, so they all felt exposed, but they hadn't had anything to drink all day and were hungry, tired, and getting increasingly careless.

Preacher got wearily to his feet when he saw a man looming over them. He looked resigned, as if he thought they had been found at last, but couldn't quite believe it.

"I found you," Chas said as he walked into the swale. He was clearly relieved. "Thank the Lord." He looked at eyes and faces around him and shook his head. "I've got a little food," he said when no one said anything, only stared stupidly at him. He climbed back up the swale.

"Wait," Preacher said, his voice hoarse and soft.

The fear on their faces was pronounced.

"It's okay," Chas said. "There are good people close."

A minute longer and he was back with a sack of rutabagas and potatoes. Joshua stared. The sun was uncomfortably hot. His hands shook as he took a small potato from Chas. His tongue felt swollen. He bit into the potato so fast he almost dropped it. Nobody said anything, but devoured what Chas had brought. It wasn't much. Joshua felt like he would never get enough food again and was sure others felt the same.

"Thank you," Abbie whispered.

"I'm sorry. I don't have anymore," Chas said. "Can you walk?"

Harrison Stimson barked a single laugh. "Seems like we been walking forever," he said.

"Joshua and I can walk," Mary said.

"As soon as it's dark," Preacher said.

Chas shook his head. "No," he said. His voice seemed loud. They had whispered to each other for so long that a normal speaking voice sounded like it was shouting. "The people here will help us. We don't have to hide. We have to be careful, but I've been up and down the road. We can go to the barn. Most of the people around here are abolitionists. There's a few we need to be worried about, but they live closer to town."

"Abolitionists are white people who oppose slavery," Joshua's mother said as if trying to tell herself something she did not already know.

His father stood by his mother, seemingly entranced to hear her speak in a normal voice that seemed to Joshua to be much too loud. Joshua didn't know how to feel. He thought the potato had been wonderful. He was still starving.

"That's right," Chas said to Joshua's mother. He turned and climbed the swale's slope again.

The rest of them, led by Preacher who, in his filthy, tattered clothes, looked like a scarecrow moving on sticks for legs, followed. The rutabagas and potatoes had not been much, but it gave them a small burst of strength and hope.

Once they were out where they could see, they found Chas standing by the horse he'd been riding when he had lost them after they'd been forced to abandon the wagons or be caught. He waited halfway to the road that they hadn't realized was there. He turned to Junebug, who had developed a limp, and smiled. She looked as tired as an old woman could look, her weariness sagging into wrinkles on her face. Chas was a handsome man when he smiled. He also looked well fed and healthy compared to the rest of them.

"You and little Abbie will ride," he said.

The old woman looked at him. "I've walked a long way," she said hesitantly.

"Time I walked a little," Chas said in a firm voice.

"I want you to ride," Harrison said, his voice weak.

Junebug nodded and took Abbie's hand.

Walking in the open before sunset with the horse ahead of them, reins in Chas's hands, felt dangerous. Joshua kept glancing around. He worried that someone was going to see them and all their escaping would end up with whips and days of backbreaking work—if they lived.

When he saw the big red barn with its loft beside a neat, two story red house, he had to hold himself back from turning around and hurrying off.

Their reception as they entered the farm's yard was not anything like he expected. At the other places where they had met white men who had helped them, one man had stood quietly in darkness, waiting to lead them to where they would be hidden. This time, when a white boy who looked to be about Joshua's age saw them walking down the road, he tore off running back toward the house. A moment later a woman, at least five children, and a man came out.

The man walked a little in front. When he got to Chas, he put out his hand, smiling.

"You found them," he exclaimed.

Chas smiled. "I found them," he agreed.

"Come," the man said. "Come meet my family. You all are welcome." He smiled and turned from Chas to Preacher. "Tom Bennett," he said. "You are a relief to my heart. I've been worried ever since Chas told me you were separated. It's been a long time."

Preacher didn't smile, but reached out and actually hugged the white man. "It's been years," he said, his voice sounding thin. "I didn't think I'd ever see you again."

The man laughed. "Please, please," he said, motioning to his wife. "Matilda, this is Tom Bennett. A long time ago on Lake Erie I served with him and Chas under Navy Master Commandant Oliver Hazard Perry." He held out his arms to the white children who stayed back from their parents and the fugitives. "Children, you've heard my stories," he said. "This is Tom Bennett. You've met Chas Bullock. This is a day you'll remember the rest of your lives."

The young people came slowly forward. The boy who had first seen them and ran to get his family came up to Joshua. "Are you really an escaped slave?" he asked.

Joshua didn't answer, but nodded his head in affirmation. What did he want to talk to a white boy for? On the other hand, maybe there'd be more food to eat. He mostly hoped they'd get to where they could hide, but he didn't want to upset anybody. He was exhausted.

"This is James Campbell," Chas said. "Matilda is his wife, and these are his children."

Joshua looked at James Campbell. He was a middle-sized man with graying hair and a steel glint in unblinking gray eyes. *The Battle of Lake Erie? Chas and Preacher had been in a battle? On a boat in a lake?* That seemed unlikely. White people were in armies, not black people. He wondered if he was imagining things.

"We've got eggs and bacon at the house," Matilda Campbell announced. "We'll bake biscuits. You look tired and hungry."

"Afterward you can rest," James Campbell said. "We'll sort this out and get you to Chicago and Lake Michigan. If you need to rest here you can, but you're probably better off out of Illinois. There's people around who don't cotton to slavery, but there's also people who'd sell their own mother to a nest of rattlesnakes if they could gain a little for themselves."

Preacher looked dazed. He reached out his hand and touched James Campbell's arm. "I had no idea I was anywhere near here," he said. "I didn't know."

James Campbell put his arm around Preacher's shoulders as Chas followed the boy who had asked if Joshua was an escaped slave toward the house. The woman—the blessed woman who had promised them eggs, bacon, and biscuits—walked in front of all of them. Slaves seldom, more like never, got bacon. That was masters' food. Joshua, when he had lived with his mother in the Master's house, had eaten bacon when it had been left over from the table and cook had slipped him some before she had gotten so angry at him, but he couldn't imagine a white person willingly giving bacon to a slave without wanting something first.

He had lived to experience some unbelievable things, he mused. White men who didn't hate slaves, strangers who were kind to people they didn't know, a white man who had served with Chas and Preacher in a war on a lake he had never heard of, and white people who said they would feed fugitive slaves bacon. He wondered what new marvel would reveal itself next.

***

By the time Joshua was on the floor lying on a blanket in what Mrs. Campbell called the parlor, the sun had set. The house was dark. They had eaten a feast. But now he didn't feel so good.

He remembered how Mrs. Hale at the church had said that they couldn't give them too much after they hadn't eaten for a while because it would make them sick. He knew he hadn't shown the manners he'd been taught in the big house by his mother when he had gulped down his food sitting on the floor beside the big oak dining room table, but he hadn't been able to help himself. He had been too hungry. Now he wondered if he had been stupid. Jamie and Jeremiah had already hurried outside and thrown up.

The whites in the room had not said anything about their lack of manners. Only his mother had been able to eat wisely. She had only eaten a small portion of the food she was given and had eaten that slowly. The rest of them had shoveled food in their mouths and swallowed.

Preacher, as tired as he was, his hands moving ceaselessly, had been animated discussing how they were going to get to Chicago and Lake Michigan. He had made Chicago sound like it was so big and crazy that Joshua couldn't imagine what he was trying to describe. Chas had sat back and looked satisfied, like he'd worked a miracle finding them in the swale where they'd spent most of the day and bringing them to the Campbell place.

Mr. Campbell thought the best thing to do was to split them up into four different wagons driven by four different men. "You'll get back together when you've gotten to the scow in Chicago," he'd said. "You can make your way to Washington Island from there."

Joshua had not heard of a scow, which he guessed was a boat of some kind, or of Washington Island before, although he slowly got the idea that the island, in Preachers' mind, was New Jerusalem. Mr. Campbell, Preacher, and Chas made it seem like a place so remote and deep in wilderness that they'd be allowed to build lives without being afraid of slavers. The three of them seemed to know all about where they were going. They sounded like they had been to this Washington Island.

Preacher hadn't wanted them separated. "I don't feel easy about it," he said over and over again. "We've managed to stay together all this way."

"But it's the safest way," James Campbell told him. "Illinois isn't Missouri, but a lot of folks don't approve of slaves escaping their masters. Slavers have free rein here. Having you together is a risk for those driving the wagons and your folks. It's just not safe."

"How's having four wagons safer?" Willie Bullock wanted to know.

"Wagons driving together looks suspicious," Chas had answered. "I agree with James. We'll be back together soon enough." He'd thought for a moment before saying, "We'll keep families together. We'll take different routes, but come together at the warehouse close to the river."

Preacher had still looked unconvinced, but, at the last, had shaken his head. "Okay," he'd said. "Okay."

Then they'd all been led to different rooms. Joshua, Jamie, and Jeremiah had gotten the parlor, shown there by Timothy Campbell, a serious boy with brown hair, a cowlick, and brown eyes. When he'd shown them where they could sleep, he'd told them, "I'm glad you're escaping. I'd escape, too. I don't like slavery."

He'd left the three of them with woven cotton blankets alone. Joshua kept touching the blanket he'd been given. He'd never felt anything so soft and smooth. It felt good on his skin. It was nothing like the burlap gunnysacks he'd slept on in the quarters. White people lived differently from slaves. The newest mystery was how he and the others were allowed to use a blanket good enough for a white person. He looked at his ragged clothes. They were filthy. He wondered if the Bulrush plantation had picked the cotton used to weave the blankets.

Before they went to sleep Jamie mumbled, "I wonder how long we'll be before we see New Jerusalem?"

"Dunno, but we're a long way from the quarters," Joshua said.

"Do you think New Jerusalem will be like Preacher says it will be? A paradise?" Jeremiah asked.

"Can't be worse than trying to avoid the Overseer all the time," Joshua said.

Jamie huffed. "He was meaner to you than to me," he said.

Joshua shook his head, knowing that what Jamie had said was true. "My stubbornness," he thought. "Always my stubbornness." Then it occurred to him that if they reached Washington Island he'd have to change and be more cooperative. He wouldn't have to be afraid all the time.

Then he thought about Jason, his father. Slaves were often ignorant of what was happening in their lives. He wasn't sure why, but he knew they were kept that way on purpose. He was still puzzled, and upset, that his mother had never let him know that he had a father who was alive. But maybe she had had her reasons. And maybe in New Jerusalem he'd find out what those reasons were.

His father had impressed him from the beginning. At first he'd resented the man who wanted to be called Pappy, but had gone along with what his mother had wanted. He'd been dealing with too much to do anything else. He hadn't had time to build up his resentment since then. They'd felt hunted, unsafe, and fearful for too long. It had taken too much energy for him to think about anything else, especially when his back had still burned.

But his father seemed to always be trying to take care of everybody. He had even carried the Stimsons, Abbie, and two of the Woodruff girls when they had faltered. When Esta May had gotten sick during the storm he'd put her on his back and kept up with the rest of them while climbing steep, rain-slicked hills.

He'd also paid attention to both Joshua and his mother, coming over to them just before they tried to sleep during the day and checking on them every chance he got during the long night runs. He did not talk as much as Preacher, or Chas, or even Harrison Stimson or Willie Bullock, but he was always asking people in his deep voice how they were or how they were getting along.

Maybe it isn't so bad having a father. I'm old enough to take care of myself, but it's nice having someone who's not mean trying to look out for Mother and me. Old Simpson had tried to look out for him before he'd died, but the idea of having a father actually felt good.

James Campbell had said they'd be on the road in their separate wagons for close to a week before they reached Lake Michigan. As he drifted off to sleep, Joshua wondered again what Lake Michigan would be like. It sounded, listening to Mr. Campbell, Chas, and Preacher talk, like it was big. Half asleep, he couldn't even imagine what a lake as big as they had talked about would look like.

Then what? Then what? Are we really going to take a boat Chas and Preacher made to an island? How could the island be so remote if it was in the middle of a big lake? How could a lake be that big?

The last vision he had before falling asleep was of the two strips of fried bacon and two eggs he'd been given by Mrs. Campbell while he'd sat in a corner by the big table. The smell had been so good he expected he would never forget it.

Chapter 8
The Place where Joy and Hope are Made

Inside the barn the memories of war
As horses ate their hay and cows were fed:

Three aging men, one white, two black, the roar
Of cannon, sight and sound of men that bled
Their lives out as the living and the dead
Were showered hot with splintering fusillades
Flung in the wave-tossed night from hell, the dread
Of battle dancing as the barricades
Of what you were in being human fades
Into the chaos burning through the night.

The preacher frowned: "Destruction serenades
Our hearts against our spirit's holy light,"
He said. The others nodded. Each had prayed
To find the place where joy and hope was made.

When Joshua woke, he felt strange. For one thing, as he could tell by
the way light from the east-facing window fell on the flowery settee to
the parlor's north side, it was morning, not early evening, the time when
he was used to waking. Another reason was that he was inside with
Jamie and Jeremiah in a room that, though smaller than rooms at the
Bulrush Plantation's big house, was clearly owned by white people. The
stained narrow-pine board floor, small library of books, roll-top desk,
and small stone fireplace were signs of wealth beyond any dream of even
a freed slave. At least, looking around the parlor, that's what Joshua felt.

What had woken him was the smell of breakfast cooking. He didn't
remember much about the day before. The journey after leaving the
wagons on the road was fuzzy in his head. He remembered being tired.
He remembered Chas's silhouette above the field's swale and the
unbelievable taste of bacon in his mouth. He also remembered gobbling
food in the large kitchen's corner while his mother, Pappy, Preacher,
Chas, and other adults sat at the table like white people.

Even the white man, woman, and five children who had welcomed
them to what was obviously a prosperous farm were vague in his head.

They seemed unreal. He had no idea where his mother, Pappy, and the other fugitives had slept. The parlor, elegant as it was, was too small to hold more than three boys, although it was bigger than the wagon beds they had crammed inside. Being separated from his mother was also strange. During their long run she'd always made sure he was close, especially when they had stopped to sleep.

The smell of frying potatoes, onions, and baking corn bread made the whole house seem like Preacher's heaven. Jamie and Jeremiah were sitting up and looking toward the kitchen, too. The sound of women moving around and talking seemed surreal after their days of constant fear and dread and silence. Their conversation seemed bizarre, as if the possibility that they had actually reached a safe place was impossible.

Jeremiah jumped to his feet and went into the kitchen.

"Wait," Jamie said, holding up his hand.

Joshua felt like rushing after Jeremiah. He was still so hungry he could hardly resist running toward the enticing smells and sounds even after he had suffered from eating too much the evening before. A second later, Jeremiah was back in the parlor with a hang-dog look. Jamie smiled.

"We have to wait," Jeremiah said. "We can eat when the men come in from the barn. They're milking cows and doing chores."

Joshua felt let down. Surely the men were as hungry as they were. He wondered if his mother and the other women had already gotten something to eat, but then pushed the thought from his mind. His stomach growled.

"Waiting's not what I want to do," Jamie said plaintively.

"Me, neither," Joshua and Jeremiah said simultaneously.

Joshua turned his head, alerted by some small sound. The white boy who'd first seen them on the road was standing in the entryway between the living room and parlor. When Joshua looked at him, he smiled.

"Hello," he said.

There was no reason for the boy not to be there; after all, it was his house. But the sight of him immediately made Joshua feel uncomfortable.

"Hello, yourself," Jeremiah said brightly. He did not seem put off by the boy at all. "You got a great house. I've never slept in a better place."

The boy smiled. He was taller than Joshua, but shorter than Jamie and slightly pudgy, showing he was used to eating well.

"I don't want to bother you," he said politely, seeing the look on Joshua's face.

"You're not bothering us," Jamie said. "We met you last night."

The boy came into the parlor and unceremoniously sat on the floor, folding his legs beneath him.

"You fell asleep the minute you had something to eat," he noted.

"You looked tough."

Joshua felt the stirrings of resentment he always felt, and fought to hide, around white people. He kept his eyes on the boy's face.

"You'd look tough, too, if you'd been running without food like we've been," he said, resentment creeping into his voice.

"Joshua," Jamie warned.

The boy looked calmly at Joshua. Nothing seemed to upset him. He seemed to have a serenity inside that Joshua did not believe he could ever have.

"I expect that's true," he said. His blue eyes and tanned, white face belonged to the parlor in a way that Joshua, Jamie, and Jeremiah did not.

"Okay, boys, it's time to eat," Esta May said, standing in the doorway leading to the kitchen. She looked rested and clean, much better than Joshua had ever seen her look. She'd combed her long, black hair, and her clothes looked like they had been washed, even though they were, like everyone else's, ragged and torn. Her dress barely held together over her body.

She was beautiful, maybe even more beautiful than Joshua's mother.

Jeremiah and Jamie did not hesitate. They got to their feet. Esta May smiled. The smile startled Joshua. "I've never seen her smile before," he thought. Neither he nor the white boy moved. Joshua thought he should let the white boy go into the kitchen first. It was his house. Another white boy, younger than his brother, came out of the living room into the parlor.

"Joshua?" Esta May asked.

"It's okay," the oldest boy told Joshua. He hesitated. "I'm Timothy. Tim," he said.

"Joshua," Esta May said again, irritation in her voice.

Joshua stared at the boy without blinking. What was he supposed to say?

"Joshua," Esta May warned, sensing something was wrong. Joshua nodded, shaking away his resentment. The food in the kitchen smelled too good, and, besides, he reasoned, he was a guest in Tim's house. "I'm Joshua," he said. He looked at Esta May. He got up off the floor as both Tim and his brother smiled. "And I am hungry."

Esta May turned and they followed her into the kitchen. It was filled with fugitives and white people young and old. The long wooden trestle table was loaded with food: boiled eggs, squares of yellow corn bread, a huge platter of fried potatoes and onions, two big bowls of oatmeal, and pitchers of milk stripped that morning from the farm's cows. The smells were beyond wonderful.

The minute Joshua came into the kitchen, Junebug, smiling widely and looking a lot stronger than she had the night before, handed him a tin plate heaped with food. "Better eat slow," she said, sounding more energetic than Joshua would have thought possible a few hours before. "Otherwise your stomach'll bust." She laughed.

His mother and Pappy were sitting by Preacher, Chas, and Mr. and Mrs. Campbell. His mother looked away from the conversation at him and smiled. Used to the ways of the Bulrush's big house, she did not look out of place.

Jeremiah and Jamie were sitting in the kitchen corner on the floor where Joshua had sat the afternoon before. The only time slaves in the quarters had gotten as much food was on Christmas when Master and Mistress Bulrush invited them to the front of the big house's porch and Cook and his mother brought tin plates out of the kitchen with the help of Massie and the other grown black women. They had eaten in the cold outside, soon filled with the season's joy as their Christmas presents went into their stomachs. The Master and Mistress never stayed after the food was distributed, but went back inside to a Christmas feast twice as resplendent.

Esta May was handed a plate by Beulah and came to sit with Joshua. She forced herself to eat the boiled egg first and slowly spooned the rest of the meal into her mouth. Joshua felt like bolting every bite, but emulated Esta May. He knew his mother would be watching to see if he still remembered what manners were even if she did not seem to be looking at him. Jeremiah looked at him as if he were crazy. He had gobbled his breakfast.

The minute Joshua finished, Pappy rose from the table and came over to him. Jeremiah and Jamie were still there, having stayed to hungrily watch Joshua and Esta May eat. Pappy nodded at each of them.

"The women have already had their turn," Pappy said. "There's a pond out back. You boys need to take your clothes off and get clean. Preacher's going to hold a service, and you need to be presentable."

Joshua glanced at Esta May and then at his mother. So that was why they looked clean. They'd not only gotten up early enough to start breakfast while the men went out to help with chores, but they'd also gone to the pond and washed not only their bodies but their clothes as well.

He looked at Pappy. He looked clean too. Pappy smiled at his son's quizzical look.

"We're not moving today," he said. "We men got up before the women and got clean before chores. Now you three move it." He laughed when Jeremiah jumped as if startled by the stern tone in his voice. Jamie and Joshua rose, too, as Esta May smirked at them.

Outside, the sun blazed. The humidity was so great Joshua felt like he was walking through a pond suspended in air. Tim and his brother were waiting by the door.

"We're supposed to take you to the pond," Tim said. He pointed toward his little brother. "This is Tommy."

"Pleased to meet you," Tommy said. He looked to be a year or so younger than Jeremiah. He pronounced his words with a precision that made him sound the way the Bulrush plantation's white preacher had sounded.

The pond was not far away. Tim led to a well-beaten path through a small copse of red pines. The pond was just on the other side. As soon as they were at its banks, Tim and Tommy kicked off their shoes and started taking off their clothes. Joshua was shocked. He had never seen a white person take off their clothes before.

Jeremiah, as rash as usual, didn't hesitate, but followed the white boys' example. Jamie held back a moment before undressing, too. Joshua felt weird, but forced himself to not think. He wanted to feel clean. Keeping his eyes averted as the white boys and Jeremiah plunged into blue-green water, he stripped and followed Jamie. The water was cooler than the air, though lukewarm, and felt good. Jeremiah, Tim, and Tommy were shoving each other and laughing. Jamie looked at Joshua and shook his head.

***

In the farmhouse kitchen for Preacher's sermon, Joshua felt better. Swimming with naked white boys hadn't felt comfortable, but washing away days of sweat and grime made him feel more like he had living in the quarters. The difference was that he wasn't on the plantation, but in the middle of an escape toward freedom. That idea still seemed even stranger than seeing two white boys scamper out of a pond over the Missouri border into Illinois and casually put on clothes without once snarling at the slaves swimming with them. Joshua and Jamie were both more self-conscious than the Campbells, although Jeremiah seemed oblivious to the gulf between him and them.

Everyone was in the kitchen, standing around the trestle table when Willie came to hurry the five boys along. He'd brought two towels with him. As they dried off, he laughed as they put on clothes still wet from Pappy's effort to clean them. They were all giddy from feeling safe, Joshua concluded, looking at Jamie and Jeremiah's father.

"I have sons beneath dirt after all," Willie joked.

The minute the six of them were in the kitchen Preacher bowed his head in prayer. The Campbell family stood between Chas and Joshua's family as Preacher looked up.

"I learned how to pray, really pray," he said, "before I got to know

Chas and Mr. James Campbell." He gestured to the two men. "We were serving under Commodore Oliver Hazard Perry in Lake Erie. I was in the flagship, the Lawrence, with the Commodore, and Chas and Mr. Campbell were in the Niagara. I was just a boy then. It was when British cannon set fire to the Lawrence that I learned how to truly pray—in the midst of smoke, flames, terrible noise, and the fear always in the hearts of mortal men.

"In Psalm 23, Verse 4, we are told that 'Yea, though I walk through the valley of the shadow of death, I will fear no evil: for thou art with me." But I was afraid every minute of that battle. Fear led me to prayer with a seriousness I had not known before. The prayers I said as cannonballs crashed around me moved my spirit toward God for the first time, even though a Godly Quaker man had freed me from my master Gwyn Harcourt and given me the opportunity to become a sailor.

"When Commodore Perry abandoned the Lawrence and had us row him to the Niagara where, later, I got to know the two good men in this house today, cannonballs splashed water into our boat. We could hear whistling as they hurtled at us. It was while pulling oars I decided I would become a preacher, dedicating my life to God and my people. As I scrambled into the Niagara, I determined I would live the life that has led to this place and time in this kitchen. After the victory by Rattlesnake Island that changed the war's course and led to American victory, I found black and white sailors who paid more attention to God, our Lord Jesus Christ, and their faith, than their race ...."

Listening to Preacher, Joshua felt detached from his own life's story. He was a slave from a particularly harsh plantation where the most important slave, the Overseer, was the tool of the master's brutality. Preacher was talking about a world and life Joshua couldn't even imagine. His story was amazing: black men serving as freed men on a warship with white sailors, a slave who determined to become a preacher and sought out black and white men who shared his beliefs! It seemed more fantasy than reality.

He looked at Mr. Campbell, whose face bore both sternness and gentleness in it. The angular cut of his cheekbones and forehead gave him the stern visage that made him look like he could stand on a ship's deck while cannon blazed and roared, although Joshua had trouble imagining what the deck of a ship like the one Preacher was talking about would look like. Gentleness was in his eyes, especially when he was looking at his wife or three daughters and two sons. Dressed in his farmer's clothes, with his brown, wide brimmed hat, he did not look like a sailor, however a sailor would look, but had an air that made it seem as if he could be courageous.

Preacher, obviously getting old, had a face that bespoke of having

72

seen and gone through storms of experiences and a ramrod straight posture, and was different when he preached. Before, Joshua had seen him as a man who was what he purported to be: a freedman preacher grateful to have a slave congregation able to get away from their plantations to services held in a swamp beneath a cypress tree. He had come to Missouri's bootheel in order to preach because he did not have the right to preach in a church like white preachers did.

But as he preached in the Campbell's kitchen, Joshua saw him differently. He was more than the preacher his mother wanted to see at service on Sundays. He was a man who had fought on a ship and experienced war and the death of those who had gone to war with him.

Joshua didn't know much about war. Old Simpson had once told him, as they shivered in their shack one night in the middle of January, about a group of white men he had tended for a master before he was sold to the Bulrushes. They were old white men, he had said, but they had fought wild Indians in the west where they'd been wounded. Two had lost legs from gangrene, and the others weren't in much better shape. War was a white man's burden, the old man had told him. Slaves were not important enough in the world's larger doings to be warriors.

The thought that Preacher and Chas, along with Mr. Campbell, had served as warriors made them bigger than life. As Preacher's deep voice rolled, dipping occasionally into a Bible verse, moving up and down in a cadence close to a chant, Joshua was mesmerized. He at last understood why his mother had risked the wrath of her owners to go to Sunday meetings.

After Preacher had finished his sermon, Mr. Campbell, Chas, and Preacher left together for the barn. On the way out the kitchen door, Joshua heard Preacher ask Mr. Campbell how he'd gotten such a fine farm.

"You were just a sailor like the other white sailors," Preacher said. "People with wealth enough to buy this didn't serve under Commodore Perry unless they were officers."

"My dad had an abandoned lot in Philadelphia," Mr. Campbell had answered. "It wasn't much, overgrown with weeds, but they wanted it for a bank after Dad died. I sold it and bought some other land ...." Then the three men were outside, out of Joshua's hearing.

Before Joshua could think about what he'd heard, Pappy came and asked him how he was doing while Mary went to the kitchen with the women to start cooking again. The thought of another big meal filled Joshua with a deep sense of satisfaction. He hoped he never again had to get as hungry as he'd been before coming to the Campbell's. When he told Pappy he was okay, Pappy hesitated, and frowned. He looked awkward.

"I've seen you looking at me and then at yourself. If you're wondering why I'm so big and you're so small for your age," he blurted, "I wasn't as small as you are at your age, but I wasn't big like I am now, either. I started growing late and didn't stop. That's going to happen to you, too."

The declaration was unexpected. He had thought about why he was so small and Pappy was so big. It had made him wonder if he was really Pappy's son, but he'd put the thought out of his mind. He was so unused to having a father he had forced himself not to think about it. He wondered if he looked like Pappy at all.

He didn't know, but suspected what had happened in the big house with his mother. He had long ago decided his behavior was only part of the reason he'd been banned. Slaves didn't have privacy, so even little kids knew about what went on between men and women. He was pretty sure Master Bulrush forced his mother to do his will when he managed to get her alone when the Mistress and his son were away somewhere. Joshua was just as sure his mother did not like the Master, not in that way or any other, but slaves did not have choices. Slave children knew about their place on the plantation, too. That was often driven home by a hard smack to an arm or leg. Was Pappy his father only in his mother's eyes? Or was he his father for real?

Clearly Pappy had been thinking about how Joshua physically compared to him. Maybe it meant something to him to know if Joshua was part of his "begetting," as the Bible put it. His mother had once told him about all the begetting around Noah and how long-lived Bible people had been. Sometimes, when he had lived in the big house, she had read to him from one of the Bibles she surreptitiously borrowed from the Master's library. She wasn't supposed to know how to read, but she did. Joshua looked up at Pappy, puzzled. The big man was nervous.

"No, forget it," he said, looking down into Joshua's eyes. "You're my son. That's what counts." He walked off toward where Willie, Bill, Franklin, and Harrison had gathered in the parlor where Joshua, Jamie, and Jeremiah had slept.

Still puzzled, Joshua went outside to find Jamie and Jeremiah. Esta May was in the kitchen with her sisters, the women talking and laughing as if fugitive women belonged where they were. Jamie and Jeremiah were talking with Tim and Tommy.

"My Dad said he was proud he served with Tom Bennett and Chas Bullock during the Battle of Lake Erie," Tommy said. "He said Tom Bennett came from Commodore Perry's ship when the Lawrence sank. He told me Tom Bennett wasn't even afraid. You think that's true?"

"What's Lake Erie?" Jeremiah asked.

"You don't know what Lake Erie is?" Tommy responded,

incredulous.

"Tommy," Timothy warned. He looked at Jeremiah. "It's a lake," he said. "A big lake. We haven't seen it, either. We've just heard my Dad's stories." He paused, looking back at Joshua. "Dad said it's not as big as Lake Michigan where you're headed," he continued. "We've been to Lake Michigan. We came around the bottom shore when we moved here from Michigan State before Ginny and Suzy were born. Tommy doesn't remember. He was too little."

Joshua's head was spinning. Too much was coming at him from too many different directions. He had hardly left the Bulrush plantation before his mother had taken him away to the swamp, and they had started their run to freedom. These boys had seen a lot of the world. They had been places he had never even heard of: Lake Erie, Lake Michigan, Michigan. They had nothing in common with him, Jamie, and Jeremiah, but if he wasn't wrong, they actually admired Preacher and Chas Bullock, black men. White boys did not admire black men even if they were freedmen. He would have sworn that on his father's grave.

The thought of the common saying about his father's grave stopped his mind from spinning. His father wasn't dead. He had just walked through the kitchen door to the barn to help with chores on a white man's farm. Even if Pappy wasn't his real father, he was still his father based on how the quarters thought about things.

Uncomfortable, he thought he owed these two white boys something. Their family was protecting him and the people he was with and promising to help them get to Lake Michigan, wherever in the far north that was. That thought of the distance they had yet to go made him feel even more uncomfortable.

"We haven't been anywhere," he said. "On the plantation you stay and work the fields or work in the master's house or feed or bed animals or work in the garden. That's life."

"Sounds confining to me," Tim said.

"You get whipped," Jamie said. "Show them your back Joshua."

Tim and Tommy's eyes widened. They were staring at Joshua as if they couldn't believe what they were hearing. "You're a kid just like me," Tim whispered.

Joshua looked sharply at Jamie. Why had he said that and put the evil eye on him? His back scars suddenly felt as fiery as they had the day his mother had forced him to leave the quarters for the swamp. The others were silent, looking at him. He thought about walking away and fleeing to the kitchen. Then, for a reason he couldn't fathom, he pulled his shirt off and turned around. He heard gasps. He dropped the shirt and looked at the white boys. Both had tears in their eyes.

He frowned. He hadn't cried when he had been whipped a second time the last day he'd spent on the plantation.

"I'm sorry," Tim said.

"I was a slave," Joshua said slowly. He looked into Tim's blue eyes. "But now I'm free—as long as slavers don't catch me."

He heard the resolution in his words. *Free? I'm free?* Where had that thought come from? Was it really true when he could hear the dogs barking on their trail in his head?

"Does your Mom know?" Tommy asked.

"She saw Silver Coats whip him over and over again," Jamie answered.

There was awe in the white boy's faces. They looked at Joshua as if he were someone other than who he was. Jamie and Jeremiah looked at them curiously, not understanding their surprise. Everyone knew slaves were whipped. That was the way it was.

The rest of that day and the next, as the Campbells waited for men who were going to drive the wagons, the five of them were mostly together except when they slept. Joshua wasn't sure why, but somehow he had become the leader. Wherever he decided to go on the farm, the other boys followed.

With every word they spoke, the Campbells showed they knew much, much more about the world than he did. They even knew how to read and write. Joshua's mother, the smartest person he knew, could read and write, but that was so unusual as to be almost unbelievable.

She didn't have the opportunity to read now, of course. When she talked about the Bible her talk came from what white people or Preacher or others had told her for the most part. But she had shown Joshua how much she loved reading when he was still at the big house. Borrowing a Bible from the Master's library could easily have led to disaster. None of the slaves that lived in the quarters could read. None of them were allowed to learn.

Joshua's mother had told him once that there was a law against white people teaching slaves to read. She said she had started to learn and knew her letters, but when the Master's daughter who was secretly teaching her was found out, Joshua's mother had been moved to the quarters and kept away from her mistress.

Joshua had never been told what plantation his mother had been sold from. He knew he'd been born shortly after she had moved to the Bulrush's, but she refused to answer any questions about her life before. He now knew she'd been sold from the plantation Pappy had escaped.

Tim said that he and Tommy were only half as good at reading and writing as their sister Sally. They were boys, he said, and boys weren't as book smart as girls, but their reading skill still seemed amazing. Joshua felt as if he had somehow stumbled into a world bigger than he had ever imagined it could be.

Mostly the five boys fooled around during the two days they spent together. They didn't rough house exactly. Joshua, Jamie, and Jeremiah were too tired, and even weak, for that, but they still did what boys do, laughed and talked, even though the black boys carried a niggling sense of dislocation and fear in the back of their minds. Sometimes they went out to the barn with the men, hurrying like deer so they minimized the chance they might be seen. They wandered the house, wanting to go outside into the sun, but constrained by eyes that might exist but could not be seen.

Esta May, her sisters, and Abbie, for the most part stayed with the women who always found work to do around the house or the big garden south of the house. They could go outside because the only thing behind the house was woods.

Sometimes she, with one or more of her sisters and Abbie, or even Tim and Tommy's sisters, joined the boys, but she was different than she had been running in the woods. She seemed more proper, as if in civilization she and the other women had remembered how domestic life ought to be and how they should behave differently from men and boys. Joining the boys in the house seemed a gift to them rather than an opportunity to be part of what they were going on about. She didn't act uppity; that wasn't her way, but there was a grown-upness about her when she was around the boys that was, Joshua suspected, absent when she wasn't close to them.

When Tommy, on the night before they were told to go to the parlor and sleep because they would be leaving before dawn, said he was glad they were all friends, Joshua was surprised but not startled. He had grown in some way, he realized. He didn't trust white people, not even Tim and Tommy, and he had no idea how any black boy could actually feel he was a friend with white boys. His experiences with white people before the escape had been anything but good.

But Tim, Tommy, their parents, and their sisters were different. They were white, but they weren't plantation white. They did not seem, at least as far as he could see into them—which wasn't all that far, he knew—to see escaping slaves as anything but equals. They sat at the same table during meals and worked side by side with them without barking out streams of orders. As he slowly drifted into sleep he thought that *that* idea was troubling and not troubling, both at the same time.

Chapter 9
Chicago on the Road to Freedom

Cacophony, noise, horses, people, smells,
A raging restlessness and energy
Unbounded from the places spirit dwells
Infected them and made them want to flee
Their fleeing even as Chicago seethed
And made them wonder if their slavery
Was more than whips and white men wreathed
In arrogance, but something in their souls,
Their consciousness, the very air they breathed
That filled their lives with loss and empty holes
Where dreams should live and let life soar in skies
Removed from fear and all the deadly shoals
That, hidden, suddenly materialize
And snatch away a slave's most longed-for prize.

Compared to the early days of their escape, the next several were easy. On the morning they left the farm that had provided them with food, rest, and safety after a long, tense time of fear and deprivation, the Campbell family came out as one wagon after another rolled into the yard in front of the red barn. People piled into the wagon bed, were covered with gray canvas, and then driven away.

"We're going to a big city called Chicago," Preacher told them. "We'll be in the poorest part where Chas and I have the boat we built stored. We're taking back roads here, but closer to Chicago we'll be going through town after town. You have to remain under the canvas and stay quiet and still. There's too many of us. We don't want to draw attention."

Joshua, his parents, and Willie, Massie, Jamie, and Jeremiah were in the third wagon to leave. Tim and Tommy watched solemnly as the three black boys crawled under the canvas cover. Joshua turned and poked his head out after he was situated and hesitantly waved. They waved back. Then the driver, a young white man they were told to call Mr. Culver, "a truly righteous man," Mr. Campbell had told them, said "Come on" to the horses, flicking leather reins. They were down the road an hour behind the wagon carrying the Woodruffs.

There was nothing to do under the canvas. At first Mr. Culver kept asking them if they were "all right back there," but after a while he was silent. The universe, like it had been the other times they had been forced to shrink into themselves hiding in wagons, became movement, the sound of horses, and the running and bumping of wagon wheels over the road. For a while Joshua occupied himself by studying his father's face in the dim light under the canvas. His eyes were like the rest of him, big, and his mouth looked like it was made for laughing. A slight smile quirked his lips even when he was serious. He hadn't laughed during their journey so far. Instead, he'd spent his time looking concerned. "Probably trying to find burdens he could put on his shoulders and take from others," Joshua thought. He wondered if he would laugh if they really made it to the island where they could live as free people.

His mother and father discreetly kept touching each other on the shoulders, arms, and face. They didn't try to hug or kiss, but even Joshua could tell how they felt about one another. He wasn't sure how *he* felt about that, but Joshua was slowly beginning to believe they had a chance to have a better life.

When they stopped, the sun was directly above them. Mr. Culver brought them sandwiches made with biscuits and salt pork and then started off again. Joshua began to try to imagine what Washington Island was going to be like. Tim and Tommy had told them about Lake Michigan. It was as big as an ocean, bigger than a plantation's fields. You couldn't see across the endless waves to another shore. Preacher had said the island was wilderness with forests, deer, small animals, berries, rock cliffs, a big hill inland, and beaches. Most of what Preacher talked about was outside Joshua's experience, but he tried to envision an enormous lake and an island that rose out of water green and wild in an afternoon sun.

The image he created in his mind was probably not right, he realized. He kept making the island more like the big swamp with its cypress and willow trees, endless brush, and openings of water. No doubt it was going to be different than that. Still, his effort to think about where they were going helped the endless hours pass.

That night, in a woods surrounded by fields, away from the wagon, he, Jamie, and Jeremiah whispered about the island and how they would feel to be free and not slaves. They could hear Mr. Culver singing beside a campfire. He'd cooked them supper, frying strips of beef, but they'd eaten in the woods away from the fire.

Jamie's face took on a dreamy expression as he started talking about the island.

"Doesn't seem real, does it? New Jerusalem? The island?" he asked.

"Reaching the island without being caught and being free?" Joshua asked.

"Yeah," Jamie answered.

"I keep seeing the Overseer every time I get out of the wagon," Jeremiah volunteered. "He's not there, but I see him."

"Preacher says we're going to paradise," Joshua said.

"I always thought dead people were the ones who went to paradise," Jamie said. "That's what your mother said when Old Simpson died. She said he went to paradise, that he was a good man who took good care of you." He looked at Joshua.

"Preacher's weird," Joshua said. "He says a lot of weird things."

After a while, Pappy came over to the tree where the three of them had their heads huddled together. "You fellas slept a lot today," he said in a near-whisper. "We're probably okay out here, but if someone comes along on the road that we don't want to know we're here ...."

"We'll sleep," Joshua told him. "We'll be quiet."

"We understand," Jamie agreed.

Pappy smiled. "You're good boys," he said approvingly. "Very good boys." He crawled back over to Joshua's mother who smiled at him as she leaned back on a chestnut tree's trunk.

***

The next day was pretty much like the first. The one after that was, too. Wagons, horses, and walkers passed them going one way or another. Mr. Culver greeted everyone they passed with a smile in his voice. They went, without stopping, through towns. Sometimes they felt twinges of fear when some small thing changed the steady routine of moving north, but the wagon kept moving day after day, north toward Chicago.

Sometimes Joshua wondered about Mr. Culver. His father had supposedly lent, as Mr. Culver explained it, three of his sons for this journey and helped provide some of the food the four wagons needed. But his reasons for helping slaves flee from their owners eluded Joshua. Ever since they'd met Mr. Jemmie in the woods outside his barn, white people had helped them.

Joshua had started to understand more about Christianity and faith. Since he'd found out that Preacher had been a sailor in a war, he'd listened to the fiery old man and his talk with his mother and others more closely.

Preacher always talked about Jesus Christ loving all people no matter what their place in life and talked about the importance of free will in God's plan. "We are all made in God's image," he said. "Slavery is an injustice that is part of man's fall from the grace of God's making."

The young Mr. Culver didn't talk like Preacher talked. He had an easy smile and way that indicated he accepted life as it was rather than how he thought it ought to be. "We got to get you out of slave country," he said a couple of times as he handed them food or signaled that it was okay to get out of the wagon after he'd stopped along an empty stretch of road. "I'm going to feel good I did this," he said on another occasion, but mostly he gave no clue about what drove him and his brothers to take the risk they were taking.

"They'll go to jail if they're caught," Joshua's mother had told him. "Their punishment won't be light."

***

Then came the night when Mr. Culver told them he couldn't let them out of the wagon to find a place to sleep. He sat on the wagon seat after he stopped the wagon and told them there were too many people in the area to ensure they wouldn't be seen. They would have to stay where they were all night. He sounded reluctant to tell them, but Willie quickly assented for all of them. "We understand," he said. "We're okay."

"We'll be to Chicago in another two days," Mr. Culver said. Then he got down off the wagon and disappeared.

That night lasted forever. The dark was as quiet as most of their nights had been since leaving the Campbells, but seemed different. Menace waited outside the wagon, waiting to end their long run and slap them into chains. When morning came, and Mr. Culver said that if they would hurry, they could get out of the wagon for a minute to do their business, as he put it, there was relief on all of their faces.

They discovered that they weren't in a highly populated area, although two houses were in sight of the wagon. Joshua's mother and Massie Bullock went into bushes beside the road, followed by the men. The sun's edge was just rising above the horizon when Mr. Culver closed the canvas flap with his twine, and they were on the move again.

As they approached Chicago the next day, the frequency of towns they passed through grew. They would huddle, muscles tense, as they made it safely through one only to tense up again a short time later. The mindlessness of traveling under canvas warred with fear that spiked every time a horse or wagon passed. Then came the time when wagons and horses followed behind them almost constantly, making thought impossible. Joshua's mother and Massie prayed.

They spent another night in the wagon. They were on the outskirts of a town. Mr. Culver disappeared again, leaving them wondering, in silence, where he'd gone. When he came back alone an hour later without saying anything, they were relieved. Joshua had been so jumpy while Mr. Culver was gone he had fought with himself to stay still beneath the canvas.

Late the next day, Mr. Culver announced they had reached the city. At first the noise was not that great, but the deeper into the city they went, the louder it became. Wagons, horses, and people passed constantly. Sometimes they heard children screeching and playing along the sides of roads and streets.

Then, suddenly, the wagon swerved and stopped. Mr. Culver cursed. "What's wrong?" Joshua's mother asked out loud. Jason's eyes were huge; he looked ready to jump out of the wagon. Joshua's nerves seemed to be out of his control. "It's okay," Mr. Culver said. He paused. "Somebody's going to have to come out here and help me. There's too much traffic."

The seven of them looked at each other. "Who's best?" Pappy asked at last.

Mr. Culver paused. "A boy," he said at last. "Joshua. A black boy won't seem strange beside me. Not in Chicago."

His father motioned to him. "Go on Joshua," he said.

Joshua panicked. He couldn't move. He had hidden for weeks. He didn't know how he could let himself be seen when he could hear city noises all around him. He looked at Jamie, whose face was a mix of emotions. He seemed both envious and relieved. Like Joshua, he wanted to be outside canvas in sunlight and seeing what the world they were passing looked like, but they had hidden so long that hiding seemed normal.

"Hurry," Mr. Culver said. "I can't stay here."

Joshua gulped and slipped out from under the canvas into daylight. He felt naked out in the open. Buildings and people were everywhere. The wagon was beside a wooden walkway in front of brick and wooden buildings that soared four stories into the air. Horses, wagons, and people were moving both ways in complicated patterns on the road. The city smelled of horse manure and smoke and a mix of other smells he couldn't identify. Men were shouting. Laundry was hanging out of second, third, and fourth story windows. The confusion was overwhelming.

"Up here," Mr. Culver said urgently. Joshua hurried around the back of the wagon and jumped up to sit beside Mr. Culver. Mr. Culver smiled at him. "Help me watch for wagons, people, and horses," he said. "I'm a country boy. This city stuff is for the birds." He jogged the two big draft horses into motion, swinging into a space between a man on a black stallion and a wagon drawn by four horses.

"Watch out!" Joshua said, pointing to a man who had darted into the road and was dancing between horses and wagons. Mr. Culver slowed the team and then urged them forward as the man darted in front of them.

"Won't people see me?" Joshua asked, the fright he was feeling in his voice.

Mr. Culver swerved to miss a wagon coming into the main road from a side street. He looked uptight. "In a city, you're mostly invisible far as I can tell," he said. "Everybody looks at you and nobody looks at you and nobody seems to see anything." His voice was tense.

Another man stepped off the wooden walkway. "There." Joshua pointed. But the man thought better of his foolhardiness and stepped backward as Mr. Culver's wagon rolled past.

This seemed to go on forever as Mr. Culver pulled on reins, then shook them, then pulled back again. "There's got to be a better way than this," he said. "But it's the way my daddy showed me. Every time I come here, I swear I'm never coming again."

Next to a building that seemed taller than the others, he said, "At last," and pulled left out of the busy street. Two blocks later, the buildings surrounding them were more poorly constructed, although people still milled about in amazing numbers. Along the busy road, buildings had been painted a variety of colors if they weren't made of brick or stone. Now their wood was weathered and gray. The people were different, too. On the road, the people had been white, black, and oriental in a bewildering mix. Joshua had not been able to fix his eyes on any one person, but strange looking people with pigtails hanging down their shoulders and strange clothes kept catching his eyes. He'd never seen people like them before.

Two short blocks later, there were still white people, but more of the people were black like Joshua. People were still riding horses, but theirs was the only wagon. More kids were playing in the street, too, dancing away from the front of the wagon just before it got to them.

"Not long now," Mr. Culver said. He looked at Joshua and smiled. He seemed more relaxed. "The warehouse isn't far from the river. We're going away from downtown to where the black laborers and their families live." He causally looked at the buildings around them. "We could let your folks breathe the air now, but we might as well get where we're going. Nobody's going to see black families as other than normal here."

Forty-five minutes later, the city changed again. Suddenly there were fewer people of any color and larger buildings. "There," Mr. Culver pointed toward a big structure painted dirty black at the end of the block. "Mr. Bullock, my brothers, and Mr. Bennett will be waiting for us 'round back in the basement."

He maneuvered the wagon around another corner, drove down an embankment, and pulled up behind the building. The wagons his two brothers had driven were tied up near closed double doors that provided a large opening from the warehouse to the small dirt road they had pulled onto. Joshua could hear his heart pounding in his ears. His mouth was dry, and he felt half sick to his stomach. The city was overwhelming.

Mr. Culver crawled down from the wagon seat. "We're here. You can get out," he said cheerfully. Joshua didn't move.

Then his mother was standing next to him in full sunlight. "Joshua?" she asked. Pappy was standing behind Mary, looking at Joshua with concern. Jamie and Jeremiah were by the warehouse door, looking dazed. Willie and Massie were peering up at the smoky sky.

Preacher came out of the black building and was greeting Mr. Culver. Joshua shook himself. He was a long, long way from the quarters and plantation life.

***

Their eyes were adjusting to the warehouse's dimness when Abbie came up to Joshua, Jamie, and Jeremiah. "You've got to see," she said, her voice excited. She reached out her hand to Joshua.

"The warehouse is owned by an abolitionist friend," Preacher was telling Pappy and Joshua's mother. "The Illinois Anti-Slavery Society provided materials for the boat."

Joshua held back, wanting to hear Preacher, but Abbie tugged at him. "Joshua," she said, exasperation in her voice.

"Come on Joshua," Jeremiah said.

"This isn't the most convenient location, but Illinois is mixed," Preacher was explaining. "It's a free state, but slavery's got support here. We're relatively safe if we don't stay long. Getting the scow on its way north to where we want to be is a challenge, but it takes time in Chicago for people to notice that somebody new's arrived since new people are always coming. In a city this big everything's just naturally confused and stirring all the time."

Joshua gave in to Abbie's tugging, and he, Jamie, and Jeremiah followed her into a large area with a high ceiling.

He had just noticed she wasn't dressed in the rags she'd worn since the swamp, but in a cotton dress, when he saw the boat. It was long and narrow with bulging sides that had two poles sticking up from the middle. Looking at it, then following Abbie when she went to touch the smooth sides, Joshua was in awe. It was as big as two, or maybe even more, wagon beds stacked front to back.

"This will get us to the island," Chas, who had come up behind them, said.

"It'll take more than one trip," Preacher, who had followed them into the big room, said. "We'll build a dory for fishing, but this will get us out even when weather is bad. That means if we're careful with nets and hooks we'll get whitefish, salmon, and trout up until ice sets in. Then we'll cut holes in the ice and keep fishing."

"Three trips?" Massie Bullock asked. "With water all around us?"

"I mean on the first trip to the island," Preacher clarified. "You don't want to overload the boat. We've got supplies as well as people."

Pappy was looking distrustfully at the vessel. "How are you going to get it up north where it's safe?" he asked. "Mr. Campbell told me it's a long way from Chicago to the peninsula's tip where you go across the lake." He paused. "None of us other than you and Chas know how to drive a boat, either."

"We're splitting up again," Chas answered. "The Stimsons, Franklin, Zelda, and Massie are going to be in the boat with Tom here," he said, pointing at Preacher. "The rest will be making it north overland with me. We'll not hide quite as much, especially north of Chicago. Wisconsin has more free territory than around here. We can't move in daylight, but we're going to chance the roads. We'll head for a place not far from Stockbridge where the Indians will meet us."

"Gordon Burr will help supply us," Preacher said. "He and the Stockbridge have been helping slaves get to Green Bay and on to Canada for years. The Indian Agent doesn't treat them right, but abolitionist churches help support them."

Joshua's mother had taken hold of his father's arm. "We'll be free," she said. Her voice had an intense energy in it. "I'll go on a boat or walk forever just to get my boy and his father free."

Chapter 10
A Scow in a Warehouse

Eyes ate the boat, the scow, magnificence
Inside the run-down warehouse, shadows deep
As hours they'd spent caught in the turbulence
Of fear and hope as hours dragged by, the creep
Of wagon wheels hypnotic, staining nerves
Until the universe was dissonance,
A time and place where senses slowly swerved
Toward disaster, dreaded slavery.

And then the scow, a tale the heart deserves,
A rush across huge waters as the tree
Of freedom looms upon a shore that sings
Into the longed-for land of jubilee,
A dream escaped from all the reckonings
That hovered in their souls' rememberings.

Silver Coats, with his narrow black eyes and beefy, snarling face, was coming at Joshua with his whip held in his right hand. His arm was cocked way back, ready to slash the leather braid full force into Joshua's back. The old black man was larger than he should have been. Uglier too. Joshua was trying to hide in a willow thicket by Fisher Creek, but he knew the Overseer could see him through the brush.

When he finally got within three feet, Joshua bolted, his heart racing. Old Simpson was floating in the air above his head. "Run," the old, dead man said. "Run!" The whip cracked behind Joshua so loud it turned the air into a wind. He could feel the leather knots tied into the whip's braid slashing toward his back. Time didn't seem right, though. It was moving so slowly he could feel the braid cut through empty air. "I'm not going to live this time," he thought. Silver Coats' maniacal laughter was so loud Joshua fled toward the darkness opening up in front of him.

Joshua woke with a start. His heart was pounding, and he was sweating. His father was kneeling beside him in the small room's darkness where the fugitives were sleeping on pads Preacher and Chas had brought them. The pads were soft. Joshua, as they had gotten ready to sleep, had been amazed at how comfortable laying down could be.

He'd slept on a small cot in his mother's room in the cellar of the big house as a boy, but he hadn't had that experience since he had been moved to the quarters. Even at the Campbells, he, Jamie, and Jeremiah had slept on the pine floor without anything beneath them. The warehouse was uncomfortably hot and humid, but the pad made everything feel comfortable.

"You okay?" his father asked. His mother was leaning on one arm and looking at the two of them.

"Nightmare," Joshua mumbled. "That's all."

Pappy nodded. "You've had a hard time." He paused. "All slaves have it hard," he said, a hint of bitterness in his voice. He shook his head. "I'm sorry. I should have been there as your pappy back on the plantation, but I wasn't able to."

His mother quietly got up and signaled. Joshua looked over to where Jamie and Jeremiah were sleeping. The warehouse was hot even in the middle of the night. He nodded, got up, and followed his mother and father.

In the room where the scow stood silently in the darkness, Pappy and Mary sat cross-legged on the warehouse floor. The room smelled faintly like the tar Joshua had once helped put on the smoke shed roof at the plantation. His mother put her arms around him and drew him over to her.

"We haven't had a chance to be family yet," she said softly.

His father smiled. "That's what we're doing," he said. "Running for a chance." He paused. "Our mothers and fathers lived out their lives in slavery. Here we have a chance."

Joshua pulled away from his mother and looked at her. She had a good, strong face. She had been considered beautiful in the quarters, but haughty. Joshua hadn't thought that was even close to the truth of what she'd felt, but he had never tried to argue about it. The sculpture of her distinct features was pronounced even in darkness.

"You never told me I had a father," he said softly, a hint of accusation still buried in the question.

His mother looked into his eyes without blinking.

"I didn't think you'd ever have a father. On the Bulrush Plantation it didn't pay to put ideas in people's heads. All you'd ever have was a whipping if you said or thought the wrong thing. It seemed safer. I wasn't wrong," she said after a moment of silence. "The risk of you knowing about your father was too great. One wrong word when you didn't even realize what you were saying could have killed you."

Pappy was looking at his big hands. "I wasn't that far away," he said, "but I might as well have been in Africa. I knew about Master Bulrush. Slaves know about him two states away. I was afraid he'd kill your mother if I showed up. My wonderful master had warned him about me. I'd been watched close, too, even though he trusted me to go into town on my own."

Joshua remained silent, although both his father and mother were looking at him expectantly. He glanced at the big boat. Preacher and Chas had said they were going to put the scow on the river in the morning. Once he reached Lake Michigan, Preacher would sail it north to the Door Peninsula in Wisconsin.

Joshua looked straight into his father's eyes. "Did you ever jump the broom?"

His father smiled, his eyes shining. He looked at Joshua's mother. "None of the masters knew," he said. "Master Samuelson thought slaves getting married was a sacrilege against the white race. But we did, out in the woods while a full moon shone down and lit the ground so well you could see grass blades as plain as day. My father was there." He paused, the light fading from his face. "Before he died. Before the master sold your mother to Master Bulrush and his plantation's version of hell."

Mary stayed quiet, although she was looking at Jason as he spoke. She still had her arms around Joshua.

"Then I'm really your jumped-over-the-broom son?" Joshua asked. He paused, thinking.

He thought about Pappy's words about how small he was. He'd suspected that his father had been Master Bulrush, but his mother had to have been pregnant before she was sold to the plantation. That's what the quarters said.

Still, he'd heard different rumors even though no one had ever said anything directly to him. The whole thing had been confusing. Why had there been the rumors about Master Bulrush and his mother if the people in the quarters had known his mother had been pregnant when she was bought and put up at the master's house?

His father saw the confusion on the boy's face. "Until Chas came with a message from your mother," he said, "neither of us expected to see the other one again unless some accident put us in the same town at the same time. And I was further away than the likelihood of that."

Joshua shifted his attention to his mother. "You sent Preacher with a message to Pappy?" he asked, his voice intense.

"Chas took the message," she said. "A boy deserves a father, even a slave boy. I wasn't sure about running until Chas came and talked at the Sunday service when you were working in the fields. Then the possibility of getting back with Jason came up.

"This might be hard, but when I met Preacher and found out he was going to lead escaped slaves north, I made up my mind that if it was possible, my son was never going to be whipped again no matter how stubborn he is. Then there was doubt about whether Jason could come or not. I delayed making a final decision. Running was going to be risky. Then Preacher let me know through Massie that Chas had found Jason."

Joshua looked from one parent to the other and back again, feeling his way into what he was being told. His mother and father had jumped the broom. He was the result of that ceremony. He was their son.

Pappy sighed. In the warehouse dark Joshua could feel how intently his father was looking at him.

"I was small for my age until I was almost sixteen," Jason said. "My father couldn't believe he and my mother had had a child so small since they were both big people. Then I started growing and getting stronger and stronger. People in the Samuelson quarters kept exclaiming that once I got started, I was going to grow forever."

"I knew him from the time he was a child," his mother said. "You can't worry so much about being small. You'll grow out of it. I mean, when Jason started spurting up, after a while nobody could believe it. I mean, what woman wouldn't fall in love with a man that grew into a giant?"

"I haven't worried about being small," Joshua responded, puzzled. Why did that subject keep coming up?

"I was sold because of Jason," his mother said.

"Master Samuelson was a different kind of master," Pappy continued for her. "In some ways he was as good a master as anybody could ask for. He was always respectful. He listened to slaves, at least sometimes. You could actually talk to him."

"Unlike with Master Bulrush," his mother chimed in.

"The point is that Master Samuelson was a single man until he was older," Pappy said. "After your mother and I had already jumped the broom, he decided to have designs on your mother."

"He told me what we were going to do," his mother said. "I was young. I didn't know much about life or what a slave really was though I'd never known any other way of life. Jason and I hadn't asked permission to jump the broom. We'd just gone out in the woods with Jason's father and done it. The first time I ever saw rage in a white man was when I told Master Samuelson I couldn't do what he wanted because I had already jumped the broom. That Master's face …."

"Two days later, he sold Mary," Pappy said. "He put her in the buggy he used to go to town and took her away. I heard about where she had been sold from Jappy June, the driver that took her to the slave market with the Master. I didn't see her again until Chas Bullock caught me in town doing errands for the Master and told me to come to the swamp in Missouri."

"We talked about this at the Campbell's and decided you had a right to know what happened," his mother said. "Up until the Bulrushes I had never slept with another man. Jason really is your father. I was pregnant with you before I ever got to the Bulrush plantation."

His parents stopped talking. Joshua was silent, his gaze directed at the shadow of Preacher's scow behind them. Their story was astonishing. A master who actually listened to slaves? Who cared whether his mother had jumped the broom or not? Who then sold her to the meanest plantation he could find?

At last he looked at Pappy. "What I don't understand," he said, "is why Chas Bullock came to find you. How did he find you?"

"Preacher needed me to get food for the escape," his mother answered, her voice sounding disembodied in the big warehouse. "He couldn't buy it himself. White people would have suspected. I told him about Jason. I said I would get the food but wouldn't leave the Bulrush's without you and Jason. I told him about the Samuelson plantation. Chas did the rest."

"You shouldn't have done that," Pappy chided her.

Joshua tried to study his mother's face in the darkness. "The Overseer's mean," he said at last. "He would have known Jamie's family had your help by the missing food." He paused. "The Overseer killed Old Simpson with his whip," he said, his voice barely above a whisper. "He *meant* to kill him."

"When Chas found me, I didn't hesitate," his father said. "I talked to him behind the General Store in North, the town nearest the Samuelson plantation. I didn't think. The two of us walked out of town in broad daylight. If there was a chance … we went south before turning around and going north. The Master wouldn't know I was gone right away. He trusted me to do his business after so many years."

Mary sat quietly, watching her son.

***

Later that morning, preparations continued the way they had the previous two days. Preacher carefully went over the boat again while different black and white people came to the door behind the warehouse with a variety of gifts: food, axes and shovels, hammers, nails, clothing, fishing gear, and other stuff they would need once they had reached Washington Island's wilderness. Above the scow there were other sounds: goods, mostly lumber, moving in and out of the warehouse's big double doors. The Culvers had sold the lumber piled above the slaves in the wagons to the business that was operated by an abolitionist.

"The caulk has to be good," Preacher kept saying as he worked. "I learned ship-building in Baltimore. You can't be too careful with the caulk."

Jamie and Jeremiah, like Joshua, were inside the scow's hull. They were fascinated by what Preacher was doing and with the boat itself. Even the feeling of being in it stimulated their imaginations. Joshua kept trying to imagine what he would feel like as the scow went on the water, rocking from a lake's waves. They had still not seen Lake Michigan, although they knew it was close to the warehouse. They hadn't been out into Chicago either, or down by the river that would take the scow into the lake. Sitting in the dim warehouse in early summer heat made it difficult to imagine how they would feel in a boat sailing in real water.

As they sat watching Preacher, Esta May came into the warehouse from the room where the back door was.

"Joshua, Jamie," she said, excitement in her voice. "They've brought us clothes, like Abbie has!"

Jeremiah was off the boat before Joshua had processed what he was being told. He glanced at the torn, ragged pants and shirt he was wearing. They were clean. His mother had taken them when he had lain down for the night and gave them a good scrubbing in the wash the women were doing. His shoes, like those of the rest of the escaped slaves, weren't worth wearing any longer.

"Come on," Esta May said impatiently.

Jamie got down off the scow. Preacher spoke to Joshua. "New clothes can be pretty important," he said.

"I can't get used to being here," Joshua said to the man who had organized the escape and led them to where they could sit in a boat he had built.

Preacher smiled. Joshua followed Jamie.

All the young people, including Abbie, were inside the small room at the back. Esta May was smiling. Her sisters were so excited they were screeching and jumping up and down. Ertha and Eunice were in constant motion, their slight bodies twitching in excitement. A white woman, dressed in a long, black dress, was handing out the clothes. She was grinning as if their excitement delighted her.

"There'll be clothes for everybody and spares," she said as she handed Esta May underwear and a brown cotton dress. Esta May's eyes grew larger than Joshua had ever seen them. For the first time in his life he felt embarrassed at seeing a girl's clothes. In the quarters privacy was limited, but here that felt different. The sudden spurt of feeling confused him. "I have shoes," the woman said as Esta May accepted the dress and hugged it against her body. "You'll need new shoes in the wilderness."

Chas was standing by the door beside Beulah and Massie, watching their daughters and sons. The three of them were smiling, too.

The woman solemnly handed Jeremiah new trousers and a shirt. "We wouldn't let people donate anything too light colored," she said. "You need dark clothes if you live in the wilderness. You don't want to stand out from the woods too much."

Jeremiah looked like he was going to cry. Joshua wondered if the white lady knew that none of them had ever had new clothes before, not even Joshua, whose mother had helped with seamstress duties in the big house. His mother looked like a mistress, dressed in a dress made out of muslin or some other rich fabric. He was surprised that she and the other women had already put on their new clothes. Esta May and her sisters ran from the room to find a place where they could put on their dresses. Beulah left Massie's side and followed them.

Jeremiah accepted his shirt, underwear, and trousers, said "Thank you, ma'am," as if the lady was a mistress, and stood aside as Jamie stepped up for his clothes, acting like the underwear was what he always wore, although Joshua knew that none of the boys had possessed any such luxury in their lives.

Then it was Joshua's turn. The lady smiled at him. She had blue eyes and dark brown hair. "Here you go," she said, handing him the same bundle she had given Jeremiah and Jamie. Joshua mumbled, rather than said, "Thank you," took the clothes and looked around. His mother was standing in the warehouse door. She looked ready to cry.

Jeremiah had left the room with Jamie on his heels. Joshua looked at Chas. Chas looked as somber and competent as he always looked. "Thank you," he told the white lady as Massie followed her sons. The white lady smiled. "If you need more donations, Mr. Bullock," she said in a formal voice, "let us know." She turned and smiled at Joshua's mother before she walked out of the room into hot Chicago sunshine.

The next morning everybody, except for Abbie, Ertha, and Eunice, the youngest of them, were given tasks to do. Joshua could not imagine how the scow was going to be moved out of the warehouse. He and Esta May were storing homesteading tools, shovels, pitchforks, and a large two-person saw for cutting downed trees into boards for construction and boat building, trying hard to follow Preacher's directions.

"Tight," he kept telling them. "We don't have space to waste."

They had just finished satisfying Preacher that the axes were stored properly when the warehouse's two large doors opened. Outside Jamie, Jeremiah, their father, and Franklin were standing beside a team of six horses in front of a large wagon on wheels. Joshua rose to his feet and stared. The flat-bottomed wagon without sides, low to the ground, was clearly made for hauling boats to the water. He could see how wooden rollers on the back would allow them to push the scow onto the flat bed.

How the wagon could be backed into the warehouse, though, stymied him. He could just make out the rumps of the first horses pointed toward the street horizontal to the warehouse. A small, bearded white man, carrying himself as if he was incredibly strong, came to the warehouse opening and studied the scene for a moment. Pappy came up to stand beside him.

"Easy," the man said. "Stand here and signal me in."

Pappy nodded. Joshua wondered why so many white people kept showing up to help them. Were so many white people really against slavery? Joshua hadn't even heard the white lady's name who had brought them their clothes and what she had called their "spares." Esta May had stored the spares in bags in front of the scow, what Preacher called the bow.

"We got to get out of the boat," Preacher said.

Esta May climbed over the side and dropped to the ground. The bearded white man moved the big brown workhorses backward, slanting the huge trailer into the warehouse and calling "Gaw, gaw." They were even larger than the plantation's workhorses. Pappy was standing calmly, motioning that the trailer had to turn sharper as if he knew what he was doing. The women and the rest of the men, except Chas, had come into the warehouse and were watching. Joshua went to stand by his mother.

Less than a half hour later, Chas was there, and he and Preacher were getting the men, including Harrison Stimson, Jamie, Jeremiah, and Joshua, along the sides of the scow.

"Just ease it forward," Preacher said. "When it's on the wagon we'll be set."

Joshua was shocked to find out how quickly the boat was on the flat bed. It was heavy, but the men, with Pappy positioned at the bow, had enough muscle power to push it off the scaffold where it had been built onto the rollers. Outside the warehouse, a small group of black men and women had gathered to watch. Joshua had no idea how they had known that there would be something interesting to watch. There hadn't been any people around any other day, but when the boat was in place they were smiling and talking as Preacher went out to greet them.

Then the bearded white man said "Gaw, gaw" in his big voice again, and the horses, without straining, walked into the street, turning right toward where Joshua understood the river was. Pappy jumped on the wagon seat and sat beside the white man as they drove past big buildings on both sides of them. The air was as smoky as Joshua had remembered from his time beside Mr. Culver, but nobody was in the street the wagon rumbled down.

The black people who had appeared at the warehouse to see the escaping slaves and scow emerge into sunlight followed the wagon. Jeremiah had caught up to Preacher and a black man with the most extraordinary face Joshua had ever seen. He had a grizzled white and black beard and a forehead that protruded out over the rest of his face. His lips were larger than normal, too, and were slightly puckered. Esta May, who had walked with Joshua as they joined the crowd, glanced at him and hurried toward where Jeremiah was. Joshua followed her.

"You brought more out of the dark places than you said you were going to," the man was telling Preacher as Joshua fell in behind them.

"Thanks to you and the others, Reverend Jemson," Preacher replied. "Without you and your congregation's help, Chas and I couldn't have gotten the scow done, no lessen found all the Underground Railroad help. We needed that help, too. Things didn't always go right."

"It never does," Jimson said. "Slavery's evil. Like all evil things, it corrupts most everybody who touches it and makes things go wrong."

Esta May tugged at Joshua's shirtsleeve and pointed at a big woman carrying a wicker basket. Then Joshua noticed other women were carrying baskets, too. There had to be two-dozen people walking down the street. They were making a lot of noise, and he wondered why nobody was trying to quiet them. During their escape, they'd learned that quietness was the world's greatest virtue. The fact that nobody in the whole group was trying to hide made him nervous. He did not hear dogs looking for them in his head the way he had in the woods, but he felt exposed.

The big woman Esta May had pointed to, who was carrying one of the baskets, saw Joshua staring at her as they walked. She smiled at them.

"You children ready for a real fried chicken dinner?" she asked. "This is a good day for having a picnic by the river. Preacher ready to lead his flock to New Jerusalem! Oh, the good Lord is good!"

"A picnic?" Esta May asked.

"We been waiting a long time for this day," the woman replied. "It's time to celebrate. This community is delivering more folks to freedom!"

Joshua, as usual, was confused. He always seemed to be trying to catch up with what was happening. That had been true ever since the moment his mother had shown up at his shack in the quarters with fire in her eyes. He couldn't believe that from that moment to this one he had managed to come as far as he had. What community? Who were these people?

"Fried chicken sounds good to me," Esta May said.

Then Joshua saw the river. With all the talk about Lake Michigan and the Chicago River, he had built it up in his imagination to be bigger than the width of a cotton field. It was obviously a river and not a stream, but it didn't look that huge in the sweltering sunlight. A barge was passing by that was bigger than anything he had even imagined seeing floating on water. There were docks and other people, mostly men, on shore, and other boats tied to posts sticking up from wooden platforms extended over the water. A lot of the people he could see were white, not black.

Pappy was off the wagon and in the river. He seemed larger than life as the trailer backed into the water. Preacher, Chas, Willie, and Franklin all ran past the horses and wagon to where the scow was. The people who had joined them were laughing and generally behaving as if it was a big holiday. Within minutes, as Willie and Franklin waded into the river, Pappy loosed the boat from the wagon and the scow floated free.

Chas was beside Preacher as Joshua, Esta May, Jamie, and Jeremiah surged toward them.

"Guess you really do know how to build a boat," Chas said. "In the Wisconsin woods, I wasn't sure. On the Niagara, you knew how to caulk. I could tell that right enough. She looks sound as a drum."

Preacher didn't say anything, but smiled, looking at the boat he'd built from scratch.

"She's a good scow," Reverend Jemson said. "Tom knows what he's doing. I knew that the minute I saw an awl in his hand."

"She'll do," Preacher said, a hint of pride in his voice. "She'll get us started on building New Jerusalem."

***

The picnic that followed was a revelation to Joshua. He felt unreal sitting beneath a giant oak tree beside the slowly flowing river that led to Lake Michigan and then north to Washington Island and his, hopefully, future home. For the first time, he started to feel that maybe slavery really was behind him, that the haunting dogs on his trail had been lost in the woods, hills, and fields of Missouri and Illinois.

The people at the picnic, other than the fugitive slaves, were all members of Reverend Jemson's Christian congregation. What Joshua came to slowly understand was that they often raised money and helped arrange for slaves to escape the South to Canada. They had helped Preacher and Chas get the warehouse space and materials for building the scow. The effort had taken over a year of work. After they had finished, they had planned to go south to free Chas's brother and his family and then, after Preacher had founded a group of Christian believers, his congregation.

Reverend Jemson was a skilled carpenter by trade and had helped Preacher almost as much as Chas had. Then he had blessed the two of them when they had at last left Chicago during a winter storm and headed south on foot.

Now they were all on the Chicago River, Preacher, Chas, Chas's brother and his family, and Preacher Jemson's congregation, ready to fulfill the stuff of dreams: a black fishing community on Washington Island in the United States rather than Canada. A true New Jerusalem that would enlighten their community with the word of God while they built new lives for themselves by fishing, building and repairing boats, hunting, and gardening.

As Joshua pieced the story and dream together in his head, it seemed as if he'd fallen into one of the tales Old Simpson had sometimes told. Old Simpson's father had told him about how his grandfather, who had lived in Africa before he had been captured and thrown into the nightmare of a slave ship, had described herds of wildebeest so large that they covered the landscape like grass. Africans had been free men, not freed men, Old Simpson had told Joshua. Up until they were captured by Arabs and sent to Africa's coast, they had never known any master but themselves.

At one point in the afternoon, Reverend Jemson told Chas, "You've got to be careful yet. Wisconsin is safer than Illinois, but slavers are looking for you folks. We've heard there's quite a stir down in Missouri. They're still searching, even though they can't believe so many made off at once. Mostly it sounds like they think you all probably went separate ways north."

Joshua shuddered at Reverend Jemson's words. He looked at the scow in the river. When they had first started, he had been afraid of the idea of freedom. He had felt the Overseer's whip cutting his back even when the cruel black man was nowhere around. Now he had run to the Chicago River's banks and was inside a city as different as any of Old Simpson's tales of Africa. He felt funny, not quite a slave, not yet free, but he was sure of one thing: he never wanted to go back to a slave's life ever again.

The amazing thing, he realized, was that he'd only seen white people aiding them, but behind everything had been Reverend Jemson and black people who had been helping Chas and Preacher for a long time.

Chapter 11
Emerging Into Freedom

Waves rolled with curving lines into the shore.
Lake Michigan horizoned into sky.
They watched a dark brown, white crowned osprey soar
Above the waves and heard its hunting cry.

Inside pinched spirits chained by slavery
And endless hours of suffocating fear,
Bonds loosened as the dream and fantasy
Of freedom suddenly seemed real, so near
To where they stood above the giant lake
They thought that they had reached a hoped-for future
Aware of who they were, the earth awake
To spirits that had passed through deadly danger.

Inside the distant swamp they'd been but slaves.
They stood up, heard the sound of distant waves.

Joshua felt stuffed. The amount of food had been incredible, not only piles of cold fried chicken, but also corn bread, cooked beans, greens, applesauce, watermelon, and several kinds of pie and cake. This was not food ever available to slaves. The picnic was a miracle.

He was surprised when Pappy came with his mother to extract him from where he was sitting with Jamie, Jeremiah, Esta May and her sisters, and little Abbie. The young people were becoming increasingly comfortable with each other.

None of the kids of Jemson's congregation had been brought to the picnic. He'd wondered why, but had been afraid to ask people he didn't know. Seeing people his age from Chicago would have been interesting. He was talking to Ella, who was always curious and full of conversation about what she was noticing, when his father had gotten up from the blanket he and his mother had been sitting on and come over to him.

"You ready to go back to the warehouse?"

Joshua glanced at the scow in the water. It looked impressive in the late afternoon light. Bigger boats were passing by, but the scow looked brand new and floated proudly with its tall mast, ready to venture to

Lake Michigan and Washington Island.

"Sure," Joshua said, getting to his feet. *What's going on now?*

Pappy did not look happy. He was frowning, and his forehead wrinkled in concentration. Nobody said anything as they started up the slight incline to the warehouse, but Pappy sighed. His wife, looking elegant in her simple donated dress, watched her husband's face closely.

"Preacher wants me to go with him and Franklin on the scow." His frown deepened. "I don't want to go."

"Why not?" Joshua's mother asked. "We're going to be living with boats once we get on the island. Chas and Preacher say we're going to be living off fishing, especially this year. You got to go out in boats to catch fish."

"I don't want to be separated," he said. "We've been separated as a family long enough. Who knows what's going to happen in the wagons or the boat? Besides, Preacher had me work with the nets, trying to teach me how to repair them. All I had were thumbs, no fingers. Franklin and Willie were both better at it than I was."

Mary smiled. "I suspect your strength is more valuable than your skill at fixing fishing nets," she said. "There's a lot of bull work chopping down trees, sawing boards, and building cabins and boats. Preacher and Chas have a lot of skills, but they'll need yours, too."

"You're okay with being separated?"

"I would've accepted anything the Bulrush's and Overseer did to me to keep Joshua and me close to you," she said. "Even if you were way south of where we were. That's why Preacher had Chas, who I hadn't even known existed, go to find you.

"I'm never going to be okay with being separated. But Preacher got us this far. I don't want to go back to being a slave in a big house. If Preacher thinks it's important for you to learn about being on the scow, we both have got to be okay with that. Joshua and I will be okay." She looked fiercely into Pappy's eyes "And you'd better be okay, too."

Pappy directed his attention to Joshua. "You okay with this, too?"

It occurred to Joshua that he was being asked something important. He shrugged.

"I don't know much about freedom," he said, surprised at his own response, "but if you going on the scow is going to help us keep away from the Overseer, and Mother says it's okay, it's okay with me."

The big man looked at the smudged city sky. Did Chicago ever lose its faint smell of manure and acrid smoke? Even down a street away from where most people were?

"Okay," Pappy said at last. "The scow it is." He cleared his throat before continuing, "If I'm going to be a fisherman, I suppose I need to learn how. I've never even been on a boat before." He paused. "And I don't know how to swim." He sighed again.

***

The next morning, Pappy woke Joshua before dawn.

"Big day," Pappy said after Joshua had sat up and put hands around his knees.

"You're leaving today," Joshua said, trying to shake sleep out of his head.

"You, too," Mother said. She was kneeling beside a sack stuffed with clothes. 'We've got to get ready. Chas will be here with the wagons after the scow's launched. Preacher slept in the scow."

"I guess I might be doing that, too," Pappy said, his voice tinged with sadness.

"I want you to carry this to the scow," Mary said to Joshua. "Your father's got to carry two oars. They look heavy."

Joshua got to his feet while Pappy went into the warehouse to collect the long, heavy oars. Everybody was moving around and getting ready for the day. Their time in Chicago was over.

***

Preacher and Chas had already attached the sail to the mast.

"Once in the lake, if the south to north wind holds," Chas was saying as Joshua came within hearing distance, "you'll make good time. At least for today."

"I've got sailors without an ounce of experience," Preacher responded. "There's learning to do before we can make the distances we need to make."

"You're not inexperienced," Chas pointed out.

Pappy dragged the big oars onto the scow as Chas hurried to help him lift them in and store them. Franklin, standing with his family, was clearly as nervous as Pappy about the unknown journey he was about to undertake. When the oars were stored, Pappy climbed out of the scow, hugged his wife, and looked into Joshua's eyes.

"I'm glad I got to know my son," he said. Then, without any more ceremony, he climbed back into the scow. Franklin hugged Beulah and his daughters. Surprisingly, Harrison and Junebug climbed into the scow instead of the Woodruff family, helped by Chas. Joshua hadn't known they were going to travel with the scow rather than with the rest of them in wagons over land.

After getting the Stimsons settled, Chas climbed out of the boat and signaled to Willie. He and Willie pushed the scow off the bank until it was floating free. Pappy and Franklin each had an oar in their hands. Preacher nodded. They dug into the water. Pappy was so strong the boat swung the prow toward Franklin's side.

"Easy, Jason. You've got to match each other's stroke. One can't overpower the other," Preacher said.

Pappy didn't say anything, but watched as Franklin dug his oar in the water, coming close to straightening the scow. The current, although not strong, was floating them away from the bank. Then both Pappy and Franklin stroked with their oars. This time the effort had a better result, although the prow still moved toward the shore. They sped up their movement downstream, zigzagging as the two men struggled to find their rhythm.

What amazed Joshua was that even though the rest of them stood on the riverbank watching, almost before they realized it, the scow was entering the mouth where the river met Lake Michigan. Joshua couldn't quite see the lake from where he was standing, but he could see the river widening into a fan that looked something like the swamp, only without the vegetation, back home.

Watching his father disappear gave him a lost feeling. For so long, he hadn't known he had a father. Now his father was on the scow, on his way to where Joshua was supposed to one day make his home. Pappy wasn't gone. Not really. But Joshua felt like he was.

***

By the time the remaining fugitives had left the river and walked to the warehouse, two wagons had pulled up behind the building. Joshua was surprised that one of the drivers was a black man who had been at Reverend Jemson's picnic the day before. He hadn't stood out at the picnic. He was a quiet, soft-spoken man who had been exceptionally polite to everyone, but stayed mostly with his wife as she handed out the fried chicken and corn bread she had brought. His presence at the warehouse seemed almost frightening. Every wagon driver that had taken them north up until that point had been white.

Joshua had been surprised to learn that Jemson's congregation had been helping Preacher and Chas plan a slave escape for years, and now it seemed that a congregation member was going to brave driving a wagon with escaped slaves as they fled further north out of Illinois into Wisconsin. Joshua didn't say anything, but he wondered about the wisdom of that and also if the black man was driving because a white man couldn't be found to take on the risk.

The other driver was a stranger, a young, silent white man. As the group approached, he nodded in greeting, but didn't speak. When the black man, who introduced himself as Mr. Gearson, had warmly shaken the adults' hands, he told them that he and Mr. Blake, the other man, would be taking them north over the next two and a half days until they met Gordon Burr, a Stockbridge Indian, not far from Stockbridge, Wisconsin.

"The Indians know about the trail from there," Mr. Gearson said. He smiled in the shy way that seemed to be his trademark. "But you all better get ready. We have a long drive before dark."

Joshua and his mother picked up the two big bags of clothes, which included coats suitable for Washington Island weather. Chas put their bags in the wagon the white man was going to drive.

Joshua had a bad feeling about going forward. Chicago had been exciting and rewarding. Seeing the scow with his father float down the river to Lake Michigan had been upsetting and even sad. The sight of the scow as it disappeared into the river's mouth had seemed filled with significance. They were getting closer to Preacher's New Jerusalem. They were getting closer to where Preacher and Chas had, over and over again, promised they'd have freedom. Trips in wagons had not been pleasant in either Missouri or Illinois and had sometimes been near-disastrous.

Loading the wagons did not take long. Another surprise came when neither of the two drivers brought out anything that could be used to cover up the escaped slaves. When Willie, as surprised as Joshua, asked why, the white man had glowered.

"In Chicago it doesn't matter," he said. "There's so many people nobody pays attention to anyone. Slavers are around, but they won't be a problem. We'll put a canvas on later, but leaving this part of town we can do what's comfortable."

Joshua, settling beside his mother in the back of the wagon the white man was going to drive, felt exposed. The day was blazing again, the sky clear of clouds. Anyone interested in escaping slaves could easily see them in the two wagons and watch their direction as they left the city. He was puzzled when Chas unleashed his brown horse from the second wagon, mounted, said, "I'll meet you on the road," and rode toward the street that led to the river.

The two drivers didn't hesitate. They drove the wagons into the street they had used to get to the riverbank, and then, after going a block north, turned west toward where a bridge, crammed with traffic and people, crossed the river.

Not long after they were across the bridge, although still in the city, the two drivers pulled the horse teams to a stop. Mr. Blake, driving the wagon Jason and his mother were in with Jamie, Jeremiah, Willy, and Massie, did not get down off the wagon seat, but Mr. Gearson came forward to them.

"We need to put canvas over you now," he said softly. "I'm sorry, but there's more eyes from here on out that we need to avoid. People won't think much of a white and black man driving two wagons, but seeing all of you in the neighborhoods could start tongues to wagging. That might not be good."

"Actually," Willie said. "I think we'll feel more comfortable. Seeing all the wagons and people jangles my nerves."

Mr. Gearson smiled. Mr. Blake handed him a large, gray sheet of canvas that he attached to the wagon sideboards. Joshua, as he had so many times before, lay down on his back and stared at canvas, pulled into a tight roof, above him. No one had talked much as they had driven through the crowded streets, noise, and constant, unpleasant smells. They had all been too nervous.

The minute they were under the canvas the habit of silence reasserted itself. Joshua felt his mother reach for his hand so that she could squeeze it in reassurance, but the truth was that he felt more comfortable, even though the canvas above their heads made the wagon bed way too hot.

***

Unlike before Chicago when being afraid dominated Joshua's time, the trip to Wisconsin agitated his imagination. Instead of constantly sensing dogs on their trail, he daydreamed about the scow with its sail out, moving steadily over water stretching forever in every direction. He could almost hear Preacher teaching Pappy the fine points of sailing. Then he dreamed about a great island soaring out of Lake Michigan with huge cliffs and green hills.

He couldn't imagine how life would be on the island once they got there. He had once had no idea how his life would change if they really escaped the Bulrush plantation and were free. He had no idea about what it would mean. He wanted to talk to Jamie and Esta May, or maybe his mother, about the confused thoughts flitting through his head, but he maintained the silence they had mastered when running in the dead of night through threatening woods.

The day passed. When they finally stopped, it was dark. The drivers had found a place to park the wagons off the road in a small meadow behind a large stand of oak trees. Mr. Gearson walked back to where the Simpsons and Bullocks were.

"We'll stay here tonight," he said, handing out pork sandwiches made with rough brown bread to each of them. "We made good time."

Mr. Blake did not say anything, but climbed off the wagon. Joshua's mother motioned toward the sullen white man as he walked off into the woods away from the road.

"He makes me uncomfortable," she said.

Mr. Gearson smiled. "He's been an abolitionist follower of Reverend Jemson for a long time. He's as dependable as sunshine. You just have to get used to him." He laughed. "He grows on you after a while."

Before spreading their blankets on the ground to sleep, Joshua, Jamie, Jeremiah, Esta May, and Ella sat cross-legged beneath a large oak and talked in hushed voices. They did not talk about escaping or how afraid they were or about how long it would take them to get to the next place where they could eat or rest. Mr. Gearson had told them that they were now in Wisconsin. "Wisconsin's a free state," he'd said. "Slaver's agents don't have much of a foothold here."

Instead, they talked about Washington Island and the scow and started trying to understand what their new lives might be like.

"Preacher says we're going to be fishermen," Jeremiah said. "I've always liked to fish."

"This is different, though," Jamie said. "We won't be fishing for fun, but to eat and get money. At least that's what Paw told me. He said it's going to be a better kind of life."

"We're going to have to build cabins first," Joshua said, trying to sound responsible. "We're going to have a lot of hard work to do before winter. Pappy told me Chas told him that winter is really mean in Wisconsin. We have to have enough food to get through the first winter."

"Preacher said God is in our life," Ella said. Esta May touched her sister's shoulder. Ella ignored her. "God and Preacher are gonna help us."

Jeremiah nodded. "They, and our Uncle Chas, have done good so far," he said. He looked up into the oak's branches. "Who ever thought we'd get away without hearing baying dogs on our trail? I was scared when I knew we were really going to run, and now ...."

"We're free," Esta May said. "Aren't we?"

***

Before dawn the next morning, Mr. Blake, after being gone all night, crept past where they were sleeping, crawled up on the wagon seat, and sat waiting. Mr. Gearson went around getting everybody up. Groggy, Joshua did not say anything before he followed his mother into the wagon bed, the canvas over their head. Jamie crawled in beside him. They were on their way.

The wagon rolled like it had the day before over the packed soil road. Everyone maintained escaping silence. When they finally stopped, the sun was high in the sky. Mr. Gearson brought them their lunch.

"Still hot," he said as he handed Joshua, Jamie, and Jeremiah corn bread, a browning peeled potato, and desiccated apples. "We might see Mr. Bullock and Mr. Gordon Burr by evening if I know Mr. Burr. He never waits the way he says he will."

"Mr. Gordon Burr is an Indian?" Joshua's mother asked. Mr. Gearson handed out a second helping of corn bread from his bag.

"Mr. Gordon Burr is a Stockbridge Indian," Mr. Gearson said. "He's an extraordinary man. We've worked with him in Mr. Jemson's congregation for several years. He says he follows what the elders of his tribe want him to do.

"Even though he's Indian, he gets along with white men without effort. He's always smiling and laughing, and he's always helping people, Indians, blacks, white farmers, slaves, whoever. I've turned over fifteen people escaping the bondage of slavery to him, and he's gotten every one to a steamship taking them to Canada. No one seems to ever question what he's doing."

The story that Old Simpson had told Joshua popped into his head. The white men Old Simpson had tended as a young man had been severely wounded by Indians. He wondered if Indians could be trusted.

"In our country, people still fear Indians," Massie, standing by Joshua's mother, said.

Mr. Gearson laughed again. As quiet as he was, he often laughed. "Mr. Burr is not an Indian to fear," he said. "The U.S. government moved the Stockbridge out of New York west to Wisconsin against their will. Mr. Burr is an abolitionist. He knows Mr. Frederick Douglas and Mr. Wendell Phillips. He is a highly civilized man."

"Mr. Frederick Douglas and Mr. Wendell Phillips?" Joshua's mother asked.

"They are the most powerful voices of the abolitionist movement of which I and the entire congregation are a part," he said, before advising, "We have a long way to go. We best be moving."

Inside the moving wagon, looking up at canvas above his head, Joshua puzzled over what Mr. Gearson had told them. There were clearly a lot of abolitionists in the country. They were also not all white. Many were black like him. A few were Indians. The idea made him feel, like Esta May's "We're free. Aren't we?", hopeful. Maybe they had truly escaped the Bulrush plantation and *were* free.

***

They were exhausted when Chas and a man they didn't know met them on the road. Riding in the wagon's bed all day jarred and jostled them without mercy. The Illinois roads had been in better shape that the ones in Wisconsin.

When Mr. Blake called out "Whoa" and the wagon came to a stop, Joshua's heart jumped. Everyone else in the wagon had wide eyes and fear on their faces. When they heard Chas's voice, relief released their tension.

"You can come on out of there, Willie," Chas said after a few moments of talking to the other wagon.

Willie pulled the canvas away and crawled out into late evening sunlight. Joshua, his mother, Jamie, and the others followed. Both Chas and the man on the other horse were standing beside Mr. Blake's wagon with the Woodruffs. Chas was smiling. The other man, balding on his high forehead with black hair cut short, middle aged, and brown skinned was looking at each escaped slave in turn. He looked friendly. Joshua was surprised how he was dressed in brown work clothes. He didn't look anything like he'd thought an Indian would look.

"This is Gordon Burr," Chas said. "He's going to lead us up the Door Peninsula to Lake Michigan. Preacher and Jason will meet us there. That's where we'll launch our trip to Washington Island. We'll meet Franklin and the Stimsons at West Harbor on the island."

Gordon Burr nodded. "Good evening," he said. "Good evening. This is a good day. I hardly believe Chas has got so many slaves out of the dark south. This is good. Really good." He started shaking hands with the men, first, and then with the women and young people. "You're almost safe," he said.

Joshua looked at the Stockbridge Indian closely. He projected an energy that reminded Joshua of Preacher. His movements were smooth and powerful, as if he had complete control of himself. He smiled continuously.

When he was through shaking hands, he looked at Mr. Gearson who had gotten down from his wagon to join the rest of them. Mr. Blake, as usual, stayed put, not even looking at the people milling around his wagon. Despite Mr. Gearson's reassurances, the man made Joshua uneasy and raised unanswered questions: Why is he always so remote? Why does he always let Mr. Gearson take the lead? Isn't he the white man?

"We're going to go long tonight," Gordon Burr said, interrupting Joshua's thoughts. "We'll stop in Old Man Mueller's barn and have some bread and butter. I'm afraid that's all we'll get to eat. From there we'll let Mr. Gearson and Mr. Blake"—he smiled up at the silent white man—"go back to Chicago. We'll take off through the woods. We're not far from Lake Michigan here. We want to avoid Lake Winnebago and go around it. I'm afraid you're going to have to walk again."

"Afraid?" Willie asked. "I'm so tired of wagons it's going to feel good to be walking again."

"I've stored a lot of stuff by where I hid Gordon's canoe," Chas said. "Stockbridgers have, as usual, worked hard to help us succeed in what we're trying to do."

"We don't need to hide these folks anymore?" Mr. Gearson asked.

Gordon Burr smiled. "It's safer here than up to here, but we should be careful. We don't want tongues wagging about this unusual sight they've seen, a bunch of negras, as they'd say, going north. I'm sorry," he added, looking at Joshua's mother.

"Once we're on Washington Island, we won't have to hide anymore," Chas said. He mounted his horse. Mr. Gearson returned to his wagon as the rest made their way to their places in the wagon beds. Within minutes they were moving north again.

They'd been traveling through a night without moon or stars. Willie had removed the canvas above their heads. The cooler air had felt good. Sitting up, rather than lying as the wagon bumped over the road, felt even better. Joshua's eyes kept getting heavy. He kept dozing off and jerking awake.

When they at last reached a small barn beside the road, Chas and Gordon Burr rode into the yard and dismounted. Joshua was surprised there wasn't a farmhouse by the barn.

As Mr. Blake pulled the wagon to a stop and got to the ground, Jamie and Joshua quickly slipped off the wagon. Chas had tied up his horse and was standing next to Mr. Gearson. Joshua and Jamie drifted over to them.

"You staying overnight?" Chas asked.

"Mr. Blake and I will get a short sleep and go on our way," Mr. Gearson answered.

"Preacher Bennett and I appreciate all you and the congregation have done." Chas looked to where Mr. Blake was still sitting on the wagon seat, making no sign he was going to get off. "We thank you too, Mr. Blake."

Mr. Gearson laughed. "Preacher Bennett is a powerful man," he said. "The truth is that if I didn't have my small home in Chicago where my family is settled, I'd start right here and go with you. A wilderness island where the white lion and black calf live together in peace and praise the good Lord is a powerful vision. Reverend Jemson's a wonderful preacher, but Preacher Bennett is a prophet. You've got to believe he has power to set all our people free just with his words."

Chas smiled. "He's always had that way," he said. "During our time in the War of 1812 on the Niagara you could tell he was changing, though. He got to reading the Bible and talking about what he was reading. When I told him about my brother and the plantation he was on, he started prophesying as if he were a prophet, for sure. Later we came to Chicago and met Reverend Jemson and you folks. Without you, none of this would have been possible." He glanced over at Joshua and Jamie and saw they were listening intently. He smiled. "But you need rest, and we've got a long way to walk tomorrow. I'll see you in the morning before you and Mr. Blake leave."

"Mr. Blake is a good man," Mr. Gearson said. He turned toward the horses and started unhitching them from the wagon for what was left of the night.

***

"Walking is better than getting jarred around in a wagon," Joshua thought as they trekked steadily through woods very different than those in Missouri. Trees were closer together, brush denser, and there seemed to be fewer open spaces. They'd been walking since dawn, and were still going north, but more east than north now. Chas had told them they would spend most of the day walking before coming to the big lake.

They were not as quiet as they had been in Missouri and Illinois. Gordon Burr kept up a constant stream of chatter. When Willie asked if it wouldn't be a good idea if they weren't quieter, the Stockbridge Indian, in his endlessly joyous way, had laughed.

"Wisconsin is a wilderness yet," he said. "At least it is this far north. We're heading into even wilder wilderness. Maybe farms will be here, like down south, in the future. Maybe even more towns rather than the villages here now, but we don't really need to be quiet."

***

In the afternoon, a wind came out of the north and clouds crowded together in the sky. Gordon Burr kept looking upwards and became more solemn and less talkative.

"We don't need wind on the lake," he said to Chas.

"No, we don't," Chas agreed.

By evening, the wind had picked up rather than died down. When the rain, once it finally started, came out of the sky, it slanted down, striking hard at faces and clothes. Within a minute after the storm hit, Joshua felt chilled.

"It's cold," he announced to no one in particular.

"No kidding," Jamie, walking next to him as usual, said.

"It's miserable," Jeremiah added.

Finally, after fighting wind and rain for over an hour, Chas stopped beneath a small hill.

"There's shelter here," he said. He tied his horse to a tree and picked up a thick pine branch. "Gather some of these," he said. "We'll build lean-tos and fires and dry out as best we can."

Gordon grunted, got off his horse, lifted Eunice to the ground, and followed Chas's directions after pulling a small hand axe out of his stuffed saddlebags. "Can't go on the lake in this anyway," he grumbled. "Not on Michigan."

By the time night came, they had a large campfire burning and were huddled under small pine branch-and-brush lean-tos. The air, whipped by wind, was getting colder. After living in sweltering heat for days on end, the sudden change was miserable; they were wet and shivering. The two horses stood away from the campfire beneath oak trees. Joshua wasn't frightened the way he had been in Missouri outside the houses by the bridge as the storm had raged above them, but he sure was uncomfortable.

After a night that seemed to go on forever, dawn finally filtered into the forest and, with it, sun from the east. Chas and Gordon Burr got them moving quickly. They did not bother tearing down the lean-tos.

"We're in Wisconsin wilderness," Gordon said again. "If somebody stumbles on them, they'll just think trappers got caught in a storm and tried to keep themselves dry."

As they walked, with the sun in front of them, what Gordon had been telling them finally penetrated Joshua's consciousness. They were in the Wisconsin wilderness. They were in country as wild as the island they were trying to reach. There were no more plantations. They had left the slave-holding states behind and were in the free state of Wisconsin. They weren't where they were going, but they had escaped. They would not hear the sound of dogs hunting them. He did not have to be afraid of the Overseer and his whip. Never again.

The sun had started to set when Chas topped a rise in the forest floor, and stood in his stirrups, and waited. Abbie and Ertha, sitting in front of the men on horseback, stared, slack jawed. Joshua, Jamie, and Jeremiah, sensing something was happening, pushed forward. Joshua heard Esta May and Ella hurrying behind them.

Joshua stopped. Not far below them, Lake Michigan stretched out as far as they could see, with white topped waves that rolled and rolled toward a pebble and sand beach. In places, pine trees hung out over the water or a birch tree with its white and black trunk rose thick and solid into the partially sunny sky. But mostly there was the shore and water that went until the horizon disappeared into the gray of endless waves.

Joshua dropped to the ground and stared. "I am free," he thought. "I didn't want to go with my mother to the preacher's meeting, and now I'm free." Tears were streaming down his cheeks. He didn't even care if Willie, Jamie, or Esta May saw them. He was free.

Chapter 12
Arrival of a Prophet in Washington
Island's Wilderness

The old black man, eyes bright as noonday sun,
Splashed from the wooden scow onto the shore.
He lifted up his voice, the waves Death's Door
Whipped white behind him, praised the blessed Son
Of God and New Jerusalem and spun
Around, his arms held high, a troubadour
Of his escape from slavery and war
To wilderness, the role of sacristan
To fisherman and men and women freed
From whips and masters and the slaver's creed
Of dominance designed to pinch the soul
And void the human spirit's vital flame.

"Praise God!" the prophet said, the roll
Of waves against his feet. "Praise God's sweet name!"

They spent the next four days walking Lake Michigan's shoreline.
Sometimes they could see the lake and hear its restless songs of waves
slapping on shore or against rocks. Other times they had to make their
way inland because of swamps or hills or downed trees. Always Gordon
Burr would lead them back to the lake.

At first, they walked through woods heavy with brush edging the
shore. Then they passed a small harbor cut into the land in a half circle.
Waves were white-capped as they stretched to a distant horizon with no
visible shore. Later the land rose into hills that humped over the great
lake as if guarding against the waves' ceaseless erosion. Later still they
came to an area where dark rocks rose into small cliffs that overlooked
the water's constant movement.

In addition to endlessly moving, the water shifted colors from green
to blue to gray, depending on the sun and whether clouds were in the
sky. Sometimes it was so bright Joshua and the others couldn't look at it
without hurting their eyes. Other times it sparkled, dancing and
cavorting with wave tops. In the early morning of the second day, when
they reached the lake it was so calm it looked like a mirror, reflecting the

bank's white pines at sky.

"We're going north and east," Gordon told them when they had stopped for a lunch of mostly hardtack and apples. "When we come to the peninsula's tip, Preacher, my canoe, and the scow will be waiting."

***

Esta May was the one who found Preacher and those who had climbed into the sailing boat in Chicago. Chas and Gordon had ridden out ahead earlier. The day was hot. As afternoon sun made them feel like they were walking through air made of water, they came upon a small depression that had dense canopy overhead and stopped. The shade's relative coolness was inviting. Esta May kept walking, not noticing she was alone.

At the top of a small rise, still in sight of the others, she paused. Then Joshua heard what Esta May was hearing. Someone on the shore was moving toward them.

They were out of slave country in Wisconsin. Slavers would surely not be in the wilderness this far north. Still, the nightmares that had plagued Joshua on their desperate journey north jumped into his head. His heart hammered. His whole body was prepared to run.

He looked at his mother, then Jamie, and then at Esta May. He could see their panic in how they were standing, staring at the woods ahead of them. Everyone had got up off the ground and was standing. They looked around for Chas and Gordon, wondering why they'd been abandoned, wondering where the two men were. Willie, then Bill, moved slowly forward, their faces grim and determined.

Esta May gave a little cry and ran toward the shore. She disappeared in the brush surrounding a small stand of cedar, then returned, hugging Franklin even though she was having trouble holding him and walking over the uneven ground. Franklin looked well fed, rested, and strong. Ella, Eunice, and Ertha cried his name and started running toward their uncle. Beulah and Bill hurried to catch up to their daughters. Tension drained out of Joshua, and his fear dissipated into morning light. There were no slavers. They were close to where Preacher, his father, and the Stimsons were waiting for them. Chas and Gordon were probably already at their camp.

A minute later, they were gathered around Franklin, all of them talking at once. Zelda and Abbie were ecstatic. Separation at the river in Chicago had been difficult. Maybe Preacher knew how to sail, but the biggest boat the rest of them had seen was a rowboat they had not been allowed to use on the small ponds and lakes around their plantations. Boats were for the use of white men, not slaves and especially not slave women or children.

Franklin at last noticed Joshua and Mary, who had clasped Joshua to her and was holding tight.

"Jason's okay, Mary," Franklin said softly. "Your Pappy's already on Washington Island, Joshua. He's started making us a home." He smiled. "I've been on the island. Preacher's right. It's a freed slave's paradise. The Stimsons are with Jason. Preacher thought that would let more of us fit in the first boat over."

By the time they reached the camp where Preacher, Chas, and Gordon were, it was already dark. A three-quarter moon was in the sky. A light wind was blowing. They saw the campfire through the trees first and wove around trees and brush until they were on a rocky beach, listening to slapping waves. The lake was calm enough to allow silver from the light above their heads to reflect off the water.

Chas and Gordon were cooking over the fire when the group of them filtered into the camp, following Franklin and Zelda. Preacher, the minute he saw Franklin working his way through the brush, jumped to his feet.

"Welcome," he said in his deep voice. "Welcome. God Almighty," he exclaimed, "I praise this day. Amen! Amen!"

Joshua found himself, with the others, repeating "Amen" after Preacher. "We are a poor looking bunch of people," he thought as he looked around. Even his mother was worn out and bedraggled. They were filthy with torn clothes and dark eyes, nothing like the way they had looked leaving Chicago.

But here they were at the edge of land looking out into the dark of a lake bigger than any Joshua had ever dreamed existed. It seemed as big as the Atlantic Ocean he'd heard some of the slaves who had been sold into the Bulrush Plantation talk about. They had escaped slavery and were on the verge of starting a new life in freedom. It seemed unreal, a dream Joshua hoped would never end.

His mother was watching him as he stood halfway into the camp looking toward the campfire, and when she caught his eye, she smiled, as if reading his thoughts.

***

By the next morning the wind had come up and the tops of the great white pines across from the camp were swaying and swirling. Where waves the night before had seemed swells of stars and moonlight, they were now running up the rocky beach, spreading out fingers of foam. Out in the small bay, whitecaps flicked in and out of existence as the lake moved frantically away from the horizon.

111

Beyond the bay, an island covered with trees invited them to get in the scow, which was floating where the bay dipped into a horseshoe shape of rock and forest, and sail across to what Joshua assumed was Washington Island. For a long time before he moved off his blanket, Joshua stared at the island. It didn't seem so far away, but at the same time it seemed unreachable across chopping, rolling waves.

Everybody but Preacher was still asleep, mostly huddled together under the protection of cedar trees, when Joshua woke. He'd gone to sleep close to the fire. The morning wind felt cool.

Joshua went into the bush away from camp and walked to where Preacher was sitting.

"We don't dare try the passage today," Preacher said. He paused for a moment before saying, "Do you know what they call the strait between Hedgewood Harbor, close to where we're at, and Washington Island?" Joshua shook his head. "They call it Porte des Mortes, the Door of Death. Even sailors in Commodore Perry's fleet talked about it. They said avoid it when that was possible. There's been so many shipwrecks here that have left souls without the grace of God and Jesus Christ our savior buried under the waves."

He stared out at the big island covered with trees and pointed. "We'll pass Pilot Island first. There's a lighthouse there. We'll try to cross so that the Lighthouse Keeper doesn't see us. Then, after that, we'll head in to Washington Island."

"We'll wait until it's safe? Until the waves calm down?"

"Chas and I are good sailors," Preacher said. "We've had experience, but neither of us are crazy enough to test Death's Door."

"Death's Door." Joshua shuddered at the words and looked at Preacher in horror. They had to cross Death's Door to get to Washington Island? Paradise?

Preacher saw the look on the boy's face and smiled. "Don't worry," he said. "We're not going out when the passage will sink the scow. We'll sit tight and wait for calmer weather."

Joshua stared at the wild waves whipped white by wind. Low lying, dark gray clouds hung heavy and moving above scudding, smaller white clouds. He pointed to the island in front of them.

"That's where we're going?"

Preacher shook his head. "That's Plum Island." He pointed at an island further out, the green of trees rising out of the lake. "That's Washington Island," he said. "There."

**

For the next two days, they were stranded in the small bay near

Hedgewood Harbor. The wind blew steadily, and, at times, squalls pebbled sheets of rain across the water. They were better set up to deal with wind and rain than they had been after escaping through the swamp. Gordon had brought two small tarps most of them could huddle under. A constantly burning campfire, impossible in territory where slavers were looking for them, was a luxurious comfort.

Mostly the adults talked about the possibilities of their new lives on the island.

"It'll be hard," Chas told them. "Summer's not long in this part of the country. We don't even have these days to waste. None of you have ever known how brutal cold and snow can be.

"Gordon's brought thread for making heavy clothes out of deerskin. We'll also have rabbits and fox or mink to make boots, though no stiff leather for soles. None of that's even talking about building at least one, or hopefully two, cabins. The men are going to have to learn to fish, too. The waters around the island are filled with fish. We'll get sick of eating fish before spring, but it's what will keep us alive this first winter. We'll have to get as many berries and other greens and roots as we can on top of everything else. It's gonna be hard."

"But we'll be free," Franklin responded. "Waiting here for everybody, I've had lots of time to think. Back in Missouri we had good times in the quarters sometimes. We're people. People can reach down into themselves and find laughing and joking and love no matter how miserable things are. But mostly we were afraid. If the Master, Mistress, the son, or that son of a bitch traitor Silver Coats got a whim, out comes a fist or a whip. Somebody suffered, or a woman got in a bad situation, and none of us could do anything about it.

"However hard that first winter is, it'll be *our* hardness, something we're wrestling with ourselves, and that's important. It's important to what makes a human a human being."

"I can deal with hard," Willie said, his hand touching his wife's arm. "If I'm building for my family and not a master who's always threatening us, I can easily deal with hard."

Bill, sitting with his daughters and wife, as silent as usual, shook his head. "As long as we can take care of our families we'll be okay," he said.

"There's white men on the island, too," Preacher said.

Joshua felt himself tensing like he had when he had been afraid that a slaver rather than Franklin was coming through the woods. He had not dreamed white people would be where they were going. He had assumed the wilderness was so huge and far away from civilization that they would be the only ones living there.

"We won't be able to hide from them," Preacher continued. "But we will need to hunker down and keep to ourselves. I don't think they'll bother us, but we're negras, as they call us, and you can't tell. They're mostly foreigners who have come to this country, so they're different, but we'll have to be on guard."

"Will they tell slavers about us?" Joshua's mother asked nervously.

"I don't expect so," Chas said. "Like Preacher said, they're not from the South, and they've got their own hardships surviving. We'll be okay."

"The Potawatomie aren't afraid of them," Gordon said, standing up from the fire as a gust of wind moaned through the trees. "Stockbridge doesn't have much to do with the Potawatomie. They live too far north, but I've talked to a couple of them. They're mad the white man took their land. They used to use Rock and Washington Islands during summers for hunting and fishing to stock up for winter, but they say they can mostly get along with the people living on their island. Mostly the whites don't get stirred up every time they see an Indian."

Gordon looked across the campfire at Chas, but Chas didn't say anything. He seemed lost in thoughts far removed from where they were.

"It'll be good on the island," Preacher said. "I've prayed and prayed about this and thought and thought about it. Ever since I was a young man, I've wanted to help a community of slaves become a community of God-fearing free men, women, and children. God is about to answer that prayer. We're going to live in New Jerusalem. Amen!"

***

Finally, on the third day, the weather broke. As soon as the men were up, they started hauling stuff to the boat. Preacher and Chas got into the boat and started checking the caulking and sails, making sure they were ready to cross Death's Door.

"I don't like the name of that strait," Joshua's mother told him as they helped carry cooking utensils to the boat.

"You get beyond Death's Door," Joshua said. "You've told me all my life. That's where you find paradise."

His mother put out her hand and gently grabbed his arm. "I miss your Pappy," she said and then let go of him and moved off toward the scow that didn't look nearly as big it had in the Chicago River. In fact, in the immense wilderness with its forest next to even larger lake waters, it seemed too small to carry them to the island.

Staring at the water, Joshua, for the first time, began to worry about how he would feel without land beneath his feet. He couldn't picture himself crawling into the boat with Jamie and Jeremiah and his mother while Preacher and Chas settled them down and hoisted the sail and set out into deep water.

Right after he delivered his last load to Chas and Franklin, who were

114

stuffing things into every corner, Preacher stopped moving and stood.

"Willie," he said quietly, "load the children and women. You and Franklin will stay here for later. Chas and I will take the others over."

"Now?" Willie asked. He looked at Beulah who was standing by the boat looking at her husband and sons already in the boat. "I thought you were going to wait until dark so the lighthouse keeper wouldn't see us going to the island."

Chas came to stand by Preacher. "The water's calm now. It won't be as calm out in the strait. You take providence when it comes."

"Help me up, Jamie and Jeremiah," Beulah said.

Joshua stood next to the boat, standing half a foot out into the lake, small waves lapping against his legs.

After Beulah was half lifted into the scow by Bill, who had quickly waded into the water, and Willie, Jeremiah crawled up by himself.

"Esta May and the girls first," Jamie said, wading into the water to stand next to Joshua.

Esta May didn't look at either of them, but helped her sisters, then Zelda. Nobody talked. There wasn't a lot of room left when Joshua's mother climbed in, but she didn't hesitate.

"I've been separated from Jason enough," she said.

Once Esta May was in, Jamie looked at Joshua. "We ready for freedom life?" he asked.

Joshua nodded and watched as Jamie leapt over the boat's side, ignoring the outstretched hand Chas held out to him. Joshua took Willie's hand. Even back in the quarters, he'd always trusted Willie. Willie slipped into the water and splashed to shore. He, along with Franklin and Gordon, pushed the scow off the gravel beach with Franklin and Gordon.

"We'll be back this evening if the waves are okay," Preacher said as Chas pulled ropes to raise the scow's sail.

Within moments, they were moving into Death's Door.

BOOK TWO

NEW JERUSALEM

North

Rock
Island

Green Bay

Boyer Bluff

Washington Harbor

Washington
Island

Little
Lake

Sand Bay

Limestone Ledge

Spring

West Harbor

Detroit
Harbor

Detroit Island

Lobdilla
Point

Plum Island

Village Sites
Corn Fields
Cemeteries
Caches
Cairns
Mound
Pits

Based on a map in Holand, Hjalmar R.
1917. *History of Door County Wisconsin,
County Beautiful*, Vol. 9. Chicago: The
S.J. Clarke Publishing Company, p. 22.

Chapter 13
Lives Lived as Prayers

They built outhouses first, then cleared a plot
Of pine and brush to plant their garden seed.
Out in the lake they fished, felt fear recede.

A Stockbridge Indian, while they'd hid, had brought
Them dreams the night the lightning's fierce onslaught
Had blued night skies, and in the cold their need
To keep on running, hiding, mutinied
Against their strength, the freedom they had sought —

But now, around a campfire as their sense
Of freedom slowly leached away despair,
The preacher dreamed alive the consequence
Of living on an island where the air
Loosed liberty in lungs, and, as, intense,
His words rang out; their lives became a prayer.

They were sitting around a campfire on the slender protrusion of land that protected West Harbor from Death's Door's wilder moods, all together for the first time since Chicago.

The landing had been dramatic. When the scow had sailed into West Harbor, Preacher had gotten out before they reached shore and splashed into the water, praising God and Jesus at the top of his lungs, thanking God for the freedom they had achieved. After he had gotten to shore, he'd knelt, dripping wet, in the tall grasses where the harbor gave way to the half circle of land.

"Hallelujah! Praise the Lord," he had shouted, his deep voice ringing into white pine, spruce, maple, birch, and cedar surrounding him.

Both Joshua and his mother had been excited to see Pappy, who'd been waiting on shore as they sailed into the harbor. Joshua had almost jumped out of the scow when Preacher did, but his mother had held him back. "Just seeing him's enough," she'd whispered. "Wait."

After landing the scow, they had all knelt in grass and prayed, crying as Preacher's deep, powerful voice described what New Jerusalem would be like without masters and overseers and whips and an endless stream of white man demands and orders.

"We have found new Jerusalem," Preacher had exclaimed as he worked toward his prayer's ending. "We have walked out of the shadows of darkness to this island wilderness where all of us, God's wonderful children, can be free. Where we can build God's house and be free. Amen, our Lord in Heaven, Amen!"

Joshua had cried with the rest of them, feeling as if he were choking out the fear and pain that had been his life ever since he had been born. He felt Master Bulrush's angry eyes disappear into the washing slap of waves on shore. In that moment, he could not even remember how the whip had burned into his back as Sliver Coats swung with all his might.

The preacher's words were powerful, describing a life and community where freedom was a natural right. The sense of having arrived, having run through swamp and fields and finding white people that didn't despise them and always having to be afraid every moment and then finding a wilderness where there were no plantations and masters was overwhelming. As Preacher said, "We have come out of darkness into the light of a new day. We rejoice in what this light means."

Joshua had been happy beyond any happiness he had ever felt, but he was also terrified of what this new life might bring.

"We'll build a civilization for black souls and freed slaves," Preacher had said.

After Preacher's praying had finished, Chas had taken oars from the scow's bottom and pushed it up on the beach. Pappy, Joshua, Jamie, and Jeremiah waded out to help. When the boat was grounded, Chas, Franklin, Bill, and Willie had jumped out and knelt as Preacher had when he had first come ashore. Pappy had swept up first his wife and then, after Joshua was done pulling on the scow, his son. Joshua's head had been a swirl of sensations: the island, the work Pappy had started by building lean-tos, his father's huge presence, his mother's ecstasy, and disbelief that they were where they were.

For what was left of the day, all of them, even Abbie and Ertha, hauled supplies out of the scow and stored them in the lean-tos Pappy had built. The afternoon was hot and humid. By the time evening shadows had spread beneath the trees, everyone was tired.

As the sun descended in the west, red and growing larger as it approached the horizon, Pappy stopped arranging things in the smallest lean-to. "It's been quite a day," he said, bending backward, stretching his back. He left the people scattered between the shore, forest, and lean-tos and strode to the spot he'd decided the evening's campfire would be. Joshua, watching him put a small circle of stones in place and twigs and small branches of dead wood into a teepee shape, felt like they had accomplished something true and momentous.

He had long since decided it was okay he had a father and that Pappy was that father. The long journey northward toward freedom and Washington Island had changed him. He was not as sullen—"and probably not as stubborn," he thought. He had hope, something he'd never even considered as a possibility on the plantation. He thought they'd all do well living on the island.

When, later, Willie started singing "Swing Low, Sweet Chariot" as if he didn't care who heard him, the rest joined in, forgetting that they would have been more restrained in Missouri. No one would have wanted to bring attention to the fact that they were having a religious meeting in the swamp. Beside the campfire, surrounded by the sound of waves, joyous that they had gathered together on Washington Island in a wilderness far from slaveholders, their spirits felt the liberation promised by Preacher all that time ago.

***

The next morning, they gathered next to the scow. Pappy had built a campfire before dawn, and everybody had gotten up early, even Chas and Willie, who had come through Death's Door in the dark.

Joshua was surprised he was awake. Their sleep patterns had been disrupted during the long escape. They'd traveled at night more often than during days. Then, after they'd spent time at the Campbell's farm, that had switched. He didn't think his body knew when it was time to sleep and when he should be awake.

Massie cooked breakfast using what was left of the deer meat Gordon had provided just before the scow had left him behind at the camp on the peninsula. After a prayer led by Preacher, Pappy, sitting beside Joshua and his mother, sighed contentedly.

"We'll start building today," he said.

"We're going to have to hunt for meat, too," Chas said. "Gordon gave us salt to preserve with, so we need to begin building provisions while we start the work that needs to be done."

"First we start on God's house," Preacher said. "If we are going to have a lamp lit in our spirits, we need to be right in relationship to God."

Joshua's mother started at Preacher's words. She glanced at Massie and then at Beulah and then fixed her eyes on Preacher.

"I don't want to be contrary, Preacher Bennett," she said, "but I don't want us to build a house of any kind first. We need outhouses first. Two, so the women can have privacy. We've been a long time getting here. We need to start reasserting the civilized part of who we are. I want a house dedicated to the Lord, but first more practical needs."

"I agree with Mary," Junebug spoke up. She looked stronger than she had when they'd started out, more energetic and bright-eyed. "None of us have had any dignity for any of our lives. It's about time we started building that for ourselves."

"With a toilet?" Bill asked, incredulity in his voice. Both Esta May and Ella glared at him. When he felt their eyes on his face, he looked cowed.

"The Bible teaches that everything ought to be done decently and in order," Zelda said. "I remember Preacher Bennett talking about that a long time ago. God knows you can't feel decent or in order when you're scared and running as if the devil is on your tail. I've got to agree with Mary and Junebug. I would give anything to feel decent again."

"An outhouse is going to do that?" Franklin queried.

Pappy, beside his wife, looked uncomfortable. Preacher stared steadily at Joshua's mother, who did not blink as she held his gaze.

At last Preacher looked away from Mary and to the sky where thunderheads were building in the south. Two great towers billowed darkly upward toward the heavens. They had reached the island between storms.

"A house to glorify God is important," Preacher said at last, eyes still on the thunderheads.

"Preacher is our leader," Chas spoke up. "If we don't follow the leader's wisdom, we'll risk falling apart."

Harrison cleared his throat. Like Junebug, he looked like he had weathered the journey well. Joshua knew he was hiding a limp, but the time he and Junebug had spent on the island with Pappy before the rest of them had crossed Death's Door had clearly helped him feel stronger.

"It's not all one thing or another," the old man said. He looked at Pappy. "Jason, Joshua, Jamie, and I can work on outhouses. Chas can go hunting. He's right about us needing to build up supplies." He smiled. "Oh, that sounds good. We're where we can actually talk about building up supplies." He laughed, causing others, especially the women, to smile. "Preacher and the women can start laying out God's house. A woman needs to make a spiritual home. The rest of us need to start making physical homes."

"We also need to think about winter," Beulah said. "We need outhouses, shelter, and food for the winter. That's a while off, but not that far away." She looked at Chas. "At least that's what we've been told."

"The men and boys have to learn what it means to become fishermen, too," Chas added. "That might seem simple, but it won't be even in waters better than any others in the world. We have skills to master before ice sets in. I've been here in winter. This is not going to be easy. We don't have enough time."

Preacher looked back at Mary and then at the other adults. Willie, who had been squatting by the fire while eating breakfast, rose to his feet and looked at his wife.

"Besides," Massie said, "unless I'm wrong, Zelda's expecting a child. We need to start protecting that child, our first child born into freedom."

Preacher's eyes immediately went to Zelda and Franklin. Joshua, shocked, looked at Zelda, too. She hadn't acted any differently than the rest of them. She had kept up and never complained. How could she be expecting a baby? She looked as thin as they all did.

The women in the quarters had always had to work up until they were ready to give birth, but even he and Jamie had known when they were pregnant. He looked at Jamie who looked surprised, too. Esta May, on the other hand, seemed to already know. He wondered if women could sense such things before men became aware of them.

Zelda didn't look at anyone but Franklin, then Abbie. "It's true," she said. "But I don't need special favors. I'm strong." Franklin smiled at her. Abbie reached out and took her mother's hand.

Preacher, clearly taken aback, was suffused with joy. His face became translucent. He looked at Mary.

"That's why you want the outhouse," he said.

"Harrison is right," she answered. "We don't have to do just one thing. The outhouses can be built while we're building the house for worshipping God."

"Praise God," Preacher exclaimed, startling them with his big voice. "This is a miracle. This is God's hand upon the souls of those with the courage to live in his love." He rose. "The time for praying's done for now. We'll finish the day with prayer."

***

The day was hot, not in the way the Bulrush Plantation was with air thick enough to cover a body with mist, but hot enough to make sweat pour down Pappy's face as he pushed the shovel blade into black dirt. As Preacher started working with Willie and Franklin on laying out, clearing, and leveling a space for God's house a little way from the beach on a slight rise of land, Pappy and Harrison decided on a spot in the woods for the outhouses. Joshua, Jamie, and Jeremiah started the digging. Harrison had gone off and found two straight saplings and began putting together a crude ladder for when the hole got too deep to crawl out of easily. After the three boys had worked their way through a layer of soil, roots, and an occasional stone, Pappy climbed into the shallow hole and took over.

Pappy was an unbelievable man, in Joshua's mind. He moved so fast it made the boys' efforts look puny. Soil—and stones when he hit them, even if they were large—was thrown out of the hole. As he got deeper, he had to throw the dirt up above his head. Harrison had the boys move the soil and stones away from where they would put the outhouse floor when the hole was dug.

"How deep does the hole have to be?" Jeremiah asked.

"Well over Jason's head," Harrison told him. "From what Gordon Burr and Chas have said, the winters here are unlike anything any of us have ever known. During the winter, we won't worry about the stink or being clean, I suspect. We'll just hate going out.

"Summer's different, though. There'll be trouble with flies and keeping things so you can stand to use the place, especially for women. Women are different from men. They want things comfortable. You got to have a deep hole, and it'd be good to have lime to put on top of the crap in the bottom."

"Chas will know what people around here do," Pappy said from the hole. "This is different from plantation country."

"Ugh," Jamie said, wrinkling his nose. "What a thing to talk about!"

The hole was already as deep as Pappy was tall. He stopped working the shovel and wiped sweat from his forehead. The back of his shirt was dripping wet.

"Crap is part of life," he said. "You boys have a choice. That's what escaping is all about, choice. You can choose to put your heads in the clouds and get away from anything that makes sense, or you can be practical and deal with what you got to deal with, no matter what you might want. Slaves only have one choice: to keep practical. Otherwise the whip will bring them to their senses."

There was bitterness in his voice. He shook his head and drove the shovel into the ground again, but stopped before lifting, and addressed his next words to Joshua, who was looking down on him in the hole.

"A man is going to be able to be a man on this island," he said slowly, his eyes boring into his son's eyes. "You're never going to be taken away from your family and forced to be shameful in how you relate yourself to other people."

He turned back to the shovelful of soil.

***

By late evening, the hole was dug and Harrison, Joshua, Jamie, and Jeremiah were out in the woods felling trees they could use to build up the outhouse's sides. Esta May and her sisters were out looking for the right size of pine, too. Preacher had told them, "Make sure you find pine; it's easier to shape. We have a lot of work to do before first snow. We can't use harder woods."

The group working on where the cabin was going to be built had made progress, too. They had cleared away the brush where God's house was going to sit and started cutting down trees. Everybody was exhausted. None of them had recovered from their hard travel yet, but nobody wanted to stop working either. They were making a new life. It might not be easy. They understood that. They had heard what Preacher and Chas had told them, but it was going to be their life, not controlled by a master and plantation. They were willing to drive themselves hard to make New Jerusalem happen.

Chas's arrival ended the workday. He came from the woods east of where they were working, carrying a doe slung over his right shoulder. He had the old Springfield model rifle Gordon had given him in his left hand. He was jaunty as he walked across the clearing above the curved shore.

"Thank the good Lord, fresh meat," Massie, who was closest to where Chas came out of the woods, shouted.

Preacher, who had been using the broad-axe delivered to the island with Pappy before the rest of them had reached Hedgewood Harbor to plane the first pine log Harrison and Willie had cut into lengths in the woods, leaned the axe's handle against the log. "We've worked enough today," he said.

Moments later, they were gathered on the land between the harbor and lake where they'd built their fire the evening before. For a long time nobody said anything. They had worked hard, were sweaty and tired, but felt good. Joshua decided he felt better than he had at any other moment in his life.

Freedom wasn't something tangible, and he wasn't really free, not really. Not yet. He had hard work to do. He wouldn't survive the words thrown at him if he didn't carry his own weight. He'd helped dig and drag small tree trunks to the outhouse all day. But he wasn't afraid of an overseer spying him from around the barn's corner. He wasn't avoiding a place just because he might run into the wrong eyes on that path. Instead, he had spent the day working without worrying. He hadn't even resented the work he was doing.

Joshua's mother stood up from the small tree she'd been leaning against.

"Well," she said firmly, "I think it's past time for us women to get clean in the lake. I'm tired of feeling dirty. What do you think, ladies?"

The women and girls were immediately on their feet. Chas had already hung the doe from a big maple's branch and was skinning it, cutting around the neck and moving the hide down to where he could bunch it in his hands and pull it downward with a swift, clean motion. He was being careful with the hide. They would need all the hides they could get for clothing, shoes, and carrying bags.

"You men can clean up in the harbor," Joshua's mother said. "The rest of us will be around the bend where we can be private."

Esta May glanced at Joshua and Jamie and smiled with the slightest smile possible before leaving with the other women.

Pappy watched them go and got to his feet.

"Boys," he said, motioning to Joshua, Jamie, and Jeremiah.

He walked to the water's edge and undressed. None of them had taken a bath since the pond at the Campbell place. Preacher was the last one in the water. Even Chas left the doe half skinned and accompanied Pappy and the boys into water much colder than Joshua had expected it to be. He gasped when he followed Jeremiah, who was whooping and hollering. The cold took his breath away even though he'd spent the day sweating and feeling so hot he didn't think he'd ever cool off.

Later, after they'd all come back to the campfire as the sun lit eastern clouds with yellow and red fire, contentment settled in. It seemed they truly had found their own piece of heaven.

***

"Tomorrow Chas, Franklin, Jamie, and Joshua will fish in the scow," Preacher said. "That's what's going to support us for the rest of our lives. Every man is going to have to learn the skill of it if we're going to survive long term. The rest of us will work on God's house and the outhouses." He looked at Pappy. "You should have one finished by tomorrow?"

Pappy shrugged after casting a glance at Harrison. "We'll see," he said.

"We'll start bringing logs for God's house in the day after tomorrow," Harrison said. "Jason's as strong as an ox. With him to help us carry them we should be able to bring logs in faster than you can trim them."

"Good," Preacher said.

The news that he and Jamie were going out on the first fishing expedition took Joshua's breath away. He looked at Jamie and Jeremiah, who seemed just as excited as he was.

"My baby's going to have its own cabin when it's born," Zelda said suddenly. "There'll be God's house, outhouses, and cabins for every family." She looked at Preacher. "Won't there?"

"We prayed for that under that big old cypress tree," he said, "before we gathered to leave." Preacher chuckled. "We're living that prayer."

Chapter 14
Beneath the Waves, Above the Waves, a
Song of Death and Light

Inside Death's Door where waters rise and fall
In symphonies of restlessness and waves,
Dark ship hulks lie, Niagara, Nichols, all
Those torn apart by storms that sunk as graves
Below deep currents powerful enough
To channel winds into a crucifix
That makes strong, hardened sailors want seraphs
To come and save them from the River Styx.

And then a young man in a wooden scow
Puts out a fishing-line and feels a trout
Begin to thrash and pull him to the prow
Where waves spit mist and shine his shout
Of pure exuberance into the light
That dances wild into a big trout's fight.

Master Bulrush's eyes dominated Joshua's attention. They were the same as they had been the day the big white man had forced him from the plantation house and his mother. The rage in them was a physical force that terrified Joshua and made him want to run, but his legs were frozen. He could not move. Then he saw the Master's hands, veins throbbing uncontrollably as they ever so slowly reached toward Joshua's neck. The world tattered as Joshua focused on clutching fingers and rigid hands, light fraying along his sight's edges as he tried to escape suffering promised in the Master's eyes.

"Joshua, Joshua," a persistent voice broke through the dream. Joshua fought away the image of threatening hands and forced his eyes open. The night was still dark and the air held a hint of coldness.

Chas was kneeling beside Joshua. "We're fishing today, remember?" Chas whispered. "You're about to become a fisherman."

Joshua was suddenly awake, but still confused. He looked east, but there was no touch of light in the sky. Franklin was getting Jamie to sit up.

"It's not day yet," Joshua complained in a whisper.

Chas smiled. "The fish get up early," he said. He swiftly moved from

Joshua's side, nodded at Franklin, and walked in the direction of the scow. It had already been pushed off the beach into West Harbor's water. Franklin followed while Jamie and Joshua frantically put trousers on, tightening them with the white string they'd been given in Chicago at the warehouse. They hurried to the boat as Chas and Franklin positioned themselves, Chas where he could work the sail, and Franklin in the stern.

"Push the boat deeper in the water before you get in," Chas directed.

Joshua glanced at Jamie. They put shoulders to the scow's hull, wading into the water. Joshua had been expecting to have to push hard, but the scow slid away from him and he almost fell. Jamie looked as surprised as he was. Both scrambled over the scow's sides.

Franklin moved back from the stern and took an oar.

"Help me, Joshua," he said.

Joshua, excited, grabbed the port side oar. When he dipped it in the water, he felt the boat move, but it moved more toward the port side rather than forward.

"Pull harder," Franklin said. "My pull's stronger than your pull. We have to match force for force."

"Learning how to sail and fish is a skill," Chas said. "It takes time."

"Can't one man do the oars?" Jamie asked.

"We've got learning to do," Chas answered. "You don't learn anything by not doing."

A few minutes later, Chas started pulling on ropes, getting ready to raise the sail. Choppy waves slapped the scow's hull. Joshua drove his oar into the water and pulled. The scow swung toward the starboard even though Franklin had tried to pull his oar in sync with Joshua's.

"Whoa," Franklin exclaimed. "You can tell you're Jason's son. I could never get the power into my oar he did even when he was trying to be easy."

His words made Joshua's heart swell with pride. He was beginning to understand what Franklin had just told him. He was growing. Jamie was still bigger than he was, but not that much. Even though they had faced ceaseless physical exertion and even starvation on their journey north, they were all so skinny their ribs showed beneath shirts, Joshua could feel himself getting stronger.

"Don't drive the oar so deep," Chas said. "You dip into the water and sweep. It takes getting used to, but that'll come." He pulled up the sail. "Jamie," he said, "get on the rudder."

The sail filled with wind and they were sailing, the oars no longer needed. Franklin brought his oar into the boat, sat it against the side, and motioned for Joshua to do the same.

East of them, over the island, the sun had brought dusk into a clear sky. A hint of pink spread over the forest behind West Harbor.

Joshua felt nothing like he had felt during the crossing of Death's Door. During that crossing, the water had, at first, been calm close to shore, but as they sailed toward Pilot Island waves had started rolling, gently rocking the boat as it sailed with wind to its port side. He had been excited and a little scared and had kept his hand on his mother's arm most of the way, forcing himself not to grip too hard.

The water was not rolling, but slapped the scow. Although they were just beginning to pick up speed, a slight spray blew wetness in Joshua's face. He felt exhilarated rather than nervous. The lake's smell was different, too. It had a fresher water smell than the swamp's fetid smell, the smell of farm animals mixed with swamp, or the plantation's pinewoods smell. He looked at Jamie gripping the rudder and smiled. Jamie smiled back.

"We're living now!" he said.

In what seemed to be no time they had slipped away from shore. Franklin moved to the bow and opened a compartment built into the boat's side.

"Come," he motioned to Joshua. "We came to fish." He pulled out a thick line nested into the compartment and a silver metal spoon with three hooks.

"We're going to use a lure and line today," Chas said as he tied the sail in place. "Later we'll get more serious and use nets. We won't have cured salmon and trout eggs for bait this year. We'll collect those and cure them in the spring. I did bring along deer fat and meat to try. But up in Sault Saint Marie they were using these lures to pretty good effect when I was last there. We'll see how we do."

Franklin, moving slowly and a little awkwardly, tied a small string to the fishing line and tied the lure to that line. He moved forward and handed the line to Joshua. Jamie was looking at what was going on with the same intensity Joshua felt.

"I want Preacher to teach how to use nets," Chas said. "There's a trick to that, but here we'll fish while we're sailing. This is a good day for it. The wind's not bad, and we've got good waters."

"Preacher showed me on the trip from Chicago after I got over getting sick every time we got into deep water," Franklin said. He laughed. "Now I feel like I'm a real sailor." He smiled. "I've put a weight on that line." He pointed at where a clump of metal had been tied four feet or so down the line's length. "You feed the lure out slowly, keeping the line tight in both hands. One hand won't be enough. Not if a big trout or salmon hits."

"Bring us even with the shore," Chas told Jamie. "Slowly. Slowly." Jamie moved the tiller to the right. He kept looking at Chas.

"Am I doing it right?"

"Slowly," Chas answered.

The scow, still moving, slowly bent its prow north, sailing perpendicular to shore. As it turned, Chas adjusted the sails to keep catching the wind.

The line Joshua was feeding into the water hummed as it sank. At first, he could see the lure flashing in bright sunlight. He kept glancing at Franklin, who was watching him.

"Slow the line down," Chas told Joshua, taking his eyes momentarily off Jamie. Jamie was grinning.

"I'm sailing," he said, exultation in his voice.

"Keep it steady," Chas demanded.

Joshua gripped the line. It pulled hard as he stopped it running into the lake. Franklin nodded his head, "Good, good," he said. He motioned with his hand. "Let it go some more," he said.

"It's got to be out a long way now," Joshua observed.

"Slowly let it out more," Chas said. "Franklin's learned. He knows what a fisherman does. This is nothing like catfish fishing. You have to prepare yourself. When something hits, it'll hit hard." He looked from Joshua to Jamie. "Steady," he said. "Good and steady."

Joshua ran the line through his fingers again.

"Slowly," Franklin directed again. Suddenly Joshua felt a sharp, quick tug on the line and then another. "Set the hook," Franklin shouted. "Strong!"

Joshua pulled back on the line. He pulled so hard he almost fell backward.

"You lose it?" Chas asked.

"You've got a fish?" Jamie asked excitedly, forgetting about the rudder.

"Jamie," Chas yelled.

Joshua pulled on the line. For a moment it was simple. He reached out with his left arm and grabbed and pulled with his right. It came in so quickly he thought for sure he'd lost the fish. It had felt big, too. He glanced in his disappointment at Franklin, whose black eyes were watching him carefully.

Then the line pulled against him so hard, jerking multiple times, that he almost let go. He was so startled he gasped, but managed to hold on even though the pulling was hard enough to burn his hands.

"You've got him," Franklin shouted. Chas and Jamie cheered.

"But I can't pull him in" Joshua cried, feeling a rush of panic.

"Hold steady," Chas said. "When he tires, you bring him in until he fights again. It's a big fish. I told you this isn't like catfishing."

To Joshua, the battle seemed to go on forever. He'd hold the line without trying to haul on it while the fish fought him. Then, when the fish stopped, he pulled it in hard, one hand over the other. Finally, Chas moved away from the sail.

"I'll get the gaff," he said, reaching down by the compartment near the bow.

"Gaff?" Jamie asked.

Chas brought up a rounded staff with a hook on one end. "Gaff," he said, and moved over by Joshua who was hauling the line again. Not ten feet from the boat the fish broke water. It flashed in sunlight, leaping into the air.

"A trout," Franklin exclaimed. "A rainbow. I thought it was acting like a trout."

"It's big," Jamie said, excitement in his voice.

Joshua said nothing, but held on, back muscles strained as the trout fought him again. The line went slack suddenly. He was startled again.

"Pull, don't give him slack," Chas said. "Quickly!"

"Chas was right," Joshua thought. "This is nothing like pulling a catfish for the evening campfire at the quarters out of the creek" He pulled up the line as fast as he could, but couldn't seem to get any tension.

"It's going under the scow," Chas said.

The line jerked again. Joshua hadn't lost his prey. He forced himself to pull against the heavy weight. Then he saw the fish flash in the water half a foot from the scow. It was huge, bigger than any fish he'd ever seen. They'd eaten trout the night before he had sailed with Preacher to Washington Island. He hadn't seen the trout dressed out. He wondered if it had been as big as this fish. His heart hammered in his ears. He kept hauling on the line, an inch forward at a time.

Chas bent over the water, the gaff in his hands. He stabbed and jerked. The fish flew in the air into the scow. It flopped wildly on the scow's bottom. Franklin had gotten out of his seat and had a large hammer in his hand. He struck the trout's head, causing it to bleed. It didn't stop flopping. It had rainbow colors on its side. Its gills moved in and out. Joshua was exhausted. He'd never thought that catching a single fish could be so hard.

"Must be twenty-five pounds at least," Chas said. He looked up from where he was kneeling by the steelhead trout and smiled. "You did good," he said to Joshua, then laughed and added, "for a beginner."

***

The rest of the day slowly became routine. They put four lines into the water and took turns when a fish took one line or another. Jamie and Joshua alternated at the rudder and sails under Chas's watchful eyes.

After settling into the routine, Joshua began noticing the profusion of birdlife on the water. Lines of black cormorants flew just above the waves, and white gulls with their squawking and strange, almost-laughing sounds were everywhere, floating on the water or flying in ones, two, threes, and larger groups, dipping white wings as they wheeled in the air. Three times during the morning the unique shapes of pelicans flew past them.

By the time lures and deer bait, which didn't seem to work that well, stopped attracting trout, salmon, and what Chas called whitefish, Joshua and Jamie were more exhausted than either would have believed possible. At last, after a lengthy time without any hits on the lines, Chas looked at the sun. It had passed zenith, but was still high in the sky.

"We've got eleven fish," he said. "That's not a bad start." He looked at Franklin. "Let's go help build God's house," he said.

Franklin saluted. "You're the leader," he said. He crawled over to the sail and swung it around. Chas put his hand on the tiller and moved them away from shore, forcing the scow to swing so that its prow pointed toward land.

"This will feed us for a few days," Franklin said, satisfaction in his voice.

"We'll clean them and salt all but one down," Chas answered. "Preacher and I will teach the women about cutting strips, drying, and hanging them out of the reach of bears."

"Bears?" Jamie asked, sounding nervous.

"The island has black bears," Chas said. "They cross the ice in winter. There's wolves, too, though you don't see them as often."

Joshua shuddered. He had never felt so good, but the mention of bears and wolves so matter-of-factly didn't seem like it made them as safe where they were as he'd expected them to be. He looked at Chas. The lean, tough man with the authoritative voice seemed to have had endless experiences since he was a slave: a sailor in the War of 1812, a man who knew the country and people of northern Wisconsin, and a frontiersman who had the skill to work out an Underground Railroad path north to freedom. Supposedly he had not escaped his master but had been freed. He was unlike any black man—or white man, for that matter—Joshua had ever known.

Both Preacher and Chas had led them a long way. They'd faced troubles, but they'd managed to get past them. "We'll probably get past bears and wolves, too," he thought as the shore came closer, and Chas prepared to take down the sail.

On shore someone had driven a thick stake into the ground near the beach. Chas kept up the scow's speed as they came into the harbor. When he collapsed the sail the boat headed straight toward the stake. Jamie jumped off the prow, splashing in cold water as they came in. Franklin followed and tied the rope attached to the bow around the log.

Beulah and Massie came to see how they had fared fishing. When they saw the scow's bottom covered with fish larger than any they had ever seen, their cries caused the rest of the community to leave what they were doing to come look. For the first time in his life, Joshua felt proud of what he'd done as Chas told the story of how he'd caught the first big trout. He didn't feel the small twang of resentment that had accompanied him even when they had reached Wisconsin and met up with Gordon Burr. His mother held back from the scow, but was looking at him with pride.

Chas, as he had promised, took the fish and carried them away from the beach south of where they were building God's house. Jeremiah, looking as envious as Joshua had ever seen him, and Esta May joined Joshua and Jamie as they followed Chas. Chas stopped at a little indentation in the shore filled with water and started slitting a trout from its anus up to its gills along the belly.

"You see?" he asked the young people.

He slowly cut outward from the gills around the head, removing the head. He kept glancing at the four of them to see if they were understanding what he was doing.

"Jeremiah," he asked after the head was off, "can you get a shovel? We need to bury the offal."

Jeremiah, still looking jealous and more than a little sullen, shrugged his shoulders and trotted off. Chas stuck his hand into the trout and pulled the entrails out in one smooth motion.

"It's not like cleaning catfish," Chas said. "You need to skin a catfish, for one thing. You don't a trout. You also don't hang a trout to clean it like they do catfish back in slave country. You keep it flat on its side. It's heavy and slick, so you got to keep a good hold."

He rinsed the huge fish in the cold lake water. After the trout was clean, he ran his thumb along the inside back ridge and forced blood out. He finished just as Jeremiah came running with the shovel. He threw the cleaned trout on the bank into tall grass.

He looked toward the lake where the gulls had moved closer, floating on the water. "We could let them have these," he said, "but I want to start out doing things the right way. We'll have to wash them again later, but we'll filet them for drying, too." He looked at Joshua. "You caught the first trout. You can clean the next one. Then Jamie." He looked up at Jeremiah. "You'll be fishing tomorrow."

Joshua could see Jeremiah's resentment disappear into a grin.

***

After Joshua, Jamie, Jeremiah, and Esta May had taken turns learning how to clean fish, they hauled all eleven—five trout, three salmon, and three whitefish—back to the camp. Harrison, working with Bill and Junebug, had laid out a mat of small logs and lashed them together to make a crude table.

Chas started laying out the fish, but they were too big to all fit. He put one salmon aside and said, "We can fry this for supper." He placed a trout on its back and inserted his knife around its backbone, working the knife toward the outside. It looked tricky, so Joshua tried hard to see what he was doing with the quick, sure movement of his hands. He knew he would be expected to follow Chas's example. A few minutes later Chas had worked the knife so that the trout's flesh separated from backbone. A minute later he had two filets lying side by side.

As the rest of them worked on individual fish using Chas's knife, Harrison stood and watched, smiling the whole time. "That's a mighty fine mess," he said. When Joshua's mother came with a small bag of salt he smiled. "You're going to dry and cure them," he said. "It'll be good eating if times get tough."

Joshua's mother's nose wrinkled up. "Before we cook a trout supper you are all going to dip in the lake and clean up," she said. "You smell like fish."

Harrison laughed. "We're going to be a fisher community," he said. "I expect we'll be getting used to the fish smell."

Chas did not crack a smile, but kept directing Joshua's hands as he heard small bones cut by the big knife. His mother threw salt on the first fish fileted. "We did this back on the plantation," she said. "Just not with fish this big."

When they had finished, the three boys wandered up to where others were working on the cabin they were calling God's house. A lot of progress had been made. Brush and small trees had been removed from the plot. The men had shoveled into the slight incline and were in the process of leveling it. More straight pine logs had been cut in the forest and moved to the beach.

Jeremiah pointed to one log that had been peeled as well as trimmed with the broad axe. "That's cedar," he said proudly. "I helped peel it. It's going to be the wood that provides the foundation. Pine logs are going to go on top of it. Cedar's a harder wood, so it'll resist rot from the ground better." He paused. "Daddy and Preacher's going to notch them on the ends to fit the cabin together."

Massie came over to them, wrinkling her nose like Joshua's mother had. "Go ahead and look at the outhouse," she said. "Jason and Harrison got one finished. You two," she said, pointing at Joshua and Jamie, "worked on it. But I want you into the lake. Now. All three of you are going to be cleaner tonight than you are now."

"Esta May smells like us, too," Jeremiah informed his mother.

"She'll get clean," Massie said. "She knows what clean is. Better than some boys I know. We've been heating water and cleaning clothes and blankets all day. One of these days we'll be living civilized lives."

Pappy and Willie were coming down the path starting to wear into the ground between God's house and the outhouse.

"I heard you boys on the scow did good," Willie said, smiling.

Jamie smiled like his father. They both had good faces, open and friendly. Jeremiah was different. He was sharper somehow and just a little wilder. More often than not his face had a cynical cast even though he was young. He wasn't really like either his mother or father.

"We did," Joshua said. "We really did."

Chapter 15
The Vagaries of Time

The Christian fires burned deep in freedom's roots.
They settled in the island's wilderness
And let the preacher's words become the shoots
Of hope that flourished as their fear and stress
Were relegated to the nightmare past,
The arrogance of whips and masters less
A worry than the way their lines were cast
Into the waters of the lake, the dream
Of lives unfettered suddenly a vast
Reality that strengthened self-esteem.

But then a man materialized from trees.
The past returned and, like a raging stream,
It dredged up terrifying memories
That made them feel time's shifting vagaries.

The next several days were endlessly busy. No one had time to think or spend a moment alone. Even though the days were hot and humid, Preacher and Chas kept telling them, "We have to be ready for winter. Winter is not that far away." Nights were cooler than they would have been in Missouri, but a single blanket was more than enough to keep warm even though they were still sleeping on ground beneath trees picked out by each family.

Joshua was given different tasks every day. He worked on God's house, helped his mother and Massie prepare ground for a garden, went out in the woods with Pappy and Harrison to find pines that could be cut down for cabin logs, tried to learn how to use a broad axe to create a flat surface on a log destined for either a cabin or an outhouse, worked on digging the hole for a second outhouse, went hunting with Chas in woods clogged with undergrowth and trees, and took his turns in the scow fishing. He even helped with meals and cleaning dishes, pots, and pans, enjoying that because he got to spend time with Esta May and her sisters.

The further they got away from their flight north's terrors, the more relaxed everyone became. Esta May, Ella, and Eunice were especially opening up, joking with each other and the boys, although mostly they teased each other. Ella had started calling Jeremiah "Ghost" because of his tendency to disappear the minute Massie tried to find him. Abbie and Ertha seemed tied together with invisible rope. Joshua, constantly on the move because of his mother and Jason's polite requests for one task after another, became "The Mule Who Couldn't Rest." The girls didn't let the adults hear them. Jeremiah tended to get defensive, but Joshua and Jamie took the teasing in stride.

God's house, just below the garden planted with peas and green beans from seeds Gordon had provided from Stockbridge gardens, slowly took shape. Every morning, Pappy, Harrison, Willie, and Bill went out in the woods, sometimes with Joshua, Jeremiah, or Jamie in tow, took felling axes, and chopped selected trees small enough to drag to the beach. There they debarked them before Preacher or Willie got busy with the broad axe to flatten the top and bottom. Preacher then used an adz, with its arched blade at right angles to the handle, to smooth out and even surfaces hewn by the broad axe.

"You can make a cabin in an easier way," Preacher told them. "You can just chink spaces between logs. Maybe, if we get too close to winter, we'll resort to that with the other cabins, but this is God's house, and it's going to be built like it should be built. We want a place where we can glorify God."

After a log was prepared, Pappy, under the watchful eye of Preacher and sometimes Chas when he wasn't hunting or in the scow with Franklin and a couple of boys, worked on the half-dovetail notching where the cabin's corners would fit together. Preacher was sad about not doing full-dovetail notching.

"We ought to do things right," he said repeatedly. "This is God's house." But they had endless chores. In the end, Preacher admitted that full-dovetail notching, although superior, was too time consuming.

To build the foundation they first laid down stones Joshua, Jamie, Jeremiah, Esta May, Ella, and the women found and carried to the cabin. Finding the right stones was not easy since they needed to be relatively flat even though they were going to be mortared before cedar logs were put in place.

No one was allowed to go alone anywhere beyond the camp. Even though they were free, they were nervous about what might lay inland. They went looking for rocks in twos and threes, always on the lookout for trouble. They spent a week looking for stones, but eventually the right sized and shaped ones piled up beside God's house as other work went forward.

Chas was the only one who seemed unconcerned and left without worrying about the island's white people. "I've wandered a long time," he told Joshua and Jamie once when he was getting ready to go hunting. "I've met a lot of men. There'll be good and bad men on Washington Island just like any place else. I'm not going to worry about what I can't change, but approach everybody with a way to disappear before I say hello."

When Jeremiah asked if the island's white people were okay with them putting up cabins, Chas had smiled enigmatically. "We'll see," he said.

God's house's design was simple. Mostly it was one big room with a small bedroom where Preacher could sleep and have his own space. After cedar logs had been placed on top of foundation rocks, they started lifting wall logs in place, fitting corners together where half-dovetail notches had been cut.

Pappy was the key to lifting the big logs and putting them on top of each other. Willy helped, wrestling one end of a log while Pappy, seemingly without effort, heaved the other end to where it belonged. Both men's foreheads poured sweat down into their eyes even during cooler days. Preacher, and sometimes Chas, directed the effort. The women, led mostly by Massie, put wood chips between logs, then dobbed and chinked moss into wherever they found a crack or opening. The dobbing and chinking was covered with a troweled layer of clay.

As the walls went up. Preacher started working on the stone fireplace and chimney. Since they did not have brick, those that had gathered foundation stones now went out to find and carry back more stone. Preacher was not as particular about flatness as he had been with foundation stones, but he still wanted good-sized ones that were not too rounded.

"I wish we had better clay," he told Massie one day as she and Joshua's mother brought in two gunnysacks with stones in them. He looked at the sky as if he were praying, but then shrugged. He stared at Pappy and Willie cutting windows into the wall and at Harrison and Junebug cutting boards out of pine logs that could be used to build the cabin's door and window shutters. They had no glass.

"Well, God helps those who helps themselves," Preacher finally mumbled and started sorting stones into piles designed to help him decide where in the fireplace and chimney they would end up. "I hate to rely only on pine tar sealing."

Not even Zelda, whose pregnancy was starting to show, was spared the endless labor. The women wouldn't let her search for and carry sacks of stone, but she worked with Joshua's mother and Massie cooking and Esta May and her sisters cleaning. Every day they fought to keep clothes reasonably clean since they had so few of them. Even keeping detritus from the campsite with so many people was a challenge. There was also

138

work in salting, drying, and preserving fish brought in from the daily trips out on the lake. Tanning deer hides when Chas brought fresh meat in from hunting was another task. They would need the tanned hides for foot coverings and clothes once winter came, not forgetting tallow for candles.

***

When the men started building the sub-roof, primarily using the adz and crosscut saw, a buzz of excitement ran through the camp. The first cabin was close to being completed. Before starting the roof, the sawing and chopping of logs into boards accelerated. Bill, who seemed to hardly move even when he was completing tasks faster than anybody else, and Beulah joined Harrison and Junebug in the work. Joshua, Jamie, and Jeremiah were continually having to help "hold things steady," or trying to sand boards smooth using the adz or an axe, although it seemed impossible to live up to Preacher's expectations. The boards produced were never straight-edged or smooth enough. Preacher also made them wash down the logs every day.

When Pappy, with Chas's help, had got the roof's angle on both sides right, they started to set the two end rafters just inches from the end of the purlins hung over the outside walls. They then notched them into place flush with the purlins. Their demand for boards after that, as they drove wooden stakes to hold the cabin together, was insatiable. Most everybody had to drop what they were doing and work with Harrison and Junebug as they labored ceaselessly through long, hard days. Franklin, now the one most in charge of the scow although he'd thought he could not stand being in it at the Chicago River, even gave up fishing as they tried to produce lumber needed for the roof, doors, and windows.

While Pappy and Chas worked on the roof, Willie and Preacher started putting down the floor. At the end of every day Harrison and Junebug, working together to make boards, were increasingly worn out. Sometimes Joshua's mother worried that the two of them, given their age, could not keep up the pace and would sicken themselves. Nobody dared suggest they stop doing what they were doing. Junebug, particularly, got irritated whenever anyone hinted they should maybe slow down.

"We made it this far," she told them. "We are going to earn our freedom just like everybody else. We're gonna work."

As the roof became visible, the camp's primary topic was about how great it was going to be to have a place to sleep out of weather. They had slept under canvas since meeting up with Gordon Burr, but dealing with wind off the lake, rain, humidity, and sun was a constant part of their lives.

"Civilization's coming," Joshua's mother shouted to Pappy pounding yet another board into place one day. Pappy, looking down at his wife, laughed. "Civilization of free men and women," he said. The banter put a spring into everyone's steps. Junebug responded with "Hallelujah!"

***

Preacher and Willie had started laying out space for the second cabin to be built after it had been cleared when, suddenly, close to the shore, a white man came out of the woods. Joshua noticed him first. He was shoveling a small mound where grass grew, trying to level it, when he glanced toward the lake. The panic he felt mirrored what he had felt the day the young girl had burst from the woods when they had been hidden in the Braxton wagons.

The white man hesitated as he looked them. Joshua dropped the shovel, causing Jamie, Jeremiah, Preacher, and Willie, working at trying to level the ground, to look up and notice the white man, too. On the roof, Pappy stood, precariously balanced where he had been kneeling pounding wooden pegs to join boards together. No one made a sound.

None of them had any idea whether the man was one of the islanders or a slaver coming to try to capture them. The man had a pistol stuffed in his belt but didn't have a rifle. He didn't show any overt aggression, but calmly walked across the open beach toward them.

Preacher moved from where he had been working not far from God's house and walked toward the white man past Joshua. The white man was not tall, but he looked strong and confident, his strides sure and long. He appeared to be a little younger than Preacher, but not young, perhaps in adulthood's middle years. He was dressed in what looked like an un-dyed cotton shirt and home-sewn pants, along with a well-used brown hat, round on the top with a wide brim. Harrison, who was some distance away from the rest of them, started walking toward the white man, too.

Joshua held his breath as Preacher approached the man, but the white man smiled and extended his hand.

"I heard a cabin was being built here," the man said, speaking loud enough so that the rest of them could hear. He laughed. "Looks like there'll be more than one cabin."

Preacher reached out and shook the man's hand. "I'm Tom Bennett," he said. "Have you met Chas Bullock?"

The man looked straight into Preacher's eyes. "Miner, Henry Miner," he said. "I'm the postman around here. That's why I need to know who's living on the island."

Preacher looked puzzled. "Postman? There's enough people for a post office?"

Joshua and Jamie found themselves edging toward the two men as Harrison came up to the white man with his hand extended.

"Harrison Stimson," he said. "Community elder."

"Good meeting you," Mr. Miner said and looked back at Preacher.

"There's three hundred souls or so if you count those on Rock Island," he said. "The post office is my cabin, although I drop mail, and sometimes supplies, off after every run to Ephraim, Little Sturgeon Bay, and Green Bay at Craw's Dock."

Preacher looked taken aback by Miner's news. A population of three hundred? They had thought they were coming to wilderness.

"Chas never said there were so many," Preacher said. "When I was here last there was only a handful."

"Are they all as friendly as you are?" Harrison asked.

"I know Chas Bullock," Miner says. "Black fella, sort of skinny and tall?" Preacher nodded. "He probably doesn't know how many people are here. We're pretty scattered."

Neither Preacher nor Harrison said anything. Harrison looked back at the rest of the community. Pappy and Willie had come off the roof, and everybody, except for Joshua and Jamie, who were now standing just behind Preacher and Harrison, had grouped together within listening distance.

Questions ran through Joshua's mind. *With that many white people, how long can we keep ourselves safe? Are we going to have to abandon the work we've done and move north again? Why had Chas brought us to a place he knew was so dangerous? What was Preacher going to do now?*

Harrison was his usual affable self after thinking for a few moments. "Preacher here's a good man," he said, pointing at Preacher. "What kind of Christians are folks around here?"

"You mean, are we Southern Christians with anti-black ways or abolitionist Christians?" Mr. Miner asked, his voice tinged with a sense of just how shrewd he was.

Joshua held his breath.

"If you want to put it that way," Preacher said cautiously.

"You a good preacher?" Miner asked. "You say the word of God and know Jesus our Lord and savior?"

"He's the best preacher you ever heard," Jeremiah spoke up, startling Joshua, who hadn't even realized Jeremiah was standing behind him and Jamie. Jamie looked terrified as he looked back at his younger brother. Black people did not speak to white people, especially if they were kids and the white man was an adult. That was asking for trouble.

Mr. Miner looked at Jeremiah, let a slight smile quirk his mouth's corners, and looked back at Preacher.

"If the boy is right," he said, "there's no preacher on the island yet. Some people will be glad to hear the word of God from the Bible spoken right. I won't say there aren't rogues in the population. You can't ever say that. No place is perfect, but you should be okay. Mostly people are too busy fishing and trying get along to worry about neighbors in a way that isn't friendly." He laughed. "Though sometimes things can get contentious, especially with women in the winter."

"We don't want to cause problems," Preacher said.

"We mostly want to be left alone," Harrison added.

Miner looked at the ground. "Yeah, I can understand that," he said. He sighed. "Well, you folks have work to do. I ought to let you get to it. I've got my own chores." He glanced at the sky. The sun was already approaching the eastern horizon.

"You sound like a Christian," Preacher said, a hesitancy in his voice that Joshua had never heard before.

Miner grinned and looked into Preacher's eyes again. "Let not your heart be troubled: ye believe in God, believe also in me," he quoted. He smiled again. "I am a believer," he said and then looked at the people standing halfway between God's house and the three boys, Harrison, and Preacher. "And this island won't suffer by having other Christians settle down and make homes here."

Then he turned abruptly and started to walk way.

"Mr. Miner," Preacher said, using his big voice. Miner stopped and turned back, a question in his eyes. "You're welcome here," Preacher said.

Miner nodded and disappeared into the woods.

***

They didn't get much done the rest of the day. Pappy and Willie got back on the roof for a while and continued fastening in boards. Massie sent Joshua and Jamie after a bucket of water for boiling after she started the evening campfire. But mostly they talked about the white man's sudden appearance.

"I don't know," Jamie said as they dipped water from where the creek ran into the lake. "Chas told us they were on the island. They had to find us, but he appeared out of nowhere."

"I saw him come out of the woods," Joshua said. "I was afraid he was a slaver."

"He wasn't though, was he?"

"He wasn't," Joshua agreed. "He was a little strange, though. Did you think he acted normal?"

"What's normal for a white man who doesn't seem to want to whip

142

you or make you do something for him?"

"We're going to have to live with them," Joshua said. He paused. "Or else we're going to have to move on."

Jamie jerked the bucket out of the water and handed it to Joshua.

In camp, the adults were talking about the implications of Mr. Miner's appearance. They seemed most concerned with the revelation that there were three hundred people on the island.

"I can't believe Chas didn't know," Franklin said. "He knows about pretty much everything. We take a wrong turn, and he finds us. He leads us to the right place. He finds game or food or wagons to haul us north. He always knows."

The talk went on until the sun was firing long clouds streaming over their heads with yellow, red, and purplish light. And when Chas came out of the woods down the well-worn trail to the outhouses shouldering a young buck with four horns, nobody said anything.

"What's wrong?" he asked in response to their unusual silence.

Preacher got to his feet. "We had a visitor while you were hunting," he said.

"Henry Miner?"

"He seems a godly man," Preacher said.

Chas knelt down beside the dead deer. "He's *the* man on Washington Island," Chas said, taking his skinning knife from his belt sheath.

"He said there are three hundred people living on the island," Pappy said, sitting on a log by the fire. Joshua's mother was sitting by him and took his hand.

"Three hundred white people," Bill Woodruff added.

"Might be," Chas said. "I never counted them. They're spread out."

"Are we all right here?" Zelda asked, startling Franklin who'd come up behind her and put his hand on her shoulder as she took Abbie's hand in hers.

Chas held his knife in his hand, looking intently at it.

"Preacher Bennett and I planned this for a long time," he said at last. "We're free here, and I think we'll stay free. Most folks here come from Europe and places that don't hold with slavery. But are we safe?" He looked at Zelda. "I think we are, but how do you know? Our skin's different from the skin of the other island people, including Indians that come and go."

"A black man's never safe," Willie said.

"A black woman neither," Massie agreed. "The good Lord knows we know that."

"Put the knife down Chas," Preacher said. He stood up. "We're gonna pray. God got us this far. He's not going to let us down now."

Chapter 16
The Metamorphosis of Zeal

Waves, choppy from the wind, flashed glints of light.
The preacher burned with words that rose from depths
Not seen by eyes and wove their meanings tight
Into the island's contours, in the steps
Of men and women trying to become
The people that they really were, souls meant
To live community, not martyrdom
To greed and power's joy in punishment.

Out on the lake the fishermen dropped lines
Into the depths, the light of who they'd be
Embodied in huge trout, bright rainbow shines
A metamorphosis of memory
Into a dream made manifest and real
By perseverance, words, the preacher's zeal.

Everybody was tired. As Bill Woodruff put it one evening beside the campfire when rain was spitting from the evening sky, "Sometimes I feel this island is fighting us and making us work twice as hard as we need to for us to make a home."

But the good news was God's house was almost done, and the second cabin was well underway.

The weather was changing. Hot days, sudden thunder, and lightning storms were over. A little way into the woods, leaves were turning a brighter orange than Joshua had ever seen on a tree before.

Preacher had hoped they could complete three cabins by the time snow fell, but that did not look likely. They were working as hard as they could, but the second cabin was not finished, and the only progress on the third was a space leveled and cleared of brush and trees.

The worst part was getting logs out of the forest. Finding right sized trees was also a challenge. Bill was the best at that. He often took Ella, as agile as Jeremiah was energetic, with him. They sometimes took hours locating a stand of pine that had more than one adequate tree. Felling trees was easy. Even Harrison could swing the axe with rhythm, sending wood chips flying. But then they had to measure the tree's trunk, make sure they could drag it through trees, brush, and rough ground, cut it if it was too large, and then, using multiple people, almost always with Pappy in the lead, employ human muscles to wrestle it to West Harbor.

Even Pappy was known to wish out loud for a team of mules. "Mosquitos and pulling and pushing don't mix," he'd complain. Then he'd look at his hands smeared with the inevitable pine pitch. "This could be an easier life."

Zelda's pregnancy was now showing. Franklin hovered around her when he wasn't out in the scow or helping with some task. Abbie was constantly at her mother's side, trying to help her every moment they were awake, irritating Zelda with her constant attention. She kept telling the young girl, who seemed more mature with every day that passed, "I'm not a china doll in the master's house." But Abbie, instructed by Franklin to look after her mother, did not listen and tried to keep her mother from bending, which was beginning to become awkward, and lifting anything other than a tin plate and cup.

Joshua was becoming increasingly aware of Esta May. There had been little to no privacy in the quarters. Love was truncated by Master and Overseer's demands. There was no safety, nor guarantees, for any slave about anything, not even love. Their lives were not their own. They were chattel handled and disposed of in any way their white masters' chose. That meant they were seldom, if ever, alone. Everyone could hear sex and see women and men in various states of undress. There was no shame in being who they were even though they chafed inside the bubble they could not escape.

The long flight north had allowed the escapees even less privacy as they had driven themselves past exhaustion. They had not had the energy or time to hide their basic human acts. Constant fear and anxiety, combined with hunger and exhaustion, had dictated that no one even think about privacy.

Now, however, led by Joshua's fierce mother, they were becoming civilized. Mary Simpson measured civilization by what she knew, the practices and sayings she had heard as a Bulrush servant in their big white house. She valued the cleanliness and good behaviors toward each other white people had demonstrated even while Master Bulrush and his son misbehaved in every way possible toward slaves and especially women slaves, including her. She was a Christian, though. Preacher had burned a Christian ethic of goodness, cleanliness, belief, and charity into her soul even while she rejected degradations of the master/slave relationship.

John in the Bible had said, "So if the Son sets you free, you will be free indeed," and although she understood the passage was about being set free from sin, she took the words another way, too. She believed in the

Son, Preacher was a disciple of the Son, and she and all of them had escaped the sin of the plantation to the freedom of wilderness. In this wilderness, they were charged from the spirit inside Preacher and his vision for their community.

They had the task of creating a civilization different from the one she had observed for so many years so closely. This civilization would not be built upon sins found outside carefully structured behaviors and attitudes in the houses of masters. It would be built upon belief in God and godly behaviors that disciplined human beings so that they became more than what their worldly bodies and souls naturally inclined toward.

It was in this new context of his mother's beliefs and Preacher's fire that Joshua's feeling for Esta May were affecting him. As they had fled day after day he, Jamie, Jeremiah, Esta May, and, to a lesser extent, her sister Ella had built a relationship separate from the one they had with the adults. They were escaping their plantations and that bound them together. They were on the Underground Railroad they had heard about, but hadn't, until they found themselves in dark woods and fields at night running, believed existed other than as a wished-for rumor among slaves unhappy in their lives.

Belonging was not a new thing. They had belonged to their plantation and their quarters and their place inside the plantation world, but belonging, as part of an escape, was different and more powerful than any other experience they had ever had. Even if they were to have been captured and punished as severely as they would be punished, their shared experience would make them different. Slavery was not who they were. Their time on the Underground Railroad had changed how they related to each other and the world.

Joshua was now noticing how Esta May was dressed in the morning and how good she looked. His feelings confused him. He knew Jamie was starting to notice the same things about her. The three of them were the same age. Jamie had always been Joshua's best friend. Joshua did not like feeling unsettled when he saw Jamie looking at Esta May. Esta May seemed oblivious that either Joshua or Jamie had started noticing her in a way neither of them could have explained if they had been challenged about it.

Inside the civilization Preacher and his mother were building, life was more complex than it had been at the plantation. He was still given orders every day, but those orders were different than those that had once gotten him into constant trouble, although he couldn't refuse any more than he could have on the plantation. Now he was told to help Pappy hoist logs up on a cabin's walls or go fishing with Franklin or help clean dishes, and now there was also the sense that even though he had to do what he was told, he still had control over his self. He felt a dignity he'd never experienced before. He could notice how Esta May was dressed and how she looked, and he had a right to those thoughts.

He fit into the civilization they were trying to build, but he had his self, too.

As he moved purposefully around the camp, aware of how his new life was coming into focus, the conflicts inside him coupled with the feeling he was where he should be stretched out indefinitely in front of him. He was concerned that fall was starting. That meant winter, with snow like he had never seen, and cold like he had never experienced, was getting closer. Still, they would have at least two cabins mostly completed. Pappy had told him they wouldn't stop building when the cold came. They'd keep on until the third cabin they had cleared a space for had a roof that could protect the two families that would live in it.

When Preacher was finally satisfied with God's house, he came outside, after going all around the building outside and inside, and made an announcement. "Tomorrow is Sunday," he said. He had spoken loud enough to get everyone in West Harbor's attention. Chas, Franklin, Jamie, and Jeremiah were out on the scow, so they didn't hear him, but everybody else stopped working and drifted to where Preacher was standing by the cabin's front door. "We are going to start living life right," he said. "The Lord rested on the seventh day. We are going to get together in God's wonderful new house and rest, too."

"This is a good start," Pappy said.

"I thank God Mary Simpson got my family and me to listen to Preacher Bennett," Willie said. "I owe him this day."

"Amen," Junebug said.

Joshua's mother walked over to Preacher and put her arm over his shoulder. "We'll have church service in a real church tomorrow and not under a swamp cypress tree. We're going to be civilized people," she said, smiling, satisfaction in her voice. "Better than any Bulrush ever thought of being."

Massie laughed.

Joshua wondered how Preacher knew that the next day was Sunday. He'd lost track of days after they had left Chicago.

***

The next morning they hurried through the camp's routine. Preacher had slept outside with the rest of them, saying that God's house would be consecrated to its purposes after the service he would lead. By the time the sun was halfway up the sky, they had all somberly, families walking with each other, filed into the church. Rows of benches Harrison and Junebug had built, and the altar Willie had put together using cedar logs, the broad axe, a knife, and a finishing stone, gleamed in their newness. The cabin's inside smelled of fresh-cut pine and cedar.

Preacher went into the small room that was going to double as his office and bedroom. When he came out, he had put on a dark blue robe that covered his shoulders and fell to the floor. He stepped up to the altar, smiling, and stood beside it and raised his arms as the rest of them sat on the plain, backless benches.

"Brothers and sisters," Preacher said in his deepest, most dramatic voice. Joshua felt shivers along both sides of his arms. "We have found freedom," Preacher exclaimed. "We have found the place every man, woman, and child knows in their bones! We have found New Jerusalem!"

"Amen," Junebug said out loud. Joshua could feel his mother startle at hearing the other woman's voice, but she remained still, Pappy beside her.

Joshua had never liked Preacher's swamp sermons. His voice had been dramatic and powerful. People gathered away from masters and plantations had been thrilled to be away from the familiarity of their captivity, but Joshua had always thought the fancy words meant nothing. Masters were in charge. If they gave their slaves a time away to hear the word of God and feel the masters' benevolence, then good. Maybe preaching, based upon the white man's religion, would make them more accepting of who they were in their master's service. The preacher's words meant nothing, not to the master and not to the slave's condition.

Inside God's house, a cabin he'd helped build, Preacher's sermon affected him in a totally different way. Freedom changed things, he decided. It was a weight lifted out of your insides and dispelled into air.

Preacher closed his eyes and lifted his face toward the ceiling. "Let me tell you brothers and sisters," he said, "we have gotten free!" His eyes swept the room. "None of us have possessed a foot of land, or a place in the wilderness. Just so, beneath a cypress tree in a swamp away from any master's ears, we let our souls feast on Jesus, and in that feasting was the courage to do what we've done. We ran and ran and ran in the darkness of night, through storms, through hunger, through the elegance of white men's homes and churches until we reached the place we were trying to find.

"The white folks in Missouri did not want their slaves to pray, to have what they stole from the Lord for themselves, the comfort of God's word. They kept the people of God ignorant when they could have been taught to read and think on the word of God. They thought it was foolishness to let slaves pray since they saw us as below them, half animal and only partly people, but the more the masters whipped us, the more we prayed. We fell asleep praying. We worked praying. We prayed doing anything that we had to do.

"The Bible says, 'For I know that my Redeemer liveth, and that he shall stand at the latter day upon the earth; and though after my skin worms destroy this body, yet in my flesh, my black flesh," Preacher cried. "I shall see God: whom I shall see for myself, and mine eyes shall behold, and not another, though my reins be consumed within me.'

"And so, with the spirit of God filling our hearts, we embraced God's purpose for us and ran, and," Preacher continued, waving his arms, "here we are on Washington Island after braving Death's Door. We are delivered, brethren! We are delivered to New Jerusalem, our spirit home. We have run from the slavers, their horses and dogs, and we are free!"

Preacher's voice, getting softer and softer as he finished the sermon, eventually trailed into silence. Reflecting on the better land they had reached and silently remembering the joy of leaving behind their lives as slaves, none of them spoke for a long, long moment.

At last, Junebug broke the spell. "Amen," she said in a soft voice. "Amen."

Preacher lifted his head, smiled, and laughed. "We need food," he said. "Fish from the sea, green beans and peas from the garden, and each other's company on a day I dreamed would come while kneeling on a ship seeing men die as cannon roared. This is a good day!"

He bent his head in prayer again. The congregation followed his example. Then they were all up, talking and laughing, enjoying each other's company as they went outside into sunshine.

***

After the evening meal Joshua, Jamie, Esta May, and Ella wandered away from where the adults were talking. Esta May and Ella both looked different than they had during the days fleeing north. Not only were they scrubbed clean, with skin that almost shined, but they were also dressed in dresses that they had been given in Chicago. During the long run north their eyes had been ringed with a purplish, bruise-like darkness. Now their eyes were as bright and sparkling as the sun's late light on the lake's waves.

Joshua actually felt shy around them. Jamie was different. He smiled and laughed, teasing them as they had always teased each other. He seemed relaxed and uplifted by the day.

"Preacher can sure talk, can't he?" he asked. "Boy, words can't spill out of my mouth like that."

"You sure?" Esta May laughed. "Seems to me your mouth is running pretty good right now."

Ella, with her dark, sad eyes looked at Joshua. "You're awfully quiet," she said.

Joshua glanced at Esta May. "It's been a good day," he said. "Seems like we've been working or running forever. It's good to stop."

"You can say that again," Jamie agreed. He looked for Jeremiah, who was now leaving the adults and walking toward them. "Even when we were in Chicago at the picnic, I was terrified." He paused. "I'm not afraid anymore."

"There's still white people around," Ella said.

"And who knows what they're all about," Esta May added.

Jeremiah joined them and slouched with his hands on the sides of his hips. "I don't care about white people," he said. "Like Preacher said, we've arrived where we were aiming, and I, for one, am not leaving. I'm not gonna spend the rest of my life being afraid of white people."

"You wouldn't," Jamie said, rolling his eyes.

Joshua glanced at Esta May again. She was easy to look at, although he saw that Jamie noticed his glance. He frowned. "I don't want to be whipped ever again," he said. "I always took it and didn't cry or even let myself be afraid, but I don't want it to ever happen again." He paused, his face getting hard. "I won't let it happen again."

Ella touched his arm. "Washington Island's a good place," she said. "Preacher said so."

"I don't think I'm ever sure of anything," Esta May said. "Maw and Paw took us and got us to run, but I wasn't sure we should be doing that. What if we're caught? I kept asking myself. I guess I'm still asking now."

"We're free," Jamie said vehemently. "We've left that behind." He looked almost angry.

"If the whites don't like us, they can stay away," Jeremiah said.

Joshua sighed. *Will they stay away?* He looked at Esta May and then Ella. *Would what we've gained last? Could it last? Or were slaves always doomed to be afraid and un-free inside memories they couldn't leave behind?* He had to admit he didn't know the answers to his questions.

"We can hope," he said. "Preacher and Chas have been right so far." He took a breath before adding, "I've even got a father I didn't know existed." Then he looked at Jamie. "And you got an amazing uncle."

Jamie laughed. "Yeah," he said. "We're here, and we're not leaving."

Esta May smiled, too, making Joshua's stomach muscles tighten. "I trust Maw and Paw," she said. She turned and looked at God's house, the half-finished cabin, the garden, and the area cleared for the next cabin. "Come on Ella," she said. "Let's let the boys do whatever boys do."

All three boys watched as she slowly walked back to where the adults were gathered, with Ella trailing behind.

Chapter 17
The Transmutation of Desperation

As God's house rose, their desperation built
Into stripped logs and fireplace stones, they felt
Cold brutalizing all their hopes, the quilt
Of winter storms a hazard as they dealt
With summer heat that generated sweat
That drained what strength was left to them from days
Of hiding, running, flinching at the threat
That gnawed at nerves and webbed them in its maze.

But then, inside four walls, the preacher's voice
A clarion of prophecy and dreams,
Their desperation, rising from the choice
To run for freedom, seeped into the seams
Of God's house, propagating alchemy,
Transmuting fear into community.

The morning after the first Sunday service in God's house, Pappy and Willie were ready to start raising another side of the second cabin. Pappy was stretching to his full height and looking at a sky starting to scud thin, wispy clouds. Nobody had told him about his assignment for the day, so Joshua had wandered over to see if he could help the two men.

Since coming to the island, his and Pappy's relationship had been pretty good. Joshua admired how his father had tried to help others as they had run north, carrying Abbie more often than even Franklin had during the journey's rougher hours. Still, sometimes he felt constrained by the adults. He was almost fifteen and had been doing a man's work in fields and around the plantation since being forced to live away from his mother in the quarters.

He had not objected to the constant stream of orders. There was work to do. Some of the work was exciting. At first fishing had seemed like a dream come true. Whether trying to haul a big whitefish in by line or working nets once Preacher and Massie had prepared them, he felt like fishing was what could easily give his life meaning. But now it was just another chore in an endless line of chores. It was not as onerous as working cotton fields while Silver Coats roamed with his short whip, but it was extremely hard, exhausting work that went on day after day.

With every reason to get things done so that a winter like he'd never experienced wouldn't catch them unprepared, he worked willingly. His mother didn't even have to give him the *look* guaranteed to get him moving. But he chafed at always receiving and following orders. He was a man, not a child. He would do his part without Pappy telling him constantly what his part in the community's life was.

Joshua reached where Pappy and Willie were working to position a log scheduled to be the next one in place on the wall furthest from the shore. As Pappy bent to grab the log's end, he looked up at Joshua. The older man had seemed out of sorts since breakfast, scowling at the strip of cooked deer meat his wife had provided and grunting rather than talking.

"Can't you help us rather than just standing there, Joshua?" he said, his voice irritated.

Joshua had been moving toward the middle of the log where he was going to help lift it, but the tone in Pappy's voice stopped him in his tracks. The faint resentment he'd been feeling boiled up in him. He glared at Pappy. "I came over to help," he said, his voice cold.

Pappy let go of the log, letting it thunk on the ground.

"Joshua?" Pappy asked, sounding puzzled. Joshua had not raised his voice to him since the moment he had agreed to let him call him son.

Joshua wasn't aware of anything other than the look on Pappy's face. Whatever had been irritating his father had vanished. Pappy looked frightened.

Joshua took a deep breath. He realized he was breathing hard, letting emotions beneath what he had been thinking for days to come to the surface.

"I'm a man, okay?" he said. "I don't need a Silver Coats telling me what to do."

Pappy stared at him without saying anything. Willie took a step toward Joshua, thought better of whatever he was going to do, and stopped.

Chas, who had been standing by God's house talking to Preacher, trotted toward them, saying, "Jason, Preacher Bennett says you and I need to take the scow to Washington Harbor this morning and find Henry Miner. We're going to need barrels to preserve the catches we're making. We should have done that a long time ago."

Joshua looked at Chas as he closed the distance. All his angry energy drained out of him.

"We'll get the log up first," Pappy said. "Then we can go."

"Come on then," Chas said. He bent down as Joshua moved beside him. Pappy and Willie grabbed the log's ends, and they all four lifted and carried it around the cabin's south corner to the back and hoisted it higher than Joshua's head, fitting it on top of the last log they'd put up.

When the log was in place Joshua shook his head, looking at his father. "I'm sorry," he mumbled.

Pappy's hand touched Joshua's shoulder. He smiled. "I'm sorrier," he said. "I got to watch myself. It's just that …."

"We've got to move," Chas said, looking steadily at Joshua. "If Mr. Miner's around this won't take long, but if he's not, well, that's another story. He's the only cooper on the island."

Willie came and put his arm around Joshua. "You and Jamie need time to your selves," he said. "Civilized life is beginning to get at both of you."

Joshua looked into Willie's dark eyes. They were as kind as they had always been. "I don't mind working," he said.

"I know," Willie answered.

Joshua watched as Chas crawled to the scow's mast. Pappy pushed the boat deeper into the water. "He's a good father," Joshua told himself. "Just, like every other adult, a little too bossy."

***

Joshua and Jamie discovered the whites after they had been sent out berry picking by Joshua's mother. Their parents had decided that the two oldest boys needed time alone. Berry picking did have a delightful sense to it. They moved from one likely clump of bushes to another through brush and trees, tasting blackberries as they filled their buckets, not really paying attention to where they were going, but following the lure of bushes that promised ripe berries just a little away from where they were.

They had both been out on the lake fishing and had seen steam ships sailing toward Washington Harbor, Detroit Harbor, and Irish Village, the places where a lot of ships stopped for supplies since they were, according to Chas, the best harbors available short of Green Bay at the Fox River's mouth. They also knew that Chas and Pappy's contact with the island's white settlers at Irish Village had gone well, making it seem like they could stay where they were building their cabins. He and Pappy had twice visited Henry Miner to collect and bring back barrels so they could preserve the fish they caught. Chas and Preacher had said they'd need a lot more barrels if they were going to succeed as a fisher community.

Carrying the small wooden buckets full of blackberries, they stumbled onto a trail that had obviously been used by wagons. Nervous, they looked around and went back into the woods just in time to hear voices coming down the road from the north. They didn't show themselves, not even after they had figured out the voices belonged to four young white people who appeared to range from Abbie to Jeremiah's ages. They watched silently as the whites came even to where they were hiding and continued south.

Even after the trail turned and the four young people were out of sight, neither Joshua nor Jamie moved. Joshua felt strange and uncomfortable seeing the children. In camp they seemed free of the outside world. They sometimes spotted a steam ship while casting nets or using lines to fish, but they'd never been close enough to see the ship's white people as anything more than moving figures on the deck. Now the outside world was closer than before. Joshua wasn't sure how far they'd wandered from West Harbor. They had gone north away from the lakeshore and inland, but picking berries had been a wonderful way to pass time. They knew they should have been working, but for the first time in a long time, at least since the days at the Campbell's place, they had felt released from constant responsibility.

At last Jamie shrugged. "That was scary," he said.

Joshua didn't know why Jamie thought that seeing white people they knew were living on the island not far from them was scary. He had not been scared, not exactly, but seeing the four children made him feel uneasy. Mr. Miner coming into their camp was one thing. Men traveled the wilderness. Chas had spent years wandering based on the little he said about himself. But the encounter reminded him that there were entire white families here.

Without saying anything, he turned from the wagon track and followed Jamie. He had spent time with white people who were not masters or the servants of masters. Mr. Jemmie and his son and the Campbells had not treated any of them badly even though they were white, but white people made him nervous. They couldn't understand who he and the other fugitives, or even who Preacher and Chas, were. They had a position that made the world more comfortable to them than it was to him, and the truth was that he resented it.

At the Campbell's he had not realized he had resented the way they were comfortable around him. The experience had been too new for him to understand his feelings. He had just felt uncomfortable. But now, watching four white children on the wagon trail, he felt discomfort and a distrust he suspected he would never leave behind.

He didn't try to catch Jamie as they walked toward the lakeshore so they could walk to the cabins. The second cabin was coming along fast; Pappy and Willie, under Preacher's tutelage, were becoming better builders. Harrison and Junebug had piled finished boards under the God's house eaves, too. Cedar logs that were to be the third cabin's foundation had even been put into place. It wouldn't be finished before winter, Chas kept reminding them of that, but they were slowly becoming, in his mother's words, increasingly confident that the winter would see them with roofs over their heads.

Joshua put his frustrations with his place in West Harbor aside. When Chas and Pappy came back with barrels, Joshua, after listening to his mother tell him he was not acting like the man she'd raised, had made a point of helping unload and store them behind God's house. Pappy had been relieved. Joshua could see it in his face, which smiled broadly when Joshua had waded out to catch the rope Pappy had thrown at him.

Getting away from West Harbor berry picking had helped, too. He needed time away. He suspected Jamie did, too, even though Jamie had not once shown either Joshua or anybody else he was getting frustrated. Growing up was hard, Joshua decided. But it was not harder than being a slave. Having achieved freedom was important even if that freedom was circumscribed by expectations of his family and others.

***

They had already gathered for Preacher's Sunday sermon when the door unexpectedly opened. Joshua jumped involuntarily as he jerked around to see what was happening behind him. What he saw was nothing short of amazing. Not only was Henry Miner standing there, but his wife and son, who looked to be about Jeremiah's age, were with him. The three of them looked uncomfortable coming into a prayer meeting just getting underway, but Mr. Miner looked determined.

Preacher did not hesitate. He cocked his head like an inquisitive bird, then, seeing who was standing in the doorway, opened his arms.

"Welcome," he boomed in his big voice. "We're just getting ready to start our Sunday meeting."

Mr. Miner seemed to stand taller. "We're here to hear your sermon," he declared, his voice steady and strong, although much softer than Preacher's voice. "There's not much religion on Washington Island yet. You are a bona fide preacher. My wife and I believe that Jesse here," he put his arm around the short boy at his side, "could use some edification from the Lord's word, especially since his grandfather was a minister to Stockbridge Indians before he died."

Preacher looked at the people on the benches. "Let's make room for our friends," he said.

To Joshua's surprise his mother motioned for him and Pappy to scoot over so that the Miners could sit with them. Joshua looked carefully at the boy. He was about Jeremiah's height, stocky, and looked like he could handle himself in a fight. Joshua could tell he was carefully controlling his face, making sure nobody could tell what he was thinking. He was dressed in homespun clothes that hung loosely on his body. His eyes were restless, darting around the room as he sat beside his mother, a plain-looking, chunky woman with dark eyes who looked nervous.

"Did the white boy want to join black people listening to a black preacher?" Joshua thought. "Or is he here because his father wants him here?" As Jesse slid in beside him, Joshua could hardly believe what was happening. He could sort of understand his mother's gesture toward the white people. She had served white people all her life and was used to them. She probably didn't think it unusual that white people might come to a black church. *But what does it mean? Are we going to be accepted as settlers on the island? Just another community of islanders?*

As Preacher started his sermon about how sin is in every man, woman, and child and how important the act of being aware of what you are thinking and doing was in light of that truth, Joshua's eyes met Jesse's eyes. The white boy didn't look away, but seemed curious.

Mrs. Miner sat by Jesse, staring steadily at Preacher, acting as if she was listening to what he was saying. One of the things that Joshua noticed was that she was better dressed than his mother and the other black women. The Miners had to have come to West Harbor through the woods, probably from the wagon track Joshua and Jamie had accidently found, but she hadn't torn her clothes even though they were too good for traipsing through wilderness.

Mr. Miner nodded every time he thought Preacher made a good point.

After the sermon was done, everybody went outside. Surprises continued when Pappy got off the bench and went over to Mr. Miner and shook his hand, smiling.

"We appreciate your barrels," he said. "We appreciate you were willing to sell them to us when you had other customers."

Chas had come from the back of God's house where he always sat with his back against the lakeside wall. He, too, was smiling. "Henry," he said in greeting.

"Chas, thank you for inviting us," Mr. Miner said. "Like you and Jason said, Tom Bennett is quite a preacher."

"He's been good for us," Joshua's mother spoke up, standing beside Pappy. "Without him and Chas, we would have never made it here."

Mrs. Miner didn't say anything, but motioned to her son. Jamie, Jeremiah, Esta May, and Ella had drifted toward where Jesse and Joshua were standing beside their parents.

"You want to go outside?" Jeremiah asked the white boy.

"Not everybody's welcoming you, I'm afraid," Mr. Miner was telling Chas. "But you know that. Even so, there are abolitionists on the island. The Danes are especially strong. I think you'll be okay here."

Jesse hesitated, but nodded. Joshua looked at his mother, who'd been watching them.

"I think it's okay," she told Joshua. She paused. "Maybe this will be okay."

Jeremiah tugged at Joshua's arm. Jamie and Jesse were already halfway out the door, with Esta May and Ella following.

Preacher joined the Miners, Joshua's parents, and Chas. The rest of the community milled about, chatting and laughing.

"It's good to find Godly folk here," Preacher exclaimed. "I cannot tell you how that warms my heart."

Reluctantly, Joshua let Jeremiah pull him toward Jamie, Jesse, and the girls. What the adults were talking about was important. What he was getting out of the conversation was that there was opposition to their being on the island, but that some people, including the Miners, approved.

When he caught up with his friends, Jesse was laughing at something Jamie had said. Esta May and Ella were hanging back, unsure of how to handle themselves around the white islander. Jeremiah, with his usual boisterousness, let go of Joshua and hurtled himself toward Jamie and Jesse.

"What's going on?" he demanded. "What's so funny?"

Joshua stopped, looked at the lake, and then to where Preacher, the Miners, Chas, and his parents were. The arrival of the Miners had been peculiar. West Harbor would have to adjust to the fact that a white family had come to their Sunday meeting for a good, rather than a bad, reason.

Chapter 18
Words' Consequence

Words ought to be just words, but when they burn
From eyes engendered by a seething soul,
Words take on flesh, create a bulging churn
That moves alive into a spreading scroll
Of lives connected to the lives that roll
Into the turbulence of all humanity.

Upon a dock a white man's cold control
Of who he is flares out his bastardly
Crazed prejudice into audacity
That stands inside his threats and hunts to find
The pathways used to flee the memory
Of chains that once bound flesh and made them blind
To hope that makes a human, human, fashions
The consequences born of human passions.

Preacher decided to send Joshua, Jamie, and Esta May to Washington Harbor with Pappy and Chas. Nights had been getting increasingly cold and they were now sleeping in one of the two finished cabins. Everyone felt crowded, but the third cabin was taking shape, although they were being forced to go further from the shore to get the right sized tree trunks. Splashed into pines, cedar, birch with yellow leaves, and other forest trees, maples were fiery with reds, oranges, and yellows, making the island's light magical.

Mary and Massie were fixing breakfast in the area built up by Franklin and Zelda. They had stacked relatively flat stones into a circular shape and chinked the space between them to form a square cooking platform that made it simple to put the pan on the grate Preacher had made using wire brought on the scow from Chicago.

Unlike most mornings, everyone was moving slower than normal, letting the early sun shouldering over the island's eastern horizon take the chill off before work started.

As Mary and Massie bent down to take the cast iron skillet containing the salmon that had been fried for breakfast, Massie sighed. "I sure miss having chickens and eggs," she said. She looked at Preacher. "Do you think we'll ever be able to get chickens?"

Mary chuckled. "Fish is okay," she said. "It's good, especially here, but I could still like fried-up morning eggs."

Preacher looked out at the lake. A small wind rustled through the trees, but the waves looked to be between two and three feet high, white caps appearing and disappearing in a dance on water.

"I don't know about chickens, but we do need supplies," he said. "Thank goodness the fishing is giving us something worth trading."

Preacher looked at Joshua and then Chas. "I think Chas, Jason, Joshua, Jamie, and Esta May ought to go into Washington Harbor and Irish Village today. We can take the barrels of fish and sell them and pick up flour for biscuits. And we need more salt." He paused. "Maybe we'll be lucky and there'll be a schooner in so we can get more for the fish. The island people need to get used to seeing more of us. I'm pretty sure Henry Miner has even let the Door County people know we're here."

Joshua felt his blood racing at the prospect of sailing over to Washington Harbor. His mother and Massie, however, looked unhappy.

"Is that safe?" Joshua's mother said. She glanced at Beulah who appeared panicked as she looked at her oldest daughter. "I mean, I know Chas and Jason have been okay dealing with Mr. Miner, but how will the rest of them react to seeing our children?"

Preacher looked steadily at Beulah, whose hands were at her throat as she looked at Bill and then at Esta May. Bill, as usual, let his wife do the talking.

"It'll be okay," Chas said with a smile. "Jason's big enough to keep troublemakers away."

Massie stood up, eyes blazing. "Chas," she said. "if you are implying there are troublemakers on this island, I want to know why Jamie is going among them. Especially with Esta May tagging along. She's a young woman."

Chas held up his hands. "Whoa," he said. "I'm just joking. Really, I've been all over the island. It'll be fine."

Esta May, Jamie, and Joshua clustered together. Jeremiah and Ella were glaring fiercely at the three of them. Joshua could tell they were thinking: *why them and not us?* Jeremiah especially looked frustrated. Ella had a shrewd, intelligent look in her eyes.

Bill rose from where he had been sitting on one of the logs he'd brought in the day before for the third cabin. "We can't hide forever," he said. "If Chas and Jason are going, Franklin and I have logs to haul in." He pointed at the frying fish. "I'd appreciate a meal before I get to work."

"Bill?" Beulah said.

"Esta May will be okay," he said. "They'll be careful." He was looking at Chas.

The building tension dissipated. Joshua smiled at Esta May. She grinned in return and took hold of Jamie and Joshua's arms. "They're going to let us go," she whispered.

***

The wind picked up before they set sail. The three boys had been out on large waves with spray blowing in their faces, but Joshua was never easy about the bigger waves. Jeremiah, on the other hand, gloried in them.

When, while fishing, the waves got high and the scow tipped up to crest one and slide into the trough, Joshua's usual exhilaration at being on the water disappeared. He didn't panic, none of them did, but his stomach roiled. He felt nervous until they turned the scow at day's end toward shore and the stability of land.

The trip from West Harbor to Washington Harbor and Irish Village did not take long even though the waves were rough, slapping hard against the scow's hull and sending streams of spray into the air. When the harbor and village came into sight Joshua became nervous. Esta May was sitting beside Chas as he steered the scow toward the harbor, which had rowboats and small fishing vessels, but no schooner. Glancing back at her, Joshua could see she was at least as, if not more, nervous than he was. Jamie was calmer, kneeling in the prow, looking steadily at the cabins built back from the shore.

The most interesting thing Joshua could see were large wooden shuttles being used to repair a score of fishing nets along the beach. At West Harbor they were always repairing ripped or tangled nets. Knots holding the mesh together untied, or lines frayed as they brought either big or smaller fish over the scow's side. Harrison had built a rough shuttle, using a big oak tree's branches to help anchor rough-hewn pine arms he and Junebug had carved from cedar saplings. Preacher and Chas had both helped with the design. It was still only partially functional. It got nets off the ground and stretched, but those fixing the knots had to stand in front and work at retying lifting their arms in the air. It was exhausting work.

Chas had taught them all how to tie the knots to repair nets. He knew an endless number of knots and the name and uses of each one. Preacher had the same knowledge, but spent more time working on cabins and preparing Sunday sermons than he did teaching knot tying.

Most of them struggled to learn the technique of repairing the nets with wooden needles and bobbins and twine brought from Chicago. Joshua's mother, with her long years as a seamstress in the big plantation house, was the quickest to master the knot-tying and weaving into small

160

corks used at critical points to give the net strength. Zelda, however, liked the task the best. She could not spend long spans of time at the nets since her back was beginning to bother her, but she sang spirituals in her high, sweet voice, much to Preacher's delight, while she stood by the oak tree with hands and fingers on the rough net twine.

Compared to the West Harbor shuttle, the shuttles at Irish Village were incredibly sophisticated. Ends stuck up over nets like small spires pointed at clouds. The nets themselves, stretched on shuttles, covered the beach by the wooden docks.

No one came to the docks as Chas guided the scow to wooden planks extended into the water. Jamie jumped out and tied the rope, the way Chas had taught them, to the pier. Pappy followed as Joshua and Esta May scrambled to climb onto the dock. Chas, who had already collapsed the sail, was last to leave the scow.

When they walked down the dock toward the two buildings where lumber, fish, and other goods could easily be loaded onto incoming schooners, Jason dropped back, holding Jamie's arm, and let Chas go in front. He seemed tense even though he had been to Washington Harbor before. Chas was nonchalant, as if what they were doing was as natural as breathing.

As they approached the small warehouse, two men, one middle-aged and the other elderly, came out of the building. The middle-aged man had a suspicious look on his face. He looked rough. Unshaven, with black bristles covering his broad cheeks, his dark eyes narrowed the moment he saw them. He wasn't as big as Pappy, but he was taller and stockier than Chas.

"Chas," the older man, who had a brisk, businesslike manner, but looked as if he was maybe the oldest man Joshua had ever seen, said.

Chas held out his hand. The older man grasped and dropped it quickly. Chas did not look at the other white man. He concentrated on the white-haired man smiling at them. "Mr. Craw," Chas said.

"You need supplies?" Mr. Craw asked. He seemed too old to be the one minding the harbor's business.

"We've got some fish to sell," Chas said. "We need flour. The women are wanting corn flour and salt. The fishing's been good."

Mr. Craw laughed. "The fishing's always good around here," he said. "Thank the good Lord. Otherwise none of us would be here."

"I heard there were negras on the island," the middle-aged man growled, his voice unfriendly and low. He looked at Mr. Craw. "You dealing with them?"

Mr. Craw looked directly into the other man's eyes. "The Danes would run me out if I didn't," he replied mildly. "The Danes don't hold with slavery or treating people different from them badly. West Harbor business is as welcome as yours, Westbrook."

Westbrook looked disgusted. He glared at Pappy, his dark eyes angry. Then he looked at the three young people. His gaze moved slowly and directly over each of them the way Master Bulrush's eyes had when he was evaluating what kind of punishment he was going to direct Silver Coats to mete out. Joshua found himself staring back defiantly at the white man. Pappy didn't lower his gaze, but he didn't challenge the white man directly, either.

"Brats, too," Westbrook finally said.

Mr. Craw smiled at Chas. "Never mind him," he said cheerfully. "Come on in. We'll get your business done." He looked at Esta May. "Who knows? I might even have a piece of candy around here somewhere for these young 'uns."

Esta May was smiling. Candy, other than sugar cane, was a rare, rare treat even on the plantation. Joshua couldn't believe that the white man would give them a piece of candy.

Westbrook shook his head. "Suit yourself," he growled and walked away toward the Irish Village cabins.

"I'll unload our fish," Pappy said, nodding at Joshua and Jamie to follow him.

"Good," Chas said. He motioned that Esta May should go with him to the warehouse.

The barrels were heavy with salt, fish, and brine. Lifting them out of the scow onto the dock took effort. Clouds were building, too, and a stronger wind was kicking waves coming into the harbor even higher.

"I didn't like that Westbrook," Joshua told his father as Pappy lifted a barrel and placed it on the dock. Joshua and Jamie pulled it from the dock's edge and made space enough for the next barrel.

"Me, neither," Jamie agreed. He shuddered involuntarily.

"We haven't seen him the other times Chas and I were here," Pappy said. "This is the first time I've felt unwelcome. Mr. Craw is always friendly. The other men have been that way, too." He wiped his brow even though the wind was stiff enough to make it seem cooler than it was. "Haven't seen any of the women or children, though," he continued. "Although Chas assures me they're here. They seem to stick inside the houses."

A shriek from the cabins caused all three of them to look up. Two boys, maybe ten years old, came running from the cabins toward the net shuttles where they proceeded to try to hide from each other. Pappy laughed.

"Sure enough," he said, "I say something, and there's the proof I was denying." He turned and wrestled another barrel over the scow's bottom hull. Joshua and Jamie watched the two boys, who were quickly joined by three more boys who ran out of different cabins.

When they finished unloading, Chas and Esta May came out of the warehouse with a low cart on wheels. "We can load the barrels on here and get flour and salt," Chas said. He seemed unperturbed by Westbrook.

Esta May was smiling brightly. She held up a handful of small candy sticks in her hands. As Chas dragged the cart toward them, Joshua and Jamie hurried over to Esta May. At the cabins, three women had come outdoors and were looking at them.

"I told him about Abbie and Ertha and the others," Esta May said. "He gave us all one apiece."

"Looks like there are plenty of families here," Jamie remarked as Joshua and Esta May looked toward where there was a sudden explosion of screaming and laughter.

"I wonder why Pappy said he hadn't seen them when he and Chas were here before?" Joshua asked.

"Candy," Esta May exclaimed impatiently, handing each of them a slender red stick.

"Did he just give that to you?" Jamie asked. "Or did Chas pay for it?"

"Preacher gave Chas some money. I saw him," Joshua said.

"He gave it to me free as anything," Esta May said.

"We'd better help," Joshua said, looking back at where Chas and Pappy were lifting barrels off the cart.

Jamie nodded. The three of them, sucking on sweet candy, went to pitch in. When they got to the cart, though, Chas shook his head.

"Enjoy yourselves," he said. "Your father's as strong as two oxen, Joshua. With him, I don't need help."

Esta May giggled, grabbed Joshua's and Jamie's arms, and pulled them away from the men. They sat on the dock, legs dangling above the water, watching the clouds moving over their heads.

By the time the supplies were loaded, rain had begun to whip through winds that had Washington Harbor crazy with white-topped waves. They secured the flour under the scow's tarps. Chas sat at the tiller, looking out at the wild lake. At last he looked at Pappy, rain running down his face.

"What do you think, Jason?" he asked. "I didn't expect the storm to come up this fast."

Pappy, soaked, glanced at Joshua and then back at Chas. "We have anywhere we can stay here?"

Chas hesitated. "Maybe the Miners," he said. He paused. "If Henry is home. Martha Lee might get nervous if he isn't home."

"What's the chance he'll be there?" Pappy asked.

Chas shook his head. "The lake's dangerous," he said. "But this is about the time Henry's off on his mail run."

"Do we have a choice?" Pappy said.

Chas looked nervously at the lake and then at Esta May. Preacher had made him take her along even though he had felt uneasy about it. He knew Joshua and Jamie were used to the scow and lake. But the girl? They had all faced bad weather often enough, including Esta May. But Death's Door was called Death's Door for a reason. A lot of ships had sunk beneath the waves.

"I could walk the young ones to West Harbor," he said at last. "You'd have to stay with the scow. With Westbrook about, we can't leave it alone. He ought to be doing his law-keeping where he's needed. Why the Danes, Irish, and others think so highly of him puzzles me."

Lightning flashes, dancing out of heavy clouds, had, when they were fishing, driven them off the lake even right out of West Harbor. A strong gust lifted the scow and dropped it as noise from thunder and waves striking the dock intensified.

"I'll stay here," Pappy said. He looked at Joshua. "Keep Joshua safe."

"We'll be okay," Jamie objected.

"Get under the tarp," Chas said, clambering out of the scow. "This storm could last a while. Come on," he told young people.

Jamie hesitated, but Esta May followed Chas immediately. Then Joshua and Jamie joined them on the dock as rain pelted down.

"What a day Preacher chose to send us to Washington Harbor," Chas grumbled. He said to Pappy, "I'll be back before morning." Pappy nodded. Chas turned and led the way toward Irish Village.

Walking through the village in broad daylight in the rain was unnerving. Joshua thought about the night they had crossed the bridge over a flood as a storm had raged. That storm had hidden them from sleeping white people. As they walked between the cabins, he saw women looking out windows as they quickly passed by, soaked from the downpour.

Not long after they passed the second to last row of cabins, Chas turned aside and went to one of the larger structures and knocked. Joshua was surprised when Jesse came to the door. "Jesse," Chas said. "Is your father home?"

Jesse looked at them, then back as his mother came up behind him. "Nope," he said. "He's gone to Ephraim."

Chas sighed. He turned and looked at the three sodden young people with him. "Okay," he said. "Thanks."

"Mr. Woodruff," Mrs. Miner said, her narrow, pinched-looking face grimacing slightly.

"Ma'am."

"You can't go out in this. You can stay in the post office shed," Mrs.

Miner said. She pointed at the small structure attached to the cabin. "It's not locked. Those children are wet enough."

Chas looked at Esta May and Jamie, then to the dock.

"We're Christians," Mrs. Miner said, "just like your people."

"Thank you," Chas said. "Okay. You three go with Jesse. I'll get Jason. We can watch the scow good enough from here."

Jesse smiled at the three of them. "Come on," he said, shrugging on the slicker he used when he was out on the boat with his father. "I'm glad you're here."

Joshua was reminded how they'd been greeted by Timothy Campbell, his serious eyes examining them quietly. Both Jesse and Timothy seemed to have the same attitude toward black people. Jesse opened the door to the post office and led them inside. It was a small room, neat, but plain.

Jesse said, "It's at least dry. Maw doesn't want men in the house with Paw gone."

None of them were dressed as appropriately as Jesse was for the weather. Joshua wondered how they were going to make it through winter if the cold and snow were as bad as Chas and Preacher had described.

"This is nice of you and your Maw," Elsa May said. "Thank you."

Jesse grinned. "You can bet Maw'll have a good breakfast in the morning," he said. "She appreciates the picnics you've had when we came to church. I like going to your church." He nodded and went back out into the storm.

***

The next morning the heavy clouds had still not dissipated, but the strong wind gusts and rain had stopped. After breakfast, Chas checked the scow.

"Let's go home," he said. He looked at Pappy. "I'm pretty sure some mothers are worrying."

"Mary'll be okay," Pappy said. "She'll keep the others calm."

Sitting around a white family's kitchen table eating breakfast had, as always, made Joshua uncomfortable, but Mrs. Miner had sent Jesse to the post office just before dawn. In her kitchen, she moved constantly, making coffee, eggs, hot jerky, and frying sourdough bread. Esta May kept getting up and helping Mrs. Miner move dishes on and off the big wooden table.

Used to fish or venison for breakfast, her guests found the meal unbelievably delicious. "The women all want chickens," Pappy said, sighing as they finished. "We can't afford any, but, man, I can see what's in their heads. That was beyond wonderful, Mrs. Miner."

Mrs. Miner looked at Jesse, who was sitting between Joshua and Jamie. "There's chicks out in the coop," Mrs. Miner told him. "Why don't you get five of them and put them in a box and give them to Esta May for helping me," she said.

"That's not what I meant," Pappy hurried to say. "I mean ...."

"It's okay," Mrs. Miner said. "I know you weren't asking for chicks." She motioned to Jesse who had stopped when Pappy protested. "Go on," she said. "It'll be a while before they can lay. And you're gonna have to get a rooster. There aren't any in this batch. You can pay me later when you have money."

Pappy and Chas both stood. Chas held out his hand. "Thank you," he told her. "You and Mr. Miner have been godsends."

Mrs. Miner smiled for the first time since Joshua'd met her. The severe lines of her face lightened, and she looked like a different woman.

Moments after Jesse had handed the small, cheeping wooden box to Esta May, they walked through the cabins again. People looked through windows as before, but didn't come outside, which left Joshua with a deadened feeling, especially after being welcomed by the Miners.

The sail back to West Harbor gave them a different feeling, however. The scow's sail wouldn't fill while they were in the harbor, so they had to resort to rowing. Then, as they tacked toward Pilot Island, a breeze came up. The sail filled out, white against the lake's greenish cast.

As Joshua looked at the island that was now his home and felt movement inside the box he had on his lap, he felt himself disappearing from the boat. He felt like the birds thick on the water, a part of lake and land, a weaving with maple fire contrasted with the shore's dark pine green, a net woven from strands that could not be seen but had become a part of who he was.

Perhaps the people looking out windows as they passed through Irish Village were not glad to see them. Perhaps no escaped slave could ever be at peace. But for that moment, watching the shore as a score of pelicans flew between them and land in long lines with flashing white wings, Joshua felt like he belonged where he was, that the island had embraced their small community.

Chapter 19
Religion as Whiteness

They fought religion as a whiteness, probed
To find a way inside their lives to let
The genius centered by His love, light robed
With justice, free slaves from the numbing threat
Dredged from the God of thunder who had touched
The white race with superiority and rights
That forged the chains that bound free spirits clutched
With anguish felt through years of days and nights.

The abolitionists reached out and tried
To build invisible, faint trails the god
Of whiteness couldn't find since he denied
The wrongs done in his name and lived a fraud
That failed to comprehend that souls of men
Could see his Christianity as sin.

The dream was so ridiculous it should have dissipated into mist the minute Joshua woke, but it stuck with him and left him feeling vaguely unsettled. The unfinished cabin where his and Jamie's family were sleeping was cold, so he pulled the gray blankets over his head. In the filtered light, he could see Silver Coats face dissolving into the face of the rough-looking white man he and the others had met at the dock outside of Mr. Craw's warehouse, the Overseer's black scowl fading into Westbrook's, the mean eyes slowly transfiguring into the white man's affronted eyes.

The dream made him shiver. Silver Coats was no white man. He could not transform himself into a white man like Westbrook—although Joshua suspected that the only time the Overseer thought of himself as black was when he had to be subservient around the plantation's white people.

He didn't know if Westbrook had spent time around slaves, or, for that matter, knew any black people. As far as Joshua knew there was not a single white man that owned a single slave on the island. If Chas was to be believed most islanders opposed slavery. A few were abolitionists.

Joshua forced himself to stop thinking about the dream, uncovered his head, and got out from the warmth he'd managed to generate.

They were all sleeping under cabin roofs now. Even Chas had given up his bed beneath the largest cedar just back from the beach. The cabin Joshua and Jamie's family were staying in still needed quite a bit of work. They couldn't cook in the fireplace yet, and even the walls needed final chinking and smoothing. He could still see the outside through some of the logs close to the fireplace.

Harrison had made tables and benches for the three cabins. He'd spent days sanding tabletops until they were as smooth as he could possibly make them. They were sleeping on cabin floors, except for Preacher, but Preacher was promising they would have beds above the cold floor before winter began in earnest. Harrison and Junebug, again, were expected to deliver the bed frames.

Cold floorboards, recently put down, made him flinch. He shivered involuntarily. He sat and put on the shoes he'd been given in Chicago. Hard use had started to wear through leather. There were no holes in the soles yet, but the sides were wearing.

When he got to the door, ready to walk to the outhouses, he was not prepared for what greeted him: the first snow.

Joshua groaned at the sight of the thin white covering on the ground and the feel of the bite of outside cold. Frost had been on the ground every morning for a week, but the snow seemed ominous. It seemed to him that winter should still be a long way off.

He knew the truth was that they were nowhere close to being ready for winter. Chas and Preacher's talk about what they would be facing as northern weather slammed the island had always seemed to be far off in the future. Now, on a morning crystal bright with sun, winter had decided to come before they were ready.

They had been working non-stop, fishing, building, planting, gathering, repairing, and making an endless number of things since they had crossed Death's Door in the scow. Bill and Harrison had even constructed a rough shack for the small flock of chickens secured from Mrs. Miner. Their accomplishments were all around them in barrels of fish, cabins, outhouses, and even piles of wood Preacher had driven Joshua, Jamie, and Jeremiah to stack up in preparation for cold weather. The women, led by Mary, had been making leather out of the deer hides, chewing the hide to make it soft and pliable so that it would be suitable for sewing into winter clothes.

But the only clothes they had were the ones from Chicago. Not only had those seen hard wear, but they felt thinner every time wind blew off the lake. Even the jackets given to them in Chicago were too thin for Wisconsin winter weather.

As he stood in the doorway his mother walked over and put her hand on his shoulder. He glanced at her as she looked at the snow.

"We're not in Missouri," she said at last. She turned from the door and back to where everyone else was stirring, getting dressed and ready for the day.

By noon the skiff of snow had melted, but, surprisingly, nobody went out in the scow to fish. The only days they hadn't had at least four people on the water that Joshua could remember were Sundays. Preacher wouldn't let them fish then, although work on cabins or tables or some other task went on, only in a slightly more relaxed fashion. Both Chas and Preacher kept insisting they keep moving forward, preparing for the coming of winter. There was no time to waste, they kept saying. The escaped slaves, used to endless work, did not question what they were told, but kept working as hard and fast as they knew how.

Not long after a breakfast of trout cooked on an outdoor fire, Harrison and Pappy went off into the woods. The snow around the camp had turned to mud, although big patches of white lingered under some of the trees and brush.

"We've got to have better coats," Harrison explained. "Deer hides are good, but there're rabbits, fox, and other animals on the island. Maybe even beaver. We can make good, warm clothes out of what we catch in a trap line."

Chas had taken his rifle and Harrison took the three traps he'd gotten from Mr. Craw during Chas's last trip.

Preacher nodded. "That's good," he said. Then he put Joshua, Jamie, and Jeremiah to splitting more wood, taking turns with the splitting axes.

Later, after Jamie and Jeremiah had used the two man saw to make wood chunks appropriate for splitting, the three of them went to the spit of land where they had built a fire that first night on the island. They had barely sat with their backs against trees when Esta May, her sisters, and Abbie joined them. Abbie and Ertha, in spite of the hardships they'd faced during the long escape, were growing. Abbie hardly looked like the big-eyed little girl who had held desperately to her parents beneath the big cypress tree when they had first started running.

"I had a bad dream last night," Joshua told Jamie after the young people had gathered, listening to the endless wash of shore waves.

Jamie grunted.

For a minute Joshua didn't say anything else, since he sensed everybody was listening to him. "I dreamed that Silver Coats with his whip and grin turned into that rough-looking white man we saw in Washington Harbor," he said in response to their continued attention. "I woke up sweating even though it was cold."

"A mean black man turning into a white man," Jeremiah said, a sneer in his voice. "That doesn't make any sense."

Jamie looked at his brother. "It was the white man's eyes," he said. "They were brown, but had the same look as the Overseer's eyes when he was trying to catch you up so he could punish you."

Esta May sighed. "He made me nervous," she said. "I didn't like the way he ... seemed."

"We're okay, aren't we?" Eunice asked nervously. "I mean, we're free here, aren't we? The way Preacher says?"

"Of course we are," Jeremiah said a little too loudly. "Chas and Preacher wouldn't have brought us here if we weren't."

"I'm not afraid," Abbie spoke up.

"I'm not either," Ertha said, echoing Abbie, her best friend.

"Maybe we should have kept going to Canada," Jamie said after an uncomfortable silence. "How do we know a place you get to over Death's Door is all right?"

"It has to be all right," Jeremiah responded quickly. "I don't want to run anymore."

"I like it here," Esta May volunteered.

Joshua looked at the lake. The moon was scudding in and out of black, almost invisible clouds. Touches of moonlight glanced off the tops of waves; the next minute clouds obscured the light and the water was dark. He was sensitive to the smell of water and vegetation on the shore. *Are we safe? Have we found freedom?* He felt like they had, but he also felt as if he could feel Silver Coats' and Westbrook's eyes watching them in the dark.

***

It was Sunday, and they were getting ready for worship. Joshua's mother and Massie were cooking outside since the cabin's fireplace was still not finished, but the others were fixing breakfast in their cabins. Jeremiah was hanging around the path through the woods where the Miners came to go to church on the Sundays they showed up. His eyes were on the ground, but he suddenly straightened up, looking startled. He hurried over to the campfire.

"There's more than just the Miners," he said, trying to whisper, but making his voice so that the whole community could hear it. "There's two other men."

Pappy and Willie got to their feet, tense. They had gotten used to the Miners, but didn't know who the two additional men might be. New visitors might and might not be good news.

Henry Miner led the way into the clearing, followed by two other white men, both wearing long coats and white hats. Jesse and his mother were walking behind the men. Pappy closed his eyes, opened them, and then walked toward the group approaching them.

Mr. Miner held out his hand to Pappy as he approached them. "Jason," he said. "I want to introduce you to Captain Stewart of the Steamer Michigan and his mate. They wanted to come listen to Tom Bennett preach, and I wanted you all to know them. They're abolitionists and have helped slaves reach Canada."

Willie had walked up behind Jason. "Don't you think we're safe on the island?" he asked, his voice troubled.

Mr. Miner looked at him in silence for a minute. The two men in their uniforms were shaking Pappy's hand. At last, as Captain Stewart reached out for Willie's hand, he shook his head. "Safe enough, I think," he said. "For now for sure."

After Preacher's sermon, which took as its Biblical text the golden rule from Matthew 7 verse 12: "Therefore all things whatsoever ye would that men should do to you: do ye even so to them: for this is the law and the prophets," the white men, Preacher, Chas, Pappy, and Harrison stayed in God's house to talk. Bill and Franklin went outside with their wives and children. Martha walked out with Joshua's mother and Massie and went over to the campfire Junebug had built to take off the morning's chill.

The young people wandered away from the adults to the lakeshore. Joshua had come to like Jesse. He had an air of mischievousness about him that made him similar to Jeremiah, whose tongue was always a little too bold. Jesse was quieter than Jeremiah, but his fearlessness was clear by the way he interacted with them. He frequently seemed to be holding back laughter. There was easiness in his relationship with them, especially with Joshua, Jamie, and Esta May, that made them like him even if he was white. He didn't show the condescending attitude they expected to find woven into most white people's skins.

Jamie picked up a flat stone and skimmed it over the harbor's water as soon as they reached the shore. Jesse, not to let his friend beat him at that game, picked up a stone and tossed it. A moment later, even Eunice had tried her hand at skipping a stone, although the stone she'd thrown was round instead of flat and sank immediately.

When Esta May sat in the grass away from the beach, they stopped skipping stones and sprawled along the line of growth outlining the deepest incursion of water into land. The early morning chill was mostly gone. The air felt fresh and calm; the day seemed perfect.

Joshua, however, kept thinking about Mr. Miner's response when Willie had asked if they were safe on the island. There had been subtlety in the way the man had answered the question, as if he thought they were safe on the island for the moment, but foresaw a time when they might not be.

Joshua wanted to feel secure in the freedom they'd found forever. Not only was the island a beautiful place, much more beautiful than the Bulrush plantation, but part of its beauty was that he felt as if Death's Door protected them from the slavers and hardness of the life they'd lived. Trees, brush, endless lake birds, and even animals entwined with the sense of freedom and rightness he felt deep inside. He wanted the life they were making, the fishing, building, net repairing, trips to Washington Harbor in the scow, all of it.

Without realizing what he was doing, he was staring at Jesse, who had at first had not paid attention, but then noticed and stared back.

At last Joshua shook his head. "Your father said he thought we're safe on the island for now," he told Jesse. "But," he paused, trying to think about how to make the words right, "he didn't seem so sure we'll be all right living here forever."

Jesse's eyes didn't leave Joshua's face. The laughter that surrounded him receded. Suddenly everyone was paying attention.

"I don't know," Jesse said after thinking about what he had been asked. "Some people that come to the post office seem okay with you here, but ...."

"Not everybody," Jeremiah piped up, bitterness in his voice.

Esta May sighed and looked at the sky. Clouds were in the far west over the Door Peninsula. There would probably be rain after dark.

Jesse was struggling to say what he wanted to say.

"The Danes and some of the Irish are strong in favor of you, and my Dad," he said at last. "But some men don't like the island being what they're calling compromised. They don't think slaves belong here."

"We aren't slaves," Ella said. She bit off her words, giving them a sharp vehemence. "We're free."

Jessie looked uncomfortable. "I know you are. My Dad and Mom know that, too. They think you're resourceful and brave. Preacher reminds Dad of his father, who was a preacher, too. He preached to the Indians. But you weren't always free," he said, his voice dropping to an awkward whisper. "That's what some of the men on the island think."

"Gordon Burr's a Stockbridge Indian," Jeremiah said.

"Like Mr. Westbrook," Esta May said, ignoring Jeremiah's comment and responding to Jesse. "We met him at the docks. He was talking with Mr. Craw."

Jessie squirmed as he met Esta May's bright dark eyes. "Like Mr. Westbrook," he agreed.

"They'd better leave us alone," Jeremiah said in a serious voice.

Jamie hummphed. "What we gonna do about it if they don't?"

Ertha looked at Jamie with her eyes wide. "I like it here," she said. "I want to stay. Everybody's been happy since we got here."

"Who is Westbrook anyway?" Joshua asked, the man's rough face in his mind.

Jesse's discomfort seemed to be growing. Joshua didn't want to frighten him off.

At last Jessie sighed. "Joel Westbrook is the Justice of the Peace for Washington Island," he said quietly.

"Justice of the Peace?" Jamie asked incredulously. "You mean a lawman?"

Esta May, Ella, and their sisters looked upset. Abbie stood. The conversation was confusing her.

Jesse nodded. "Yeah," he said. "The man who upholds the law on Washington Island."

"He doesn't like us," Esta May said. "I saw that at Mr. Craw's store."

Jesse didn't say anything. He looked at the ground. Impulsively, Joshua reached out and lightly touched his shoulder.

"It's okay," he said. "We don't blame you." Later he thought that what he had said was dumb. Of course Jesse wasn't to blame. He didn't act anything like how Westbrook had acted in Washington Harbor. But Jesse had looked up from the ground and seemed grateful for Joshua's soft words.

Preacher and the white man who had been introduced as the Michigan's captain chose that moment to come out of God's house. They looked serious. Jamie got to his feet, followed by the rest of the young people. Jesse's face reflected his relief at seeing his father come out of the cabin. They walked toward the campfire where the adults had gathered.

As they reached the adults, Captain Stewart shook Preacher's hand. "Just remember," he said, "if there's trouble the Michigan can be counted on."

"Jesse," Mr. Miner said. "Martha." Moments later their guests were walking toward the path that led into the woods.

That night, still thinking about the warning hidden in both Mr. Miner and Jesse's words, Joshua dreamed again. Not of Silver Coats nor Joel Westbrook, but of an osprey, rangy, slender, brown and white, with a kink in its wings, flying over white-capped waves foaming and disappearing in the lake's endless dance. At first Joshua was looking down on the large hawk from a vantage point high in the sky. Then, suddenly, he was seeing out of the hawk's eyes. He felt spray from waves as his long legs dangled just over the whitecaps as he flew. He moved his wings powerfully and soared over the tops of cedars and a small grove of birch, wheeling as he cried into the rush of forest beneath him.

When Joshua woke, the sensation of being an osprey was still with him. He did not feel human, but a part of the lake, island, and its forests, his white head gleaming with early morning sun, claws ready to plunge into the lake to seize a trout as large as he was. He sat on the floor in semi-darkness and looked mindlessly at the cabin's interior that he and the others had worked so hard to build, his thoughts as random as the roiling waves beneath the osprey's flight. Winter was going to be difficult. He thought that he belonged on the island. He believed it had become integral to how he was becoming as a man. The question was would they be able to live in peace, fishing and creating memories out of freedom.

Chapter 20
Chicago's Gift

The wilderness was difficult enough.
As winter loomed they didn't have the clothes
To deal with minus zero days so tough
The winds would howl in blizzards wild with snows.

They worked, preparing, trying to avoid
The looming threat as flocks of geese and crows
Spoke prophesies about their dreams destroyed
By consequences flowing from the time
They'd spent in fleeing north, their hearts all buoyed
By freedom's lure, the promise of a paradigm
Embedded in the preacher's fire, their trust
In New Jerusalem, deliverance the rhyme
That resonated through a paddle's thrust
Toward salvation, springtime's Eucharist.

The temperature in mornings was cold enough for frost, and geese
were gathering in huge numbers in West Harbor and on the lake,
preparing for their great southern migration. Black crows appeared, too,
searching for seeds in clearings around the cabins and further afield. As
Zelda, whose belly had continued to grow larger, said at breakfast on a
morning when they were around the fireplace in God's House to cook so
they could get out of a sharp northern wind, "It's too early. The trees
shouldn't be turning, but they're crazy with colors more blazing than I'd
have thought was possible."

Chas had, a few days earlier, returned from a trip to Washington
Harbor with more traps. "We need small animals for better winter
clothes," he'd said, handing the traps to Franklin. Franklin, who had
trapped in the great swamp back in Missouri, was enthusiastic. "Now
we're talking," he said. "I can run a real trap line now."

Chas, intent on taking Joshua and Jeremiah out fishing, left Jamie to
work with Franklin. That evening Franklin and Jamie came into camp
carrying four rabbits, providing not only good material for winter hats, as
Joshua's mother said, but also a change in diet. They'd been too busy to
concentrate on food variety for months, but the different meat was

welcome. The only sardonic comment was Beulah's, who said that with all of them needing warm hats for what seemed like unbelievable winter to come, they were going to have to clean out the island's rabbit population.

"We set snares like we did in the swamp near the quarters," Jamie told Joshua later. "There was nothing in the traps, but the snares were tripped. There're rabbits everywhere, though. They're easy to hunt."

That night, in God's house, they had filed in and sat on the benches when Zelda sighed. She looked directly at Preacher. "How bad is the winter going to be?" she asked. "I know what you and Chas have told us, but I don't think I understand." She touched her belly. Franklin took her hand in his and looked worriedly at her. Abbie, on the other side, touched her shoulder. "I'm worried about our baby," Zelda added. "How does a baby survive a place like this?"

Preacher looked at her solemnly. "The reason we've driven the boys to pile up firewood is that we're going to be inside a lot," he said. "We've got to worry about wind and cold and snow. This will be our roughest winter. We didn't get here in time. We'll fish on the ice no matter what. We need the few dollars that brings, but we're going to have to have more than fish to eat, and that's going to be hard to come by."

He paused. "But God will provide. He said in Genesis, 'For it was little which thou hadst before I came, and it is now increased unto a multitude; and the Lord hath blessed thee since my coming: and now when shall I provide for mine own house also?'"

"The biggest problem we've got," Chas added, "is foot coverings, boots. We can make hats and share the heavy coats Mary and the women are making. With any luck the traps will provide material to supplement the deer hides you women have been making into leather. I've been hunting hard for bear with no luck, though there's got to be bear on the island. But the shoes we got in Chicago are wearing out. We need gloves, too. It gets cold in Missouri, but not twenty or thirty below with four feet of snow."

"The fishing's better than I ever thought fishing could be," Franklin said, still holding Zelda's hand. "But it's not going to provide enough money to get us what we need even if we won't starve. I suspect we'll be eating better than we were on the plantations, depending on," there was bitterness in his voice when he said, "the master."

"We've done tremendous work," Harrison agreed. "Two cabins months after running for what seemed forever. The fish we've caught. Deer hides and even vegetables. The third cabin isn't done. It's going to be crowded with two cabins if it gets too cold too quickly, but we couldn't have asked more of ourselves."

"We can work inside if it's cold outside," Junebug pointed out. "The framing's done, and walls are going up. We've worked a miracle with God and Preacher's guidance."

"We're sharing now. We'll have to share more later," Joshua's mother spoke up, her voice stern. "I understand about boots. That's a problem. I see that. But the truth is we are free," her voice rang with conviction. "Free men and women can get through anything. None of us women have to worry about a master or master's son or overseer hulking around shaming us. I don't have to worry about Joshua being beaten. Winter's going to be hard. Zelda's right to worry. A baby's going to be vulnerable, but we can and will survive what we have to and live to see spring and summer and know just how good a free life can be."

Massie sighed. "You're right, Mary," she said. "But that doesn't mean we shouldn't worry."

"No," Preacher answered. "We're imperfect humans. We can't help but be concerned about people we love and ourselves. But we also have to do for ourselves. Tomorrow's going to come. Like Mary says, we'll share food and shelter and even boots if necessary. Under the cypress tree in the Mingo swamp we found the spirit of power God instilled in us, and it got us to freedom. We can't forget the power we have. We can face trials and tribulations and make it through. There might be suffering, but there's suffering and suffering. The suffering we're facing is physical, not spiritual. Human beings have been getting through physical suffering since the beginning of time."

Joshua looked at his shoes. They were not in good shape. They'd been wet and muddy, dry and hard used not only during the flight north, but after they had gotten to the island. In the scow water and flopping fish had soaked them time and again. He knew that nobody was in better shape for shoes than he was. Chas and Preacher had boots. He'd spotted them while the scow was brand new in the Chicago warehouse. Chas had told him they were seaman's boots and were designed to handle challenges seamen faced. What the rest of them had were hand-me-downs.

They had done so much work, driving bodies and minds to their limits day after day, sometimes making Joshua, Jamie, Jeremiah, and even Esta May, her sisters, and little Abbie resentful of not having time of their own. But it still wasn't enough, not when the threat of winter was in the riotous color of maple and birch leaves.

He thought again that he couldn't imagine how cold could get so fierce the waters of Death's Door would freeze over and allow ice roads to be built so that wagons could cross wild waters as if they were an extension of land like Preacher and Chas had told them. And he was pretty sure Preacher never knowingly told a lie, even if he seemed a little out of control at times, burning convictions driving him past practicality.

Looking at his shoes, he wondered if they could be covered with hide and waterproofed in some way. If the cold was going to be as brutal as Chas and Preacher told them, frostbite could easily get to toes when feet got wet. They were lucky, he knew, to have Preacher and Chas. At least they knew to prepare for what was coming.

Before the meeting broke up and they went to the cabin they were staying in for the night, Preacher rose to his feet. "There's one more thing," he said. "I've been worrying about this for some time. We can't address it yet; there's too much work to do, but these young people need to learn how to read. Only Chas, Mary, and I are literate. I've sent word to Gordon Burr through Mr. Miner for some books and Bibles to help us with a winter school. I don't know if he can get them to us, but regardless, we're going to start a school this winter. We should have the hours we need. Even adults can learn to read if they have a hankering to."

Joshua's heart pulsed softly in his ear. His mother could read. She had read Bible stories to him when he had lived in the master's house. He knew about letters and how they represented sounds, but slaves were not allowed to read. His mother had broken the law when she had taught herself with the quiet, illegal help of the white mistress she had served as a child. The idea that he and the rest of them could learn their letters both dismayed and excited him.

"That's the most wonderful news I've heard since I realized we were going to run for freedom," Joshua's mother said. "We're going to be civilized. We're going to make this community something special."

"I want to learn to read the Bible for myself," Pappy said, as serious as his wife had been. "If there's going to be a school, and if I can, I'm going to attend."

Joshua glanced at Esta May. Her face seemed almost angry as she looked toward Preacher. Joshua wondered what she was thinking. Didn't she want to learn how to read? He suspected she was brighter than either he or Jamie. Jeremiah's expression was another matter, even if his tongue and attitude was so sharp he could drive anybody crazy. His eyes held an eagerness when Preacher started talking about teaching reading.

***

The third cabin's roof was mostly in place. Harrison, Junebug, and Preacher were working on the stone fireplace, carefully chinking stones together with clay into a chimney. Joshua's and Jamie's family had, at last, moved out of the second cabin. In the mornings, though, they were dealing with the cold without the protection a finished cabin would provide.

They were all still sleeping on cabin floors, but Preacher was promising they would have beds above the cold floor before winter began in earnest.

When Joshua opened the door after waking up before his parents, and even Jeremiah, he flinched to see the thin white covering on the ground and feel the cold's bite. The snow made him realize just what the discussion in God's house the evening before had been about.

Joshua stood in the open doorway and took a deep breath. "Snow," he said. "It's white outside."

His mother got out of the blankets where she and Pappy had been sleeping and crossed the cold floor barefoot. She put her hand on Joshua's shoulder, looking out the door. Jamie and Jeremiah got up, too, although they looked longingly at the fireplace that couldn't hold a fire without causing billows of choking smoke.

After a moment of silence Mary sighed. "We're not ready," she said. She looked at the heavy clouds in the sky. She shivered, hugging herself with her arms. "We've got to get prepared. Preacher and Chas have warned us." She turned back to where Pappy, Willie, and Massie were getting up and folding blankets to get ready for the day's work.

***

By mid-morning the snow had melted, but there was nervousness in the way everyone glanced at the blue sky every little while. Jeremiah had gone out fishing with Franklin and Chas. Joshua and Jamie had been put to going through the laborious process of sawing tree trunks Pappy had dragged close to the outhouses. Once trunks had been sawed into round chunks, they set about splitting them, taking turns with the axe as each of them got tired. Firewood was stacked in neat rows higher than Jamie's head. He'd grown taller than Joshua, even though he had been a little shorter when they had been younger. That realization constantly irritated Joshua.

Preacher, when he looked in on them after leaving the third cabin where he was working with Joshua's mother on the fireplace, shook his head.

"We'll need a lot more before the cold sets in," he said. "With three cabins to heat we'll go through a lot of wood." He walked away to check on the progress of other projects, including the vital one of turning leather into clothes occupying Massie and Zelda.

When Pappy came toward the two boys with another small pine trunk, hardly straining as he dragged it down the path worn through the woods, Joshua's mother called that it was time for a break and dried jerky. Joshua dropped the axe he'd just picked up after Jamie had handed it to him, glad for the reprieve.

On the way down the well-worn path between outhouses and cabins, Joshua saw Esta May lingering not far from the shore, looking out toward the Door Peninsula across from West Harbor. Without thinking, Joshua veered away from Jamie and walked toward her.

Esta May did not look at him as he came across the long grass still thick along the lake's edge. Joshua cleared his throat to alert her of his presence, but she kept looking out at the lake. The scow wasn't in sight. Joshua couldn't see anything that might hold her attention. He quietly stood beside her.

Joshua really hadn't thought much about women. He knew he was old enough and that they should be attracting him. He hadn't known Esta May that long, but the experiences they and the others had shared seemed to have lasted forever. He felt funny when he looked at her, as if somehow he had suddenly woken up and was aware of more than just himself and his thoughts. He looked away from her and out at the lake.

At last she sighed and glanced at him.

"You looked upset in God's house last night," he said softly. "Why?"

She didn't answer at first. She sighed again and looked back at where the others were getting together for their break. "We're working so hard," she said at last. "My Maw's upset. She's worried about Zelda and the baby that's going to be born and all us girls and how we're going to get through winter. Paw's upset, too, although he's upset about whites on the island. He's afraid they're not going to accept us being here in the long run. He thinks this land we're on is too valuable, and whites always take what they want."

"Preacher says things are going to be all right," Joshua said.

Esta May looked at him. "You think he knows? Really knows?"

Joshua looked into her dark eyes. She looked right through him. He couldn't look away from her.

Do I really believe in Preacher? When his mother had first taken him to the swamp meetings he'd gone because she had insisted. He hadn't believed the fiery black man back then. If he hadn't come to truly believe in Preacher, how had he reached Washington Island? Preacher had kept urging them on, but he'd felt surer of Chas, especially when they'd reached the safety of the Campbell place after half starving to death.

But Preacher had told them the truth. He had said that he and Chas would get them to freedom in a Wisconsin island wilderness, and that's where they were. Even white men listened when he preached. The visits of the Miner family and steamer captain had meant something. Even Mr. Campbell's recounting of the Battle of Lake Erie had meant something. Preacher was a prophet, a real prophet.

But do I really believe in him?

"He got us here," he told Esta May after a long silence. "Now that we're here we're going to have to do the best we can. Pappy says that, and I believe him."

Esta May looked away from him back at the lake. "I'm afraid of winter," she said.

***

The next morning, ice edged West Harbor's shoreline. It didn't last long, especially after waves swelled as they rolled in to shore, but it was another sign of what was to come.

Joshua had been told that he and Jeremiah were fishing when Abbie came running up from the harbor toward the cabins. "A canoe! A man's coming in a canoe!"

Everyone hurried to the harbor. Jeremiah and Eunice had run out ahead of everybody else. "It's Gordon Burr," Jeremiah yelled.

As Joshua, flanked by Pappy and Mary, got to the shore, they could see that the big Stockbridge Indian was smiling and laughing at the excitement he was causing. His canoe was packed to its gunwales with goods stuffed into canvas bags. Chas, smiling, walked up as the canoe's bow softly slid up on the beach.

"Gordon Burr," he exclaimed, smiling. "This is a surprise. Welcome."

Gordon got out of the canoe and splashed to shore without flinching at the water's cold. Pappy rushed down and pulled the canoe further out of the water. Preacher stood calmly in the midst of them. "You dared Death's Door in a canoe?" he asked. "This time of year?"

Gordon shook Chas's hand, touched Pappy's arm as he stood from pulling the canoe on shore, and looked up at Preacher as the young people, including Joshua, milled around him. The rest of the community, all of them smiling, waited further back nearer the cabins.

"You wanted books," Burr told Preacher. "Miner told me. And you need other things." He looked up at the two mostly finished cabins and the one cabin still being built. "You've been working hard," he said. "Anyway, the Potawatomi have been coming to this island by canoe since time immemorial. A battle was even fought in the waters between Rock and Washington Island by the Potawatomi and Winnebago. A Stockbridge should be able to do what those braves have been doing for centuries."

An hour later, they had unloaded a small number of books, including two Bibles, and a larger volume of blankets, coats, soft and hard leather, two bolts of heavy cloth, and were sitting in God's house during hours when they normally were working. The women and girls couldn't stop touching the cloth Burr had brought.

"Jemson's congregation in Chicago collected the goods from their abolitionist friends," Gordon told them. "But the Stockbridgers and Munsees got the hard leather for boot soles and some of the cloth and books. We don't have much, but we have determination and humanity. You'll need this stuff once serious storms start."

"Our Lord in Matthew says, "Therefore take no thought, says, What shall we eat? Or, What shall we drink? Or, wherewithal shall we be clothed?'" Preacher said. "And off the lake comes Gordon Burr in a canoe with what we aren't going to be able to provide for ourselves."

"We're grateful," Joshua's mother said. "Truly grateful."

"We can make boots," Harrison said. "Good boots, too. We won't have all of them finished in time, but there's enough hard leather here to make a pair for everybody."

"You're an angel," Zelda said, fingering a rough wool blanket. "An angel."

"And you're going to have a child." Gordon laughed. He sobered. "It will be a child born in freedom. No man, woman, or child should be born in any other way." He paused. "I'm rooting for this community to succeed," he said fervently. "Me and every other Christian Stockbridger."

"We're going to learn how to read," Abbie blurted. "Preacher and Mary Simpson are going to make a school!"

"Are they really?"

"Yes, yes," Ertha responded, supporting what her best friend had said.

"That's good, really good," Gordon said. He turned to Chas. "What about the islanders? The white people? What are they saying about you being here?"

Chas shook his head. "Some are good," he said. "You know Henry Miner, though how he got to you so that you know what we need puzzles me. Still, there are others. We don't know them. Not really. We have our friends, but we'll see."

"A steamer captain came to church and said he'd help us to Canada if need be," Pappy said. "We thanked him, but told him we'd be okay. We've worked pretty hard to run the minute we've gotten settled."

"It won't be necessary," Preacher said. "I saw the community we are building in a vision while fire was burning as Commodore Perry swore and loaded boats to get to another ship to carry on the fight. That vision was true. It won't change just because a white man or two doesn't like what God has ordained."

A silence greeted Preacher's intense words. His eyes burned. With his wild white hair and beard, neither of which he had been trimming, he was increasingly looking like a Biblical prophet.

At last Massie stirred them out of their thoughts. "Time for a feast," she said. "Bill's been bringing us braces of rabbits for hats. I think we can make some pretty good eating out of what we have."

***

Overnight, a cold wind swept down from the north. By morning, the lake was wild with waves. The wind was so strong it bent over trees, and voices were swept away by the constant roar.

Gordon threw up his hands in the air and turned in a full circle. "Ah, Mother Earth is stirred up today," he yelled. "I'm staying here until she finds her calm again."

The community took up tasks that kept them out of the big wind. The women worked on putting together hats or clothes, while Harrison worked at cutting hard leather into the soles for shoes.

The old man amazed Pappy. "Is there anything you can't do?" he asked as he watched Harrison's sure, steady cuts with the knife he was using.

Harrison smiled, looking up at Junebug, who smiled back at him.

"A man who lives long enough and is more curious than he ought to be gets in a lot of trouble," Junebug said. "Masters and overseers don't like a curious slave. Harrison never learned that at the Billard place, though he should have." Her voice sounded rueful. "But that same man learns a lot over a lifetime. He maybe doesn't keep up so good when you're fleeing cross-country, but he's handy to have around."

In the third cabin, Pappy and Willie worked on the floor while the boys were put to work chinking in spaces between stones stacked up for the fireplace.

The day passed quickly, filled with laughter and goodwill. Gordon's unexpected arrival had dissipated tension underlying what had been happening since Henry Miner had told them about opposition to their presence by some of the islanders.

Going to the outhouse, Joshua heard a tree fall in the woods not far from where he was walking. Branches were strewn everywhere on the ground. The storm was frightening. As he half ran down the short path to the small structures he had helped build, a sharp retort of thunder shook the ground. The wind not only made it difficult to keep his balance, but it was cold, too. Lightning traced forks across the sky, lighting up the black underside of clouds.

Inside the outhouse, he wondered for the millionth time how they would survive the winter. He was so cold he could hardly stand to pull down his pants even though he had to go so bad he felt panicked. On the Bulrush plantation he had always dreaded winter cold, but sitting in the dark, frozen, he realized that none of them, other than Chas and

Preacher, even knew what cold was.

He realized, although he hadn't really thought about it before, that a Washington Island winter could kill. Even though Gordon's arrival had made survival more possible, it did not guarantee all of them would survive to spring.

On the way back to the cabin, freezing rain pummeled him, paralyzing his face into a mask that did not belong to who he was. Enormous shadows from trees twisted wildly in the wind. He wondered about the baby about to born. How could it survive weather worse than the storm whipping rain and cold in waves through the trees? How had white men and women who had settled the island survived their first winter?

Back in the cabin, he bolted through the door and leaned his back against it, relieved to be out of the wind and cold. He was surprised to feel himself shaking. Then the realization hit him. The storm was frightening him. He'd seen many bad storms. The one at the bridge during their escape had frightened him, too, but for different reasons. The cold in the rain and wind had implications that had been worrying him unconsciously for days.

His mother came over and looked into his eyes. "You okay?"

He nodded. "It's pretty bad out there," he said.

An especially powerful wind gust made the cabin roof rattle as a large tree branch was flung across it. She didn't say anything, although Joshua could tell the storm was making her as nervous as it was him.

"God, what a country," she said at last.

Joshua didn't say anything, but he agreed with her. The coming of winter seemed like a nightmare that he could sense, but not really imagine.

***

The next morning dawned with clear skies and calm waters. West Harbor didn't have a ripple on the water's surface. Gordon was out of God's house and in his canoe almost before anyone knew he was leaving.

Just before he shoved off, however, the whole community had made it to the shore, led by Preacher. As Gordon pushed the canoe off the beach where Pappy had pulled it, Preacher solemnly shook his hand. "You're God's messenger," he told Gordon. "We are grateful."

Gordon laughed. "I'm a strange kind of Indian messenger," he said. "I'm not Potawatomi. They belong here." He shoved the canoe off, took up his paddle, and canoed into the calm waters out of West Harbor toward Death's Door.

Chapter 21
Beyond Fear and Depression

Doubt, fear, a question asked at night, the stakes
So high they eat at confidence and sap
The energy from fire in eyes that hurled mistakes
Into the wind and laughed at how the gaps
Between success and failure complicates
The desperation drummed into the feet
Of children, men, and women daring fates
Defining who they'd been, their lives' heartbeat —

And then the preacher sat alone and tried to grasp
How prophecies could be ambiguous
When hatred came to suddenly enclasp
The shores that terminated exodus —

But spirit born of fire transcends despair
And pulls determination from the air.

Joshua woke up crabby. His mood was inexplicable since the day before had been unusually successful. He and Jeremiah had been in the scow with Chas and Franklin, and they had hauled in more fish than anyone had managed to date. Lake trout, salmon, white fish, perch, walleye, and even a huge, unexpected sturgeon were part of the catch. At times they had not been able to haul fish into the scow fast enough. Jeremiah had spent most of his time making sure ten to thirty-pound fish did not flop from the scow into water.

The sturgeon was the largest fish any of them had ever seen, almost swamping the scow as they brought it over the side. Joshua and Franklin, with the help of Jeremiah, had hauled the big fish with the long snout and four lower snout whiskers into the boat, ruining the net they had caught it with in the process. Joshua's hands and feet were already numb from water-soaked gloves and shoes. His muscles strained, feeling as if he were damaging his back permanently, as the huge fish almost tipped the scow over. Chas said that it had to be at least a hundred and seventy pounds. By the time they were finished for the day, even Jeremiah was sitting in the boat, silent and exhausted.

Fishing had been difficult for a while now. Catches were good, but getting used to wading through snow to where they had stored the scow high on the beach to ensure it didn't get caught by high tide, and dealing with cold biting through flesh into bone, was difficult. Joshua had been thrilled with the sturgeon. He knew what the enormous catch meant to them. Funds the fish were bringing in would help them get through winter, but dealing with elements so different from what he had grown up with was hard.

They had been jubilant returning to West Harbor. The scow was heavy with fish and so low in the water Franklin said that if the day had been different, stronger winds would have sunk them. When word of their day spread, everybody came out of the cabins to celebrate. What the catch brought in would be a welcome addition to money already saved.

***

Joshua had been dreaming of Esta May as he woke up in the cabin's dark. Something about the dream, he couldn't remember what, had upset him. His mind felt sluggish and filled with a heavy, emotional cloud.

Esta May had begun to take up more and more of his thoughts. On the run north he had not realized she was beautiful. Constant fear of slavers had been too consuming to leave room for anything else. Freedom from constant fear now allowed him to be more aware of the world around him than at any other time during his life. In that awareness, Esta May and how she moved and laughed and teased him, Jamie, Jeremiah, and her sisters was increasingly prominent.

Unfortunately, Joshua could feel Jamie's relationship with both him and Esta May changing, too. Jamie had always been his best friend, with Jeremiah a close second. Jamie wasn't much like Joshua. For one thing he was more careful about doing anything that might cause trouble. Joshua, struggling with feelings of resentment, had always thought Jamie's caution was smarter than his own stubbornness, even while he had no idea how to contain the feelings that caused him to do whatever he could to upset what the masters wanted.

Now, however, Joshua could tell that Jamie was subtly forward with Esta May, trying hard to get her attention. He was better at it, too. Joshua usually paid little attention to Ella, Eunice, and Ertha, but Jamie was attentive to them. This attentiveness drew Esta May's notice as sure as dawn was created by the sun rising. Joshua had figured that out. He genuinely liked the younger Woodruffs, but he usually woke up to them after Jamie had taken the lead and started talking to them, especially to Eunice or Ertha.

Neither Jamie nor Joshua talked about the rising tension. They worked at giving the outward appearance they had the same relationship they had always had.

Joshua didn't think that even his mother noticed what was happening. She was aware of everything else going on in the community, so much so that Joshua sometimes thought she had an extra sense beyond touching, hearing, smelling, and seeing that allowed her to know what people were thinking before they did. But to all appearances, Jamie and Joshua still were best friends, which was true, and were working in tandem in every way they knew how to help them all succeed.

Joshua climbed out from under the warm blankets Burr had brought and pulled on boots Harrison had made and went out of his family's bedroom to build the morning fire in the newly finished fireplace. Pappy and his mother got up moments after he did and dressed. On the other side of the cabin, behind walls put up just the week before, Joshua could hear the Woodruff's stirrings.

As soon as the fire was started and Pappy had come and said good morning to him, Joshua, after grumbling "Morning," in reply, went outside. Yesterday the sky had been clear, and only the softest of breezes had been blowing. Now heavy clouds promised another snowstorm that would add more inches to whiteness stretched from forest to the lake's edge. The water along the beach was frozen for over a foot out from the beach. To get the scow out they would have to break ice again.

What was the hardest to deal with, though, was the cold. Joshua understood the weather was still mild by Washington Island standards, but it was already as cold as it got in January in Missouri.

Without thinking, Joshua walked to the trail the Miners used when they came to church on Sunday mornings. He was still trying to recapture what had bothered him about the dream when he stopped. A white man, not Henry Miner nor the steamer captain that had visited them, came out of the woods. He stopped momentarily to glare at Joshua and then started to approach him.

Joshua forgot about the dream. Joel Westbrook, face unshaven and looking as rough as he had at the Washington Harbor dock, was walking toward him. He turned and looked back toward the cabins. Pappy was standing outside and had seen Westbrook and his son. Joshua turned to look back at his father. Pappy yelled, "Chas," and, without waiting, started walking toward them.

Joshua turned back to face Westbrook. Watching the man stride toward him as if he owned what Preacher and the rest of them had built through weeks of hard labor, Joshua glared.

The white man stopped uncomfortably close to where Joshua was standing, staring steadily at him, but Joshua did not move. He knew that he should step backward. A black man had to show obeisance to an aggressive white man or face a beating or worse. Westbrook was taller than he was, but Joshua was calm, as if this confrontation was part of what his mood expected from the day. Behind him, Pappy and Chas, followed by Preacher, walked up to them.

"Mr. Westbrook," Pappy said, "I believe we met at Washington Harbor." Pappy's voice was calm and respectful, soft, not like his normal voice at all.

Westbrook's eyes left Joshua's face to look at Pappy and then Chas. Chas's head was slightly cocked, as if he were puzzled by what was taking place.

"West Harbor's a good place," Westbrook drawled. "I understand James Jesse Strang's talking about getting a foothold on Washington Island by taking over here. All kinds of anti-American misfits seem to think this place ought to be theirs."

"James Jesse Strang?" Chas asked. His voice was not quite as respectful as Pappy's, but still had a sense of carefulness.

Joshua moved a step back from the white man to let Chas move slightly forward. Westbrook smiled, clearly feeling he had established dominance. He glared at Chas.

"A so-called Mormon prophet over on Beaver Island," Westbrook said. "Seems like he wants to capture fishing grounds in all the islands and needs a harbor to move his plans forward."

"I've heard something about Mormons on Beaver Island," Chas responded. "The fishing there's as good as fishing here. Why would he need to come to Washington Island?"

Westbrook smiled. "He's probably heard a bunch of escaped darky slaves wanted by their masters down south have taken over West Harbor and thinks that that's a spot ripe for the picking."

"I was a veteran of the War of 1812 and Commodore Perry's fleet," Preacher said loudly. "I don't think Commodore Perry's command had any slaves in it, only free men eligible to serve in this country's Navy."

"Anybody can say anything about anything," Westbrook said. "That doesn't make it true. I heard you all are escaped slaves from down south who think Washington Island's far enough away to make a good hideout."

"We're improving this property through our labor," Pappy said, drawing himself up to his full height. "Just like any other group of people who have had that opportunity."

Westbrook looked Pappy directly in the eye. Aggressiveness oozed from him. He leaned toward Pappy. "You're a big man," he said.

"He's an uncommonly strong man," Chas said.

Westbrook smiled. "He'd bring a pretty penny from a master who wanted that strength back," he said. He paused. "I bet there's a master who wants it back badly."

The white man's threat made Joshua draw in his breath.

"You threatening us?" Preacher asked, his voice as soft as the white man's had been.

Westbrook smiled. "The Danes wouldn't like that," he said, his voice flat. "They're abolitionists," his voice snarled the word. "Still, I'm officially the law around here. I've been meaning to visit West Harbor ever since I heard you'd all settled here. I'm just making sure none of you are going to make any kind of mischief."

"We haven't bothered anybody," Chas said firmly.

"Yeah, Craw told me he's been doing business with you. He's a big man, Craw. Old. Lots of money. He and Henry Miner, the Washington Island do-gooders." His eyes turned to Joshua. "This boy's got attitude. You can see it," he said. "I figure the rest of you got attitudes, too. You're just not so young you can't hide it. Fugitive slaves with attitudes don't belong on this island."

"I haven't done anything wrong," Joshua said, his heart hammering. He couldn't believe he was speaking up for himself. He felt the same tremor of fear mixed with excitement he'd felt when he'd spoken inappropriately to Silver Coats.

Pappy put his hand on his shoulder. "This is my son," he said, his voice stern. "He's a good boy who works hard."

"We've got every right as Americans to be here," Preacher said.

Westbrook didn't say anything, but stared at Preacher with his hard, unblinking eyes. At last he glanced over his shoulders at the woods he'd come through. "I'm warning you about the Mormons," he said at last. "They'll be coming into your fishing grounds pretty soon I suspect. They want West Harbor. And I don't feel," he paused, thinking through his words, "comfortable about who's here to defend it."

"We just want to make a life for ourselves," Preacher said, eyes sparking with the dark fire that often came into them. "Like any other people. 'Thou wilt shew me the path of life,' the psalmist says. 'In the Lord's presence is fullness of joy.' We're here to live in the Lord's presence."

"I heard you fashioned yourself a preacher," Westbrook said. "But in my experience, those who mouth religious words can be more righteous in their wrongdoing than the drunkest wild man on this island. I'm just telling you. All of you. I'm watching."

"The abolitionists on the island will support us," Chas answered, his voice assured. "I've talked to them."

Westbrook smiled. "The law is about who enforces it," he said. "Just remember." He turned and walked back to the path through the woods, deepening the trail in the snow.

After the white man had disappeared Chas said, "Well, that's that," but Preacher mumbled, "Behold, how good and how pleasant it is for brethren to dwell together in unity!" Frowning, Preacher had turned back toward God's house with his shoulders slumped. Pappy spat on the ground. "Seems like a man can't escape masters," he grumbled.

Later, Jamie, Esta May, Jeremiah, and Ella got together on the land between the harbor and lake. Joshua was no longer out of sorts. The confrontation had driven out his early-morning mood. Now he felt shaken. Pappy's words had brought back memories of Master Bulrush watching him as he struggled to move stacks of hay from a wagon into the plantation's big red barns when he was too young to carry what Silver Coats piled on him. He kept wondering how he could ever escape the past that had shaped him. The universe did not seem to have justice, not even in the paradise Preacher had found for them in the wilderness on an island across water called Death's Door.

Jeremiah, as usual, was the first to speak after they had wandered around the harbor's curve to look out at restless lake waters. He looked directly at Joshua as if he were challenging him. "Seems like we can't get away from what we've been," he said, bitterness tingeing his words. "I thought that after we got here, we'd be free and wouldn't have to worry for the rest of our lives."

"Women know better," Esta May said quickly. "Where there's human beings, there's trouble. Maw's always taught us that. She says women are what knit a family so that it can handle whatever trouble is over the horizon."

"Uncle Chas says abolitionists on the island outnumber those who don't like the idea we're here," Jamie said. "I heard him talking to Paw right after Mr. Westbrook left and you all," he pointed at Joshua, "came back to where we were all standing."

"That doesn't mean things are okay," Jeremiah said. "There's only one master on a plantation, but everybody dances his tune."

"I'm tired of running," Ella said. "I don't want to be running and hungry for days and days ever again. I like it here."

Joshua looked at the endless roll of waves, the way they swept in arcs toward shore. He felt dark inside. He hadn't been afraid of Westbrook. He'd never been afraid of Master Bulrush nor Silver Coats nor the whipping that had left long, ugly scars on his back. He figured that was part of his problem in life. Normal people were afraid, but he was stubborn. When he should back down and act properly, like even Pappy had when confronting Westbrook, he forgot who he was. He'd been that way as a child. He knew it frightened his mother almost to death. He suspected his mother hadn't believed he would survive into adulthood there, which had made her doubly eager to run.

The others waited for him to say something. He'd been with his father, Chas, and Preacher when they'd gone out to see what Westbrook wanted. He'd been the first one to face the white man.

At last he turned from the lake and looked at Esta May, who was frowning. "We've earned our place here," he said last. "I, for one, am a man. I'm not leaving because some white man thinks I can't live where he lives. There are a lot of woods between him and us."

He then turned to Jamie, who seemed to be measuring what he had just said.

Esta May said, "We'll see," and walked back to the cabins. Something about the way she had turned from him made Joshua's heart sink. He was pretty sure that, without knowing, he'd said something that made her think less of him.

***

The next few days were difficult. Preacher had been the heart of dreams that had led to Washington Island. The confrontation with Westbrook seemed to have taken some of the power that had led them out of him. He had dreamed of helping slaves escape captivity for years, found a Chicago community willing to help him build a scow and find resources, found slaves, including Chas's family, who believed in his power as a preacher and prophet, and led them, as he expressed it, out of the wilderness of despair.

After the unpleasant encounter with Westbrook, Preacher spent the evening without saying much. They had eaten supper out in the open even though cold was beginning to make outdoor community times difficult. He'd been withdrawn, mumbling in response to Chas's question about whether he was all right, "We are troubled on every side, yet not distressed; we are perplexed, but not in despair,'" quoting from the Bible.

During the next two days he only came out of God's house to go to the outhouses. He wouldn't talk to anyone, not even Chas, who had kept in touch with him for so many years after the Battle of Put-in-Bay.

At first the adults took his dark mood in stride. "Every man has to have a down time," Pappy said. Chas shook the whole thing off. He's faced tougher things than Joel Westbrook, he told them, and none of them stopped him from going where he was determined to go.

But then his mood began to affect them. Westbrook was one man, albeit a white man, but he had power no one else on the island had.

Chas wasn't sure that meant much. He said that in a community as isolated and small as Washington Island, most men were busy trying to survive by fishing and planting garden plots. They didn't have time for titles and duties out of the everyday jobs they had to do to bring enough in to get through winters. Less effective men ended up taking jobs the more respectable men refused to do.

Henry Miner was an exception, Chas told them. He was a hardworking man who took on Post Master duties because no one else would brave the dangers inherent in the job. Getting and delivering mail, and sometimes goods, across Death's Door was essential to everybody's well-being, even though winter made the job treacherous. Death's Door froze over, and you could sometimes walk or drive a wagon across it, but there was always the danger of soft ice that could give way and send you to your death.

Chas didn't really know Joel Westbrook, he said, although he'd run into him now and then, but he did know his reputation wasn't the most exalted on the island.

After a second day when Preacher stayed in his bedroom, his head bent over his Bible, even Chas began to get worried.

Joshua was having a hard time understanding why the confrontation with the white man was affecting Preacher so much. When he'd first met Preacher in the swamp he had not been impressed. His fiery voice and eyes that burned with his faith's fierceness were powerful. Still, he had never really believed in Preacher the way his mother had. His belief in the old man had not developed until they had reached the Campbell place and listened to Mr. Campbell, Preacher, and Chas talk about their service in the War of 1812. The man had been a warrior even though he was a black man. Even a white Commodore, whatever kind of leader a Commodore was, had allowed him to serve with white men. Preacher was different than any other black man he'd ever met. Men as competent as Chas, as well as a rich white farmer like Mr. Campbell, respected him.

Now the man who had led them to freedom was clearly deeply troubled. His eyes were dull, their fire dimmed, and he was silent, his mood so black he'd barely lift his head. As far as anybody could tell, he wasn't eating. His already hollow cheeks seemed to shrink further into his cheekbones. Joshua wondered what had happened when Westbrook had come down the path, what had happened to Preacher.

No one talked about what was happening. They went out to catch fish even though ice was increasingly a problem, especially in the harbor, and they continued to work on the cabins, build the woodpile, turn hides into clothes, cook, and do the other chores that filled days from sunrise to sunset. But a pall was over everything they did. Their leader had retreated into himself. They felt a heaviness that weighed down even the youngest among them.

Finally, after three days, Joshua's mother had had enough. She got up before Joshua and Pappy and scrubbed the sanded pine floor as soon as she came back from the outhouse. Pappy looked on helplessly as she stared fiercely at an already clean floor. By the time Joshua had gone out and come back, she was rearranging pots and pans on the shelves Pappy had built the week before, trying to help organize their side of the cabin. Massie was fixing buckwheat pancakes for breakfast, using flour Chas had bought from Mr. Craw's store. Her expression made it obvious that she was clearly wondering what was going on with Mary. Finally, Joshua's mother stopped wiping shelves with the rag from one of Joshua's tattered shirts and came out of the room separated from the fireplace.

She stopped in the doorway and looked at Massie flipping a pancake with the wooden spatula Junebug had made for each cabin by whittling and polishing pieces of cedar.

"We got to do something," Mary declared.

Joshua and Pappy had just come in after splitting wood. Willie, Jamie, and Jeremiah were still in the Bullock's room. Joshua mother's pronouncement, made in a too loud voice, caused them to come and stand just outside the room's doorway.

"It's time," Massie said. Joshua had no idea what the two women were talking about. "Get Abbie. That'll help." She glanced at the buckwheat pancakes. "After breakfast, though."

Joshua's mother sighed. "After breakfast," she agreed.

Without waiting to help do the dishes, Joshua's mother got up as soon as she'd eaten a single pancake. Massie had served her first so that the rest of them were just getting pancakes when she stood up and stretched. "I'll get Abbie," she said. She marched, rather than walked, out of the cabin.

Minutes later, the entire community was gathered outside God's house. Even Chas had come out from where he slept beside the congregational benches. Abbie looked bewildered while she stood holding Joshua's mother's hand. Nobody said anything.

Just as Mary put her hand out to pull the cabin's door handle, however, the door opened. Preacher stood in the open doorway, looking out at them. For a long couple of minutes there was complete silence. Preacher glanced at the heavily clouded sky before looking down at Abbie.

"I wasn't always free," he said, making sure his voice was loud enough for all of them to hear. "I told all of you that. Gwyn Harcourt, the master I served when I was young, was not a bad man. He was a small shipwright who built boats for people, fishermen and others, not far outside Baltimore, Maryland. He taught me most of the skills, other than preaching, that have let me build boats and do so many other things. He even taught me my letters, even though he could have gotten into serious trouble with the authorities if either of us had been found out. He hated paperwork and used that as an excuse for teaching me what I shouldn't have been taught.

"But when he was drunk, he changed from being a good master into a vicious animal that would beat slaves until either he or they collapsed, him from drink, the rest of us from the beating. I don't think it ever occurred to us to fight back or even to try to protect ourselves. We were mostly terrified.

"He'd taken me with him to Baltimore one day to buy supplies. My job was to do the carrying and loading after he purchased what he needed to finish building a big boat for an outer banks fisherman. After we'd bought supplies, he decided to go into a saloon across from the docks. I was told to stay with the supplies and watch them.

"Everyone here knows the dread you get waiting for what you know is going to happen. I was Joshua and Jamie's age. After a while, staying by the wagon made me more and more nervous. He was getting drunk. I knew what that meant. I didn't want to face it. So—" Preacher shrugged. "—I left the wagon. I didn't have any place to go or even anything in my mind. I was just nervous and upset, and I walked away.

"I walked for about an hour into town when this tall white man stopped me. He was wearing a funny hat and somber, plain clothes. When he said, 'Boy,' my heart went out of me. I must have looked terrified, because he smiled and told me not to be afraid. He asked if I was lost. I've tried for years to understand what made him stop me and ask me that. Not being smart enough to know better, I told him the truth, that my master was getting drunk and was going to beat me. That I'd gotten scared and left the wagon full of supplies I was supposed to be watching.

"I'm not sure why I was so open with the man. I could have ended up in Baltimore's jails, which, for slaves, were nightmares of squalor and abuse. But there was something about him, some kindness in his manner and blue eyes. I still remember his eyes. When I'd said my piece, my heart hammering because I knew how wrong I was and what that would probably lead to, the man told me to come with him.

"And that's how I became a freed man. The man was Johnathan Pitt, a Quaker and abolitionist. He took me into his house for a week and let me live with his wife and seven children. Even though he was a Quaker and a godly man, he took me to a man who forged papers that named me a freed Negro man.

"Then he put me in a wagon sitting next to him and drove me to Philadelphia and put me with a free Negro, Jasmin Freeman, who had never been a slave and was also an abolitionist. Jasmin's the one who got me into Commodore Perry's Navy. He wasn't Quaker. Quakers don't believe in war and don't like it when people agree to fight in wars. But

Jasmin wasn't well off. I had to do something to pull my own weight in his family. The Navy was desperate for Great Lake sailors. I knew how to caulk boats. That was good enough to make me a prime candidate for the battles I would end up in."

Preacher, still standing in the doorway, reached out to Abbie. She gave him a sweet, trusting smile and took his hand. Ertha went up and took his other hand. The rest were silent, looking at him, trying to understand what he was telling them.

He smiled at last, the first smile they'd seen from him since Westbrook came out of the woods.

"What I'm trying to say," he said, "is that there's good and bad people everywhere. Some have streaks of both good and bad in them like my master Gwyn Harcourt. I've spent days praying and fasting, trying to discover if I have really brought you to New Jerusalem or some other place different than what my vision had showed me. I've been frightened. Having a vision and having that vision roiled up like Lake Michigan during a big storm confuses you in your mind. Certainty becomes uncertain and troublesome.

"But what I've come to understand is that "the Lord is the Spirit, and where the Spirit of the Lord is, there is liberty." We've got the spirit of the Lord here. So whether this is New Jerusalem or not, this is like the moment when I stood terrified before Johnathon Pitt and told him the truth of who I was.

"That led to good things that led me to Missouri and a swamp where I preached about the Lord. Not in the way Johnathon Pitt believed, but in the way I learned after the Battle of Put-in-Bay searching for a way to keep my promise to God during the thunder and lightning of ship guns. We belong here. In this place on Washington Island, we belong. We're going to have to find the good people who are abolitionists and willing to help us make New Jerusalem out of a place where sinners live in abundance and hatred."

He finished with his voice deepening and becoming as powerful as it had been in the great swamp in Missouri. His eyes were burning again. Joshua's mother looked at him holding Abbie's hand and smiled. "Amen," she said loudly. "Amen!" Everyone else echoed her.

***

Later that day, after delivering logs to the cabins, Joshua and Jamie, freed from chores for a change, walked down the path Westbrook had used to get to West Harbor. Biting cold, made worse by clouds pressed down on the earth, encouraged them to keep moving. Several hundred yards down the path Jamie veered off toward the lake. They could hear the crash of waves piling onto the shore before they got to where they could see enormous swells rising until they collapsed in sprays of white foam. Half in and out of the woods they stopped. There wasn't a lake bird to be seen.

"It's been a hard day," Jamie said over the crashing sound of waves.

"Preacher's story was pretty strange," Joshua answered. "It sounds like he isn't as sure we belong here as he's been up until now."

Jamie was silent. He pointed up the shoreline to where a white-tailed buck was walking up the open strip of beach. "I don't know," he said. "Whatever Preacher thinks, I think we'll make it here. Just like that buck. It could die tomorrow if it runs into Chas with his rifle, but it's not worried right now. It's just living."

Joshua laughed. "What would Jeremiah make of you sounding all philosophical?"

Jamie smiled. "I'm not leaving, not easily, Westbrook and his kind or no. We wanted freedom. We found freedom. Maybe not New Jerusalem, but a lot more freedom than we had on the plantation."

Joshua stared at the huge sweep of the waves. "That's for sure," he said at last, thinking about his mother in the master's house, Silver Coats with his whip and mean grin, the sudden appearance of Pappy in the swamp's woods, and Preacher standing with his flock beneath the big cypress tree beside the small pond in the swamp. A sharp gust of wind pushed against them and sang into the forest. The few leaves left flew off bare tree branches. Pines, firs, and evergreen branches twisted. "We'd better get back," he said, "before it starts snowing again. Winter's here."

Chapter 22
Throwing Off Old Chains

When words upon a page connect to where
Electric currents spark alive the mind,
Atrophied thoughts once bound by self, confined
Inside awareness looking, feeling, breathing air,
Begin to learn, to walk the thoroughfare
Of human revelation, knowledge, mind
From lives of those we've never known, that shined
Their possibilities into the flare
Of what a human can become, or make.

The preacher, as the Bible's verses swirled
Out from his eyes and heart, used words to snare
Free students into words designed to shake
Alive their learning in an unsafe world.

    Ice covered West Harbor so fast it was startling. In the morning, Franklin and Joshua were breaking ice along the shore so they could get the scow into the water. Overnight, the entire small harbor was covered with a shield of ice.

    Chas said the ice was very early. It was barely December. He said it usually started later in December or early January and that the signs they were getting foretold a tough winter. "That's bad luck," he said. "We could have used something milder this year of all years."

    Chas joined Franklin, Joshua, Jamie, and Jeremiah, looked at the opaque covering, and shook his head. "We can drag the scow over to the spit," he said. "I think we might be able to break through enough to get out where the water is still clear." He paused. "But maybe not." His voice sounded regretful. He turned from the harbor and walked back toward God's house, mumbling, "A good day for hunting." The four of them stared out at a sight none of them had seen before. Ice had filmed over Missouri's small ponds, but always melted before it could thicken. Washington Island seemed to always present difficult-to-believe discoveries.

***

Later that morning, Preacher came out and started rounding up the young people. "It's time for school," he said over and over again. "In Missouri, you weren't allowed to read. Here, you have an obligation to learn. You can't learn God's word if you're not capable of reading it for yourself."

Surprisingly, not only the young people but even Pappy trudged from their cabin through ankle deep snow to join them. Joshua wasn't sure why he was surprised that Pappy wanted to learn how to read, but he was even if he had heard his expressed interest earlier. Since that startling evening when he had first learned he had a father, he'd come to see Pappy as self-sufficient. The huge man, compared to his son, seemed to be able to do anything. He was constantly moving and working. He was too larger than life to need anything like reading in his life.

The only one not coming to God's house was Harrison. Even Junebug got up from her work stitching a pair of leather gloves for Eunice and followed Preacher. When Joshua's mother looked curiously at Harrison, who always followed his wife, he grinned sheepishly. "I'm too old to learn a skill that complicated," he explained. "I've done enough learning in my life."

Joshua's mother smiled at the old man and nodded her understanding.

After they were sitting on the benches, Pappy coming to sit beside Joshua and looking sheepish, Preacher brought out ten slates. Joshua hadn't seen them before and was curious about where they came from. His mother handed them out. "We don't have enough for everybody," she said reluctantly. "We'll share."

Preacher distributed a piece of chalk and a small rag with each slate. "Be careful of the chalk," he said. "Don't press down too hard. If it breaks, it doesn't last as long, and getting more's not easy in the wilderness."

Joshua's mother went to the front of the room while Preacher sat on a chair placed behind her. There was something different about her, as if she could hardly contain her excitement. She cleared her throat.

"I wanted to say something first," she said. "We all know what would have happened if we got together like this in Missouri. No slave was allowed to learn to read, even though some of us learned anyway. When I was a young girl, I was assigned to watch my even younger mistress. I sat in on her lessons when she learned to read. I wasn't supposed to. I wasn't given a book or slate to help me, but you can't keep a determined mind imprisoned. If it's given a chance, it can soak up anything.

"At night, after the lessons were done, on my own, I wrote letters, then words in the dirt and repeated them over and over to myself. I snitched books from the piles in Mistress Claudia's room and pored over them even when the light was so bad I could hardly make out the letters.

She knew what I was doing, I believe, but let me get away with it. I took what they denied me and taught myself how to read."

She looked at them with eyes blazing. "We're here now," she declared. "Free. No master is keeping us from making our own civilization or learning what we want to learn, including how to read. To me that is what freedom is about, setting a dream and having the right to work toward achieving that dream.

"I want you to learn how to read as part of making civilization in this community on Washington Island. If there are those that chase us off this land we've occupied, we'll still have what we've learned to help make our way in a hard world. If the good people on the island support us and help us stay, we'll be able to watch out for ourselves since all of us will be able to read better than most of them can."

She smiled. "That's what I told Preacher Bennett I wanted to say before we started learning letters," she said. "Now that I've said it, he's going to show you how to write letters, A, B, C. Then we'll practice writing them to fix them in your minds. After that, we'll learn how letters make sounds that make up words." She turned to Preacher. "Preacher Bennett?"

As Mary Simpson turned to sit in Preacher's chair, Preacher stood and smiled. Seeing him beside his mother caused Joshua to think about how old he was. His hair was streaked and becoming increasingly gray; his face had deep wrinkle lines.

During the times he'd heard Preacher preach in the swamp and the long run north and the days since they'd been learning how to commercially fish and build their community, he'd never thought of Preacher as old. But after hearing his mother's words and looking at the man so dominant in his life, he realized he *was* old. He'd escaped slavery, been to war, learned how to become a preacher who knew more about the Bible than any person any of them had ever known, mastered the art of building and repairing boats, and gone south to free people he didn't know from slavery. That was a lot to do during any lifetime.

"Take up your slates, the young people first," Preacher directed. "Then I want you to write an A like this." He wrote an A on the slate he was holding and held it up so that everyone could see it. Joshua's mother got up to walk around and see that everyone was following directions. Joshua, without thinking about it, easily wrote an A on the slate. He didn't hesitate, just did what Preacher had told him to do.

His mother smiled, wiped the slate clean with one motion of her hand, and handed it to his father. Pappy was hesitant, much like the rest of them, other than Ella, Joshua noticed, in carefully trying to trace out an A.

"I want you to listen and say the ABCs to yourself over and over again until you've memorized them," his mother whispered to Joshua. Then she went around the room helping young people and adults alike.

When they'd finally finished writing down each of the alphabet's twenty-six letters, Preacher and his assistant told them to relax. "You can write letters in snow or on slates in your mind's eye," Preacher said after he told them to lay down their slates. "You've done good today, but we'll see who's ready to move on tomorrow and start learning how to put letters together into words."

"Tomorrow?" Esta May asked, consternation in her voice. "We're going to be doing this every day?"

The tone in which she asked the question startled Joshua. She seemed dismayed. Joshua had been thinking that he was really happy to learn how to read. The letters hadn't been hard. He'd do what his mother had whispered. He'd go over them until he had them memorized. He was pretty sure he could do that without any effort at all.

Pappy was in the process of getting to his feet. "If an old fool like me can come to school to learn my letters, you can too, young lady," he said.

Several of the older people smiled. Joshua kept his eyes away from Esta May. He'd never had a doubt about her since she'd first approached him and Jamie in the barn that first night during the escape. It made him uncomfortable to think she'd said something that didn't seem perfectly in line with his perception of her.

They walked outside into a heavy snowstorm. There wasn't much wind, but huge white flakes drifted downward, covering even the ice in the harbor. The cold seemed less intense than it had that morning, but at least three or four inches of snow had fallen while they'd been working on their letters. They were staring into the heart of winter.

When Chas and Franklin came outside together, Chas chuckling at a story Franklin was telling, they both stopped and looked shocked. "The scow," Chas exclaimed.

They plowed through the deepening snow, followed by Joshua, Pappy, Jamie, and Jeremiah. When they got to the harbor Joshua saw what had alarmed the two men. The first day of school had let them forget, for a moment, about what they needed to be doing. The inside of the scow was filled with steadily deepening snow. They had cleaned the scow's bottom before going out fishing several times, but now the scow had to be stored for the winter.

Without a word, all six of them started scooping snow out of the hull. Then Franklin started handing the boys oars, buckets, fishing equipment, nets, and other stuff stored in the scow. Preacher, who had followed behind the rest of them, said, "Take it to God's house. The other cabins are too crowded. We'll store it there." He was calm and even looked amused. They had worked so hard at building, fishing, and hunting; a

200

moment's lapse in thinking reminded them that they were in a wilderness a long way from any real civilization.

After the scow was emptied and the mast taken down, Pappy and the other men, including the three boys, put their hands into the snow and heaved it up. Pappy made the huge weight look effortless to lift, but the others staggered. Joshua thought his arms were going to dislocate from his shoulders. Once they got the scow to where Preacher wanted it, they sat it down and Pappy, alone, flipped it over so that the hull was toward the pine branches and sky, out of the worst weather that would come.

What they had achieved since coming to Washington Island was a miracle, as Preacher kept telling them. But they had a long way to go before they could manage what was to come.

***

Just before nightfall, Pappy and Willie went out in the woods and cut down two straight pines for making into boards and dragged them through the snow to the cabins. Preacher and Harrison had decided to build what Chas called a "fishing shack." After the two men had gotten back to the cabins, Joshua and his father stayed in the small room the three of them slept in and practiced saying the alphabet they had learned during their first school day. The memorization wasn't too hard for either of them. By the time the candle Zelda had made started sputtering, they both felt like they could say their ABCs without error.

***

The next morning dawned with brutal cold. A wind came off the lake and tossed trees into frenzied dance. Rushing to the outhouses was miserable. When Joshua saw Chas and Harrison ahead of him with three women waiting outside the second outhouse, he took off into the woods, his feet and hands numb. He had just stopped behind a screen of brush when he heard a sound behind him. He turned. A green-eyed wolf, larger than any dog he had ever seen, was standing not twenty feet away, staring at him. Not one of the freed slaves had ever seen a wolf. Joshua's bladder dried up. He gasped. The wolf, seeing him looking at it, calmly turned and faded into woods, leaving a trail in the snow.

Joshua could hardly contain the mixture of fear and excitement when he ran back to the outhouse to find Chas. They had done well so far, but were they prepared for wolves? How could wolves get across Death's Door? No animal could swim that far.

Chas smiled when Joshua reached him, half gibbering. "It must be a holdover from last winter," he said. He did not look half as cold as

Joshua felt. He'd spent winters in this country before. "They come over on the ice," he continued. "Remember me hunting for black bear? There aren't many wolves around, but sometimes you see them, usually in a small pack. The island's not big enough to support too many of them."

Jamie, who had come up the trail while Joshua had been in the woods, looked incredulously at Chas, his eyes large and round. "You didn't tell us there were wolves here," he objected. "They're dangerous."

Preacher had come out of the outhouse and held the door for Harrison. Massie, hearing the fear and excitement in Joshua's voice, had come over to where the men were standing.

Chas shook his head. "They'd have to be pretty hungry to attack an adult human," he said. "You don't want to challenge them. If they're on this side of the island, we'd better be careful with Ertha and Abbie, but the Indians have been living beside wolves forever."

"If we're careful, the Lord will take care of us," Preacher added.

Joshua looked at Jamie. He'd seen a wolf, a real wolf. He felt disassociated from what he was hearing. They were living in a wilderness, and wolves were living where they lived. Jamie didn't say anything, but shook his head. Massie started to say something to Preacher but held back her words. They'd lived for months on the island and never dreamed wolves were in the forest. They were free, but the place where they were free was filled with dangers, some human made, others a part of nature and the wilderness they had run to in order to end their dread of becoming slaves again.

Back in the cabin, Joshua and Jamie had just started recounting Joshua's story about the wolf when Preacher came to the door. He stomped inside, letting a cold blast sweep through the small room. He looked at Joshua's mother. "School again today," he announced. "I got the books out. We'll work with those who've memorized the alphabet on starting to learn to read. The others'll have to work on their ABCs."

Pappy looked at Preacher bundled in the long, brown coat Gordon had brought from Chicago. "Joshua saw a wolf this morning," he said, his deep voice calm. Joshua's mother stood up from kneeling in front of the fireplace and looked at Preacher.

Preacher shrugged. "There were panthers near the plantations," he said. "I heard them at night sometimes."

Massie had come out of the Bullock's room and looked from Preacher to Joshua's mother.

Joshua's mother shook her head. "We just have to be careful," she said after a moment of silence.

Massie frowned. "Are panthers here, too?" she asked.

Preacher nodded. "There's all kinds of dangers," he said. "The lake's dangerous, storms are dangerous, some men are truly dangerous. Then there are wolves, bears, panthers, and cold so fierce we won't be able to walk a mile in it. But we'll survive. The white people have survived. We will, too."

"Yeah, that's right," Pappy said solemnly. "We'll survive."

After breakfast everyone but Chas, who already knew how to read and was going to work the trap line, and Harrison headed to God's house. Joshua noticed Jeremiah and Massie were looking forward to the day's lesson. Jamie and Willie seemed less enthusiastic. The greatest surprise, though, waited just inside the cabin's door. Esta May was standing beside the door looking distastefully at the hastily set-up classroom. Eunice and the other Woodruffs had taken benches in the semi-circle Preacher had set up.

When Joshua saw the look on Esta May's face, he stopped and looked at her. She was beautiful, even if she looked decidedly unhappy. He especially appreciated the curves of her body beneath the long dress she was wearing.

"What's going on?" he asked.

She looked at him. He felt like she was pushing back at him even though he had, as far as he could tell, said nothing to upset her. "You want to learn to read, don't you?" she demanded.

Confused, he said, "Of course. The masters were afraid to allow us to read, so it's our duty to learn. We want to create paradise. Like Preacher says, you can't have paradise without learning."

Esta May frowned. "You sound like your mother," she said.

Joshua bit his lip, realized what he was doing, and put his teeth back in his mouth. He looked steadily into Esta May's dark eyes. He supposed he sounded like his mother in a way. He remembered crying for weeks in Old Simpson's cabin after Master Bulrush— "No," he thought, "Bulrush, not master"—had forced him out of her small room by the pantry cellar. She had never abandoned him. He knew that what she believed had imprinted strongly into everything he thought. That had always been true, even when he had defied her.

He sighed. "I suppose so," he said at last. He paused again. "She's not a bad person to think like." He was startled to discover how soft his voice had become.

Esta May stared at him with a discomforting intensity. "You have to understand," she said, "I am who I am." Joshua was suddenly aware that several of the others were staring at them as they stood by the door. Esta May half gestured at the room, slightly raising her arm. "I mean," she said, "this is what my life is going to be. I'm going to marry either you or Jamie, live in this place we've built, be a fisherman's wife, have children. I don't need reading or anything else. That's enough. That's who I am and who I am going to be."

Beulah had gotten to her feet, but stopped before going to her daughter. Bill was looking at Joshua with a bemused look on his face. Esta May noticed her mother was standing and looking at her and, to Joshua's horror, he saw tears in Esta May's eyes. He didn't know what to do.

Esta May turned, opened the door, and walked outside, leaving Joshua standing where he was, dumbfounded. Everyone was looking at him and the closed door. His confusion was so great he felt paralyzed. No one moved. Then Jamie got up from where he was sitting beside Jeremiah and Massie and rushed to the door, brushing Joshua as he went outside.

"What is going on?" he thought. "What's happening?" He loved Esta May. He knew he did, even though he hadn't done anything about it because he didn't really know what to do about it. Now Jamie was outside trying to comfort her while he was inside confused.

"Come sit down, Joshua," Preacher said. "We've got a lesson to get through."

"But—."

Preacher held out his hand. "Let Esta May and her family work this out amongst themselves," he said.

Joshua wanted to learn how to read. He loved the idea of Preacher's and his mother's school. He might be facing a life as a fisherman, but that didn't mean he couldn't show the masters what he was capable of achieving. He didn't have to accept the slavery they'd imposed on him since he was a baby. The truth was, he suddenly realized, he didn't understand Esta May at all, what she was thinking and feeling, what her dreams were. He didn't have any idea.

He looked at the door closed against the winter's cold. This was a cold, harsh country. It bit people. It especially bit those who were more about dreams than lives lived. Awkwardly, he walked over to his mother. Jamie had gone after Esta May. Joshua had failed her. He understood that, but the whole incident seemed wrong. She'd seemed okay the day before when the school had started.

He had noticed she'd been reluctant to start Preacher's school, but she'd followed the rest of them without protesting. He felt so roiled up he didn't even feel his mother touch his arm gently as she led him to a place on the bench beside Pappy. His life had turned upside down. His mother handed him a thin book with the big letters of the alphabet. He glanced at it, but only half saw it. Preacher was in front of the room again. Joshua had no idea how he'd gotten there.

Neither Jamie nor Esta May came back. Preacher and his mother started the lesson they had intended to teach as if nothing had happened, testing them on how well they knew their ABCs. Even Beulah, after looking at the closed door for a long time, gave in to Bill's gentle urging and sat on the bench next to him.

At first Joshua hadn't been able to concentrate on what Preacher was trying to get him to do. He could still remember the alphabet and call up the look of the letters in his mind, but the book he'd been handed didn't register until Pappy frowned at him. Then he focused on the book and making sense out of what he was seeing on the pages.

His mother pointed at a word, said the word and each letter in the word, and then had him repeat her teaching.

"The fact is that I learned to read better than either of the mistresses, but Mistress Mary, a born snitch, and Miss Wilma and Miss Melanie never knew. Miss Melanie probably guessed, but if she did, she never hinted at it. Learning by picturing words in your mind and getting their sound down combined with letters, even if you don't have your own slate, works miracles."

She looked at Joshua to see if he understood and then smiled at Pappy. Joshua, still upset about what had happened with Esta May, thought about how different his mother looked from when they had been on the plantation. Her joy at being with Joshua and her long-lost husband was obvious.

Suddenly, looking at the page and the letters his mother was pointing at, he saw what they were trying to get him to do. He started to, silently, in his head, puzzle out letter sounds so they fit together into words. *The American Spelling* book with its long list of words, almost like magic, made sense. All he had to do was learn what the word looked and sounded like in his head, and he could remember it and have the word he'd captured forever.

He looked up at Pappy, who was trying to follow along, but had not had Joshua's revelation. He looked confused.

The minute his mother saw that Joshua understood what to do, she smiled. "You've got it," she exclaimed. The Woodruffs were staring at them, looking away from Preacher who was working with them the way Mary Simpson was working with her family.

Joshua nodded, his face serious. His mother looked at Franklin, Zelda, and Abbie. "Good," she said. "Work with your father while I help Zelda and her family. We've got to work together to make learning happen."

The morning flew by. Joshua kept remembering the look on Esta May's face when she had turned away from him to flee outside, but working to help Pappy kept his mind and emotions occupied. Pappy was determined and was amazed his son was picking up what his wife had taught them so fast. Joshua kept mimicking what his mother had done with him with the few words he had figured out as Pappy tried to do what Joshua had already accomplished, trying to learn by rote what Joshua had picked up with sudden insight.

Glancing around, Joshua saw that about the only one working to teach her family the way he was teaching his was Ella. Looking at the way she was working with one little sister after another gave him an unexpected feeling that he had no idea how to explain to himself.

***

After a midmorning break, they were all given tasks to do. Snow dancers whipped off the ground by the shore. The harbor was completely enclosed in ice. Being outside, the way Harrison had been all morning while working on making boards out of tree trunks for the fishing shack, seemed impossible. Joshua's skin burned just on the quick walk between God's house and the cabin.

Irrespective of how reluctant he was to work outside, Harrison came to get him as soon as he had scurried to the cabin. He was surprised that Jamie and Esta May weren't either beside the fireplace or in the Bullock's room.

"I can use some help with the saw," Harrison told him.

Joshua groaned out loud. Pappy, who had come over to the cabin with him, smiled, but gestured him outside. "One fishing shack's not enough," he said. "We need to keep catching fish. Not everybody's going to fit into a tiny shack pulled out on the ice, so we need to get done what we can get done."

Joshua had just gotten out of the layers of clothes he'd put on that morning, but started the process of getting back in them. Harrison, who had been stamping on the wooden floor, trying to get circulation back in his feet, leaving snow clumps wherever he stamped, didn't say anything, but smiled.

They had just reached where Pappy had dragged logs when Ella came out of the cabin the Woodruffs were occupying. She was smaller than Esta May, but, at only a year younger, not by much. Joshua looked curiously at her as she crossed the open area to where he was standing. Harrison ignored the two of them and picked up the two-man saw. Joshua saw he'd been trying to square the trunk sides with a single saw so that they could use the two man saw to slice off boards that could be used to build walls over the shack's frame.

Ella looked serious as she came up to him. "Esta May doesn't have many dreams," she said in her soft voice. "Her one dream was to escape the plantation. Once we did that, she's decided she knows what her life is going to be like."

The shock of Esta May's rejection of the reading school went through

Joshua again. He didn't understand why someone wouldn't want to read after they'd been denied the possibility all their lives. Esta May took his breath away, but he clearly had no idea who she was.

Ella waited patiently for him to say something. At last he shook his head. "You seemed to be learning fast enough," he said.

Ella's smile lit up her face. She wasn't as pretty as Esta May, or as old, but her smile made her more alive, more attuned with whom she was talking to than Esta May was.

"I've got dreams," she announced. She gestured vaguely at the three cabins. "This is only the start of what we can be."

Harrison cleared his throat. "We've got to get to work," he said. "You two can talk later."

Only the start? Joshua wondered. But instead of asking her what she meant, he took the handle of the saw Harrison was handing him. "I've got work," he said.

Ella nodded. "We can talk later," she said.

Joshua watched her for a few seconds as she walked back to the cabin, noticing how straight her back was as she walked away from them, but then turned his attention to the log they were going to saw perpendicular to its squared top to make a board. He wondered where Esta May and Jamie were. His thought made him sad. He wondered if they had fallen in love with each other, leaving him out in the cold.

Chapter 23
In the Throes of Having Lost Expected Love

The nightmare slipped into his sleep, the lash
Slow-moving, curled, until its black tip snapped
Into his flesh, blood oozing where it wrapped
Around his side, the welt an ugly slash
Of fire and slicing pain that made him thrash
Against the ropes that bound him, spirit trapped
Inside a silent, burning rage that mapped
Itself into his breath and made him smash
Against the white man's wall of slavery
And long for wings so strong he could fly free.

He woke, a free man who had reached his freedom,
But in the darkness as he contemplated
How life could lurch into a yawing chasm,
He mourned his true love lost, felt empty, scalded.

Joshua forced himself awake. He quietly got out of bed, dressed, found his coat in the dark, desperate to be totally silent so that he wouldn't wake anybody, and then, without building a fire, slipped outdoors. That he was upset was an understatement. Jamie hadn't come back to the cabin until after he and his parents had crawled under covers to escape the cold. Joshua's vague plans, never fully formulated, and dreams about Esta May had disappeared in an instant. He could not have guessed that she wouldn't like learning to read and that that would, mysteriously, drive her towards Jamie.

The stars were bright in the early winter sky. The moon was a sliver in the darkness. There was hardly any light, but he walked through snow toward the spit of land where they had built so many fires. Once on the point extending into the harbor, he stood silent, looking at the lake.

For a minute his mind was blank, but then he felt uneasy. The dark was intense enough to make seeing distances hard, but light was filtering into the cold eastern sky. He felt even colder than he had when he had first come outside. Even after West Harbor froze, he had felt, rather than saw, how ice edged the horizon's dark waters. Now he could see no end to the ice. Whiteness stretched from where he was standing beyond the horizon, looking ghostly. He shivered. He felt shaken, as if the world had changed and would never be like it had been again.

He suddenly wanted to be back in Missouri, not on the plantation, but in the swamp. He wanted to feel warm again and feel like he knew where he was. Oddly, he missed where he was born in a strange, inexplicable, way. He certainly didn't want to go back, but his memory of warm winter days seemed emblematic of something he was missing.

He felt like crying, but was determined not to. The universe, with its stars, moon, and dark spaces between stars above more ice than should have ever existed was immense. His father was huge, and he was small, smaller than Jamie, but even his father was small underneath a night sky lightening toward dawn. He couldn't fathom how he had reached a place in his life where he was stuck.

As he watched the rising sun, he could see in his mind's eye Esta May smiling at him as they made their way up the Door Peninsula to where Pappy and Preacher were waiting for them. He wondered why he hadn't known how beautiful she had been at that moment. He'd been so involved with seeing Lake Michigan and feeling freedom and the safety wilderness represented, he'd not been able to look outside himself. He saw her, beautiful with her perfectly proportioned face, thinner than she should have been from their long running, but he hadn't seen her. He'd always been too involved with himself.

Then he saw Jamie rushing to God's house's door as Esta May turned away from learning how to read. The confusion he'd felt at that moment washed over him again. He could understand Jamie's reaction. He could even see wisdom in it. But he could not make sense of Esta May's rejection of learning, not even in the dawn of the morning after it had happened. He sighed unhappiness onto the endless ice.

He heard the door to one of the cabins open behind him. Someone was up and making the cold journey to the outhouses, his mother's demand for civilization. Ice had silenced the world. No waves slapped the shore; no birds flew through morning light. There was only him and the cabin door opening and feelings about being lost in a too-large universe.

Lost in his thoughts, Joshua was startled to hear Pappy calling him. He raised his hand in acknowledgement and walked toward him.

Once he got to God's house, he was surprised to see Esta May and Jamie sitting inside with everyone but Harrison. Preacher motioned to him the minute he got in the door. He realized he'd missed breakfast.

"I want you to work with Ella and help everyone else with their lesson today," Preacher said. "Jeremiah's not far behind you, but you two are the furthest along."

Joshua glanced at Esta May. She looked at him, then at the floor. She was sitting by Beulah and Zelda, who was starting to act uncomfortable whether sitting or standing. Her belly was getting bigger and bigger. Joshua absently wondered how long it would be before she had her baby. He glanced at Jamie, who studiously looked away from him. Before he could feel jealous, Joshua forced the emotion out.

In the quarters they had been taught that they had to control emotions. If they didn't, they would be verbally abused or whipped or given an onerous task. They had to live together. They couldn't walk away and never come back.

They weren't slaves anymore, but the same rules held, Joshua realized with a start. Not only did they have to battle, making a place for themselves against Washington Island's wilderness and weather, but they had to stick together in an effort to avoid being overrun by white people who wanted them gone. They could not afford to dissolve into jealousy, hate, or any other negative emotion that could split the community apart.

Joshua had never been good at controlling his emotions. But that was what Preacher was really all about. He preached Christianity and love in order to give them something besides themselves to hang onto. Joshua shook his head. His introspection was leading to ideas and thoughts, one after another, he'd never had before. Without saying anything he went to sit by Ella, who looked at him with bright eyes. "She's proud she's ahead of everyone but me in mastering reading," he thought. "She's different from her older sister."

**

At the end of the morning lesson, Preacher asked Joshua to come to the front of the room. "I want you to read the Bible to us, Joshua," Preacher said. He opened it to the middle of the book. Then he turned several pages before stopping and handing it to Joshua. "Read Psalm 133 to us," he said.

Joshua swallowed. *Can I really do it?* He looked at Preacher, feeling a twinge of panic. Preacher smiled and nodded encouragement. Joshua had figured out how to piece together sounds out of letters. He knew he was further along than even Ella, but to actually read from the Bible? It didn't seem all that possible.

He took a deep breath and looked at the book in his hands. A Bible had been placed in each cabin after Gordon's visit, carefully put on the small mantle built above each fireplace, but Preacher's Bible was different. The ones in their cabins were bound in stiff paperboard covered with rough cotton fabric. Preacher's Bible was bound in leather and was bigger.

"Behold," he read. "How good and how pleasant it is for …," he tried to sound out the word silently in his head.

"Brethren," Preacher told him.

"… brethren," Joshua repeated, "to dwell …"

"Together," Preacher prompted.

"… together in …"

"Unity."

"… unity!" Joshua repeated, puzzling out the sounds. "It is like the …"

"Precious ointment," Preacher said.

"… precious ointment upon the head, that ran down upon the beard," Joshua said, stumbling through the verse.

Preacher, smiling broadly, took the Bible back from him. "Even Aaron's beard: that went down to the skirts of his garments; As the dew of Hermon, and as the dew that descended upon the mountains of Zion: for there the Lord commanded the blessing, even life for evermore," Preacher read in a triumphant voice.

He looked up at his congregation. "We're coming along," he declared. "Joshua just read from the Bible, God's word. We're coming along!"

Joshua shook his head. He hadn't done well. He'd stumbled on almost every other word. "I didn't do so good," he mumbled.

His mother was standing and looking at him. Her pride in him was obvious. "A good beginning," she said. Beside her, Pappy looked as happy as she.

Joshua fled to his seat next to Ella, who was looking at him in pretty much the way his mother was looking at him.

"We're reading," she whispered. "Both of us. We're not good yet, but we're going to be good."

***

Outside, Junebug had joined Harrison, Pappy, and Willie as they tacked together the fishing shack's frame. Esta May and Jamie had disappeared again, making Joshua feel unsettled all over again. He flinched when Junebug got up from where she was kneeling and holding a board in place on the ground and came over to him, smiling. Her old face, with wrinkles around her eyes and down the smile line of her cheeks, looked like his mother's face had when he had finished trying to read Psalm 133.

"It did my spirit good to hear you reading from the Bible," she said.

The memory of how exhausted she had looked before Chas had found them in the swale not far from the Campbell farm flashed through Joshua's head. She looked healthy, not emaciated from starvation.

"I didn't do so good," Joshua said, still smarting from knowing how far short he had fallen from what his expectation of his reading ability had been before Preacher had called on him.

Junebug shook her head vigorously. "Oh no, child," she said. "You did better than good. I'm not doing so good at learning to read. I'm too old, I suspect, but you were a slave boy always being beat up by your master. You stood up in front of that room and showed us all where we might get if we work hard enough." She glanced at Harrison, who had stopped working to listen to his wife. Pappy and Willie had stopped, too. "I'm proud of how you read from the Bible," she continued.

"I am, too," Pappy added. "Your mother's always been a reader. Now we have two readers in the family."

Joshua hung his head. He tried to lift his spirits to meet their praise, but felt half dead inside, as if Esta May's choice of Jamie instead of him had ended his life.

At that moment, Preacher and Jeremiah came out of God's house and stood looking at the five of them. Seeing Jeremiah panicked Joshua. He turned from Junebug's expectant face and walked away from the cabins toward the outhouses and veered north into the woods.

He cussed at himself. What was he doing? Why was he acting how he was acting? He was a member of a free community. He had a responsibility to help make that community work. He was not free to wallow inside his emotions. At the plantation he could get stubborn against Silver Coats and even, to a lesser degree, the master and his family. The only one he was hurting was himself. But here, in the wilderness, after they had taken such terrible risks and endured so much, his behavior wasn't right. He was a different person here, with different responsibilities.

He was still angry inside, as he had been before their escape. But the run north had taught him lessons. He was not doomed to being a slave until the day he died. He did not have to fear the burning whip's sting as leather slashed his back. Even though whites could not be trusted, some were willing to go beyond who they were and find a conscience that helped slaves escape their masters. He could no longer feed his deep anger in a way that would endanger what all of them together, following Preacher and Chas, had earned.

He wanted to jump the broom with Esta May. He wanted to rage against Jamie and fate and how whatever had happened had happened, but he couldn't. He had to bury his hurt and accept what was instead of letting his anger out in destructive, all-consuming rage.

By the time Joshua was aware of where he was once he stopped walking furiously through the woods in snow well over his ankles, he was lost. He didn't even know how much time had passed since he'd left.

He was hungry. He hadn't eaten since the evening before. Nervous, he turned around in a circle in an effort to get his bearings, beating a circular depression in the snow. His feet ached from the cold.

He'd lived on the island for months now. They'd come in the summer. Now it was winter. He had tramped, mostly with Jamie, all over the country surrounding the cabins, but it looked different in the snow. He had no idea where he was. He wondered how long he'd been wandering lost in his thoughts.

Then he glanced at the circular depression he'd made and smiled at himself. He wasn't lost. All he had to do was follow the trail he'd made and backtrack.

An hour later, he saw smoke rising from the cabins' chimneys. He hadn't gone so far after all. Then he heard someone walking through the woods toward him. He stepped forward, but stopped. Esta May was following the path he'd made. She looked small walking through huge, barren maple trees. With a start she looked up at him. The silence in the forest seemed to have substance.

"Joshua?" Esta May's voice sounded hesitant.

"Esta May," he whispered.

"I thought this was your trail," she said. She shook her head, not vigorously, but just enough for Joshua to see her head move. "I'm sorry," she said.

The mix of emotions Joshua was feeling scrunched up his forehead and the space between his eyes. "Sorry?" he asked, his voice just more discernable than the silence around them.

"I'm going to jump the broom with Jamie, not you," Esta May said, a hint of defiance in her voice. "I thought it would be with you, but—" her voice faltered.

Joshua felt like he might break down and bawl in front of her.

Esta May squared her shoulders. "You're too different from me," she said. "Jamie's plainer. He knows what I need from a man."

Man? Jamie's a man? Jamie knew what she needed, and I don't?

Of course, he'd already known. The minute Jamie had followed her out of God's house, the verdict had been clear. And it was his fault, because he'd not made any effort to tell her how he felt about her earlier. Because he hadn't been sure until it was too late.

He forced himself to release his tension and smile. "It's okay," he said at last. "It's your choice. Jamie's my best friend, and it's okay."

The happiness in Esta May's smile shocked him. She glanced back over her shoulder. "People are worried," she said. "They didn't know where you went. We need to get back."

"Yeah," he said.

Esta May walked in front of him, following two sets of tracks in the snow.

The next day, after another night of tossing and turning beneath blankets on the cabin's cold floor, Joshua again got up early, but this time he built a fire in the fireplace and decided to fix breakfast before he went outside.

"The cold makes it nice to store the meat the men have been bringing home," his mother said as he stomped in from the small wooden storage bin Pappy and Willie had built outside the cabin's door."

"Beats walking somewhere to get something in this cold," Joshua responded, getting the heavy black frying pan off the shelf beside the fireplace where both families had put their cooking utensils.

"You all right?" she asked after a moment of studying his face.

Joshua looked into the fire in the fireplace. "Yeah," he said, trying to hide the sadness in his voice. "I am." The strips of deer steak he'd put into the pan started to sizzle.

His mother didn't ask further, but she'd heard the sadness he'd been trying to hide, and, like him, hid how it was affecting her.

After he'd finished eating, he went outside and walked to the harbor where Chas was standing on the shore, looking at the endless fields of white ice. There was still open water out on the lake. Joshua thought he could almost see a dark line where the ice ended and the water began, but he couldn't be sure.

"You ready to test the ice?" Chas asked.

"Is it safe?" Joshua asked, thinking of what his mother would say.

Chas grinned. "This from a boy who ran from Missouri to Washington Island with slavers and dogs after him?"

In spite of himself, Joshua barked a short laugh. "We edge out carefully?" he asked.

"We get a branch that acts as a staff," Chas said, turning toward the cedar grove mixed with pine and maples just east of the harbor shore. "We go slow and probe the ice ahead of us." He paused. "This bitter cold's been going for days now. My bet is the ice is pretty thick." As he said his last sentence, he was already walking toward the trees.

A few minutes later, he returned with a hand axe and a straight branch covered with bark. "After we're out a ways, we'll see how thick the ice is," he explained.

Without pausing, he nodded to Joshua and casually stepped off the shore onto the harbor ice. Joshua and some of the others had already walked out a few feet from shore, but Chas didn't stop. He kept walking, with Joshua a couple of steps behind, past where the rest had ventured and then past where the spit of land enclosed the harbor. The ice was nosier than the forest. As they walked their feet crunched; every once in a while, Joshua felt creepy when the ice groaned softly from somewhere around them. Chas didn't hesitate, but kept walking with his long, steady stride.

When they finally stopped, Joshua was astonished to look back and see how far they were from shore. If the ice gave way, they'd have no way to make it back to safety unless they could somehow crawl out of freezing water and drag themselves up on ice that didn't collapse because of their weight.

This is nothing like Missouri.

Chas used his right boot to clear snow off the ice. "Help me," he said.

Feeling apprehensive, Joshua started using the side of his Harrison-made boot to clear snow.

"This is how we'll fish," Chas said. "It's hard to use nets through ice, so we'll put lines down holes we cut and fish that way. Later on we'll need a full-size axe to make holes, not a hand axe, but for now this should be enough."

He knelt down, gestured at Joshua to move away, and took a hard swing. Ice chipped into the air, but he hadn't cut through Without pausing, he brought the axe up and swung again and then again. On the fourth swing, the axe splashed water that filled up the small hole he'd made.

Chas looked at the black water and nodded. "A few inches," he said. He stood and looked at the sky as if he were measuring it, too. "I don't think we can bring the shack out yet. A warm day might make Harrison's work go under." He sighed. "We don't have enough shacks to keep us warm anyway," he said. "And we can start fishing." He smiled at Joshua. "We're going to have to buy goods before winter's over." Chas turned back to the shore and started walking again. "Come on," he said.

Back on West Harbor ice, Jamie, Jeremiah, Franklin, and Bill were watching them as they walked toward the shore. When Joshua saw Jamie his heart jumped into his throat. He swallowed hard. What could they say to each other?

When they were less than a hundred yards out, Franklin hollered, "Fishing?"

Chas raised his right arm and put his gloved hand up in the air. "The ice is good. Not thick enough for the shack yet. We'll drag what we catch on a pine branch to shore."

Franklin smiled. Joshua thought about how strange it was that Franklin had taken on the most responsibility for becoming a fisherman. Back in Chicago, he'd seemed like the one most involved with his small family. He had been a cotton picker on his plantation, a man known for following orders and keeping out of the Overseer's way, as Joshua understood from talk during the days when they'd had campfires. But the minute he'd learned how to sail the scow, it seemed like he'd fallen in love with sailing, water, and fishing. His lean, black face had been weathered all summer and fall by winds and waves.

Jamie fell in next to Joshua as Chas and Joshua kept walking toward the shore. He looked tense and a little bit afraid.

"You all right?" Jamie asked Joshua softly enough so that the other men couldn't hear. "Are *we* all right?"

Joshua looked straight ahead and kept walking. He didn't know how he could answer either of those questions. As the men walked off the ice toward the cabins he stopped. Jamie stopped, too. The two boys studied each other's faces.

After a silence Joshua knew was lasting too long, he shrugged. "We've got to live together," he said. "I know that."

"We've been through a lot together," Jamie said. "Our whole lives."

"Yeah," Joshua said. "Since I was moved into Old Simpson's place at the quarters."

"Esta May and I ...."

"I know," Joshua said quickly, then impulsively held out his hand.

"I want to stay friends," Jamie said, accepting Joshua's hand and shaking it gratefully.

"Me, too."

Joshua buttoned up what he was feeling and walked with Jamie toward the cabin they shared with their families.

Chapter 24
The Working of Hope and Dreams in Being Human

Shape shifting swarms of gnats, their worries gnawed
At them as long days drained their energy
And taxed their strength as dreams of being free
Materialized in walls, fish caught, the songs to God
That echoed through the trees, the paths they trod
To carve from wilderness community,
A feeling of impregnability
Against gnats buzzing that in hope was fraud.

Their labors sang a hymn of glory rooted
In faith that they could toss away the past
And seize a future drenched in human sweat
As safety wrapped well-being sewn and quilted
Into days shining, stormy, overcast
With liberated time freed from regret.

In spite of Joshua's expectations, they did not attempt to try fishing through the ice the next day. Chas went off into the woods hunting. Harrison started fashioning what he called runners for the fishing shack with an axe, and the rest of them went to school. Joshua could tell that Esta May, who was not doing well at learning how to read, wanted to be anywhere but where she was. As her little sister Ella and Joshua went around with Preacher and Joshua's mother to help those struggling to move forward, she studiously ignored them. Still, she was obedient to her mother and Preacher, sat beside Jamie, who was not that far from Ella in his efforts to learn, and dutifully worked at what she disliked.

Before class ended for the morning, Chas' shouting brought them all outside. He stood in the sunlight, holding the legs of a rooster squawking and trying desperately to escape his firm grip. They laughed at the sight of him holding up the rooster and looking like he had conjured up a miracle.

"I found him in the bush," he said. "Nobody lives anywhere close to where he was. I suspect he got loose from somebody, but we got ourselves a rooster!"

Massie didn't hesitate, but trotted toward the chicken shed. The young birds in the shed had grown into respectable chickens under Massie and Zelda's careful supervision. The two women fed them and spent time cleaning the shed and making sure they were healthy. They hadn't lost a single chick.

Chas laughed and followed Massie to the shed. The whole community, including Preacher, followed. When Chas tossed the rooster, with its brown and black feathers and flaring red comb, into the shack, wings fluttering wildly, all of them cheered. Even Joshua felt good. For once he wasn't thinking about Esta May.

"Out in the bush?" Willie asked his brother.

"I kept going over there," Chas answered. "I saw him in the brush a week ago, but if I even spotted him, he spooked. The strange thing is he's still alive. With all the predators, you'd have thought something would've gotten him by now."

"It's a good thing to have chickens," Zelda said. "It's a good omen for my baby." She patted her stomach and smiled.

"The girls'll take good care of him," Massie said, exiting the chicken coop, smiling broadly. "I was beginning to despair of having a rooster they could look after."

"We can't eat all the eggs," Junebug contributed. "We need more chickens. The ones we've got won't be enough for everybody, especially not long term."

Everyone was excited as they filed back inside. Laughter lit up the day. Esta May and Jamie were holding hands. The sight saddened Joshua, but he told himself yet again that he had to live with what was, not what he wished could be.

Just before he reached the doorway, Pappy touched his shoulder and motioned him away. Puzzled, Joshua followed his father. They were on the ice before Pappy stopped.

"You're pretty upset," he said quietly.

Joshua, startled, looked into his father's dark eyes. He didn't say anything for a moment, trying to feel for he wanted to say. His mind was blank. At last he sighed, his unhappiness blowing out into cold air. "Is it obvious?"

"Esta May and Jamie."

Joshua shrugged.

Pappy looked out at the white cold of ice beneath heavy snow clouds bent to the earth. "You could keep trying," he said at last.

"What's happened has happened," Joshua said. "I suspect it was my fault. I kept going along assuming the two of us would be together, but that wasn't a done deal in the bag. Jamie was always better at letting her know he was interested." His face screwed up in puzzlement. "What I don't understand is how reading turned her to Jamie. My reading good made her see me in a different way. It seems mysterious."

Pappy smiled. "You never really figure out women," he said. "They got their own minds and own ways. I think that's part of the reason men are always thinking about them. I don't think we're supposed to understand."

Joshua didn't answer, but studied the ice and snow beneath his feet.

Pappy touched his shoulder again, his touch so light Joshua could barely feel it through his coat. "Ella's interested in you," he said.

"Ella's young," Joshua said quickly.

Pappy sighed. "She's fourteen going on fifteen. You're a little over sixteen. Your mother and Preacher just figured out you turned sixteen a month ago. There's not much difference in your ages." He paused. "Preacher's been getting everybody's birthdays down and putting them in his Bible. Chas is making a calendar. As your mother says, we're going to be a civilized people."

He paused and then continued in an almost fierce voice. "One of these days we have to start doing something for birthdays, not so much for the older people, but for you younger ones. We've been too busy and involved in our affairs. We haven't got a life rhythm down yet, but that's going to end.

"And anyway, I'm just under two years younger than your mother. That's no problem. Age doesn't make boundaries that keep love in containers made out of what people think."

Joshua looked strangely at his father. He could not have known the man was younger than his mother. For the flash of a moment he saw Ella, slender, earnest, always deferring to her prettier big sister, moving around God's house, helping smaller children sound out words in the speller. He quickly shook the image away.

"We got to get along," Joshua said. "I understand that. I love this island. Nobody beats or whips me. I see my mother every day. She doesn't have to hide that from the mistress or anybody else. I've got a father." He looked up into Pappy's eyes. "Back on the plantation I was stubborn as a mule and hated going along with anybody in anyway, but I've changed. Here, I understand. There's too few of us. If we want to be okay, we've got to get along and work together."

Pappy nodded. "You're going to be quite a man."

Joshua snorted his disbelief at what his father had just said.

Pappy clapped him on the shoulder. "We'd better be getting back," he said. "They'll be missing us." He paused, looking at Joshua. "Do you know you're growing?"

"Growing?"

"I wasn't big for my age," he said with a smile. "Not when I was young. I didn't start shooting up until I was your age. I think maybe my blood is starting to show in you. You getting cramps in your legs at night?"

"You're a giant of a man," Joshua protested, not answering Pappy's question about the cramps that had started bothering him most nights. "You're stronger than any man I ever met."

"I wasn't always that way," Pappy said. "I started growing late, but I didn't stop. I outgrew everybody bigger than me, including every man on the plantation, black or white. You've almost caught up with Jamie, if you haven't noticed, though he's still taller. I can almost see you growing."

Joshua smiled. "You're crazy," he said.

Pappy laughed. "We'd better be getting back. Preacher'll be getting irritated that his best reader isn't helping."

***

The minute the cabin's door opened, Preacher smiled. "Good," he said. "You're here." He pointed at Joshua. "Why don't you read with Jeremiah? One of you can read aloud and then the other one can. You're both doing really well."

Joshua saw that Ella May and Jamie were sitting together away from both their families. He clenched his teeth without realizing what he was doing and went to sit beside Jeremiah. Jeremiah had followed Joshua's gaze and grimaced, shaking his head, but didn't say anything. Instead he picked up the Bible from their cabin and opened it to Genesis. He looked at Joshua.

"Go ahead," Joshua said.

"In the beginning God created the heaven and the earth," Jeremiah read, stumbling over every four words or so, in his high-pitched voice. "And the earth was without form, and void; and darkness was upon the face of the deep. And the Spirit of God moved upon the face of the waters."

He stopped. The cabin door opened to admit Harrison and Henry Miner. Harrison was frowning. Henry Miner looked like he always looked, full of a brisk energy and over-charged sense of purpose, although Joshua noticed that he did seem disconcerted, as if he hadn't expected to find them together.

"Excuse us," Harrison said, "but Mr. Miner wants to tell us all something."

He looked at the white man in a way that made Joshua uncomfortable. It wasn't subservient exactly, but it seemed as if he were giving the white man more respect than he gave the people he lived with every day. There was something in the way he stood beside Miner that seemed to say that he had to be both careful and respectful around the man.

Henry Miner's face was pinched, his eyes narrowed as if he were trying to see more than there was to see. After a moment's silence he turned and addressed Preacher.

"I think I warned you about James Strang on Beaver Island," he said. He waited until Preacher nodded his head.

"The man who says he's a king," Preacher acknowledged.

"That's the one," Miner said. He paused again. "Well," he said, "this seems foolish to me, but after thinking about it I decided I should come out here and tell you." He shook his head slightly. "This is just a rumor, mind you, but in Irish Village they're saying Strang has gotten more serious about Washington Island and is planning a raid to get the foothold he's supposedly been talking to his Mormon folk about." He stopped and looked around the room. "The rumor is that after the ice firms enough he's going to come with an armed force to West Harbor and establish here."

"He's a Mormon?" Preacher asked. "Is that a Christian faith? I don't think I know about Mormons."

"Christian?" Miner sounded puzzled. "They don't sound Christian to me. At least not in any way my father as a minister would have recognized someone being Christian. They say Strang has more than one wife. He follows a man called Joseph Smith who was killed in Missouri by Christians who didn't think he was a Christian. They thought he was of the Devil's party." He cocked his head slightly, still looking at Preacher. "I'd have thought you might have heard of him."

Preacher shook his head. "No," he said, "I haven't. But why is this Strang interested in Washington Island and West Harbor? We're here now."

"Someone, I don't know who, was over on Beaver Island this fall," Miner said. "The rumor is that a king needs a kingdom. Beaver Island's pretty small to be considered a kingdom. A lot of folks have followed Strang, too. They're saying he needs more fishing grounds to support them all."

"Who's them?" Pappy asked from his seat on the bench.

"Do they know we're here at West Harbor?" Willie added. "It seems like we've done what we need to do to make a claim here."

"I've never met this Strang, although I have run into a couple of his followers," Miner said. "From what I understand, he claims to have seen an angel who came to ordain him as the ruler of God's people. Supposedly there's a letter from Joseph Smith, who started up the Mormons, that appoints Strang the Mormon leader after Smith's death."

"He knows we're here?" Willie prompted again.

"I only know what I'm told," Miner said. "That's why I hesitated to come tell you. I've heard he thinks West Harbor is the perfect place for a Mormon outpost. He thinks you might put up the least trouble for him and his people coming over the ice."

"So he knows a group of black families have settled here," Preacher said, his voice troubled.

Joshua felt chills running up his spine. The Mormons were white. They didn't sound like slavers, but you couldn't trust white people.

"Jason asked who they are." Joshua's mother said. "Who told you all this? Are they reliable people?"

Mr. Miner looked decidedly uncomfortable, like he didn't want to tell them who his sources of information were. He looked at Pappy and Joshua's mother and then back at Preacher. "That's why I almost didn't come," he said. "I knew you'd ask. You have every right to ask. I'd ask too." He shook his head. "I heard it from Joel Westbrook. He's the magistrate. I know he doesn't like you here on this island, but I don't know that he's a liar."

The silence was tense. Joshua felt like he'd been nailed to the bench where he was sitting beside Jeremiah. He could feel the fear that had crept into the room, into God's house.

"You think Westbrook's planning something and is going to blame it on Strang?" Harrison asked.

Jeremiah had gotten to his feet.

"He's got to be careful," Miner said. "There's enough abolitionists on the island to make his life difficult if he tries anything on his own." He looked like he only half believed what he was telling them.

"Chas has a rifle," Jeremiah said, his voice louder than he had meant it to be. "We won't leave without fighting."

"Jeremiah," Massie warned him.

"I'm sorry," Mr. Miner said.

"Sorry?" Preacher asked. "What have you got to be sorry about? You're a friend who came to warn us about possible trouble so we can prepare ourselves. You don't have to be sorry about trying to be our friend."

"Mr. Westbrook frightens me," Zelda said.

Franklin, who had been struggling with his reading like the rest of the grown men, touched his wife's shoulder. "He frightens all of us," he said. "But that doesn't mean we should run." He looked at Henry Miner. "Do you think West Harbor is in any danger?"

Mr. Miner shook his head. "Not from Westbrook, not really, I don't," he said in a matter-of-fact voice. "Not if you don't let him spook you." He thought for a moment. "But I don't know about Strang. I don't know what to think about that. Maybe there's something to the rumor and maybe not." He bit his lip. "I also heard he's an abolitionist like the Danes. If he is that would mean you maybe don't have any worries about him and his followers. But as far as I know, that's rumor, too."

Preacher looked around at the tense room. Everybody had turned from Mr. Miner and was waiting for him to speak.

"How's the lake, Mr. Miner?" Preacher asked. "Are fishermen around Washington Harbor going out on the ice yet?"

Miner bowed his head, then raised it again. "There's open water yet," he said. "Ice is still thin. You can't see open water, but I can't deliver mail by walking across the lake yet. Maybe soon, but you can get far enough out to catch fish, and a lot of fishermen have started."

Preacher smiled. "Chas has been telling us it's time," he said.

"Well," Miner said. "I've done what I came to do. I can take any mail you folks want. If the cold holds, I suspect a man walking can make it across in a week or less. I go out every day and check."

"Isn't that dangerous?" Ertha asked, concerned. "I'd be afraid to go out on that ice so far." Beulah put her arm around her daughter.

Mr. Miner smiled. "I'm careful," he said. "I've been doing it for a long time now."

"We don't have mail," Pappy said. He looked blankly at the cabin floor. "Maybe someday."

Miner nodded. "I'd better be going," he said.

Harrison went to the door and opened it, letting a cold gust make the flames in the fireplace waver.

***

The next morning, Joshua woke when Pappy crawled out of the blankets covering him and Joshua's mother. Willie had already built a fire, although it still hadn't warmed the cabin. In the dark, Jason looked more like a hulking shadow than a man as Joshua followed him into the cabin's shared room. Pappy laughed as he saw how Willie was holding his hands out to the fire still climbing up the teepee of sticks put together to help the flames breathe and dance toward larger chunks of split wood.

"Think we'll ever get used to this country's cold?" he asked Willie good-naturedly.

"Chas says we will," Willie said. He smiled, firelight flashing briefly on his white teeth. "He also said that today will separate the men from the boys."

Pappy sobered. "Yeah." He sighed. He slapped arms across his chest, his hands hitting his shoulders.

A few minutes later, Joshua's mother, Massie, Jamie, and Jeremiah were all in the room. It wasn't as crowded as most of the quarters' shacks had been.

They had built good cabins. They were living in cold country, but weren't, inside, any colder than they would have been in Missouri except during the nighttime before the morning fire had been made. Massie and Joshua's mother didn't say much, but got a heavy black frying pan off the wall. Jamie was already going outside to get frozen meat and the stuff for frying pan bread that Chas had bought in Washington Harbor.

When they finished their hurried breakfast, they made their way to where Chas, Harrison, Franklin, and Bill had gathered axes, wooden buckets, lines, hooks, and small cut-up pieces of venison for bait. "Not like going out in the scow, eh?" Harrison asked.

Chas hmmphed. "We spread out," he said. "The ice is thick enough to support all of us standing close to each other, but there's no sense tempting fate. We're gonna walk a quarter mile out, knock a hole in the ice," he lifted up one of the axes they'd used to fell trees, "then bait hooks on a single line." He held up a line that looked like it might have anywhere from four to five leaders, each one with a hook on the end. "You put the baited hooks in the hole you've made. When you get a bite, you pull the line up." His gaze caught each of theirs in turn. "Anybody got a question?"

They were smiling when Chas led the way out on the ice.

As they left the harbor's protection, snow on top of the ice was whispering in long, ghostly lines in a southerly direction. The cold, already biting, cut into them, but nobody hesitated.

"We can't be this close together," Chas said once they were where he wanted to be. "Here, Franklin, Bill, take axes and walk about fifty yards or so and cut a hole." He added as they started to separate from each other, "Baiting's not easy in these conditions. You might have to take off your gloves. You have to be careful of frostbite. We don't want to lose any fingers."

He swung the axe in his hand back and struck the ice hard. Shards flew in all directions. A few minutes later, he had a hole through four or five inches of ice and was forcing frozen venison onto hooks.

Looking out to where the Door Peninsula jutted into Lake Michigan while waiting for someone to get a fish on their line, Joshua felt an enormous hole in his life. Emptiness seemed to be one with the soft whisper of wind and scuttling of snow. He felt lonely even though the men he knew best surrounded him.

No one talked. They were trying to cope with the cold, fingers and feet growing numb, and the waiting for fish. Joshua knew they would have to catch fish all winter, no matter how cold it got. They hadn't been able to store enough during the short summer and fall after they'd arrived to get them through. He didn't think they'd starve, but he could see days with skimpy meals. They also had to earn cash to buy supplies they would inevitably need. A thin winter was in the offing no matter how good they were at ice fishing.

No one felt a tug on his line for what seemed forever. Then Jeremiah gave an excited shout. Willy quickly pulled his line out of the hole he was hunching over and moved to help his youngest son. Less than a minute later, Jeremiah pulled a five-pound trout out of the ice. Five minutes later, Franklin had a larger trout on his line. Then, off and on, with long minutes between bites, they started catching trout, a few in the twelve, fifteen-pound range, but most smaller.

When Chas finally called an end to the day, Joshua was exhausted. His cheeks burned from wind and winter sun, and his hands and feet were numb from cold. The number of fish they'd caught hardly seemed worth the pain. After they gathered up the buckets holding thirty-one trout, and lines, hooks, bait, and other stuff they'd scattered on the ice during a long day, they dragged toward home.

As they came ashore, Harrison, looking especially tired, asked Chas, "When do you think we can take the outhouse on the lake?" he asked. He glanced toward the three boys. "I've got the runners done."

Chas stopped his trek up the slope to the cabins and looked at the sky. "Close to time," he said. "A week or so?"

Harrison nodded. "After all that work, I don't want it to break through and sink."

Joshua was surprised by the conversation. Outhouse? It sounded to him like the ice shack Harrison and Junebug had built was an outhouse and not a shack they'd use to keep out of the lake's cold to fish. He had imagined the small structure would somehow keep them warm through long days on the ice. He shook his head and walked resolutely toward the cabin. He didn't see the smiles behind his back as he walked away.

Chapter 25
Washington Island Ice

They did not notice when the mist began
To tendril off the ice, the brutal cold
Horizoned by the lake's huge winter span
Of white that wrapped them in an endless fold
That barely separated how the heavens
Knelt down with heavy clouds and fiercely gripped
Their spirits in a subtle separation
Of white from white, lake, sky an arching crypt.

Then, in a moment, rising mist became
A covering that muted any hint of sound
And made a silence suffocating flames
Of who they were, the dense, white wraparound

A spell that snuffed away direction — fog
An absent, blind, and disconcerting bog.

    The daily fishing was exhausting and, often, miserable. They moved Harrison's fishing shack onto its runners and, after moving around for several days, placed it where the fishing seemed to be the best. Increasingly cold weather and days of wind burned their faces and the fierce light reflecting off snow and ice hurt their eyes. Keeping the ice holes open was a constant struggle. If ice that filmed over the water wasn't kept cleared, when the fish, or sometimes more than one fish on the line, was pulled up, the surface ice somehow seemed to help the catch slip off the hook.
    Snowy days created another problem. They made trails through the snow to where the ice shack was, but then a storm would dump a foot of new snow on top of the ice. Chas, who fished and hunted alternately, could move over the snow with his snowshoes, but the rest of them weren't as well equipped. Harrison and Junebug, with Beulah's help, had finished deer hide boots with the hard leather brought by Gordon, but there was work on the cabins, with the chickens, on the woodpile, and on the grounds. Essential work took time, leaving little extra for making things like snowshoes. Their need for leather to make things seemed

endless, and turning hide into usable leather took the women hours of effort.

Some days fishing was good. On other days the fish were not biting, and though they always put fish into the barrels they got from Mr. Miner when Chas and others walked along the shore to Washington Harbor, there were times when ice fishing was painful as they stood around holes and waited into a time that felt forever empty.

The problem with a good day's catch was that there was no way to avoid getting their hands wet. They could use a shovel to keep ice out of the hole, but fish, flopping out of the ice, made it difficult to stay dry. On the coldest days, when the snow crunched a hollow sound as they made their way to the fishing shack, getting even a little damp was dangerous. The ice was deep enough to allow small fires, so they were constantly holding their hands over small flames. Still, avoiding frostbite was a very real struggle.

The problem was, Joshua thought repeatedly, especially in mornings when cold sun filtered light into the sky, Chas and Preacher had experience with northern climates, but the rest of them had spent their lives in the warmer south. The fishermen from Washington Harbor not only had better equipment than they did, but they also had a better idea about how to survive ceaseless cold. They'd learn, Joshua supposed, and the money from the fish they were catching would help them buy better clothing and gear, but in the meantime, they had to survive.

***

Disaster struck. Zelda fell on the way to the outhouse at dawn. Joshua was on his way back to the cabin and breakfast when he saw her slip on an icy rise on the snow-covered path beaten down by people going up and down the slight slope. His heart jumped when he saw her go down hard, sliding backward toward the cabins. He gasped as he ran to help her.

She didn't make a sound when she fell. Instead she looked up at the sky with a puzzled look on her face. Kneeling beside her, Joshua could see that she didn't feel right. Her eyes seemed strangely distant, bloodshot, and she looked scared.

"Are you all right Miss Zelda?" he asked anxiously. "Are you all right?"

She had fallen on her back, so she looked from the sky into his face. She shook her head so slightly Joshua barely could see the movement. Her forehead creased. "I don't think so," she said, looking at her extended belly.

"Can you get up?"

She strained to lift herself so that she could sit, but couldn't move. She cried out involuntarily. Joshua tried to help, but was out of his depth and awkward. The child. The unborn baby. He glanced toward the cabins, but couldn't see anybody.

"You'd better get Franklin," Zelda said. She seemed calm, but Joshua could see her pain.

Without thinking Joshua got to his feet and ran to the cabins. "Franklin," he shouted. "Franklin!"

Pappy was standing in front of Joshua before he reached the back of God's house. "Son?" he asked.

"Zelda," Joshua said, pointing up the hill.

He moved so fast Joshua hardly felt him go past him up the hill. Chas and Franklin came around God's house's corner, too. "What?" Chas asked and then saw Pappy running and then saw Zelda. A minute later Joshua, Franklin, and Chas were kneeling in snow beside the path. Pappy was carefully examining Zelda, running his big hands along her side.

"Do you hurt Zelda?" he asked.

Zelda, looking distant, shook her head and grimaced. "I don't feel right," she said, but she didn't moan or cry or do anything else to make it seem like she was hurting.

"I can carry you," Pappy said.

"What if her back's broken?" Chas asked.

Franklin's face paled. He had looked like he'd gone into shock the minute he saw his wife lying flat on her back on the trail. At Chas's words, he looked sick. "You've got to be careful," he said, his voice trembling. "Zelda's the best thing that ever happened to me. You've to be careful."

"We've got to get her out of this cold and beneath warm covers beside a fire," Pappy said. He looked at Chas. Franklin had grabbed Zelda's hand and was rubbing it. Joshua felt helpless.

"How do you feel Zelda?" Chas asked. "Can you stand to have Jason pick you up and carry you?"

Zelda looked at him as if he were a stranger. "You've got to be careful of the baby," she said.

The rest of the community had come out of the cabins and were standing along the trail. Joshua's mother was standing behind Joshua. He hadn't been aware she had come up the trail. "Lift her slow, Jason," she ordered in that voice that always compelled Joshua to do what she wanted him to do. "And if she cries out stop,"

Pappy didn't look at her, but carefully slid his hands underneath Zelda's knees. She gasped. He froze. "I'm cold," she said.

"Do you want him to lift you?" Joshua's mother asked. "Is there too much pain?"

Zelda didn't look at her, but at Franklin. Her breathing was shallow. She wasn't breathing normally.

"May God protect her and our child," Franklin said. Preacher, standing where the path started up the slight incline, said, "Amen."

"Careful, Jason," Franklin said, his voice anguished. "Careful."

Pappy slowly slid his right arm under her shoulders. Zelda closed her eyes and gasped. "Lift me," she said, whispering.

Pappy looked at Franklin. "God's with us," Franklin said loudly. "He's got to be with us."

In one movement, Pappy was on his feet and carrying Zelda toward the corner of God's house. She screamed, her pain ringing through the silent trees. Pappy didn't stop, but rushed around the corner so fast he didn't seem to be carrying any weight at all, especially not a woman heavy with her pregnancy. Zelda, after that one cry, was silent. Franklin, caught by surprise when Pappy lifted her, was a step behind. By the time Joshua and his mother and the rest were around the cabin's corner, both men and Zelda were in the Woodruff cabin out of sight.

Joshua's mother, Massie, and Beulah hesitated a moment after seeing that the men had Zelda inside the cabin, but then, thinking the same thought at the same moment, rushed toward the cabin and went inside.

For a long time, there was no hint about what was happening. Esta May took charge of Abbie, who clung to her as if she were frightened that she would be left alone. She didn't cry, but looked like she could start at any moment.

Jamie, Jeremiah, Ella, and the rest of the Woodruffs milled around the big cedar in front of the cabin. Jamie asked Joshua if he thought Zelda would be all right, but Joshua shrugged. He'd seen her fall, but there was no way he could know. Ella tried to talk to him, too. He looked at her, half smiled, and looked at the cabin again. He felt like everything had happened so quickly he hadn't had time to think. He tried to think about what he'd done and what he could have done differently.

At last Preacher came over to where the young people were beside the cedar. He looked serious, but calm. "We need to pray in God's house," he said.

Joshua looked at him as if he was crazy. "Zelda's in the cabin," he said, a hint of exasperation in his voice.

Preacher captured his eyes. Joshua wondered how he always knew how to command everybody's attention whenever he wanted to do so. "You did what you could," Preacher told him. "You got help." He paused. "Good help." He took Joshua's arm. "Come," he said, and Joshua and the rest of them followed him to God's house.

Preacher didn't try to give a sermon through his prayer once they were on the benches. "We'll each pray for Zelda and her unborn child," he said. "The hope of our freedom." He bowed his graying head. "We'll pray silently." Abbie, who had been unbelievably strong all the way north during their escape, sitting between Esta May and Ella, whimpered so softly she could just barely be heard. Her best friend Ertha reached over Ella's lap to hold her hand.

Joshua was trying to find a prayer inside him when God's house's door opened. His head jerked up. Pappy slipped inside and closed the door. "Zelda's going be okay," he said. He sounded tired. "She's not feeling good, but Mary said she thinks she's mostly sore. Chas agrees with her."

Relief flooded into Joshua. "Thank God," Preacher said. "Thank God for all our blessings."

Abbie stood. "I'm going to see my Maw," she declared. Esta May rose and took her hand.

The problem was, however, that after he and Jamie had split wood for the woodpile and carried several armfuls of kindling and wood into each cabin for the night, hardly speaking to each other as they worked, Joshua's mother still hadn't come into their cabin. Pappy was frying trout in the big black frying pan for supper. Massie wasn't in the cabin, either. Jamie had gone to eat with Esta May's family, so Pappy, Willie, Jeremiah, and Joshua were alone. Pappy, working over the fire, looked worried.

"Where's my mother?" Joshua asked after he realized Pappy wasn't just helping with the meal but was making it.

Willie, looking as stressed as Pappy, came out of the Bullock's room with Jeremiah. "There's still trouble at Zelda's and Franklin's," he said. "They've sent Abbie to be with Bill, Jamie, and the girls."

Joshua had a funny feeling. Jamie had delivered wood to the second cabin while he had taken his loads into God's house for Preacher and Chas. No one had told him anything. He saw Zelda's frightened eyes as she stared up at him when he'd first reached her on the path. He shivered.

"The preacher's praying," Pappy said.

Joshua had seen the preacher praying. He'd been on his knees in front of the sanctuary, facing the benches where they sat every Sunday, but that wasn't anything new. Joshua had hardly noticed him when he'd put another chunk of wood on a fire starting to die down. When Preacher wasn't working, he was either reading the Bible or praying. That was central to who he was as a man.

"What's wrong? I thought Miss Zelda was all right," Joshua said.

Willie shook his head. "The worry isn't Zelda," he said. Then he was silent.

Joshua stared blankly into dancing flames below the black tripod holding the frying pan and fish. The baby. He'd forgotten about the baby.

***

Massie and Mary did not come into the cabin until late in the night. Jamie had come in earlier, slipping into the Bullock room as quietly as he knew how. No one was sleeping. Joshua and Pappy got out of warm covers the minute a cold wind burst came into the cabin. Both women looked exhausted and grim faced. The fire had mostly died down, with only a flickering flame toward the back of the hearth. Joshua and Jeremiah both went to the wood racked beside the fireplace to throw logs onto the embers. Jamie had gotten out of bed, but he stayed by the door to their sleeping room. He seemed like an unhappy shadow in the cabin's darkness.

Massie was shaking her head. "The baby's gone," she said quietly. "Mary did all she could, but it's gone."

Joshua, staring at sparks that went up the chimney when he'd placed wood on the embers, didn't move. Zelda's pregnancy had been part of the joy of coming into freedom on the island. It had spoken of a future different from what any of them had imagined on their plantations. Zelda's child was going to be the first one born of their escape to freedom.

"Mary?" Pappy asked.

Joshua's mother was silent. She was looking at Joshua. She shook her head. "I'm going to bed," she said. Abruptly, she walked past them and walked into their room.

After she left, Massie shook her head. "She's taking it hard. She kept thinking she could save the child and Zelda both." She looked toward her family's room. "When something like that's happening there's no way," she said, her voice sad. "No human hands or love words are going to stop the terribleness coming."

"How's Zelda?" Willy asked.

Jeremiah had gone over to his mother and put his arms around her. She looked at him and smiled. "Upset," she said. "The same as any woman who's just lost a child would be." She paused. "Franklin and Junebug are with her. She seems to be tolerating Junebug better than the rest of us. Abbie's with her cousins."

Pappy nodded and headed toward the bedroom and his wife. Joshua didn't know what to do.

There had been unborn children that had not lived in the quarters. Doctors attended white women, but not women slaves. Sometimes a child died, too. He remembered one energetic little girl who had just collapsed in the tobacco fields one day and never came out of a feverish, restless sleep. The day had been so hot, and Silver Coats had been so mean, it had seemed a miracle any of them had survived, they'd been driven so hard. The girl, though, had woken up feverish and said she wasn't feeling good and that her stomach hurt, but the Overseer had been in a bad mood and made her mother get the girl up anyway.

But this was different. This was family.

***

The next morning, no one felt like breakfast. Everybody but Zelda and Franklin ended up in God's house. Preacher greeted each of them as they came in the door. He looked like he'd been up all night praying. Joshua's mother, still shaken, said he'd been with Zelda and Franklin after the baby had been stillborn. That was the word she'd used, stillborn. But then he'd left after Zelda refused to even acknowledge he was in the room.

After they were seated on Harrison's benches, sitting like they were ready for Sunday service, Preacher slowly made his way to the front of the room. He had his head bowed. Before he spoke, however, he lifted his head and looked at them, fire in his eyes.

"Tragedy has come to this community," he said. "The Apostle John in the Bible tells us 'These things I have spoken unto you, that in me ye might have peace. In the world ye shall have tribulation: but be of good cheer; I have overcome the world'. Well, we have tribulation this morning, and we are in need of peace inside the troubles that have visited Franklin, Zelda, and Abbie with such force, but the idea of good cheer is not really in me this morning.

"I have asked so many times during my lifetime, how can this be? How did friends who believed in Jesus and worshipped the Lord die when cannon balls struck them in the midst of battle? Why has the Lord allowed His word to be used by slavers, and those who are supposedly His servants, to enslave people and subject them to whippings and other violations? Why did the Lord allow an unborn baby who would have been the joy and pride of everyone in this room to not be born?

"I have never found an answer to these and other questions that stir me up in the middle of some nights. But I always take comfort remembering this hymn."

He took a deep breath, and in a soft, deep voice, sang to his bereft congregation.

"The truth is," he said. "We are nothing but poor human beings who used to be slaves. None of us, including me, have the answers we need. All I can tell any of you, including our grieving sister and brother Zelda and Franklin, is that by going to Jesus in prayer, our hearts will ease, and we'll be able to go on. It is the going on that counts. We have made a great journey and found freedom, but it's the going on that counts."

He let his hands fall to his side. Joshua was confused. If even Preacher had no answers for the terrible sadness everyone was suffering, he wondered if there was truly any answers to be had. Preacher turned and went to his bedroom, leaving the rest of them to their silence.

Outside, the sun was shining, but the day seemed dark, even out on the lake beyond the harbor where light was glinting off miles of snow and ice. Joshua's mother, Massie, and Beulah went purposefully into the cabin where Zelda and Franklin were. Abbie kept close to Ertha, Eunice, and Ella, while Jamie and Esta May disappeared. Chas brought his rifle out of God's house and walked into the woods. Pappy, Willie, Bill, and Harrison quietly started doing chores. Pappy and Bill took shovels to the outhouse path and started chipping at the hard snow and patches of ice that had made it so perilous for Zelda. Willie and Harrison took a saw and followed Chas into the woods.

Jeremiah, sticking with Joshua, walked with him out onto the harbor's ice. They didn't pick up fishing gear, but instead trudged out past the harbor mouth onto the frozen lake's broad flatness. For a while neither spoke, each intent on trying to walk off the feeling that their world was disintegrating. There was no wind. The endless ice was as peaceful as Joshua had ever seen it.

***

At last Joshua sat down on the ice and stared up at Jeremiah. "I should have done more for Miss Zelda," he said, his sadness so overpowering he could hardly stand it.

"*What?* Maw said you did everything you could do."

"There must have been something."

"What?"

"Something."

Jeremiah sat beside him in the snow. "My parents called me Jeremiah," he said. He smiled. "They didn't ask me if I wanted the name. Reading in the Bible I found out that Jeremiah was okay with God, but not a peaceful man. He kept prophesizing about Jerusalem's destruction. If I had my way, I wouldn't have that name. I can't change it, so I'm going to have to live with it. You weren't near Miss Zelda when she fell. You couldn't have kept her from falling. You went and got help as fast as you could. That's what I understand, and, like with my name, you can't change any of that."

Joshua sighed. "Things aren't going good for me right now."

"You're free," Jeremiah said softly. "You couldn't have imagined that not long ago. Not any more than I could have imagined it, or Jamie, or anybody else that came with us."

Joshua looked at Jeremiah for a long moment. "What is freedom about if it doesn't make you happy? I mean, look at Zelda, Franklin, and Abbie right now. What good has freedom done for them?"

Jeremiah looked at Joshua and, as abruptly as Preacher had left the sanctuary, got to his feet. "We're going through a hard time," he said. "But there were hard times on the plantation, too." He paused. "You know that as much as anybody. I'd rather be free and dealing with hard times than a slave that can't do anything they need to do to make things better." He turned and started back to the harbor and land.

Joshua didn't move. The lake's silence grew until it swallowed him up. He watched Jeremiah until he disappeared into the cabin they shared and then looked at the lake. He'd lost Esta May. His relationship with Jamie wasn't as good as it had been most of their lives. He hadn't been able to help Zelda when she'd needed help more than at any other time in her life. He'd failed Franklin, who had constantly been taking them out in the scow before winter had come, and Abbie, a child who had never complained even when she was starving during the run north. He wondered what Abbie's brother or sister would have looked and been like if they had been born into freedom. Would they have been any different?

At last he realized he was getting cold. There was still no wind and the sun was shining, but it was winter. He reluctantly got to his feet. Jeremiah was right, of course. He knew that. He'd done what he'd been able to do after Zelda had fallen. His life was as it was. He couldn't change it. He was free—even if he wasn't sure what that meant.

Chapter 26
A Time of Aftermaths

Events can shock through lives and rip apart
The weave of hours infusing sapience
Throughout the complex expectations chart
Into the early morning radiance
Of rising sun, the comfort of continuance
Across the ceaseless ebb and flow of thought
Concealed until its conscious utterance
Shakes spirit out of heart, a juggernaut
Of self adjusting to emotions caught
By staggering realities, the song
That is, though we have always looked for, sought
A future feeling right and good, not wrong.

But when events upset the flow of days,
What destinies are born out of malaise?

The next morning Preacher came to their cabin. He looked solemn as he stood beside the fireplace as Joshua and his family and the four Bullocks joined him. Blue-black rings were heavy beneath his eyes.

"I've prayed all night," he said. "I talked to Franklin and Zelda this morning. They want to have a Christian funeral for their son."

Joshua's mother bowed her head. "That's only right," she said.

"When?" Massie asked.

"This afternoon," Preacher said. He paused. "You'll help Zelda prepare?" he asked, looking first at Joshua's mother and then Massie.

"So soon?" Joshua's mother asked.

Preacher shook his head. "Franklin and Zelda both are thinking of past times," he said. "Zelda's fragile. She's afraid a funeral won't be held even though here we would not deny the child the dignity of what he meant to his parents and all of us. Our mortality is always entwined into the days we have." He closed his eyes and grimaced as if in tremendous pain. "This is difficult," he said. "But the Lord is with us, and we have to persevere."

***

No one thought about fishing. Instead, they busied themselves with other tasks. The women joined together to prepare the baby's body for the funeral and comfort Zelda. Franklin didn't stay in the cabin with his wife, but took Abbie outside. He started planing boards made out of maple stacked up behind the cabins. He said that the chicken coop needed expanding. He kept asking Abbie for tools and even help with sawing, just to keep her occupied.

Harrison and Junebug, working together, started putting together a small casket out of boards left over from their various projects.

When, at last, it came time for the funeral, they gathered not far from the spit of land that reached out into the lake. Pappy and Willie had dug a grave in the frozen ground. Joshua, Jamie, and Jeremiah had taken their turns chipping at it, but Pappy had done most of the work.

When Preacher finally led Zelda, Franklin, and Abbie out of their cabin, afternoon shadows were spreading out from beneath the trees. Franklin carried the small wooden casket. Joshua's mother and Beulah were on each side of Zelda, holding her arms, while Massie walked hand in hand with Abbie.

Zelda was pale. She shuffled rather than picking up her feet, and appeared to still be in pain. Preacher's face held a storm of emotions as he walked. Chas, Pappy, and the men waited at the gravesite. Nobody said anything until all of them were in a circle around the grave.

Preacher clasped his hands and bowed his head. "We are gathered here in grieving, Lord," he said in his deepest, most sonorous voice. His words sounded like a song.

Zelda gasped and almost fell into Beulah. Preacher didn't open his eyes, but took a deep breath.

"At times like this it's easy to doubt the goodness in life and the Lord, Lord," Preacher continued. "We remember, when we've gone through tragedy, our ancestors who were brought to this far land against their will. We start to ask if heathenism, in its innocence, did not have better answers than what we find in the Holy Bible, your word.

"But, of course, that thinking lays a false path. It does not find the place where hope gives us the promise of reaching your side after we have walked the valley of death." He suddenly looked up toward the sky. "We have lost a child," he said loudly. "An innocence too innocent to breathe air in this difficult world."

Zelda broke down, sagging to the ground. She moaned loudly. Franklin turned and handed the small casket to Chas who had quietly stepped to his side. Joshua's mother and Beulah helped hold Zelda off the snowy ground.

Joshua felt himself crying. He didn't raise his head enough to see if everyone else was, too, but Zelda's wild, uncontrolled sobbing bound the universe into her pain and desperation.

Preacher took another deep breath. "Your word tells us, Lord, 'And I heard a great voice out of heaven saying, Behold, the tabernacle of God is with men, and he will dwell with them, and they shall be his people, and God himself shall be with them, and be their God.' We are giving an unborn child, a pure spirit into your hands, Lord, with grieving and suffering. We want to tell you that in spite of our heritage in the black heart of slavery, we are free now, and we choose to be your people.

"So we ask you, Lord, you and your son Jesus Christ, to accept this pure spirit into your keeping and your kingdom. We ask you to bless and comfort his parents, our sister Zelda and our brother Franklin, and his sister, Abbie, for they need your care right now. And we ask you to bless and comfort this community of souls who have fled to this island wilderness in hopes of building a life in the name of our protector and Lord." Preacher paused for a long moment of silence, then sighed. "We pray this in Jesus' name," he concluded. "Amen."

Preacher nodded at Chas, who brought the small casket forward and got down on his knees and carefully put it into the grave. Preacher then nodded to Pappy and Willie, and the two men picked up their shovels and started covering the casket with frozen dirt. Joshua heard it clunk as it hit the casket's wood.

***

The day after the funeral, neither Franklin nor Chas came out of the cabin where Zelda laid in bed all day. The next day, the two men came out, but neither Zelda nor Abbie left the cabin. Neither of the Bullock men spoke about what had happened, and no one else referred to it, either.

Then, on the second Sunday after the funeral, Zelda, Abbie, and Franklin came out of their cabin and attended the service. The weather was miserable. Wind violently tossed the tops of the white pine and a hard sleet whipped faces as the community gathered.

Inside the cabin the fire had been built up and, compared to what they had just hurried through, made the sanctuary warm. Preacher was in his room putting the finishing touches on his sermon, so the rest of them quietly went to their benches and sat waiting. Unlike other Sundays, the men didn't talk, but nodded to each other and especially to Franklin. The women, one at a time, went over to Zelda and bent their heads close to her face to whisper condolences. Joshua's mother touched Abbie's head tenderly as the little girl looked at her with large dark eyes.

Finally, Preacher came into the sanctuary and took his place in front of them. During the week he had stayed in God's house and prayed, spending hours with hands clasped in front of him and his head bowed. Pappy had said he was taking the baby's stillbirth hard. They had all had an incredible run of good fortune, starting with the escape through the Mingo swamp. Now their fortunes had turned, although, Pappy confessed to his son, he wasn't sure why.

"He's a preacher, though," Pappy said. "In the end he'll comfort us. That's what preachers are supposed to do."

Preacher didn't speak for a long time after he stood in front of them. He seemed to be searching for what to say. At last he took a deep breath.

"This is a special day," he said. "John the Baptist baptizing disciples in the waters of the Jordan River once said, 'A man can receive nothing, except it be given from heaven.' As we join together this day, I want us to think about what John said. The Bible also tells us that God's judgments are unsearchable, that in the ways of an old English hymn, 'God moves in a mysterious way.'

"The truth is this morning that these Bible words are affecting me deeply. We have lost a child before it could be born. It would have been the first child among this company born into freedom and would have been loved. The loss has hurt our sister Zelda and our brother Franklin deeply, but this hurt has not hurt their spirit nor their belief in God."

He paused and took a deep breath. "Instead, Zelda and Franklin, with the love of Abbie, have made a special request. They want to have a Christian wedding, not in the old way of jumping the broom like we have been forced into by circumstances in the past, but in the way of Christians where there are abolitionists and freed slaves and other free Christians."

He looked seriously at his congregation, his face filled with wonderment. Joshua and the others looked at the three Woodruffs who had their heads bowed.

"This is a miracle," Preacher said, his voice rolling with passion. "Out of this terrible tragedy this family and group of believers has faced, comes something so powerful with the love of the Lord and a man, woman, and child that it surpasses any words any preacher could ever preach."

The rest of the sermon went on, but Joshua stopped paying attention. Preacher's announcement, and the Woodruff's reaction when they looked up from the floor to see how everyone else was reacting, seemed right somehow. They were mourning what might have been but moving beyond sorrow into doing something that bound them to each other and the free community they'd helped build.

Later that day, talking to Pappy and Joshua, his mother smiled when Pappy asked her if she'd known what was going to happen during Preacher's service. The three of them were in the small room they shared, getting ready for bed. Pappy had just stoked the fire enough to keep the room reasonably warm for most of the night.

"I knew what Zelda was thinking," his mother said. "She was thinking that if she and Franklin had been properly married like good Christians her son might have been blessed and given life. In a way, she's trying to atone for what she sees as their sin in not being married the right way. What's she's been thinking doesn't make sense. Married or not married Christian it's common enough for babies to die before they're born. Still, I think this is going to help their family."

"We didn't get married like good Christians," Pappy said, his voice more intense than he meant it to be.

Mary looked at Joshua sitting on the quilt on his side of the room. "I think we were blessed anyway," she said.

"But do you feel like Zelda?" Pappy pressed. "That we ought to be married like good Christians?"

Mary was silent, careful, her eyes glued to his as their son looked on. "Of course," she said. "But not until Zelda and Franklin are married in that way. They need the healing. We were healed the night Chas Bullock brought you to the swamp so we could be together again. I had no dream we could ever make that happen."

Pappy smiled. "We'll have a Christian wedding," he said. "We're Christians. We ought to be married in a Christian way."

"In the spring we'll get baptized, too," Joshua's mother said. "I was reminded about that when Preacher talked about John the Baptist. I wanted to be baptized even back in Missouri." A fire of determination came into her voice. "We're going to be civilized and not in the way Bulrush and his family were civilized. We're going to be real people."

Pappy laughed, looking at Joshua. "Your mother's a fierce woman," he said.

Joshua laughed, too. He was amazed. He had been a slave child prone to getting the Overseer to whip or beat him. Now he was free in a wilderness with a family that felt the way a family ought to feel.

***

The next morning Joshua walked out on the ice at dawn with Pappy, Willie, Bill, Harrison, Jamie, and Jeremiah. The day was cold and gray, but the sleet and snow had stopped. Thankfully, the wind had died down, too.

Joshua had caught two whitefish in a hole he'd only pulled trout out of before when Jamie came over to him slapping his arms against his sides in an attempt to keep warm. "Joshua?" he said.

Joshua smiled. "Jamie," he replied, teasing his rival and friend.

"I got something to tell you," Jamie said.

"Okay," Joshua replied as he started pulling up the line with another fish fighting him.

Jamie waited until Joshua had pulled another good-sized whitefish from the hole. "Nice one," he said.

Joshua fumbled to take the hook out of the fish's mouth. They had pliers that they shared to help them now. Early on they'd had to struggle to work the hook out by hand. Chas had made their work easier by bringing pliers back from a visit he'd made to Washington Harbor to sell the barrels of fish they'd caught. Joshua looked up expectantly at Jamie.

"It's Esta May and me," Jamie said.

Joshua grimaced. "I'm over that," he said.

"Good," Jamie said and then paused. "You're my friend," he blurted. "My oldest friend. But I have to tell you, Esta May and I are going to get married. We're going to have a Christian marriage like Franklin and Zelda. Not now. In the spring. After we've got a cabin of our own."

Joshua stared down at the whitefish he was holding in his hands, its mouth moving as it tried to breathe. He turned from Jamie and threw the whitefish into the small wooden bucket he'd carried out on the ice with him. He was surprised he didn't feel much of anything, perhaps a hint of numbness. He'd already known what was going to happen and had accepted it.

"Good." He smiled. "Don't worry," he said. "We're still friends."

The smile on Jamie's face was testament to his relief. "I'm glad," he said.

Without waiting for Joshua to respond, he walked quickly away. Joshua watched him go.

***

That night, toward morning, Joshua had another powerful dream. He was alone in a woods where trees towered over him, trunks so huge three men could not have gotten their arms around them. The top branches were so high that even if he strained his neck and bent backward to the point of falling he could only make out a hint of blue sky. The loneliness he felt was immense. He was trapped in the trees with no way out. Where he was looked incredibly beautiful and peaceful, but it was the beauty of a clever trap that offered no path for escape.

He woke with a start. The cabin was dark and cold. He was warm beneath the covers. He could hear Pappy's breathing across the room and his mother's slight snoring.

After struggling to get back to sleep, saying his ABC's frontward and backward, he finally quietly got up and slipped on his clothes and boots. He went to the fireplace and carefully placed an oak log on the fire, trying to not wake up anybody else. When the fire was burning brightly, he went to the carved wooden hanger by the door, put his coat on, and went outside.

The moon was so bright it glistened silver off the snow and ice in the harbor. He took a step toward the light and saw two deer jumping and playing on the ice. He could hardly believe his eyes. How could they be so confident with the slickness of ice beneath their sharp hooves? He seemed caught inside a magic vortex where the Milky Way smeared silver light across the night sky in a great river flowing from horizon to horizon.

He took a deep breath. The air was cold enough to bite his lungs. Halfway feeling like he was in a trance, he walked toward the two does. At first, they didn't see him, but when he walked off the shore onto harbor ice they stopped their play, froze, and scampered away from him up the north shore, staying on the lake.

He wasn't sure how long he walked out onto the lake; he felt tired and had started worrying about walking onto thin ice as he got further and further from shore. He looked at the Milky Way again, turning as he felt its wonders.

***

Pappy woke him up. He had been sleeping deeply and blinked when he opened his eyes. Nobody other than Pappy was in the cabin with him. He could feel the cabin's silence. When Pappy saw he was awake he crinkled his forehead.

"You got up in the middle of the night," he said.

Joshua nodded. "I couldn't sleep," he said. "I took a walk out on the lake."

Pappy looked hard at him. "The others are fishing or doing chores," he said. "Your mother thought you might be getting sick."

"No, I'm all right," Joshua said.

He did feel a little woozy, Joshua realized as he crawled out from beneath the covers. He wasn't used to being unable to sleep. The dream that had woken him was still with him. He no longer felt trapped in it, but it seemed to him that everything since Zelda had fallen seemed more dream than reality.

When he got to the cabin door he stopped and thought about making himself something to eat, but then thought about what his mother would say: "If you can't get to a meal on time, you're just being rude to the cooks."

He grimaced and went outside. He should get down to the lake and help catch some fish. He knew what starvation was, and he wasn't anywhere near close to it just from missing breakfast.

He hadn't taken three steps toward the harbor when Ella came around the cabin's corner where she'd obviously been waiting for him. Joshua, surprised, looked at her. She looked determined.

"You've got to stop this mooning around," she said in a voice that had a hard edge to it.

Her phrasing caused him to stop and turn to look at her. It seemed too appropriate to his long, cold walk through the moonlight. "Mooning around?"

"Esta May has a right to her happiness," Ella said.

"She does," Joshua agreed.

Ella looked exasperated. "She's not the woman for you anyway," she said bluntly. "You're … you're … too smart and ambitious. All Esta May has ever wanted was a life with a man and babies and everyday things like chores and taking care of her family. She doesn't care about reading or much of anything else. You've got dreams popping out all over you." She paused, looking him in the eye. "You're like me that way." Her voice had softened.

"I'm not mooning over Esta May," Joshua objected.

"Why are you walking around like you're carrying a wagon full of people on your back all the time then?"

Joshua shook his head. "You're asking that after everything that's happened? Zelda falling, losing her unborn baby, and going through the funeral, and then the Christian wedding announced by Preacher? Isn't that enough for you to feel like you're carrying a weight around?"

"You don't understand yourself very well, do you?" Ella challenged.

Joshua stared at her. She stared back.

"What?" he asked.

"You're a reader," Ella exclaimed. "You want to learn. You like going to school."

"How does that fit together?"

Ella threw up her hands. "May the Lord protect and keep us," she said. She abruptly turned and stalked off.

The emotions Joshua felt as she walked away tumbled through his thoughts. What had just happened? Ella was too young for him. He knew what Pappy had told him, but she was too young. She wasn't as pretty as Esta May, either, although she was smarter. He could see that. She was his equal as a reader. The two of them, along with Jeremiah, were getting so that they could almost read as well as either Preacher or his mother. He suspected they read better than Chas did already.

Had he been mooning around? Jamie telling him that he and Esta May had decided to get married as Christians had shaken him a little, he had to admit. But he'd already figured that out. Esta May had made her decision plain enough to the whole community. Besides, the loss of Franklin and Zelda's unborn son had shaken him more than Esta May's rejection of what he'd thought was going to happen between the two of them.

What did Ella ambushing me like she had mean anyway? Is she in love with me? Or does she see me as a numbskull upsetting her older sister? What had the confrontation been about, really? How do I feel about Ella anyway?

He looked at God's house, but he didn't see an answer in the cabin's plain look. The problem was they only had themselves. There weren't any other black people on the island. And there wasn't likely to be any more. Preacher and Chas had picked out Washington Island for their dream of a free black fisher community a long time ago. The Captain from the steamship that had come to Preacher's sermon had said he could carry them north to Canada, away from any possibility of being caught by slavers. They had not thought about running to Canada.

If they were the only ones they could look to in order to make their lives, then, at least for the young people, they had to look from cabin to cabin for husbands or wives. That was the practical truth, and Ella was, if anything, practical.

He suddenly realized he was still standing where Ella had left him. He shook his head and looked out at the lake. The men, as usual, were moving around, trying to deal with cold that made hands and faces numb. Their eyes would be hurting by now from the late morning sun's brightness.

What am I thinking? That Ella is the only practical answer for me as a prospective wife?

He tried to find where his heart was. Hearts were a difficult affair. She was interesting, he decided. She wasn't Esta May. Her mind was alive, different from the way even his mother thought. If she wasn't as beautiful as Esta May, she had something inside, an energy he didn't know how to define. That energy was really just as appealing. He wasn't sure what she had been about confronting him, but she'd managed to seize his attention.

He snorted and set off to where the men were out on the lake.

Chapter 27
The Healing Human Spirit

Inside great pain a melancholy rises,
A sadness paring down the blood-song
Rived from normality and all the choices
Which constitute our sense of right and wrong
And help us navigate the waves along
The axis of glad days without the sorrow
That surges into storms where demons throng
In feelings deadening our life's ebb-flow.

Then, from her pain, a mother feels the floe
Of ice inside her heart begin to thaw,
And though the pain burns deep, she starts to sow
A rightness that can ease the endless gnaw
Inside her heart and let a wedding's light
Leach darkness from depression's heavy night.

The planning for Franklin and Zelda's wedding was straightforward. Everybody was to gather at God's house. Preacher would go through the ceremony that would make them Christian husband and wife, and then the women would put on a feast.

They were already a Christian husband and wife. Nobody doubted that. They had both been born on plantations that practiced Christianity, and, although both had been sold as teenagers, they had taken their beliefs with them to the plantation where they had first met.

Their master at that plantation had not approved of slave marriage. "It ruins their value when you move them around," he'd claimed. "They get to thinking they're too much like white people with ties."

But they'd jumped the broom anyway in secret out in the woods with the quarters celebrating with them.

They were free people now. After the horror of losing her baby, Zelda wanted to reaffirm the bonds she felt to Franklin and Abbie. She wanted to do it inside what she said was "the temple of freedom," the idea and place that now defined who they were. They were no longer property, but people with their own dignity, minds, and wills inside a Christian community. Zelda wanted a ceremony that reflected who they had become during their long run to freedom.

"We're out in the open Christians now," Zelda had told Joshua's mother, trying to explain why she wanted a wedding ceremony so soon after the death of her stillborn son. "Not hidden in the swamp Christians." She'd then paused for a long time. "I know children that ought to be born aren't born and that too many children die. I know that, but sometimes I can't help but feel that Franklin and I should have been married the right way. Maybe that would have made a difference."

Then Zelda took her wedding idea one step further. She and Beulah were talking about how it was about time there was an excuse for singing and dancing again. In all of the quarters there had been times when, no matter how bad things were going, the slaves got together and celebrated.

Since coming to Washington Island, they had celebrated around a campfire the night they had arrived, but mostly work had come first. Fears about a winter they were not prepared for caused Preacher and Chas to drive the rest of them relentlessly. They had not even taken time out for birthdays.

Now it was time to sing and dance even though tragedy had seared into their spirits. It was time to move beyond what had happened.

Then the wedding plans became more complex when Zelda suggested that Beulah and Bill ought to be married at the same time she and Franklin were. Beulah, like Zelda, could renew her marriage commitment to her husband and Christianity at the same time, giving their Washington Island community the start it deserved. They would ensure their lives would be moral from that day forward. A day later, Joshua's parents and Willie and Massie had been wrapped into the plans too. Harrison and Junebug, as usual, were the only holdouts.

"I've been with Harrison a long time," Junebug said in her most sassy voice. "We're just fine the way we've been."

***

Then, during a Monday at the start of the three hours dedicated to beginning math lessons, taught mostly by Chas, Zelda, who had, before the death of her unborn child been one the quietest of them, spoke up again. "I've been thinking," she said in a loud voice, getting everyone's attention. "I was talking to Chas. He said Christmas is in twelve days. I think we ought to have our weddings on Christmas Day."

"Christmas is a holy day," Preacher said, his voice gentle. "It is the Christ child's birthday."

Zelda nodded. "That's what I was thinking," she said. "We want to celebrate Jesus. We want to celebrate the fact he was born and lived and came among human beings to work out salvation in heaven where my son is. By holding our marriage ceremonies on Christmas we are making the day doubly special. We are acknowledging the power of Jesus and the Lord in our lives, celebrating with the holy power of marriage in His name as it relates to how central He, and the promise of heaven, is to who we are as married human beings."

Preacher looked confused, his eyebrows scrunching toward each other. "Don't you think we ought to focus on Christ on his birthday?" he asked.

Joshua could tell he was treading lightly, not forgetting what Zelda and the rest of West Harbor had just gone through.

"How in the world do we prepare for four wedding ceremonies in ten days?" Joshua's mother asked in her most matter-of-fact voice.

Zelda, her eyes large, looked at Mary. "We've all been married for years," she said. "Whether masters recognized that or not. There's no preparing really." She paused and looked down at the floor so carefully put together by Pappy, Willie, Preacher, and Harrison. "We have no way to make fancy dresses. We just need to finish the dresses we've been working on. Besides, saying Christian vows isn't about fuss. It's about heart and spirit and what each of us means to each other and our families."

Pappy, sitting next to where Joshua was standing, helping him to puzzle his way through the addition problem assigned by Chas, shifted on the bench. "It's about freedom," he declared in his deep voice. "It's about getting married when we want, using the ceremony we want to follow with people we want to be with, and doing what's important to us when we want to do it."

Preacher looked from Zelda to Pappy and then around the sanctuary turned classroom. "I've got to say this is a surprise," he said. He sighed. "The question is, is it right?"

He apparently came to a decision, because his puzzled look dissipated. "White people changed our ways," he said. "In Africa we were different peoples, but here we found Jesus and the Lord, and we aren't white people. We can make our own way and do it so that it fits who we are, rather than what white people might think we are.

"I don't think Jesus Christ, our beloved savior, would object to glorifying him on his birthday by celebrating our belief through a celebration of our own making." He looked increasingly convinced as he spoke. He struck his fist into his hand to emphasize what he was saying.

Jeremiah whooped and stood up. Jamie and Esta May, grinning from ear to ear, stood up with him. Joshua found that he and the rest of those in the room were standing and grinning, too. Zelda, for the first time since she had lost her baby, looked pleased, smiling with the rest of them.

The work and bad weather didn't cease because Christmas was around the corner. Big wedding or no wedding, Christmas or no Christmas with all its Christian significance, the daily life they were living in freedom continued. They had to continue building their resources.

As Christmas Day approached, the excitement was palpable. Chas and Franklin hiked down the shore to Washington Harbor and bought flour and sugar so that the women could make Christmas cookies, a treat rare enough on the plantations, but certainly had not been a part of their Washington Island lives. Chas bagged two wild turkeys for the Christmas Day feast planned for after the wedding ceremony.

For Joshua the biggest problem was keeping out of his mother's and Massie's way in the cabin. All the cabins were being scoured, but the two women were determined to make their cabin gleam for the big day. Joshua thought they had surely gone over every surface at least a dozen times with water, soap, and rags. They usually expected Joshua, Jamie, and Jeremiah to help.

Esta May and Jamie slipped away from the rest of them once or twice a day. Joshua was getting better at not dwelling on what he still thought about as his loss, but sometimes, when he noticed they were missing from the buzz of anticipation around the cabins and fishing holes, he felt a slight tinge that could have been irritation, or maybe disappointment, in the way his life was turning out.

Somehow, when this feeling jolted him, Ella was usually close to where he was. He still thought of her as a little girl, but she wasn't really all that little. She was growing so fast she was now taller than Esta May.

What was really unexpected was that he now was sure that he was growing, too. What Pappy had foretold was coming true. After spending his entire life shorter and skinnier than other boys near his age, he woke at night with leg spasms Pappy told him were growing pains. Even he could see that he was shooting up, approaching Jamie's height.

"Those happened to me, too, when I started getting so big," Pappy said. "Nobody expected me to grow the way I grew."

Joshua could hardly believe what was happening. During their run north neither he, nor his mother, nor anyone else had noticed he was growing taller. Now even Chas noticed the difference.

***

On Christmas morning, the largest flakes Joshua had ever seen drifted lazily from the sky. Jamie was already up, building the morning fire, so Joshua went to the door and looked outside. A hint of light promised dawn, but giant flakes fell straight down out of the darkness.

Jamie and Esta May had been giddy in their excitement over Christmas and the coming wedding. As the day approached, they were always together, holding hands and looking into each other's eyes as if no one else in the community existed. The only time they were separated was at night when their parents insisted they stay in their family's cabins. Joshua kept having to bite back the irritation he felt at seeing them mooning around.

But they were all caught in a whirlpool of suppressed excitement. The old folk's confirmation, as Joshua had started thinking about the coming ceremony to himself, was a statement that the suffering and work they had experienced as they had made their way toward the most significant Christmas Day of any of their lives had been worth the risk and effort. It was confirming the commitment they were making to themselves, their Christianity, and the fellowship they had formed. Somehow, out of the tragedy Zelma and Franklin had faced, they had changed an expression of their freedom from bonds imposed by masters into a choice about their individual and community life.

Joshua turned from the darkness, went back inside, and walked over to Jamie. "Big day," he said.

Jamie, face flickering from fireplace flames, looked at Joshua and smiled. "It's hard to believe, isn't it?" he asked. "Not that long ago we walked around cringing every time we saw old Coats or a white man. Lordy, lordy, what's going to happen to us? Now we're having a Christian wedding on Christmas day preached over by Preacher. I think it's—" he looked for the right word. "—a miracle."

Joshua smiled, but didn't respond. Pappy and Willie exited their separate bedrooms at the same time.

"The women have to get ready," Willie said. "And that's a fact."

Pappy and Willie grinned at each other.

As soon as Jamie had the fire going, the menfolk left the cabin for God's house. Light was a soft yellow along the eastern sky's edges. The two grooms seemed relaxed after a time of such feverish activity. The men, working together, had even built a small wooden bathtub sealed so that it wouldn't leak, working with Harrison and Preacher's help, so that they and the brides could take turns taking baths after heating enough water. Both Junebug and Harrison had spent two full days sanding to ensure that people could get into the rectangular tub without getting a splinter.

After it was finished, Chas had said he would travel to Ephraim with a sled after the ice was safe and get tin to line it with. "A tub ought to have a tin lining to be right," he said.

Then everyone had been chased out of the cabins as one and then another used the tub placed by fireplaces in each cabin. The days of bathing in the lake were long past.

***

In God's house, Preacher and Chas were already at work. They had put up a small pine Christmas tree on the table where Preacher normally kept a Bible and decorated it with cloths the women had sewn into different, colorful shapes: stars, circles, squares, and even abstract children. They had also arranged the benches into a large half-circle. Tallow candlesticks, rendered from deer fat, had been placed on logs brought in from outside and set at the end of each row of benches.

Willie, seeing what was going on, shook his head. "Not as grand as Christmas at the master's house," he said. "But better."

Preacher looked especially pleased. "This is a special day," he said.

The three boys had just sat on the bench nearest the door when the other men came in out of the storm picking up outside. Preacher, Chas, and Harrison were calm and talked to one and then another of the grooms, but the grooms themselves settled on a bench for a moment and then got up and moved to another part of the sanctuary. Nobody seemed to be saying anything substantive. Instead, the grooms looked perplexed, or maybe confused.

Interestingly, none of the women or girls came into God's house while the men and boys waited. At one point, after the wait seemed interminable, Joshua went over to Jamie who was sitting beside Franklin, neither of them saying anything.

"What's going on?" Joshua asked.

Jamie shrugged. "Who knows?"

"I thought maybe Esta May might have said something," Joshua said.

Jamie shook his head.

At last the door opened and the women and girls filed in. They were clothed, even Abbie and Ertha, in deerskin dresses they had been working on for months. The smallest girls came out of the snowstorm first, flakes of white snow in black hair, followed by the brides. They were smiling.

Joshua was stunned. His eyes, in spite of his intentions, went straight to Esta May. She was truly beautiful. Black hair, flecked with the white of melting snowflakes, framed her perfectly proportioned face with its high cheekbones. Her dress, with fringes cut into the hem, was as wonderful as she was. His heart skipped a beat. He forced himself to look away to Ella. She was taller than Esta May, not as filled out, and her face, although pleasant enough, did not look like it had been fashioned by a master artist. Instead her face had a distinctive, angular look that made her more striking than beautiful.

The dresses themselves were exquisite. Chewed to softness and cured, they hung from the women's shoulders, culminating in an irregular or fringe hem. A rough, dark thread seamed from the neck around the shoulders. The edges were natural, fashioned from the shapes of the various hides used to make them. The effect of seeing all of the women with new dresses together was stunning.

The minute the women were in the cabin Preacher moved toward the center of the benches. He suddenly was a different man. The gray in his hair glowed. The darkness of his trousers and shirt was powerful inside the sanctuary's small space. His eyes, as they so often did, burned.

"I've been wondering how to do this since Zelda first convinced me a wedding on our savior's birthday is all right," he said in his deepest, most musical voice.

The grooms had stood when the women had entered. Brides and grooms, the minute Preacher spoke, gravitated to each other's sides. The rest of the congregation stood back, the celebrants in front of them. Joshua thought that Pappy, so large and tall, and his mother, eyes and face shining, a well-made woman a foot shorter than his father, made a wonderful couple.

Preacher smiled and waited until everyone had stopped rearranging themselves. "What I've decided," he said at last, "is that we should celebrate Jesus, our savior first, and use the power of his name and his time on earth to give us a powerful understanding of how the Lord weaves sacred bonds between a man and a woman." He lifted his hands into the air. "I'd like us to join hands with each other," he said.

There was a general shifting, and the four couples moved closer to each other. The rest moved forward to hold each other's hands.

"Now, make a circle around me," Preacher said after everyone was in place.

Joshua and Jamie, who had ended up at the end of the lines, moved sideways until they were holding each other's hands, and the circle was made. Jamie had a firm hold on Esta May's hand. She stood next to Ella. Joshua had his hand in Pappy's large, callused right hand.

After the circle was made Preacher closed his eyes. "This is a Christmas Day different from any Christmas Day any of us have had before," he said as they bowed their heads. "No master is around to force a woman to accept a man she doesn't want or to force a man to accept a woman. Although these couples have committed themselves by jumping the broom in the old way, they are choosing today to take a different path to marriage and everlasting commitment. Lord, we are a blessed people."

Joshua was startled when most of the people in the circle repeated "a blessed people," the sound reverberating through the cabin.

"They are making vows," Preacher continued, "in the presence of the spirit of Jesus Christ. We are taking this opportunity to not only celebrate our Christian faith, but to also pledge Christian constancy in our relations with each other by joining men and women already joined together.

"In enjoying this day, we want to remember the child lost, and Zelda Woodruff's role in moving beyond that tragedy into what we are about today. The people here had the courage to run from slavery into freedom in spite of all the risks. We have left old lives behind. Zelda has helped us, out of her own special courage, to see this new life with fresh eyes and renewed hope for the journey we are making.

"We are praying, Lord, for your blessing on this Christmas Day on all of those gathered here in this wilderness, and especially on those pledging to each other, through an understanding of the Christian faith, vows that link their spirits into the spirit of both you and Jesus, the most precious joy in our lives." He paused for a long time without lifting his head and then sighed. "Amen," he said. Everyone followed by saying "Amen" with a soft reverence.

Preacher lifted up his head and smiled. "This is a good Christmas," he said. He waved his hand. "Now the rest of you can sit down, and we'll get on with the wedding. Then," he paused and looked at Harrison. "I believe Harrison and Junebug have a celebration planned that's been hidden from the rest of us."

Joshua glanced over at Junebug, who was smiling.

The wedding ceremony itself was simple. Preacher asked the four couples to line up in front of him. He said another prayer, asking for the Lord's blessing on the ceremony he was about to perform. He named each of them by name. Then he started the ceremony with Franklin and Zelda, moving through each couple in turn. He told each of them that this was a serious day and that they were renewing the commitment they had made to each other when they were slaves, but that they were now renewing their marriage in freedom. After they had promised to be faithful to each other and their faith, he ended the ceremony by asking each of them to promise a lifetime of love and caring for them and their children "no matter how many troubles might visit them in the days to come."

Pappy made the pledge in a voice so soft that Joshua could hardly hear him. When Bill and Beulah made their pledge, Joshua saw that Esta May was wiping tears from her eyes. She was so concentrated on her parents that no one else, including Jamie sitting beside her, seemed to hold her awareness. Ella, sitting next to her sister, was smiling, but not crying. She looked suffused with a powerful, pure joy.

The minute Pappy and Joshua's mother had whispered their "I do's," everyone, including Preacher, started clapping. They all, together, had made an important statement. They were moving beyond memories into their lives. Joshua's parents came over to him the minute Preacher had said, "and I name you husband and wife," and, together, hugged him.

Joshua, feeling his father and mother's strength, felt the powerful change that had come into his life beneath the old cypress tree in the Missouri swamp. At that moment he had moved beyond his physical self and reached for an impossible dream that was now his life. He had not been born without a father. He had a father. He deserved, like all of them, freedom. They all had their freedom.

They had reached Washington Island in Lake Michigan. The only bonds he had were those forged from the people in that cabin, God's house. He hugged his mother even tighter when he saw she was crying as she held her husband and son.

Harrison went outside a few minutes after Preacher had finished. Junebug stood by the door, her eyes sparking. Then Harrison came back in carrying two small drums he'd made. He'd stretched thinned deer hide tightly over an octagonal birch wood frame.

"This is a celebration," he said loudly.

"A celebration deserves a shout," Junebug exclaimed, taking one of the hand drums.

Pappy and Bill grabbed their wives' hands and pulled the whole room, including Chas and Preacher, into a circle. Harrison and Junebug started pounding a fast beat on their small drums. There were cries of exultation. "Freedom," Harrison shouted. "Freedom," Junebug yelled. Everyone, including the young ones and Preacher, were stomping feet as hard as they could on the cabin's wood floor.

"When Israel was in Egypt's land," Preacher sang in his deep voice. "O Let my people go! Oppressed so hard they could not stand, O Let my people go!"

The combined voices of everyone dancing took up the refrain and the singing got so loud the cabin reverberated with voices and the pounding of drums and stomping feet. Abbie, Ertha, and Eunice's faces blazed with excitement and flashing eyes. They had never been around such excitement in their lives, not even in the quarters when the master, his family, and the Overseer and his assistant had gone away and left them to build up a celebration on their own.

At first Joshua was swept up in the exuberance and dancing, not quite sure what he was doing inside the noise, but then everything that separated him disappeared. He danced, like they all were dancing, as if he were no longer who he was, but part of a universe so filled with light and joy that eternity was filled with who he truly was.

BOOK THREE

A MYSTERY

Chapter 28
An Incident on Washington Island

As Ambrose Betts gulped down the whiskey shot
That Gullickson had given him, his face
Was flushed, the muscles in his neck a knot
So tight he winced, his outrage out of place
Inside the cabin's half lit single room.

"A Winnebago Chief! I tell you Gullickson,"
He said. "As large as life inside the gloom
Of Miner's kitchen, Bullock looking drawn,
As if he'd seen a ghost, as black as coal.
I've never seen the like before!" he yelled.
"An Indian, white man, black man like a shoal
Of pebbles on a beach. The Indian held
His hand up, said, I swear, to Bullock, "You,"
He said. "First white man that I ever knew."

"Old Bullock, black as night,
Smiled with those teeth of his
So dazzlingly bright white.
My head began to fizz,

"And Miner looked like God
About to haul back, smack
The Indian into sod.
A white man that is black!"

Chas shocked the community on a late Sunday morning after Preacher's sermon. They had gotten through their fifth winter. Each winter seemed easier than the one before, although their integration into the larger Washington Island community wasn't going as well as any of them would have liked.

A lot of islanders were abolitionists, but there was a group, many of them rougher edged men led by Joel Westbrook, that wanted every black person on the island gone. Some of the abolitionists weren't all that friendly, either. When a group from West Harbor, especially the men, came to Washington Harbor, they could always expect one or two of the white people to hurry out of the store or warehouse they were visiting.

Still, the Miners always greeted them like they were glad to see them. They, and others, sometimes made the trip from the docks to West Harbor to attend Preacher's sermons. Some of the fishermen, too, learning about Preacher's skill in building and fixing boats, brought their boat problems to him along with some of their hard-earned cash.

Preacher no longer had the energy he had possessed fleeing the Missouri swamp. He would have much preferred to contemplate, pray, and preach away his days, but when fishermen came into the harbor he walked to the shore to greet them and make an arrangement for doing whatever repairs were needed. Harrison and Franklin were usually in charge of the work under Preacher's supervision, but Joshua, Jamie, and Jeremiah had learned most of the skills, too, and were often conscripted to help.

Preacher's hair, once black and gray, was becoming increasingly long and white. Joshua thought that, with his still burning eyes and long white hair, he looked like an ancient prophet from Israel before the coming of Jesus. Joshua also thought it was weird he was aging so fast, although no one seemed to know his age. When asked, Preacher always danced around the question, saying he didn't really know.

Jamie, who had married Esta May and had his own cabin, had tried to figure it out by getting Mr. Craw to tell him when the Battle of Put-in-Bay had been that Preacher, Chas, and James Campbell had talked about in Illinois. Mr. Craw had told him the battle had occurred in 1813, but when Jamie, Jeremiah, Joshua, and Esta May, who was pregnant again, talked about it, they decided that knowing the date didn't really help since they had no way of knowing how old Preacher had been when he'd been in the battle. Neither he nor Chas could have been that old. When they'd then asked Chas about Preacher's age, he'd just shook his head and laughed at them.

They were used to Chas disappearing into the woods. It hadn't happened much during the first year on the island, but after that he often didn't tell anybody when he went off and sometimes stayed away for weeks at a time. The first time it happened everyone had been worried. A missing black man on an island without a boat to cross over Death's Door felt ominous. Preacher had not been concerned. He told them he wasn't sure where Chas was off to, but that he had wandered the Wisconsin wilderness alone for a long time.

"He has wandering feet," Preacher said. "I've been surprised he stayed still so long. We've got to allow him his own kind of freedom. He's been a lot of places since his master freed him all those years ago."

After that first time, Chas had wandered off at least a half dozen times. A year, then another, then another passed. They got comfortable in their lives' rhythm in spite of the uneasiness they felt when they visited where white settlers lived. Three children had been born since they had come to the island. Massie had given birth to a boy that was the same age as Jamie and Esta May's girl, and Beulah had, at last, gotten herself a boy after wanting a son for Bill ever since they'd first jumped the broom in Missouri. The tragedy was that Zelda and Franklin had not had another child.

Then Chas shocked them. He'd been gone longer than normal when Jeremiah saw him, in the company of an Indian woman, walking up the wagon path the Miners used when they were coming to Preacher's sermons. Jeremiah's eyes had grown large at the sight of them. For a reason that he couldn't later explain, he turned from where he was going to hunt with the new rifle the community had purchased and ran toward West Harbor.

The first person he'd run into as he came out of the woods was Ella. She was still not as striking as her older sister, but Jeremiah kept his eyes on her as she ran toward her cabin and mother. At nineteen, she had a healthy energy that was enough to stir the blood of any man.

She and Joshua had gotten into the habit of getting together before the day's light died and reading from books Joshua was sometimes able to borrow from Jesse Miner when he went to town or Jesse came with his parents to Preacher's sermons. Most of West Harbor believed the two of them would be married in the natural order of things.

They were both highly intelligent and obsessive readers. Ella helped Joshua's mother run the winter school, when work wasn't incessant, still held in God's house. But the truth was that the subject of marriage had not come up once in their time together, so Jeremiah was starting to get his own ideas about the inevitability of their lifelong pairing.

As Ella ran, Jeremiah moved purposefully toward where his father and Joshua were splitting wood behind their cabin.

When Chas and the Indian woman came out of the woods the entire community, except for Preacher, who had not seemed surprised at the news when Jeremiah told him, had gathered. They were silent as the pair stopped and looked at their greeting party.

The woman, dressed in a loose deerskin dress and wearing old moccasins, was not young. She seemed timid as she regarded all the black people standing in front of her. Her face and figure looked slightly round, although she was thin. Her hair was thick, black with peppered gray streaks, and long, hanging down behind her back.

Chas protectively put his hand on her arm. "These are my people," he said. He led her to where they were all standing.

Joshua's mother, as she often did, took the lead. She walked forward and held out her hand to the woman, nodding first to Chas. Chas let go of the woman's arm and nodded to Mary.

"This is Weayaya," he said cautiously. He paused as Weayaya started to raise her hand in the air, but then tentatively held out her hand. "She's my wife," he said.

Joshua's mother could not hide her surprise. She glanced at Pappy who had also started to approach the couple.

"We've been married a number of years," Chas said.

"How could you be married and spend so much time apart?" Joshua thought. Then he thought about how life had been in quarters where wives and children could be sold off without any notice at all. Sometimes husbands and wives stayed loyal to each other even if they had no idea where the other one was.

After a moment's hesitation, Chas's words shocked the married women forward. In an instant, Chas had been separated from Weayaya. The women had surrounded her. She kept calm, eyes carefully surveying each woman in turn, as if she weren't surprised at their reaction. She didn't answer the greetings offered her, however.

"She's quiet," Chas said over the heads of the women. His eyes were glued on his wife. "She hasn't had an easy life."

"Where did she come from?" Joshua's mother asked without looking at Chas. "Where have you been?"

There was an edge to her voice. Chas had never hinted at having a wife during the years since they had come to the island, and especially not an Indian wife. The women had discussed how he never appeared to be interested in women, but they'd always thought he was waiting until he found the right one.

"She's been living with the Potowatomi up north not far from the Pine River," he said, "though she's not Potowatomi."

"Weren't the Potowatomi here before the white settlers?" Pappy, now standing beside Chas, asked.

Without taking his eyes off his wife, Chas nodded. "Yeah."

"We want to welcome you to West Harbor," Joshua's mother greeted the new arrival. "Chas helped us come here. His wife is also part of who we are."

At that moment, Preacher came out of God's house. *What a grand man! He looks like a character from a book.*

When Preacher reached them, the women moved aside. Weayaya tilted her head. "Tom Bennett," she said, her voice soft, musical.

Preacher smiled. "Weayaya," he said. "It has been a long, long time." He touched her shoulder as a flicker of a smile appeared and vanished on her face. "You brought her at last," he said to Chas.

Most of the community was confused. Not only had a secret existed none of them had imagined, but Preacher, their shepherd, had never said anything about it. Joshua wondered why anyone would keep a wife secret.

Preacher and Chas had a history the rest of them knew nothing about.

"Will it work out?" Chas asked, looking at Preacher as if he were challenging him.

There was a sudden, deadening silence. Weayaya looked into Joshua's mother's black eyes. She seemed to be searching for an answer she needed to find. "I will try this place," she said, her voice just above a whisper.

Chas pointed at the cabin he and the rest of the men had built beside Jamie and Esta May's. "That's our place."

No one had wondered why Chas had wanted to move out of God's house. Having to make up his bed every night and pack it away during the day wasn't something that appealed to any of them. But now old assumptions were suddenly being reordered.

"May I see it now?" Weayaya asked Joshua's mother. She seemed to have decided that Mary was a figure of authority.

"Of course," she said. "I don't know how far you've come today, but you must be tired."

***

When Ella and Joshua got together to read by the fire pit just before sunset, they talked about Chas and the Indian woman rather than Charles Dickens' *The Cricket on the Hearth*, a book Jesse had talked his father into buying on one of his trips to the Door Peninsula. They had both been excited when Joshua had gotten the book and brought it to West Harbor. It was supposedly the most read book in the whole of the United States, Jesse had said. But the appearance of Chas's wife seemed more momentous than a new book, even if it was a story about Christmas. Christmas was a long way away.

"Can you believe Chas never said anything, not even once in all these years?"

Ella, looking pensively out over the gently rolling lake waves, was wrapped deep in her own thoughts. "I think it's romantic," she said. "Preacher knew about her, too. They acted like they'd met before."

"A black man married to an Indian," Joshua said. "I'd heard about that happening back in Missouri. Some of the old folks said some slaves had escaped and gone to live with Indians where their masters couldn't find them, but I didn't believe them."

"Chas didn't escape," Ella said. "He was freed of his master's own will after he and Willie had been sold away from their parents. That's partly why it's so romantic. He traveled into the wilderness and found a wife."

"She's pretty quiet," Joshua noted.

Ella smiled. "You're just used to girls with lots of words," she said and laughed.

Joshua looked seriously at her. He'd gotten over Esta May a long time ago. The truth was that he spent most of his free time with Ella, either reading books together or just sitting and talking. They had achieved so much by running away, but both of them kept picking at the future. What did it mean to be part of a black fishing community in the Washington Island wilderness? Was that what they were meant to do with their lives? Or was there something else waiting for them?

The one thing they couldn't escape was that they were young black Africans who had escaped their masters. They sometimes talked about Jesse Miner and his friends and how they had a different future simply because they weren't black or fugitives. They thought maybe they should be satisfied with their lives where they were. They had good families. Living as Christians in a strong community gave them a strength that kept the former plantation lives' nightmares away. But they were young and intelligent. Sometimes they yearned for something more, although neither knew what that more could possibly be.

Joshua sighed. "I ought to be in love with you," he blurted, startling himself as well as Ella.

"You mean you're not?" Ella asked without a second's hesitation.

Joshua stared at her, her black eyes and dark skin and teeth that flashed white every time she opened her mouth. He had been watching how Jeremiah looked at her. He'd lost any chance at Esta May because he'd not been as bold and direct as Jamie. He wasn't so sure that he hadn't already made a mistake by holding back from Ella.

Esta May was beautiful. She seemed even more beautiful after giving birth to one child and becoming pregnant with another. The West Harbor women were always fussing over her, especially Zelda. But the truth was that Esta May was dull. She was a hard worker and would help anybody without a moment's hesitation, but she never read anything, not even the Bible, and mostly she talked about chores or Jamie or little Emily, her and Jamie's girl. That was what interested her.

Ella was different. Words poured out of her as if she had stored so many they were a lake in her spirit. Inside the words were ideas that took flight into a place beyond the everyday world into an imaginative universe where anything could happen. She was interesting and vital and full of life.

"I wonder if Chas loves Weayaya?"

"She's his wife," Ella said, clearly shocked by the question.

"Yeah, but she's Indian," Joshua said. "What does he have in common with her? I mean, Indians can be wonderful. Look how Gordon Burr helped us. But an ex-slave and an Indian woman? I mean, why didn't Chas bring her back to West Harbor the first year we were here?"

Joshua's thoughts were jumbled. He was trying to say something, understand something, but he was stumbling around trying to discover the thought in the back of his mind.

Ella's eyes drilled into him. "You'd think you didn't approve of an Indian woman and black man being married," she said.

"No," he said slowly. He stayed silent for a long time. "I just don't understand it," he said at last.

"I think I do," Ella said. "Chas had to wait until it was right to bring her here. He wanted us settled before he ran the risk of having to lose us or leave her again."

Joshua looked at the lake. Its restless movement was always beautiful. The water was almost green. Sometimes it looked gray or blue, or tinted with sunlight, but at that moment the evening sunlight made it look green. He bit his lip and turned back to Ella.

"You're describing a different kind of love," he said.

"A protective love?" Ella suggested. "We're established enough now to let him feel comfortable bringing her to meet us?"

Joshua watched her as she spoke. Her eyes changed with her moods. Sometimes they shined. Sometimes they looked cloudy, especially when she was puzzled. When she was angry, they burned.

"There's no way I couldn't love you, is there?" Joshua asked. He paused. "There's just different ways of loving, isn't there?"

He had no idea what she was thinking.

***

The next morning, after Joshua and Jeremiah had built the morning fire for cooking breakfast but before they went down to the dory Preacher and Harrison had built the year before to give them a second boat to fish with, Willie came out of the bedroom and told them to hold off going to the lake. "Preacher wants to see us in God's house," he said.

When Jeremiah asked him what that was about, he shrugged. "I suspect it's about Chas and the Indian woman," he said.

Forty-five minutes later, Joshua's mother and Massie had finished fixing fried eggs and potatoes, corn bread, and hot coffee. Then both families trooped off to the sanctuary. Everyone other than Chas and Weayaya was already there.

Ella surprised Joshua by moving away from her parents the moment he came into the room to stand beside him. In spite of the daily times when they read books, they had been keeping their distance during Preacher's sermons and at other parts of the day. Joshua wasn't sure why. With everybody assuming they were destined for marriage, no one would have remarked about how they gravitated toward each other

When Ella was suddenly by his side, Joshua realized she was making a statement neither of them had made before. She didn't say anything as they shared a look. Joshua took her hand in his. His mother had gone to talk to Beulah, who had sat down on a bench, waiting for what was going to happen, but Joshua could hear a small intake of breath when she saw Joshua and Ella holding hands.

Preacher moved to his usual place beside the lectern Harrison and Junebug had made out of birds-eye maple. When he cleared his throat, conversation stopped. Chas and Weayaya opened the cabin's door and quietly came into the sanctuary. Everyone's eyes were on them.

"Chas asked me to call this meeting," Preacher said. "He thinks he owes you an explanation. With all we owe him, I don't think that's necessary. He and Weayaya are welcome as part of our community. I, for one, find it a blessing Weayaya has joined us. But Chas insisted."

Chas didn't move from beside his wife. Something about Weayaya made Joshua think of a place in deep woods on the slopes of the mountain located near the island's center where sunlight filtered through a birch grove. He hadn't been to that spot that many times, but after he had discovered it, he had made a point of finding it again. Noonday sunlight made the grove unearthly as leaves rustled from a small breeze. The trees looked like they were marching up the mountain's peak toward an eternity of blue sky.

"I'm pretty sure everyone's wondering why I haven't mentioned I had a wife before," Chas said. He looked self-contained and competent like always. "The fact is, Weayaya asked me not to. She didn't feel comfortable coming here after I came back from Missouri, even though she'd urged me to go with Preacher in the first place." He looked at the woman with her long, straight hair, still eyes, and round face. "She's not had any easy time in life and had settled in after we had met and married over a decade ago.

"Weayaya's tribe was called the Noquet by the French. She is the last member of her tribe alive. Her parents survived after white man's diseases killed most of her relatives not long after Americans took over this part of the country. She lived with the Menominee during the last years of her parent's lives, but had moved north and was living with the Potowatomi when I first met her. I was wandering like a lost soul after the war.

"The war didn't treat me well. Black sailors were considered trash by Commodore Perry and his officers and were treated even worse than the whites, although they thought the white sailors were trash, too. Friends I'd made during my service died, some of them horribly, and, as a young man, little more than a child really, I was having trouble finding a place where a freed ex-slave who had been a sailor on a warship could feel like he belonged.

"Weayaya didn't belong where she was, either, and it was that sense of not having a place that brought us together. We've been married ever since.

"When Tom Bennett came and found the two of us living in woods near the Pine River, he sold me on going south with him to get my brother Willie and his family free from slavery. I didn't want to leave Weayaya, but all her family and tribe are gone. She thought that rescuing a brother I hadn't seen since we were separated as children was important. We talked it out, and Preacher and I set out to Chicago where Tom had made connections with Reverend Jemson where we built the scow.

"When, after that first winter here, I went to find Weayaya, she wouldn't come back with me." He looked at Weayaya. "I wanted her to, but she'd lived in that place I'd built near the river and been alone for over three years. The Potawatomi visited her off and on, but mostly she'd been alone, and didn't want to see what it was like being a part of my people." He paused, still looking at his calm wife. "She surprised me when I said I was going to stay with her this time. I knew Preacher could explain what had happened, but she packed us up and got us moving before I knew what she was thinking, and now we're here."

He fell silent. Weayaya nodded her head so slightly Joshua almost missed it. Chas wore a hesitant smile. Joshua's mother, with Beulah following her, went up to Weayaya, smiling broadly, and touched her shoulder. The Indian woman flinched slightly.

"Welcome again," Joshua's mother said.

Then the other women came and said the same thing as if they were enacting an important ritual. Ella left Joshua's side and followed Esta May as she came up to Weayaya. The men milled around, wondering what was expected of them.

Preacher cleared his throat again. "I don't think we ought to work today," he said in his most sonorous voice. "We ought to give praise to the Lord for the miracle of our sister Weayaya and her decision to join us. This is a special day indeed."

Weayaya bowed her head. "I'll cook," she said

Chas held up his hand. He had a strange look on his face. Before he'd looked like a man who was torn between fear and hope, wanting this moment to work out, but unsure of what was going to actually happen. Now he looked like another thought had occurred to him. "There is one other thing," he said.

The movement and noises that had been building silenced. Chas was the center of attention again.

"Before I set out north, I stopped by the Union Congregational Church in Green Bay to see the Reverend Jeremiah Porter. The Porters are friends with Gordon Burr and the Stockbridge. Eliza, the Reverend's wife, has been especially involved with them and the Underground Railroad and knew Henry Miner's father. Reverend Porter helped us with some of the contacts that allowed our escape from Missouri to be successful.

"Anyway, I thought everybody ought to know there's talk of a new law happening between the south and north that will give slave owners the right to come to Wisconsin to take back escaped slaves." He paused. "I don't know that it means anything, but I thought everybody should hear what I heard."

Preacher, standing by the lectern, looked troubled, but then got control of himself. "For God hath not given us the spirit of fear; but of power, and of love, and of a sound mind," he said in the voice he used for quoting the Bible. "This is a day for celebration, not worrying about what might come down the road someday."

There was a profound pause as everyone tried to absorb both Weayaya's story as well as the news Chas had brought. The story was powerful, as powerful as any of their stories. The news was dreadful. It hooked its teeth in them and bit hard. Joshua wondered why Chas had brought his wife when the future was roiled up again. *Will we ever be free from the past? How could we ever be truly, truly free?*

Joshua could hear the worry in Ella's voice when she spoke his name. "Joshua?"

Joshua wiped his arm across his lips. "Washington Island's our home," he said. "We found it. We're not going to let any slaver come here and take it away. We won't!"

Chapter 29
Remembering a Winter Sky

The rising sun on ice exploded fire
Upon the surface of the lake as light
Burned in the clouds, the bowl of sky a choir
Of gold and reds upon, above the white
Expanse that glinted, danced in flowing swells
That turned the universe into a trance
So stunning winter fishermen felt spells
Ensnaring them into the light's romance.

But even as the sky transfigured how
They felt their lives, the grind imbedded deep
In human hands and minds began to plow
Into the wonder that was theirs, the sweep
Of fire from other people's greed a cloud
So dark it seemed to be a burial shroud.

Less than a week later, Joshua, Jamie, and Jeremiah came back after a difficult day fishing in the dory and found the community in an uproar. Joel Westbrook and his son had hung around half of the afternoon, asking questions and hinting that things were about to change at West Harbor. As soon as Joshua had jumped from the dory and pulled it ashore, Ella and Esta May came down to the grassy beach. Esta May was clearly upset. Ella's face wore the stubborn expression Joshua was familiar with, especially since he knew he had the same streak.

"Joel Westbrook and his son were here," Esta May told Jamie as he climbed out of the dory. "He kept saying we should leave the island."

"Who did he talk to?" Jamie asked.

"Mostly Preacher," Ella answered. "We were all there, though. We heard what he said." Her soft voice seemed, to Joshua, to have iron hidden in it.

"The children all right?" Jamie asked.

Esta May, her eyes focused on him, nodded.

Jeremiah and Joshua unloaded fish and gear from the dory. The fishing had been poor. All they had were a few whitefish netted from deep in the lake far from shore. They had worked until their muscles ached, but had little to show for the day's efforts. There weren't many days when fishing was lousy, but when it was, it set them back.

When the fish and gear were unloaded, Joshua leaned backward and stretched his lower back. "Did he let on what had him stirred up?" he asked. "He's tried to make us nervous before. He's a low-down snake in the grass, but nothing's ever happened."

"What got Preacher upset, though he didn't let on to Westbrook or his son," Ella said, "was he said he had heard from what he called 'fugitive slave hunters'. When Preacher asked him what he was talking about, he refused to say, just looked at his son and smiled."

"Chas told us about his meeting with Reverend Porter in Green Bay before he got together with Weayaya," Jeremiah said. "What he told us didn't sound good."

"We've always known about slavers," Ella responded.

"But Westbrook and his son have some evil idea in their head," Esta May said. "You could see it in their eyes. They don't mean good for my daughter."

"Mr. Miner and the other island abolitionists are okay with us being here," Joshua pointed out. "Johannson, the Swedes, and even the Irish have had Preacher help with their boats. We aren't like we were running and hiding through Illinois and Wisconsin and up the Door." He looked at the poor whitefish catch he and Jeremiah had put into a single bucket. "We're fishermen," he said. "We've even got a little cash saved, something that when we first got here we couldn't have imagined."

Jamie looked hard at him. "Esta May and I are about to have a second child," he said. "Little Emily is precious enough. The question is will those children born on this island in freedom be all right? Will they be safe? They're not going to know a minute of slavery."

Joshua looked at his best friend. He didn't smile, but reflected Jamie's seriousness back at him. "We've got to be all right," he said. "Washington Island and West Harbor is home."

That evening they gathered in God's house. Sensing the general unease, Esta May and Jamie's toddler and the other two babies were fussy. Abbie, Ertha, and Eunice, all of them eager to grow out of childhood, seemed strained, but were maintaining an air of calm. They had been through more trying experiences. Although they understood the seriousness of the Westbrooks, especially since both men had carried rifles, they had talked and decided they wouldn't act like children. And adults, as their parents kept telling them, held close to their faith as Christians and faced trouble, looking for a solution that could improve their lives. As Bill kept telling his girls, "the way might be dangerous and hard, but those who've been slaves have lived worse."

Both Chas and Preacher took the Westbrooks' threats seriously. "I'm not much for understanding white men's laws," Chas said at one point, "but we all know they can be used against black people. The Porters warned me. They said some new law was dangerous to us. What Westbrook's visit means is that what the Porters told me is true."

"Take Westbrook's rifle away, and he can't stand up to a real man," Pappy said in response.

Harrison touched Pappy's shoulder. "Your Master Samuelson couldn't have stood up to you, either," he said gently. "You're the strongest man I've ever seen. But sometimes the situation doesn't allow a strong man to use his strength."

"We can't let them chase us off," Joshua said, supporting what he thought his father was trying to say. "We can't run forever. We've got to hold what we've made for ourselves sooner or later."

"We're not slaves or ex-slaves," Ella, standing beside him, said. "We're free people." She paused, looking at Preacher. "Living in New Jerusalem."

Preacher started and a wistful look came over his face. "I haven't used those words for a while," he said. His voice deepened. "'Be ye glad and rejoice forever in that which I create: for, behold, I create Jerusalem a rejoicing, and her people a joy.'" His eyes smoldered with powerful emotions as he looked at Ella. "But they're true, aren't they? We've started making New Jerusalem."

"What I want," Esta May said, "is for my babies to be able to grow up as free people, safe from the white race's ugliness. If I never saw a white person again, I wouldn't feel deprived."

"We've made lives for ourselves here," Zelda said, panic in her voice. "My baby is buried here." She put out her hand and pulled Abbie toward her.

"I don't think anybody's saying we have to run again," Chas said. "But I think we need to be careful. Westbrook is not a man to mess with."

Weayaya, who had been standing beside her husband and looking discomfited by the passion flowing through the sanctuary, shook her head. "The white man cannot be trusted," she said. "But not all white men are completely white. Some have human in them. You can learn from what those white men say."

A long silence followed Weayaya's words. Nobody looked at each other, but they were all thinking.

Finally Preacher sighed loud enough for everyone to hear him. "Weayaya's right," he said. "We need to go to Washington Harbor and talk to Henry Miner and Mr. Craw and some of the abolitionists. Something's happening. We need to understand that better so we can figure out our response."

They talked for another hour or so, trying to decide who would travel to Washington Harbor in the morning. Almost everybody wanted Preacher to go, but he kept refusing.

"Even the whites respect you," Joshua mother had said in exasperation at one point. "Look how many have been out here to hear you preach."

"They're Christians," Preacher said. "Tomorrow we don't want to hear what the Christians think they ought to say to a man they believe knows the word of God. We want to know what they have to say about the reality of what we're facing." After a pause he shook his head. "The truth is," he said slowly, "I am getting old and am satisfied to spend every moment I have in New Jerusalem."

In the end, his will prevailed. It was decided that Chas, Pappy, Franklin, and Bill would go to see whoever was around in Washington Harbor that might have sympathy for West Harbor. Harrison was asked to go, too, but refused, saying, "No, I belong here."

Joshua was a little upset that he and Jamie had not been chosen to go. His mother, after they were outside walking to their cabin, told him that he had gotten too literate. He got along well with Jesse, who liked books as well as he did, but she suspected the last thing white people wanted was a black man who was better read than they were. "You can't hide what you and Ella are," she told him. "Neither one of you even talk like the rest of us anymore, not all the time. You're way too bold with words."

***

The next morning, everybody went outside when the men were ready to leave for Washington Harbor. The sun was shining and warm. Lake waters danced with light and moving lines of long waves, gulls were landing and taking off out of West Harbor's waters, and a breeze not only made the air feel clean and fresh but rustled the leaved trees with their earth song. Joshua was disconcerted when Weayaya walked down the trail to Washington Harbor before the men did. He hadn't understood she was going to go with them, but Chas, seeing her start, moved quickly with the others on his heels.

After they were gone, Joshua realized, as the community watched the now empty trailhead, that what the rest of them thought did not bind Weayaya. Her life had been different than their lives. She was used to fending for herself in a wilderness, which would challenge the resources of most men, including him. She had lived a lifetime freedom the rest of them were still learning. They might not ever reach what she had possessed since she had been a child grieving for the loss of her tribe and all those close to her other than her parents. None of them, including Chas, were going to govern what she chose to do.

After everyone had filtered back to the cabins, Jeremiah came over to Joshua with Jamie. "They're going to be a while," he said. "We might as well go fishing."

Joshua hesitated. They had an excuse to spend a few hours without anything specific to do, but he shrugged and started for the dory. The scow was still where Franklin and Pappy had pulled it up on the beach, but the boys were most often assigned the dory, which, since they had to use oars, made fishing more difficult.

They didn't get too far out of the harbor before they put nets down, even though they knew the fishing would be better further out. "I want to hear what happened," Jamie said. "We've got to be able to see when they come back. I'd better be there for Esta May, too."

The miracle was that they found a large school of lake trout right away and were soon fully occupied with their fishing.

The sun was over halfway through its journey in the sky, and they had nearly filled the hold built into the dory for fish when they saw movement near the trailhead. Without even speaking, they hauled the net they'd just put out in and started getting ready to return to shore.

Yet another surprise was waiting for them. Gordon Burr, who they'd not seen in over a year, was with the four men and Weayaya. Gordon always brought stuff from the peninsula the community needed. Reverend Jemson's congregation never seemed to forget them.

But this time, neither Gordon, nor anybody else, was carrying supplies when the three of them yanked the dory to shore. Instead he, like the others, looked serious as they talked to the people of the community, all of whom had come out of the cabins and met the men and Weayaya in the clearing. The three fishermen secured the dory and hurried to where everybody was standing.

"Good Lord," Gordon exclaimed as the three of them approached. "You boys have turned into men."

In spite of how he felt, Joshua smiled. All three of them *were* men who helped make a living for their families. Gordon always made him feel happy. He suspected the Stockbridge Indian had the same effect on everyone he met.

Preacher didn't smile. He looked sober. "Gordon Burr has some serious news," he said.

"We didn't find Henry Miner or Mr. Craw," Pappy said. "We found Gordon on Craw's dock instead."

"A good substitute," Joshua's mother said.

Gordon smiled at her. "I guess I'd better get on with the telling then," he said.

"Let's go to God's house," Preacher said. "The telling will be easier there."

Inside the sanctuary, everybody, except for the babies, sat on the benches. Gordon stretched his legs and then pulled them up beneath where he was sitting. "Well, it's not good news," he said. "The fact is that it's not good news for you folks at all.

"Reverend Jemson sent word three weeks ago that I needed to come to Washington Island. He'd sent a young black man on his way to Canada. Stanton Younger, the young man, told me that a lot of blacks are fleeing Chicago. Based on what I was told, Senator Henry Clay of Kentucky got a new law through Congress called the Fugitive Slave Act. It requires all citizens of the United States to help southerners recover escaped slaves. The law provides a bounty for every slave returned. It also says that no man, woman, or child recovered has the right to appeal to any court. Even black people born free can get sent to a slave owner without any protection. Stanton said several members of Reverend Jemson's congregation had already fled and that more were getting ready to."

Gordon stopped long enough to take a breath before saying, "I caught a ride from a steamer over here to tell you. I think you folks are the largest black community outside Milwaukee in Wisconsin. There's another fisher community north of here in Michigan, but they're a whole lot closer to Canada if there's trouble. You've got to be a target. Plus, as we all know, you're escaped slaves. You had masters that want you back. They spent a lot of money trying to capture you when you ran here. You've got to know how much risk you're at."

No one spoke after Gordon finished. Most stared intently at the floor they had put down in such haste that first late summer after they had arrived on the island. Gordon stared at it with them.

At last Preacher got to his feet. "Sounds like they've declared extermination war on free black people," he said.

"Chas told me about Westbrook poking around," Gordon said. "He's never been a good man."

"But he's the Justice of the Peace," Massie said, her voice bitter.

"Well, what are we going to do?" Joshua's mother asked. "I don't hanker to go running again. Still, that steamer captain, what was his name?"

"Stewart, Captain Stewart," Pappy said.

"He volunteered to take us to Canada," she said. She looked at the walls of God's house. They had spent the last winter sanding them all over again and making them gleam. They had spent endless hours peeling and sanding bark off the rough logs. They had worked hard at building Preacher's dream of New Jerusalem.

"What will the islanders do?" Harrison asked, looking at Chas, the one they always looked to when dealing with the outside world. "Will they let Westbrook and his like send us back to our old plantations?"

Chas stared at Harrison, thinking through what he should say. "I don't know," he admitted at last. "We didn't find Henry Miner or Mr. Craw. Mr. Miner might be willing to guess, and his guess might be pretty good. But I don't suppose there's a promise in that. There are more people coming to the island, especially Finlanders. We've even been told we've been threatened by King Strang and the Mormons."

"That's not serious, though," Franklin said. "The Swedes told us he's crazy. He wants to build a Mormon empire out of the Michigan and Wisconsin islands, but he's an abolitionist. He's not about to threaten us, at least not directly."

Preacher sighed. "You'd think building New Jerusalem should be surer," he said. "You'd think that if you'd put down a plank and fastened it to another plank that would be it. 'If ye have faith as a grain of mustard seed, ye shall say unto this mountain, Remove hence to yonder place; and it shall remove; and nothing shall be impossible unto you.' I saw this place when cannons roared and flames burned as men died from cannonballs and grapeshot. I guess if you're a black man you're never free of the human condition that afflicts you."

Preacher stared into empty space. Joshua felt the stubbornness he'd felt as a boy coming back to him. He'd misplaced it for a while, but it was still there. "They're going to have drag me in chains off this island," he declared loudly. "The Westbrooks aren't going to make me run off that easily."

Ella grabbed his arm and squeezed. She looked frightened.

***

The next morning Joshua was just behind Pappy, still in his nightclothes, when they heard the sound of gunshot. Willie and Jeremiah and Massie and Joshua's mother moved fast.

As soon as he hit the ground outside the cabin door Pappy stopped. People were standing in nightclothes outside the cabins. Westbrook was walking calmly across the clearing toward them, smiling.

"Nothing to worry about folks," he called. "I'm just doing a little hunting. I shot at a big doe, but missed." He laughed, his laugh sounding phony. "Nothing to worry about."

Gordon, Preacher, and Chas walked slowly in front of the five cabins to where Westbrook was standing. Weayaya was behind her husband. She looked as calm as she had when she had first walked with him into their lives.

When Westbrook saw them, he shook his head with an exaggerated swagger. "Well, I'll be," he said loudly. "Gordon Burr and an Indian woman. Looks like negras aren't the only ones we settlers have to worry about. I thought those two boys on Rock Island who drove off the braves a few years back had settled things. This is a white man's place, not a place for Indians."

"You ought to be careful what you wish for, Mr. Westbrook," Gordon said as he walked, his voice good-natured. "You never know what a bunch of wild Indians might get it in their heads to do even in this day and age. They've got firearms now, you know."

Westbrook sobered. "That a threat? I am the law around here."

"What do you want, Mr. Westbrook?" Chas asked.

Westbrook did not take his eyes off Gordon Burr, who smiled at him.

"I was just hunting," Westbrook said. "I didn't intend to get all of you out of bed. An early hunter gets his deer meat."

"We've heard about the Fugitive Slave Act," Preacher said. "I don't think you have any reason for threatening us with it. You've known for a long time that Chas Bullock and I are veterans of the War of 1812 and served under Commodore Perry. We're veterans."

Westbrook shook his head. "I know you've put that about," he said slowly, "but how does any inhabitant of this island know that that's true? Runaway slaves have to have a story, or else they're north of here in Canada. I've been hearing from my law enforcement brothers. What they tell me is that they're catching escaped slaves who claim not to be escaped slaves all the time."

"You're not the only one on this island," Chas said.

"Oh." Westbrook laughed. "You think the Miners, Swedes, and abolitionists will save you?" He shook his head. "What you don't understand is that the Fugitive Slave Act is a national law signed by President Fillmore himself. You see, the southerners don't want California to come into the union as a free state. Congress doesn't want a war between slave and free states, so now every citizen of the United States is required — I say required — to assist slave owners recover escaped property. That means Henry Miner, Johannson, and even that idiot Irishman O'Reilly who likes to play songs on his fiddle that he says are made up by slaves. Those men are law-abiding men, I tell you. They'll follow the law I am sworn to uphold."

Joshua felt a chill pass through him. His mother tried to grab his arm as he suddenly moved toward Westbrook. He was smiling. "You want to whip me?" he asked loudly. "Isn't that what white men really want to do? Whip negras? Men?" He smiled even more wildly. "Women?"

"Joshua," Pappy roared.

Westbrook's eyes bored into Joshua's. They glittered with manic excitement.

"You been whipped boy?" Westbrook asked eagerly. "You telling me you're an escaped slave that's been whipped?" He took a step forward. "Why don't you take off that shirt you're wearing and let me see your back? That's where they whip you slaves, isn't it? On your back?"

Chas and Weayaya moved as one to stand side by side between Westbrook and Joshua.

"He's a boy," Chas said. "He's not any of your interest."

Westbrook looked Weayaya up and down, ignoring Chas. "Too bad it's against the law to murder Indians anymore," he said. "I swear they're more worthless than negras."

"We are a God-fearing community," Preacher said. "Everyone here has pledged their faith and lives to Jesus Christ our Lord." He took a deep breath. "In Proverbs," he said, "the Bible tells us 'When the righteous are in authority, the people rejoice: but when the wicked beareth rule, the people mourn.' I trust you're a righteous man, Mr. Westbrook. I trust that."

Westbrook looked at Preacher, licking his top lip. "Oh, fugitive slave Tom Bennett, I am a righteous man who believes in the law of the United States of America. Oh, yes. I am a righteous man." He smiled again. "Besides, I didn't come here to arrest anyone this morning. I was only hunting." He looked directly at Joshua. "I'll be seeing you, boy."

Still smiling, he turned and walked into the woods.

Joshua's mother touched his shoulder. He saw her anger when he looked into her dark eyes.

"When you were a child, I could never understand why you goaded white folks the way you did," she said, almost whispering. "I used to think you were born with a self-destructive spirit. You didn't think for a moment about what you were doing to yourself when you got the unholy masters or that fool Silver Coats after you. For years now I've thought that spirit was gone, but now—"

"Mary," Pappy interrupted as her voice started quivering from the rage she was feeling.

Preacher waved his arm, indicating that he wanted them to get into a circle. Even the children's eyes were on Joshua's mother and the anger contorting her face as she stared at her only son.

"I think it's time to pray," Preacher said.

Neither Mary nor Joshua moved, although Pappy did. The turmoil Joshua was feeling as his mother kept her eyes locked on his was so great he was shaking. *What possessed me to challenge Westbrook? My idiocy could damage everything we've worked so hard to achieve.* Then, suddenly, he was aware that Ella had separated from the circle and was standing by him, her eyes on the ground. His mother's eyes did not move when Ella broke from the forming circle.

"Lord," Preacher began. His voice for the first time in Joshua's memory sounded shaky. "We don't understand your ways at this moment. In Proverbs we are told to 'Trust in the Lord with all thine heart; and lean not unto thine own understanding.' But sometimes we are weak vessels without understanding. Sometimes even this servant of yours feels doubts that trouble his sleep and make him mourn his weaknesses.

"The Apostle John taught us that we must love one another no matter what faults we find in each other, but sometimes finding that love is hard. When we are frightened we protect ourselves and ours. Sometimes that's necessary, but, Lord, we know that the only real protection is in you and the example of love Jesus set before all his children ...."

As the prayer went on, Joshua and his mother bowed their heads. Preacher was overwhelmingly powerful sometimes. Joshua could sense the anger draining from his mother. He felt differently too, although he wasn't sure why. He knew he hadn't acted like a man ought to act, but like a child whose stubbornness was stronger than his sense.

When Preacher finished, Joshua's mother looked at him with tears in her eyes. "I love you," she said. "I've always tried to find a way to protect you, but you don't make that easy."

Preacher touched Joshua's shoulder, started to say something, but thought better of it and walked away. Joshua could tell that Jamie had wanted to come over to talk to him, but Esta May had jerked his arm toward their cabin. After a few minutes Joshua and Ella were standing alone.

"Guess I wasn't so smart," he said.

Ella shook her head. "No," she said. "But the thing is that we shouldn't still be dancing to the master's tune. Westbrook is the white man's fiddle. You scared the life out of me, but I was proud anyhow. If we go all meek and humble every time the white man rumbles at us, we'll be in a slavery that's just different from the one we escaped."

He studied her face carefully. Strangely enough, he'd never tried to kiss her, not once. They had been so close, but he'd always been determined she was a little girl, a sister he'd never had. That wasn't true, of course. He'd seen how Jeremiah looked at her. He'd seen her that way, too, but he'd read with her rather than desired her, fighting off feelings that didn't seem right. He couldn't fathom why he'd felt that way.

"I've got to be more careful," he said at last. "I've got my mother and father and you to think about, along with the babies and the others. I got to unknot who Silver Coats and Master Bulrush made me and become the man I'm meant to be."

Ella took his right hand in her two hands. "You're smart," she said. "You'll make your way in the world."

He bent his head and pressed his lips to hers.

Chapter 30
From Inside the Gates of New Jerusalem

And then a breeze, as gentle as a kiss,
Came billowing into the scow's white sail
Until the lake and island left travail
To sink into the water's dark abyss
Where no soul had to dream or reminisce
About days when raw courage couldn't fail
If voices were to someday tell the tale
Of how they'd found their sanctuary's bliss.

They reveled in the way the breeze confirmed
Their sense that they had found auspicious winds,
A shore where lives could live in Christendom
And flourish on a distant island bermed
With rock and soil against the storm's life sends
To batter down the gates of New Jerusalem.

    The next few weeks were tense. Joshua knew his mother and father were talking about what they could do about the fugitive slave law, but no one confronted the situation out in the open. They seemed to have all agreed that there was no use talking about something they couldn't change. The only ones who had even been in contact with anything to do with the government were Preacher and Chas when they had been sailors under Commodore Perry. No one had an idea about how to do anything about Westbrook and his friends on the island.

    Gordon and Chas visited Washington Harbor and saw Mr. Craw and Henry Miner two days after Westbrook's visit. In their report to the community, they basically said that the two white men did not give them much comfort. They didn't think Westbrook would try anything too drastic, since any kind of action could threaten his livelihood, but neither had any idea about what would happen if plantation agents came to the island in search of runaway slaves. The white island people did not approve of slavery and did not like the legislation that had been adopted, but the law had been passed.

    Mr. Craw had told the two black men that it had passed almost two years before. The good news was that so far it had not been a concern.

"As you know, though," Mr. Craw had said, "sometimes consequences of what happens in the larger world reach Washington Island later than other places."

***

Life continued as it had before Westbrook's fake hunting expedition. The men took the scow and dory out to fish. They spent Sunday mornings listening to Preacher's sermons. When they had to repair nets, or sew clothes, or cook, or collect eggs from the henhouse, or do any of the other dozens of things common to the community, they did so.

One of the women's delights was Weayaya. Although completely independent, wandering off whenever she took a notion, whether Chas was aware of where she was going or not, she turned out to be a prodigious worker. When she spoke it was always to the point with as few words as possible. And she especially liked the huge garden planted south of the cabins. They had carefully harvested seeds from plants Reverend Jemson and Gordon's original gift of seed had grown that first late summer and fall and added to their stock by acquisitions from Craw's store funded by fishing income.

The garden now had a variety of crops ranging from rows of corn that Junebug and Harrison would grind into cornmeal for baking, to potatoes, beets, rutabagas, carrots, lettuce, okra, beans, peas, and squash. Beulah had even planted a small garden of wildflowers she had gotten Bill to search out and replant where the community could see them every day during the spring and summer.

Ella told Joshua that Weayaya was popular partially because she was different. Not only did she have a spirit at the heart of what freedom meant, but in the mornings, before dawn, she went to the lake, knelt on shore, and said prayers in her language as the sun came up. None of them thought she said Christian prayers, although she attended Preacher's sermons with the rest on Sundays, praying in English with the same reverence they exhibited.

"It's good to have someone different to think about," Ella said. "She helps the rest of us know who we are."

To everyone's relief, Westbrook hadn't given a repeat performance of his threats, although none of them thought he'd hold off forever. Pappy and Willie, talking one day in their cabin before getting ready to walk down to the fishing boats, agreed he was determined to scare them off. He hadn't succeeded, so he'd inevitably try again.

***

One morning in the third week after Gordon came to the island, he told Preacher he had to get back to Stockbridge. He said he'd been gone too long and that a steamer heading to Green Bay was due in Washington Harbor.

That evening, after the men returned from the lake and packed the day's catch in Miner's barrels, Preacher called a meeting. Before everybody got to God's house, the sun, a huge red ball, had set. Zelda and Preacher lit a dozen tallow candles to give the sanctuary light. Since they knew Gordon was leaving the next day, they were solemn, remembering what he'd done for them as he'd led them through Wisconsin to near Hedgehog Harbor where they'd launched to Washington Island.

Preacher started with his usual prayer, but then was silent as he looked at them, his eyes as fiery as they always were when he was preaching. "I'm not concerned about Gordon leaving tomorrow," he said. "He goes away and comes back. He's always bringing a blessing with him. All of us understand, deep inside, the gratitude we hold for those who helped us in our escape.

"But with him leaving tomorrow, the time has come to discuss the challenge we're facing." He bowed his head. Joshua had the idea that he was feeling a deep sadness. "This dream of mine, this community," he continued, lifting his head to look at the walls surrounding them, "this New Jerusalem has become reality. It is no dream, no promise from God. It is a blessing from God brought about by Christians with strong backs and determined faith. I can't tell any of you how blessed I am to have lived and seen what you have built and Gordon helped make possible.

"Still, as ex-slaves we know we can't control all the circumstances of our lives. We've taken action and run from whips and white masters. We've proven we can act in defiance of obstacles binding us. But the question is can we stay in this New Jerusalem we have built or do we need to go further north to Canada? I have thought much about this these past few weeks. New Jerusalem is not a place, but a spirit endowed with the Lord's spirit and His people.

"Before Gordon leaves, so he doesn't lose track of us, so that he can let Reverend Jemson and others in the Underground Railroad know, I think we need to talk this through." He quietly moved from his usual place at the lectern to the bench where Chas and Weayaya were sitting.

"We've got to stay here," Zelda spoke up, her voice intense. "Franklin, Abbie, and I have to stay here."

Franklin took his wife's hand but said nothing, while Abbie squirmed uncomfortably in her seat.

"I don't want Jamie and I to leave either," Esta May said. She looked over at Zelda. "I saw how Zelda and Franklin struggled to bring Abbie when we fled the swamp. She was so small and brave. But Jamie and I have even a younger child with another on the way." She looked at Beulah and the baby cradled in her arms. "We have two babies who can't walk yet."

Chas looked at Weayaya and subtly nudged her. Weayaya glanced calmly at him. She nodded. "For little ones, that one over there," she gestured toward Harrison, "can make a cradleboard."

"A cradleboard?" Joshua's mother asked.

"You wrap the baby in a tight blanket," Chas explained. "Then you strap it, using soft leather straps, onto a wood board and put the cradleboard on your back. All the Indian tribes use them to carry babies, especially if they're going long distances." He smiled at his wife.

"Would we try to catch the steamer Michigan in Washington Harbor?" Bill asked.

"We've got boats. That seems to me to be safer," Willie said. "We can float away at night and let the islanders find we're gone. Besides, we're a community of fishermen. We're going to need the scow and dory to prosper wherever we go."

Pappy, nervous, rose to his feet. He always seemed too big for small rooms. His energy was too restless to be contained in small spaces. Out on the lake, hauling in nets or rowing, or hauling tree trunks through the woods to West Harbor, he was in his element.

"The question seems to me to be," he said, "what's the risk of staying put?" He looked at Esta May. "We don't want any of the young ones born free to know slavery. There's no way any of us can allow that."

"We can't run," Zelda said, sounding distressed.

"If my grandbabies are going to be put into chains or face the whip, we'll run," Massie said bluntly. "It won't be easy or right, but we'll run."

Silence greeted Massie's statement. The only untroubled ones seemed to be Gordon and Weayaya. Gordon shifted on his bench. "I can't advise you, I'm afraid," he said. "My people were driven from our homelands in New York even though those who came to Wisconsin were Christian and knew how to farm and make do for themselves. You can make peace with some white men, but you can't trust them. There's too many of them. They seem to always want everything they can have even if their Christianity says they shouldn't have some of what they want."

"I don't think we ought to abandon West Harbor, at least not yet," Chas said. "Westbrook's not been making trouble. Mr. Claw and Henry Miner seem to think he'll have to be careful not to upset the island's abolitionists too much."

"In Luke we're told to 'fear not, little flock; for it is your Father's good pleasure to give you the kingdom,'" Preacher said. "Fear, though, is not a bad thing in a man or woman who's been a slave." He turned and said to

Gordon, "I wonder if we'll be here when you come to look for us."

"You're not ready to move on yet," Gordon said. "Be careful, though. You don't want to hesitate too long if your masters have an inkling of where you are."

"You wouldn't think they would," Junebug said. "We didn't send them notice of where we were going."

A brief titter of laughter circled the room. Junebug was smiling broadly.

Chas smiled, but he also shook his head. "We're not a secret on the island or Door County," he said soberly. "We don't know how far news of us has traveled. Like Gordon said before, we're the largest black community living north of Milwaukee that isn't in the upper peninsula of Michigan or Canada. That's noticeable to a lot of people, especially to those who want to notice it."

Jamie was staring at his uncle. "If Esta May and I need to run, we'll run," he said. "No Bullock's going back to the Bulrush Plantation."

Joshua, who had not said anything during the discussion, found himself disagreeing with Jamie. He had no intention of leaving Washington Island. To him it was Preacher's New Jerusalem. When he was out on the lake with gulls, pelicans, and cormorants flying around him, looking back at the shore's wildness, he sometimes felt that this must be what heaven was like. In the winter when his thumbs burned from the cold while he tried to handle fishing tackle and nets, he didn't have quite the same feeling, but he didn't intend to leave.

He looked at Ella quietly sitting beside him, then at Preacher. He decided that he and Ella should get married. At least that would make something certain in an uncertain world, something bound to be a lifetime good.

***

That Sunday, two days after Gordon Burr left down the trail that headed north to Washington Harbor, the Miner family, for the first time in months, came to Preacher's sermon. After the service, while the West Harbor community and the older Miners talked to each other, carefully avoiding the topic of the Fugitive Slave Act, Joshua, Jamie, Jeremiah, Esta May, and Ella went with Jesse Miner to the spit between the lake and harbor. Esta May left Emily with her grandmother.

Jesse seemed excited to be with them. Joshua knew he had his white island friends, and he also knew that none of those friends had come with the Miners to Preacher's sermons, although several people from around the island had come over the years. Still, Jesse seemed to think of the West Harbor young people as his friends.

After they'd sat on logs placed around the fire pit for a long time, Jesse laughed. "You know what I've heard?" he asked.

"What?" Jeremiah responded.

Jessie lifted out his arms. He seemed exuberant. "Washington Island might get a teacher," he exclaimed. "A real teacher. I heard my Dad and Ambrose Betts talking about it in the post office."

Jeremiah looked at Jesse with a puzzled look. "That sounds good," he said. "But we already have teachers here." He pointed at Joshua and Ella. "There's two of them sitting right there. Preacher and Joshua's Mom are the others. Besides," he added, "we won't be welcome at a school set up to teach whites."

Jesse looked shocked. "Why not?" He looked at Joshua. "Joshua borrows every book I can get. You all can read. Teachers like students who want to learn."

"That's not the point," Esta May said. "The point is that there are some people on the island that won't approve of us coming to a school where their children are students. That just won't happen."

Jeremiah, looking mischievous, shook his head. "Why not?" he asked. "I bet hardly any of the white students can read half as well as Joshua and Ella—maybe even me."

"It just won't," Esta May said. "It won't. Anyway, Joshua and Ella are good enough teachers for my children."

"All of you are good readers," Jesse acknowledged. "But I bet none of you know Latin. How about arithmetic? Or history? I read novels when I get them, but knowing history would be a good thing. That's what Daddy says. He says my grandfather was a learned man who knew a lot about the Bible, but also about history."

"I bet not everybody on the island will be glad to go to school," Ella said. "All of us have jobs to do. In the winter, school's a good thing. We have time. But, unless you really like to read, school interrupts what you ought to be doing."

"Tommy O'Reilly says he hopes they don't get a teacher," Jessie admitted. "He says he already knows what he needs to make his life on the island, but Tommy's not the brightest anyway. That's why I think you'll be invited. A teacher likes students who like to read. You all like to read more than anybody else I know."

"We're black," Jeremiah said. "Blacks aren't supposed to be smart enough to know how to read."

An uncomfortable silence followed.

Jesse shook his head. "It's obvious you're black," he said. "Look, I didn't mean to upset anybody." He abruptly got to his feet. "I guess I ought to be seeing if my Daddy's ready to go home."

The others stayed where they were. Joshua started to say something, but couldn't find the right words. He didn't want Jesse mad at them.

"Why were you so tough on Jessie?" he asked Jeremiah. "The Miners have been the best friends we've got on the island. They've supported us."

"You think he'll miss us if we have to run to Canada?" Jeremiah asked.

"I don't think so," Ella said. "He might remember us, but I don't think he'll hardly know we've gone."

"We ought to be able to stay here," Esta May said.

"We ought to," Jamie said. "The question is are we going to be able to? Even Preacher hasn't been able to answer that one. We ought to fight for our place, but what's clear is that we have to protect ourselves first. We can make lives elsewhere. In the end, the way I've thought this out, I can't imagine saying yes, sir to Silver Coats while he lords it over us while we walk behind him in chains. They'll chain us for sure if we're ever caught. Just because we're here now doesn't mean it's the only place we can be." Jamie got to his feet.

"I'm tired of it all," Jeremiah said. "Stay? Not stay? Sooner or later we're going to have to decide." He looked at the lake. "Actually, a school with a teacher sounds good. Too bad it's not possible." Then, like Jesse, he walked away, leaving Joshua with a sick feeling in his stomach.

***

On Wednesday, three days later, Westbrook showed up at West Harbor again. The fishermen were already done with their day on the lake. The wind had been up, and fishing had been nearly impossible. Westbrook didn't stop as he and his son walked between the cabins and lake, but before he was out of the clearing into the woods, he stopped and fired his rifle. Pappy and Willie, who had been the only ones outside watching him, heard him laugh like a crazy man as he and his son disappeared into shadows beneath the trees.

After they'd all gathered to discuss what had just happened, Chas said, "He's just trying to rattle us. If he had slavers coming, he wouldn't bother with what he probably considers a big joke. He'd come on us after everybody's asleep. Fewer of us would be able to run that way."

"I'm not afraid of him," Pappy said. "But he does know how to make lives uncomfortable."

***

After that weeks went by without any sighting of either Westbrook or his son. Even when Chas, Weayaya, and Franklin went to Washington

Harbor with a load of fish, he was nowhere to be seen. The rhythm of their lives, preparing for winter, harvesting, fishing, canning, chopping wood, repairing nets, cooking, and doing all the other necessary, endless tasks slowly forced their tension into the background.

Then, as the weather got cold, Chas was out hunting when he ran across Shamus O'Reilly in the woods. Chas often described O'Reilly as a good-humored man with unruly red hair and a ready grin who'd talk the leg off anybody who'd listen. And he had news. He saw Chas sitting with his back against a big white pine, watching a deer trail, and went over to talk to him.

"You don't have to worry so much about Joel Westbrook," he said. "Not now anyway. The Mormons came over to the island and murdered that half-breed John Laframboise with a bowie knife. They're saying King Stang has spies on the island with orders to murder Joseph Lodbill and take over his place and the rest of the northwest. They're planning to burn places to the ground for sure. Westbrook's so busy looking for Mormons and trying to figure out how whiskey from his warehouse showed up in Craw's warehouse he hasn't got time to bother you folks right now."

After coming back to West Harbor, Chas said that O'Reilly's endless stream of talk had made him feel better than he had for months. When O'Reilly had told him most of the island was angry with Westbrook because they thought he wasn't doing his job and was too soft on Mormons bothering their efforts at fishing, Chas said that he didn't tell him West Harbor hadn't had any problems with the Mormons. Instead he had decided that Westbrook had suddenly become a lot less of a problem.

As winter gathered force with its usual snow, wind, and brutal cold, and the ice froze, New Jerusalem started feeling like New Jerusalem again. The winter school started up. Ella was in charge of toddlers while Joshua and Jeremiah worked with the others on reading and mathematics. Most of the adults had stopped coming to the classes. They could all read enough "to get along," as Willie put it. Even during days when the weather was too dangerous to allow fishing on the ice there was still lots of work to do. Jamie and Esta May had given up on the lessons years before.

The younger children, though, had a longer road of opportunity that learning represented. Joshua, Ella, and Jeremiah did not feel all that accomplished, and were constantly asking Chas or another of the men when they went to Washington Harbor, or, in Chas's case, to Ephraim or Green Bay, if they'd managed to find a new book for them. They didn't care what kind of book they got. Books were too rare to worry about that.

The strangest part of the winter was Weayaya and Chas's constant trips away from West Harbor. They both were restless. Chas kept leaving for Washington or Detroit Harbor or even trips to the Door Peninsula over the ice. Most of the time Weayaya went with him, although sometimes she went off into the wilderness alone. Neither of them seemed to fear strapping snowshoes on their feet, or, sometimes their backs, depending on snow conditions, and walking into a treacherous white wilderness.

The best part of Chas and Weayaya's restlessness was that Chas kept bringing tidbits of news from the outside world. Wisconsin was aflame in its opposition to the Fugitive Slave Act. During a particularly long trip with Weayaya when the two of them had visited the Potawatomi village she had lived near during the years Chas had spent rescuing his brother and the rest of them, Chas had heard of an incident in Milwaukee where a captured slave had been freed by an abolitionist mob from jail, enraging most of the racist south, including Missouri.

Then, in late February, on the coldest Sunday of the year thus far, Henry Miner showed up moments after Preacher had finished his sermon. Everybody turned to look at the man dressed in a heavy brown fur coat crusted with frost as the cabin's door opened and cold slammed in from the outside. Miner shook himself like an animal, stomped his boots, getting off snow he'd been unable to shake off outside the door, and grunted. Preacher went over to him, smiling. They hadn't seen him since the young people had made Jesse uncomfortable.

"Come in, Mr. Miner," Preacher said. "Take off your coat. We have a warm fire going."

Miner shrugged off his heavy coat and ran his eyes around the sanctuary. Everyone was seated in their usual places. They waited respectfully until he had acclimated to the cabin's temperature. No one was eager to go back out in the cold.

After Preacher had taken Miner's coat and big leather mitts and put them beside the pile of coats by the fireplace where they could dry off, Chas got up, smiling like Preacher, and extended his hand. Mr. Miner reciprocated.

"So cold the snow crunches," he said to Chas. He slapped his hands against his shoulders and looked at the benches. "I thought I ought to come and tell you," he said, casting his voice loud enough for everybody to hear. "I know you've been worried about Westbrook, but I don't think you're going to have to worry for a while.

"He's been in jail in Green Bay as of a month and a half ago. Westbrook was making a lot of noise that Mr. Craw's men had taken some of his hay. He went over to Rock Island to try to replace the hay he was supposedly missing. While he was there, his yellow dog Bose started making a fuss. He said that when he went to see what was getting the dog so excited, he found the bodies of two boys and a keg of his missing whiskey tied to a sled.

"He left the boys there, he said, and came back to Washington Island to report what he'd found and get help. When he got home, a couple of men from Door County were there and arrested him and his son. After he'd made all that fuss about Craw's men stealing his hay, Craw's barn burned down. It looked like arson, so they arrested the two of them."

Miner looked around the room, his eyes shining. "The point is," he said, "Westbrook won't be bothering any of you for a while, not from where he and his son are. The other point is that when a group of men went over to find the dead boys, the whiskey keg, and sled, nothing was there. Everybody on Washington Island other than you folks are talking day and night about this." He smiled. "There, that's what I came out here to tell you."

Preacher, who had been standing by the fireplace while Mr. Miner talked, came forward as the room got noisy with conversation. "I don't wish any man ill," he said. "Not even Mr. Westbrook. But that is welcome news!"

Joshua was watching Chas as Ella watched him. He could feel her eyes on his face. Chas was frowning. "Did Westbrook burn down the barn?" he asked Mr. Miner.

Miner shook his head. "I don't know," he said. "Joel can be a rough man sometimes. His boy's the same as he is. Mr. Craw says there'll be a jury trial in Green Bay. Most people think the Westbrooks are guilty."

"What about the two dead boys?" Preacher asked. "What happened to them if nobody can find them?"

Mr. Miner sighed. "Maybe Westbrook used that as his cover story for burning the barn," he said. "He could have thought people would be so stirred up about a double murder they'd need him to solve the crime. On the other hand, rough as Joel is, nobody has ever known him to make something like that up."

Joshua's mother and Pappy had gotten out of their seats and joined the three men. "But we can be more relaxed for a while," his mother said slowly, both a question and a statement in her voice. "And I, for one, can be glad about that."

Joshua turned to Ella. He didn't know why the conversation by the fireplace was troubling him, but in spite of what Mr. Miner had tried to accomplish by traveling through a brutal day, he felt that something was missing. He was glad Westbrook was in jail, but he wasn't sure the Fugitive Slave Act wasn't going to affect them. "I'm not sure this is the end of our troubles," he said.

Chapter 31
Love Singing Alive the Moon

Upon a shore where sheets of ice had stacked
Into a shadowed sky, the full moon round
And silver in a field of stars that tracked
The darkness with eternity, the sound
Of waves beyond the ice a lullabye
That serenaded who they were, they walked
And held each other's hands and felt the sigh
Of what they'd lived inside the talk they'd talked.

And in between their words, love sang the moon
Alive to whom their dreams said they would be
As passion beat against soft silver strewn
As light across ice shards, a filigree
That echoed pulsing waves, blood stirred, inflamed
Into two lifetimes that was love exclaimed.

By March, Joshua was beside himself. He had learned that Ella could
set him on fire, especially when they were alone and could explore each
other's bodies. She might not be as physically beautiful as her older sister,
but everything about her had come to seem to be a miracle. And her
mind was a match to his.

What he was happiest about was that he had never had to pursue Ella
the way Jamie had Esta May. She had, instead, made herself available to
him, even pushed him, before he'd had the faint idea she might be the
love of his life. Sometimes, on the lake when brutal cold made him and
the other men so miserable they wondered why they had ever taken up
so difficult a life, he looked back on his behavior the first year on the
island and was chagrined. He'd never once seen past his experience of
Ella as a little, plain-faced sister. He had not been able to understand that
people, all people, were more than how they looked. He had not even
seen that he and Ella had much more spirit in common than any others,
including the married couples, in the community, or that her spirit made
her unbelievably beautiful.

Joshua's mother and Beulah had set Ella and Joshua's wedding for
the spring. Both Ella and Joshua, after Joshua had finally woken up, had

wanted to get married right away. After all, Joshua was as old as Jamie and Esta May, and they already had one child with another on its way.

But both mothers were insistent. "Spring, when the blood starts to stir out winter, is the time for a wedding," Beulah had said as Joshua's mother nodded, smiling. "Not winter when the world is so cold the blood in your veins is frozen."

The biggest problem was that Joshua's mother especially, and Preacher, insisted that the two of them had to "behave" themselves before the wedding.

"We are civilized people," his mother had said in her fiercest voice. "We will not act like white men that claim to be Christian while acting like rutting cats."

"'For this cause shall a man leave his father and mother, and shall be joined unto his wife, and they two shall be one flesh,'" Preacher had told them when they'd gone to tell him they wanted to get married. "Marriage is a great sacrament. You cannot be one flesh without the sacrament. If you do that, you're committing a sin that Moses brought to us in the Ten Commandments. We have to be true in the flesh to the joining of a man and woman. That means you bring purity to the marriage bed."

Both were tempted to go beyond what the adults were demanding, but in the end they always stopped. Mostly because opportunity was not as easily had as it would have been in better weather. They couldn't sneak into a cabin and go beyond touching and kissing. There was too much risk of being caught.

They also understood what their mothers and Preacher were telling them. With freedom came responsibility. As intelligent people they needed to exercise that responsibility so that it became one of the hallmarks of their lives as a couple and as individuals.

In this waiting period, the idea of teaching seemed especially important. The books Joshua had been able to borrow from Jesse had dried up. Jesse hadn't been back since the awkwardness of his last visit. Joshua wasn't sure he should ask Chas to try to borrow any new books Jesse might have. He wasn't sure about how Jesse was thinking about West Harbor.

That meant the only books available to them were the three Bibles they'd had since Gordon Burr's visit that first fall, battered copies of *The American Spelling Book*, the single arithmetic textbook that they used to teach what little mathematics any of them, including Chas and Preacher, had mastered, and a few battered novels, like *Deerbrook* by Harriet Martineau, that Chas had been given on one of his trips to Ephraim.

Joshua's mother's idea about building a Christian civilization better than the white master's plantation civilization called for a community that could exercise its imagination through books as well as hard work. It was a different notion, but one that occupied a lot of their conversations when they snatched time together from chores, work, and Sunday meetings. They even talked about how someday they might be able to have half a dozen books like the ones Jesse talked his father into buying so that West Harbor's young people could stretch their minds. The books they knew about all had white people as their subjects, but imagination extended them into lives so different from those they were living. They knew that the community's children, including their own, and they meant to have children, deserved to discover the blessings of imagining.

The whole thing about blacks and whites was complicated, they told each other. There was no reason, however, that blacks couldn't take what was useful in white society and fashion it so that it fulfilled black dreams and aspirations, fashioning their own society in the process. Preacher and Chas were proud of having been a part of the American Navy with Commodore Perry, even though neither had been pleased with the way they had been treated. They had taken pride in having been a part of history and molded it into the dream of becoming larger-than-life heroes who used the Underground Railroad to stage an escape for a group of Missouri plantation slaves.

For the first three weeks, March seemed as perverse as winter had been. Strong winds and cold blew off lake ice. The cold wasn't quite as brutal as it had been, but it was raw and harder to take. Not only was everybody tired of bad weather. But Joshua and Ella wanted March to go away so that they could finally be married in April.

***

They had not talked about where they were going to stay after they got married, and so were relieved when Harrison told them it was time to build them their own cabin.

Less than a week later, Pappy, Bill, Franklin, and Willie sent Joshua, Jamie, and Jeremiah out on the ice to fish while they went into the forest to find trees suitable for building. When they'd first come to West Harbor, such trees had been plentiful not far from shore, but their constant effort to feed fireplaces with logs and build cabins, outhouses, fishing shacks, and the chicken coop had depleted the best trees that were nearby.

"We need to get the trunks hauled in before the snow goes," Pappy said. "It's going to be hard enough hauling what we need. What we really need is a mule or a horse."

"Lot of money," Chas had responded laconically.

While the three young men got ready for fishing, Joshua's mother and Massie arrived to talk to Joshua. They'd brought Ella with them and pulled Joshua aside from Jamie and Jeremiah.

"The cabin won't be built in time for the wedding," Massie told them. "We've talked to Esta May. She'll let you move in with her, Jamie, and Emily until it's done."

The fact that Massie, rather than Joshua's mother or Beulah, was giving them the news struck Joshua as puzzling, but he didn't say anything. Neither did Ella. Instead, they looked at each other in dismay. They would have to share each other in a house with Joshua's best friend and Ella's sister. They couldn't imagine how uncomfortable that would be.

"In the quarters, as the two of you know, there was no privacy," Joshua's mother said, answering their objection before it could be stated. "People still got along."

"Yes, ma'am," Ella said, bowing her head.

Joshua started to blurt out his feeling that the plan didn't sound right to him, but held back his words. Ella, looking at the snow on the ground, abruptly walked away toward her parents' cabin. Joshua felt like he should follow her, but Jamie called, "You coming?"

"You're fishing today," his mother said softly.

***

Following the progress as Pappy and the other men hauled the trunks of logs that would become his and Ella's cabin became a daily ritual. Harrison had long before built sleds the men could use to drag tree trunks through the snow with ropes. The worst problem was choosing a path that would allow straight logs to move through places where thickets of young white pine or birch blocked the way.

As the logs took shape on the ground, however, with one man after another, including Joshua, Jamie, and Jeremiah, flattening tops and bottoms with broad axes, the weather started, in fits and starts, to warm slightly. It was still cold. They could still get out on the ice, but there were hints of coming spring.

By the early days of April, preparations for their marriage ceremony were underway. Ella, Esta May, and Beulah were making Ella a new deerskin dress for the ceremony. The women were talking about the wedding feast they'd all have. But it seemed like the day would never come.

Part of the problem was that the closer to May and the wedding they got, the less time Ella and he had together. A conspiracy seemed to be in place to purposefully keep them apart. There was always this or that chore to do or some reason why one or the other had to help somebody with something. Preacher was a special nuisance. He decided that Joshua

288

had the duty to help him put together his sermons. "You know the Bible the best among the men," he told him on a particularly blustery Sunday after the service, "so we need to prepare you for the time when I'm not here anymore."

Consumed with his own life, Joshua hadn't really noticed that Preacher was slowing down. In his eyes, Preacher had always been old, even on the day when his mother had first taken him in the swamp to go to Preacher's secret meeting. The old man with the pepper and salt beard, black hair, deep voice, and flaming eyes had frightened him. He'd sensed even then that Preacher had an ancientness inside that had nothing to do with his age.

But Preacher, as he knew from all the stories he'd heard, had not had an easy life. He'd worked hard and been beaten as a child, lived hand to mouth after the Quakers had spirited him away from slavery, and gone to war on Lake Erie, surviving while many he and Chas had known had died. He'd built and repaired boats after the war and eventually found Chas in the wilderness and talked him into the dream of freeing his brother and his family. Then he'd run with the rest of them, almost starving, until they had reached Washington Island where they'd worked desperately to get through that first winter with poor rations and barely enough shelter to survive.

Talking to him after everyone else had left them in the sanctuary, hearing what Preacher was saying, he realized the man who had led them to freedom was working less and less outside of God's house. He'd spent most of the winter by the fire while the women brought food to him and took care of him in innumerable small ways. They owed him more than they could ever repay.

He was older than Harrison and Junebug even, who, in spite of their relentless industry, seemed to Joshua to be really old. Now Preacher wanted Joshua to start learning how to preach the way he did.

Joshua didn't want anything to do with the responsibilities being thrust on him because he liked to read. Ella didn't like the idea, either. To both of them it seemed like an imposition on time they wanted to spend together, but, in the end, Joshua sat with Preacher and helped pick out Bible verses he could use in his sermons, even though Preacher didn't seem to need help with the task. His mind seemed as sharp as it had always been.

Preacher would ask him questions like "What do you think we should say about being kind to each other?" "What verse fits with glorifying the Lord and sanctifying Him as our Creator?" His questions seemed endless and, to Joshua in his anxiousness to get to his wedding day, irritating. He'd never be a preacher. He was more interested in reading, teaching, and building the kind of West Harbor civilization he and Ella were always talking about. But he sincerely didn't want to upset the old man, so whenever Preacher called for help with his sermon, Joshua walked to God's house.

***

One day, after Joshua had spent an especially trying morning with Preacher, Ella found the first hepatica poking up through the snow in the woods beside the Washington Harbor trail and came running to get him. He was helping Pappy lift a log up onto what was slowly becoming their cabin's back wall, getting rid of some of his frustration by doing physical work. Ella called to him excitedly as she ran down the well-worn path through melting snow. Pappy saw his future daughter-in-law in the clearing, shook his head, and said, "Go on." Bill, working to fit the corner together where they'd placed the log, snorted. Joshua didn't have to be told twice.

When they met halfway through the clearing, she took his hand, said, "Come," and led him into the woods. He had no idea what she was excited about. They weren't far in when she stopped. "There," she said, pointing at a small plant's green, curling head poking out of snow. "Spring's coming," she said. "The hepatica's proof."

Then, as he looked at the plant, understanding what she was telling him, she startled him by kissing him with such passion she took his breath away. The woods, shadowed even though the day was bright with sun, was a wonderland filled with a bewilderment of birch, maple, oak, black walnut, and other hardwoods and the rich green of junipers low to the ground, pine, and cedar. The white winter world, contrasted against the bareness and greenness of trees, was as beautiful and vibrant as Ella herself.

As Joshua tried to press against her with all the urgency he felt, feeling her body's heat in the cold, she whirled away, pushing against him and laughing. A moment later he was alone as she ran back to the clearing toward the cabins, making him raise his arms toward the sky half in frustration and half in supplication. At that moment he had no idea why he listened to either his mother or Preacher.

***

As the weather warmed, the lake ice cracked and groaned, softly at first. They moved the fishing shacks off the lake as soon as Bill saw a fissure in the ice while he was out early in the morning looking for a new place to smash a hole with an axe. They had the task down to a routine. They put the shacks on their side after Harrison had planed down the runners he'd put on each one, then they pulled them to shore. They stored them next to the chicken pens, disturbing both hens and roosters. The flock of birds cackled and fluttered around as they hauled shacks behind God's house and set them upright again.

The ice didn't last another three weeks. During earlier years, the ice had melted, piling up ridges of white chunks along the shore for miles in either direction. This year the cracking and groaning boomed and a storm gathered enormous black clouds from the south and lit the sky with continuous flickering of blue and white lightning. The unbelievable noises kept up all afternoon and through the night. No one slept well.

Then, in the morning, they went outside to find enormous walls of ice piled up along the lake's shores, although not as high inside the harbor. Instead, the harbor was filled with enormous, flat icebergs, but on the spit of land and in both directions of the shore jagged ice mountains were as high as a man with his arms extended standing on another man's shoulders.

The force of what had happened was awe-inspiring. Everyone, including the children, had to walk to the enormous, jagged walls and look upward toward the early morning sky, feeling the cold that flowed off ice floes in the lake. A sense of ruin and destruction about the way the ice had broken apart and piled up made the natural forces involved intimidating. What had been a stable world all winter was shattered and left towering on the shore.

The storm's heavy rain had reduced the piles of snow left by the spring's warming, too. Although the ground was still a dirt-streaked white, clear patches could be seen here and there up to the tree line around the opening around the cabins. They had to take off their boots when they came back to the cabins. For the first time since late November, there was mud on the ground.

The usual spring miracle continued to unfold. Warm weather melted more snow. Pretty soon hints of green were everywhere. Small white and red flowers started blooming in the woods. Not long after the first small blue flowers bloomed, trilliums with their three petals of white carpeted the woods, with sprinklings of blue phlox, celandine poppy, bloodroot, Jacob's ladder, and foamflower popping up at different places. Chas and particularly Weayaya were always willing to share what they knew about each plant anyone brought them, including uses that the community had never known about.

***

On the evening before the most important day of their lives, Joshua and Ella were, for a change, left alone. They walked where waves lapped gently on the shore. The moon was close to full and gave the darkness an unearthly silver tinge. The air was neither cold nor warm. They felt like they were in a universe made up of only the two of them, a union that could face and shove off all the bad things that might happen in the future. They didn't stop, as had been their habit when finally escaping from everybody else, to kiss or get close to each other. Instead they walked in silver light and felt the power of the moon surrounded by stars.

"Do you think we'll feel different after we're married?" Ella asked.

Joshua shrugged. "Jamie tells me that you do for a while," he said. "But he said you get used to each other. You start feeling like you're part of each other in a way you can't imagine until it happens."

Ella was looking up at the moon over the edge of one of the last of the higher ice walls. The ice loomed in darkness, faintly luminous, but dense and cold. She snuggled into Joshua. "We're going to be a team," she said. "We're going to live a future better than our past has been."

Joshua looked down at her face. "Our families and Preacher have already helped us take control of our lives," he said. "We owe both them and ourselves for that. We're free." The wonder of his statement flowed through him. "We're free to love each other. If we hadn't managed to do what we all did, that wouldn't have been possible even if we'd met."

"Funny," Ella said, standing on her tiptoes to reach up and kiss him.

"What?" Joshua murmured as he lost himself in the moment.

"I can't imagine any other present than the one we have," Ella said after they'd separated. "I can't imagine us ever being apart."

***

Their wedding day started with feverish bustle. Pappy got Joshua up before first light, and the two of them went to build the morning fire only to find Jeremiah had beat them to it. The day before the women had spent most of the morning heating water and using the small bathhouse Harrison and Junebug had built. The children had not escaped the tub, to some a delight and others a chore. The women were determined to ensure that people and cabins were scrubbed immaculately clean in honor of the special event.

Joshua hadn't even gotten breakfast when Pappy ushered him out of the cabin to the bathhouse where they built a fire and then went to the harbor to get the buckets of cold water that would have to be heated. Preparations for baths took a while as water heated in the huge tin bowl Chas had made. They dipped wooden buckets into the bowl and dumped them into the tub. They'd filled more buckets than they'd need for the initial baths so that colder water could be thrown outside into the woods

292

and replaced with warmer water as the morning ritual was consummated.

Joshua was the first to take his bath, but then Pappy and the other men filed into the bathhouse. When Joshua finished and went outside the morning chill made him want to dance around, but instead he went back to the cabin where his mother and Massie had fixed a light breakfast of eggs and cornbread.

"You'll get full enough at the wedding feast," his mother told him as she handed him his meal. She smiled. "Preacher was by while you were taking your bath. You're wanted at God's house, something about the ceremony."

The rest of the day was a blur. Preacher, waiting for him, asked him to pick out the Bible verses he was going to read before the ceremony. Then his mother and Massie came into the cabin and told him he wouldn't see his bride until he was standing with his father ready for her entry into God's house. Then they went off, one at a time, making sure he didn't go outside, to prepare fried chicken, shriveled up potatoes from last fall's harvest, spring herbs Weayaya had gathered from the woods, and venison that would provide the feast. During the preparations he got lightheaded, as if he were moving around in a daze.

Suddenly, everyone but Ella, Esta May, Beulah, and Bill were in God's house, sitting on benches. Later Joshua could hardly tell what had happened. Preacher had asked him to come up and stand by him. He'd then motioned to the door. Ella and her parents came into the cabin. Dressed in her new deerskin dress and shining with joy, dark face and eyes so beautiful Joshua could hardly believe he was actually going to be able to marry her, Ella walked gracefully and slowly over to him, taking his hand in hers.

Preacher had preached a short sermon based on a passage from 1 Peter, "Wherefore laying aside all malice and all guile and hypocrisies, and envies, all evil speakings, as newborn babes, desire the sincere milk of the word, that ye may grow thereby.'" The two of them had then been asked if they loved each other and would stay true to each other through all the challenges, joys, and tribulations of life. After they'd said yes, Preacher had announced that they were now a Christian man and wife, dedicated to praising the Lord and holding to the Lord's commandments.

After the meal and a wildly celebratory hollering and singing, where both Joshua and Ella danced crazily inside their joy, the two of them were led by Esta May and Jamie to their cabin and left alone. Night shadows crept long from fading light as their married life began.

Chapter 32
Upon the Edge of Sanity and Fear

The edge where sanity and fear collide
Whirls passions that are uncontrollable
Into events that spark effects that tide
Across the barriers of shores and scull
Destruction, pestilence, a flood of woe
Fermented in assumptions drawn from trials
That litter through all human lives and flow
Like water over hopes, beliefs, denials,

And on the edge, in ferment's shifting shape,
Decisions ratchet back and forth; dreams lure
The spirit as dire consequences scrape
Against the future suddenly obscure
Enough to paralyze the strength from hands
That long to civilize life's hinterlands.

Married life was different, Joshua contemplated as he walked out to the dory he, Jamie, and Jeremiah were taking out on the lake. He felt better, and even more secure, than he ever had. Jamie had been right when he'd said the early months would make him feel different. The difference wasn't only in nights when Ella seemed all flesh and fire, drawing him out of himself into a fusion of the two of them, a single pulse inside a swelling of life. It existed in the way he saw her when he was awake and she was asleep, and even when she got after him for not doing some chore she wanted him to get done. His life had a different, richer rhythm than before.

Living with Jamie, Esta May, and Emily had not been as awkward as he'd feared. They'd all lived in close quarters without a lot of privacy for most of their lives.

Joshua couldn't understand what he'd ever seen in Esta May, now that he was living in such close quarters with her. Jamie was a man, but his wife had a will as strong as Joshua's mother. When she spoke, Jamie immediately moved to do whatever she wanted him to do.

Joshua, forced from the master's house, had rebelled against his mother's strong personality and commands. He had no doubt that if he had actually gotten what he had desired with Esta May when he had believed he was in love with her, his life would not have worked out. Esta May had been wiser than he had been when she had chosen Jamie. He was more comfortable with her demands and strength of will.

Ella was almost the opposite of her sister. Joshua felt like they were equals, intelligent and responsive to each other, always talking things over even when they disagreed. Not that they had many disagreements. In the first flush of marriage, they seemed to be inside a stream of warmth and light that gave deep meaning to their lives.

***

Spring had melded into early summer so quickly none of them seemed aware it had come before days were so hot and humid they were uncomfortable. Joshua and Ella spent any few minutes they could steal from work and chores to work on their cabin. Pappy, Joshua's mother, Bill, and Beulah spent almost as much time as they did, putting on the roof and caulking. When they had spare time the others helped, too. Harrison and Junebug, as usual, were making chairs, a kitchen table, frame for a bed that would have a mattress made from a mixture of broken up twigs, chicken feathers, and no longer wearable, torn-up old clothes. Willie and Jeremiah had started to put down the pine floor.

Jamie and Jeremiah came down from the cabins to join Joshua at the dory, which was already stowed with nets and other gear they'd need for the day's fishing. Jamie was bringing jerky and bread they'd eat somewhere around high sun when the fishing slacked off.

No one had forgotten about Westbrook, but the news had been mostly good. Neither he nor his son had been released from the Green Bay jail, although both were protesting their innocence. Westbrook was using the two dead young men as the reason he couldn't have burnt down Craw's barn since, he claimed, he would have been traveling to Rock Island at the time. The problem was that the dead men had never been found, so most people on the island doubted that part of his story, even though it was accepted that he had bought hay on Rock Island. There were witnesses to that.

As Jeremiah shoved the three of them off shore into the water, following the scow that already had its sail up with Franklin at the rudder, the day seemed perfect. Afternoon heat and humidity was in the future. The sky was cloudless, the waves small and easily managed, and a mix of seagulls, Canadian geese, ducks, cormorants, pelicans, and other birds were in the sky and floating on water.

The fishing turned out to be slow, but they kept bringing in a trout or a salmon or two every time they spread the net and brought it back into the boat. West Harbor wasn't going to get any wealthier due to their work, but at least they were catching something.

The sun was nearing the time when they could eat jerky and bread when Jeremiah saw the canoe slicing through the small waves. He pointed toward the birch bark and laughed. There were canoes big enough to challenge Death's Door, especially with a big crew of men. The French voyagers who had been the first Europeans to ply Lake Michigan had used huge canoes. Before they'd stopped seeing each other, Jesse had loaned Joshua a book that had described the voyagers and their journeys. But this was a small canoe with a single paddler too far out on the lake even for calm weather.

When the canoeist saw them, he changed direction slightly and paddled toward where they were. "It's Gordon," Jeremiah exclaimed. Jamie laughed. "Who else?" he asked.

"Let's get the net in," Joshua said. "The fishing's not good right now anyway."

Gordon was all smiles when he came up to them and pulled his canoe close. He named each of them in his hearty voice and clasped Jeremiah's hand.

Jamie, hauling the net up with Joshua, called over his head, "Come aboard, Gordon Burr. We'll tow your canoe and row to shore."

"Okay," Gordon said. He reached down and handed Jeremiah a rope. Then he was up and over the dory's side.

The net had two small salmon in it, so they stowed those in the fish bin and started rowing. They had been fishing just south of West Harbor toward Detroit Harbor, but the waves, even though against them, were small, so not much time passed before they could see the harbor.

As Jamie and Joshua pulled the oars, Gordon told them that the Stockbridge were going to be moved off their farms on the Fox River to a Reservation and that they were trying to identify a place where they could go. "Even I'll move," he said. "Brotherton and some Stockbridgers are determined to become U.S. citizens and hold their farms, but most of us understand what we learned New York. If the white man decides they want your land, you have to negotiate the best deal you can and move."

When they pulled the dory up on the beach Gordon was the first one on land. "Can you take care of the canoe?" he asked. "I've got to see Preacher." He stopped and looked at them. "I'm going to ask everybody get together after the scow's in," he said. "I've got news." He looked sober. He turned and walked toward God's house.

Joshua found Ella scrubbing the floors in the bathhouse. When she heard why he had shown up in the middle of the day, she frowned. "What kind of news does Gordon Burr have?" she asked. "Every time he canoes over Death's Door he takes an awful risk."

Joshua shook his head. "He wasn't smiling when he told us," he said.

The two of them then went to the cabin where they found Esta May, Jamie, and Emily, who was fussy. The four adults sat by the cold fireplace and talked. At first Esta May thought they should go to God's house to find out what the news was. When Ella pointed out their father might not appreciate that and that, anyway, Preacher would probably just make them wait for the others, they tried to talk about Joshua and Ella's new cabin and what still had to be finished before they could occupy it.

"We're lucky, aren't we?" Esta May asked at one point. "When we were young, we could never have dreamed we'd ever have a cabin to live in with just our family."

They'd moved outside to be sure not to miss any summons when Ella saw the scow coming into harbor. They had hardly taken four steps before they realized that the whole community, with the exception of Preacher and Gordon, was walking to the beach. Even Harrison and Junebug had left furniture making behind and were joining the rest of them.

When Chas and Pappy heard their news, they didn't hesitate. They let Bill and Franklin finish unloading the catch and gear and walked resolutely toward God's house. The men, women, and children milled around until the two men had packed the day's catch, which was only a little larger than the one Joshua, Jamie, and Jeremiah had brought in. Then everybody followed Chas and Pappy.

Joshua didn't wonder why there was such a sense of foreboding. Gordon had just told them, without a smile, that he had news. On the way to shore he'd been quiet about why he was visiting West Harbor. He hadn't said he had bad news, but that seemed to be what they all were expecting. They had been living inside good news for longer than any of them had ever experienced.

As they went to their customary places on the benches, Preacher and Gordon came out of Preacher's bedroom. The day had become uncomfortably hot. Chas and Pappy left the cabin door open, hoping to catch a breeze. The way Preacher and Gordon came out of the bedroom just as everyone was in their place meant that they had been waiting for them. Joshua took a deep breath and quietly took Ella's hand.

Preacher went immediately to the lectern and faced them. "Gordon brings us troubling news," he said. "I'm glad everybody's here." He smiled at Beulah's young Jacob who was beginning to stand and take a step or two. "Even the children. I know Gordon was careful to make sure he wasn't followed out of Stockbridge to here, but I think we're going to have to discuss this development seriously."

He looked at Gordon, then moved behind the lectern and leaned his back against the wall as Gordon took his place. The seriousness on his face and in his dark eyes made Joshua dread what was coming. He glanced at Ella, who looked as worried as he felt.

"I came as soon as Reverend Jemson sent a messenger to me out of Chicago," he said without a greeting or any other preamble. "I was relieved when I saw Joshua, Jamie, and Jeremiah on the lake fishing. That let me know I wasn't too late." He paused. "What you have to know is that Preacher Jemson is recommending you leave Washington Island for Canada as soon as you can."

People gasped or groaned all over the sanctuary. Preacher didn't move, but looked down at the floor.

"Reverend Jemson says to tell you there's two white men hanging around the white people who donated building materials for the scow, clothes, and Bibles to this community," he said. "He said they've been asking specific questions about a big black man by the name of Jason Billings, a valuable domestic who calls herself Mary Simpson, and the domestic's son. From what I'm told, the two men are assuming there's other escaped slaves with those people. They even have the idea that a black preacher might have helped in the escape.

"Reverend Jemson doesn't think the men have been told you were in Chicago, but he's not sure. The young man who talked to me told me that the Reverend said a lot of people donated things. He's not sure who was told what about Washington Island, but he does think, given the Fugitive Slave Act of 1850, that you're at terrible risk and ought to run."

The silence greeting his words shouted in Joshua's ears. Nobody said anything. Westbrook was in jail. With Westbrook in jail they were safe. They had to be safe. All of his old resentments stirred.

Gordon looked uncomfortably back at Preacher. Preacher caught his eyes, but then looked at his congregation, waiting. Pappy shifted on the bench beside his daughter-in-law. He'd had a wonderful time at his son's wedding. He hadn't known he had a son, and he'd found both his son and wife and been to his son's wedding. He had known miracles.

He cleared his throat and stood up. "I'll go to Chicago," he said without flinching. Joshua's mother, startled, jerked to her feet and looked at him with panic in her eyes. Joshua stared at him, wondering what insanity had infected his mind.

Pappy looked at Mary and saw the slender, elegant girl he'd been raised with on the Samuelson plantation. As he'd grown into a giant, she'd grown into someone more beautiful than any woman Jason Billings had ever seen. Then she'd been sold, and he hadn't even known what master she'd been sold to at first or where that master had taken her.

"If they have me, maybe that'll throw them off their looking," he said. "I can give them a good old run around. If they get me, well … I know the way north."

"You're doing no such thing," Joshua's mother said in her most matter of fact voice. "You're my husband, and you're going to stay my husband and Joshua's father."

Chas, who always sat in the back row of benches, had leaned forward and was looking intently at Pappy and Joshua's mother. "Sacrificing yourself won't do any good," he said. "You'd only let them know we're still in the United States. You'd stir them up, and everybody but me would have to run anyway. They're after escaped slaves. There are lots of escaped slaves at West Harbor."

"Wisconsin's a free state," Harrison said on the heels of Chas's words. "We heard about how the abolitionists freed the man slavers had captured outside of Milwaukee. How would they get us across the whole state without stirring up abolitionists?"

Gordon shook his head. "You have to remember that Joshua Glover was caught in Racine on a foggy night," he said. "They drove him to Milwaukee without anyone knowing he was captured until they put him in jail. Bounty hunters won't make that mistake again, not in Wisconsin. They'll set up a capture and make sure no one sees the light of day until they're where they can slap on chains."

Zelda was becoming increasing upset. Franklin had been trying to keep her quiet, but she was squirming. "I already told you," she said loudly, her voice hysterical. "I'm not leaving this community. They're going to have to drag me out dead. I have a baby buried here."

Beside her, Abbie, looking half shocked and half angry, turned to her mother and put her arms around her. Franklin, always so competent, especially in the scow where he had become the best sailor and fisherman, looked lost.

"Mama," Abbie said in a clear, adult voice. "The baby's gone. I'm gonna be married some day and have children. Those children are going to need a grandmother. That grandmother is you. You need to leave what's happened behind and look at what's going to be."

Zelda broke into pitiful crying. Pappy, with everybody's eyes off him, took his wife's hand and slowly sat back down on the bench. His shirt was wet from perspiration.

Preacher moved off the wall and put his hand on Gordon's shoulder. "Paul, in 2 Corinthians said," he said, "'And he said unto me, My grace is sufficient for thee: for my strength is made perfect in weakness. Most gladly therefore will I rather glory in my infirmities, that the power of Christ may rest upon me. Therefore I take pleasure in infirmities, in reproaches, in necessities, in persecutions, in distresses for Christ's sake: for when I am weak, then am I strong.'"

He paused. Zelda kept crying, although some of the hysteria had leached out of her sobs. Preacher held up his hand and looked at it as if he were seeing it for the first time. It had dark liver spots and shook slightly. Joshua thought about how he had started to think the indomitable Preacher he had known for so many years was starting to feel the infirmities that were part of getting old.

"When men who I had known were around me," Preacher continued, "I heard their cries. In my despair at that moment I had the vision that set me on a path that led to West Harbor. It took a while. I had to get my head together to walk a long path first. Then I had to find help to make a vision turn into a sailing scow and a journey. At the same time, I spent endless hours learning the Bible, trying to master how to take strength and resolve from words I memorized deep in myself."

He looked at Gordon. "The point I'm making is that what all of us together have accomplished so far is not done. I'm getting old and tired. My bones ache even when I wake up warm now and not just in the cold. But no matter what we have to do, we can find strength in Christ and know that when we're weak and listening to despair inside us, we can find our strength."

When he'd finished reading from 2 Corinthians, Zelda had stopped crying and started listening. Joshua felt Preacher's words rumbling around in his head.

"What are we going to do?" Ella asked. "Run or stay put for now?"

"We need to start watching," Junebug said. "We got to see who's coming before they know we're watching."

Harrison nodded. "There's three of us that are pretty worn out from our last run," he said. He gestured toward Preacher. "We maybe got some strength left, but whatever we decide to do, we need to prepare. We aren't as poor as we were when we came here. We've got clothes, stored food, lots of supplies, and fishing equipment. Even some money. If we prepare, even old folks can start again."

"The scow and dory aren't enough," Willie said. "If we crowded in we might be able to get all of us in them, even if there are more of us than before. But Death's Door, as we know only too well, is dangerous on a calm day. We couldn't sail and take even a portion of our supplies and gear."

"Maybe Mr. Miner would help us," Beulah said. "He's been the best one to us on the island."

Chas was shaking his head. "We talked about this one other time," he said. "If we run, and I don't think we're ready to do that yet, not until we get some idea that those men are out of Chicago and in Wisconsin, we don't want anyone to know we're gone. The longer they don't know, the less likely they'll find our trail."

"Chas and I won't need boats," Weayaya said softly. "We can make it to the shore opposite Ephraim and meet you there and take you to

Canada."

"You've been to Canada?" Willie asked. "You know the way?"

Weayaya nodded.

Joshua looked at Jeremiah, who had stood. He looked back at Joshua and Jamie. "If it comes to it," he said, "Jamie, Joshua, and I can lead a bunch of people from the mainland in circles if we see them coming. We've learned this island. We're young and strong enough to get them running in circles even if they have dogs."

Ella sighed and glanced at Joshua, raising one eyebrow.

"It's not going to come to that," Massie said firmly. "It won't."

Gordon frowned as he looked around the room. Some faces were defiant, others frightened. Some looked confused. "I can't stay too long," he said at last. "The Stockbridge have their own troubles. I'm needed there. I, and the elders, had hoped we had done a good thing helping you escape and settle here. I only wish that neither my people nor you should have to face what we are facing. We decided, as a people, to walk the Christian road, like you decided. But I'll admit, walking that road hasn't always brought the peace promised in the Holy Bible."

"Jesus was crucified on the cross," Preacher said quickly. "We are promised salvation, not an easy life." That theological point taken care of, he held out his hand to Gordon. "I can't tell you how grateful we are and have been for you and all of those who've helped us."

"I'm going to leave the canoe," Gordon said. "I can catch a steamer heading to Green Bay."

Preacher said, "If we have to flee, and I will admit these old bones are hoping we'll find a reason not to, it won't be unwelcome. Thank you."

Weayaya and Chas were the first to leave, followed by everybody else in family groupings. Outside God's house, Ella stopped Pappy before he and Joshua's mother could go to their cabin. "You can't leave us," she told him. "Abbie said she was going to have children and her children were going to need a grandmother. Well, Joshua and I are a little closer to that eventuality than Abbie, and our children are going to need a grandfather."

Joshua's mother smiled, her eyes fierce. "You tell him, Ella," she said. She unceremoniously grabbed Pappy's arm and half dragged him toward the cabin.

Alone, Ella and Joshua wandered toward the spit of land between the lake and harbor. The evening had turned cooler, and a breeze was ruffling the lake's waters rather than causing it to sweep with waves. A large crow sat watching them from a low branch on one of the pines near the beach. It didn't move even when they looked at it. Stars blinked into existence as a quarter moon sailed above the horizon into night.

After they'd sat on a dead tree trunk, arms about each other, Ella shivered. "I'm frightened," she said.

"If Westbrook was around," Joshua said, "we'd already be gone. But I keep thinking about how things worked out last summer and winter. One piece of good news followed another. Westbrook threatened us, the Mormons stirred him up and took his attention away, and then he and his son were in jail."

He listened for a moment to the sound of the waves. "I can't help but think that God's inside Preacher," he said. "If that's true, we're going to be all right."

Ella lifted her lips to his face and kissed him. Her kiss was as soft and gentle as the sound of the water. "I hope so," she said. "I'm thankful you decided to fall in love with me."

Chapter 33
In the Unsettled Homeland of Dreams

The preacher sat upon a rocky hill
Above a cave where waters from the lake
Crashed angrily above the soaring shrill
Of gulls excited by a splashing wake
Of fish caught by the afternoon's harsh light
Flashed back into the early fall's blue sky.

He sat upon the hill, his second sight
Unmoored and wild, and listened as the lie
He'd told himself when struggling to find
The island where his people could be free
Wrapped round reality, the awful bind
Of white men, dark men in the company
Of humankind, their kind, the hunger spun
From dreams once dreamed beneath a noonday sun.

The tension in West Harbor over the next two weeks was unrelenting. Complex, unspoken emotions occasionally surfaced out of the masks they had all put on in an effort to be brave and face what they didn't know how to avoid.

When the morning dawned after another restless night caused by Gordon Burr's news, Joshua, Jamie, Ella, and Esta May got out of bed and wandered over to the unfinished cabin, with Emily in her mother's arms. Given another week of work, the roof could cover the inside and finishing work could begin. The four of them stood looking at Joshua and Ella's dream, one of many dreams that had turned West Harbor into a community.

Ella at last shook her head. "I can't imagine being a slave again," she said. She turned from the unfinished cabin and walked toward the woods.

Joshua panicked. He had been about to show his defiance by climbing on the cabin's roof and starting to work. Ella walked so swiftly she was in the woods before he could get his mind to grasp that she had left his side.

Esta May looked sternly at him. "You'd better go get her," she said.

With a start, Joshua bounded, without saying anything, across the clearing.

Inside the woods, by the small birch grove where she'd found the spring's first hepatica shoot, Ella had stopped. When Joshua came up to her, she didn't say anything, but looked through the pattern of leaves at blue sky. Joshua had no idea what to say or even how he should act. He wondered what they should do, if they should continue living their lives in West Harbor's wondrous freedom or protect themselves by searching for a freedom they had believed they'd already achieved. The dilemma made him feel sick.

"I'm okay," Ella said after a long silence. She looked into Joshua's eyes, tears running down her cheeks. "It just seems unfair."

Later that morning Chas, Weayaya, and Gordon set off for West Harbor in the canoe, Weayaya in the stern and Chas in the middle. When Joshua and Jamie came to the shore, Gordon said, "We'll listen for rumors without saying anything about anything." He smiled. Then they were riding over swells rising into shore in a staccato slapping.

No one suggested going out on the lake to fish. After an afternoon meal that everyone spent with their family, the women got together and talked about what they could start to prepare if they needed to leave West Harbor. Even Zelda seemed resigned to the idea that it would be better to leave than risk being caught and watching Abbie and Franklin thrown back into slavery. She was sullen, but all of them felt the weight of what was making them afraid.

When Gordon, Weayaya, and Chas paddled back, the sun had descended beyond the horizon. They had just entered the harbor, and the entire community, Preacher, children and adults, walked to the shore.

Gordon shook his head when Preacher looked at him as he jumped out of the canoe. "Nothing," he said. "West Harbor's the way it always is. We went to see Henry Miner. I talked about his father and how he'd served the Stockbridge as a missionary, bought some corn flour from Mr. Craw, listened hard, but the only thing we heard even remotely concerning was that Westbrook and his son's trial has started in Green Bay."

Joshua didn't know whether to feel relieved or not. Surely there would be some rumor if strangers were visiting the island. Henry Miner always knew about everything happening. He could conceivably even have an idea about what was going on in Door County.

Joshua fastened his gaze on Weayaya. "Do you think the white people on the island will protect us?" he asked her. "Do what the people in Milwaukee did?"

She looked steadily into Joshua's eyes, slowly shaking her head. "White men can't be predicted," she said. "Their words mean this or that, but then the people in your tribe are dying."

***

The next day Willie came to get Jamie and Joshua before dawn. They had not built the cooking fire when they heard the loud knock on the door. "We've decided we'll fish," Willie said. "The other fishermen might notice if we're not on the water. Anyway, Gordon, Chas, and Franklin are going to take our filled barrels to Mr. Craw in a day or two on another listening tour."

Ironically, at least in Joshua's mind, the fishing was as good as it had ever been. Nets were so heavy with fish as they brought them to the surface Joshua, Jamie, and Jeremiah had to work together to pull them up. The good thing about the catch was that it kept them working hard. They didn't have time to worry, although off and on Joshua thought about Ella and how she was getting along. He knew the women intended to start putting up what was ready from the garden and do other tasks related to preparing for leaving West Harbor, but he suspected they still had time enough to mull over what was happening. As he sweated in the afternoon sun, he decided he was the lucky one, because for once in his life, he didn't have time to think.

***

As time stretched out life resumed more of a sense of normalcy, although their tension didn't go away. Junebug even got angry with Harrison, something that never happened, trying to deal with an arthritic morning while Harrison chattered on without noticing she wasn't feeling well. On Sunday, Preacher gave his sermon, as usual. He didn't try to address what was happening, but instead talked about how they all had to feel joy in service to the Lord and trusting in the love of Jesus. Then, on Monday, they put the barrels of fish they'd caught in the scow and watched as Franklin, Gordon, Weayaya, and Chas sailed off to Washington Harbor.

When they returned, the four of them were in good spirits. The community trooped to the shore again to see what they and Weayaya had to say. Chas shook his head and said, "Nothing. Everything seemed absolutely normal."

"We sold the fish," Franklin added. "Gordon visited the Miners again. Henry wasn't home, but he talked to Jesse. Everything seemed as usual as possible. I saw O'Reilly at Mr. Craw's and heard that the fishing's been especially good lately. He said he'd be out here one of these days to see about a problem he was having with his hull."

That night, in Jamie and Esta May's cabin, the two sisters and their husbands had a quiet celebration. Maybe the fears stirred up by Gordon's news from Chicago were unfounded. Maybe Reverend Jemson had been wrong to tell them to flee to Canada. Maybe they could get on with their lives, enjoying their freedom and what they had achieved at West Harbor.

***

Another week went by, and Gordon, seeing how quiet and normal everything was, started saying that he should get back to Stockbridge. "I'll wait for a really calm day," he said. "Preferably one without clouds." He laughed. "But I'll go home."

Preacher was the one most upset by Gordon's decision. "I hate to see you go. Reverend Jemson isn't a man to get upset over nothing. Still, I know there are negotiations going on. You want to be there to keep track of what's happening."

"I wish this was a better world," Gordon said.

***

That night heavy clouds gathered. A storm was threatening, so Gordon made no preparations to leave, but went out in the dory with Joshua, Jamie, and Jeremiah. A stiff wind came up late morning, but quickly calmed, and then heavy rain dumped out of the sky, drenching all of them. In addition to dealing with the rain, they started to catch fish like they had the day after they'd come back on the lake after hearing Gordon's news. Jeremiah spotted a boat further out during the rainstorm. It started toward them, but then tacked away, its sail more limp than full.

After the rain slackened, and it was late enough to justify coming in to West Harbor, they saw a steamer. It looked like it was heading toward Detroit rather than Washington Harbor. It was an unusual sight, but not an entirely unheard of one. It might not have been stopping at Washington Island at all.

As they disembarked, Gordon stretched and held his arms up in the sky. "Maybe tomorrow will be calm after the storm," he said. "You West Harborites work too hard. I'm ready for Stockbridge." After they'd unloaded and packed the fish in barrels, he walked slowly toward God's house.

***

Joshua was on his way to the outhouse when the shot rang out. "Slavers!" The word startled through him. He ran toward the sound before he realized what he was doing. A vision of them as fugitives in the field's low point starving before Chas had found them and led them to the Campbells' flashed into his mind. He felt the moment Old Simpson died in the dirty quarter's shack where they were living.

The men were out of the cabins when he came around the corner of God's house. Gold and pink light streamed across clouds remaining from the storm. Out in the clearing, unbelievably, Westbrook was walking toward the cabins, his big body shambling like a bear. None of the women had come out of the cabins.

Joshua slowed, but moved resolutely toward Jamie and Esta May's cabin, the one closest to where Westbrook was. The other men, including Preacher and Gordon, were walking toward the white man, too. *What's he doing out of jail? How can be out of jail? He'd burned Craw's barn!*

When Jamie and Jeremiah were in front of Westbrook the white man stopped walking toward them and waited for the rest of the men to get to where he was. He was smiling. Joshua reached them just as Preacher and Chas confronted Westbrook.

"I thought you were in the Green Bay jail," Chas said.

Westbrook had grown a thick brown beard and looked grizzled. His grin grew even broader. "Found innocent of all charges," he said. "My son and I didn't burn down that barn. The jury saw that."

"What do you want, Westbrook?" Preacher asked in his deep voice. "I'd think you'd be celebrating your good fortune."

Westbrook turned his grin into a mocking sneer. "Oh, we celebrated right enough. We've been free for a while now." He put an emphasis upon the word "free." "I thought I'd visit you folks and see how you're doing." He paused, staring hard at Preacher. "Anyway," he continued, "I thought you might like to know." He looked from Preacher to Pappy. "In jail one of the deputies asked me about a big black man with the name of Jason. A man big enough to lift a wagon all by himself."

"There's lots of big men in the world," Willie, standing behind Preacher, said.

"Is there?" Westbrook asked. "A big man with a woman that looks like she could be a domestic, and her son?"

"Everybody in West Harbor, except for the children born here, have their papers," Preacher said. "Your threats don't mean anything."

Westbrook's eyes narrowed. "There's a pretty reward for the capture of this big negra and those with him," he said. "I was told that by the deputies holding me in Green Bay. They asked if I had seen any negras like that."

"Why are you standing telling us that then?" Chas asked. "Seems like it would make more sense to just arrange to collect the reward if you think we're the ones being looked for."

"You think I'm an evil man," he told them, shaking his head. "But

I'm not. Even though I've felt how the law can be unjust, I still believe in the law. I was Justice of the Peace." He paused. "I didn't tell the deputy anything. I thought I'd rather collect the reward for me and my son."

"Why are you telling us?" Preacher asked. "A visit late at night would make more sense. We could run now, knowing what you're thinking."

"I've always thought this place wasn't right," Westbrook said. "Maybe I just want you to disappear."

Gordon took a step forward to stand by Chas. "How do Mr. Miner and the abolitionists feel about that?" he asked. "Mr. Miner's father was a missionary. He's a man who practices his Christianity."

"Mr. Miner and Mr. Craw," Westbrook snarled, a sharp edge to his voice. "Law abiding citizens of Washington Island." He looked directly at Gordon. "Go back home, Indian," he said. "White men won this island fair and square from the likes of you. We know how to make it pay and not just sit here in the middle of the lake."

"We've broken no law," Preacher said. "We are a Christian community harming no one. We've as much right to be here as you do."

"Squatting on land that isn't really yours," Westbrook said.

"We don't need your like here," Pappy said. "We're God-fearing people. Those who improve land not in use in the wilderness can claim it for their own."

Westbrook reached out his hand toward Pappy. Joshua found himself stepping forward without intending to move. He had learned his lesson the last time he'd confronted Westbrook. Pappy glared at the white man. "You must be Jason," Westbrook said.

The sound in Westbrook's voice jolted Joshua. He lunged at Westbrook, but suddenly couldn't move his arms. Both Jamie and Jeremiah had grabbed him. "There's more of us than of him," Joshua spit out, his voice angry and loud. He felt his heart racing. He wanted to smash Westbrook's face in. He struggled, but Pappy had grabbed him, too.

Chas casually looked over at Joshua and shook his head. He glared at Westbrook. "About time for you to go," he told Westbrook. "Like we said, we're God-fearing people and don't want trouble."

Joshua stopped struggling. The white man huffed and smiled again. "This is just a friendly visit," he said calmly. He turned and walked back the way he had come.

Pappy let go of Joshua and patted his shoulder. "It's over, son," he said. Jamie and Jeremiah let go of him. Looking at the woods where Westbrook had gone, Joshua imagined he could see Silver Coats, his black face shining with sweat as he picked up his black whip and fingered its lash lovingly. He shook the vision away and turned toward the cabins. Ella was standing in front of the other women. They all looked scared.

Joshua's mother was looking as hard as Pappy and Ella was at Joshua. "The weather's going to be calm tonight," she said. She hugged Pappy quickly and fiercely.

A moment later, the whole group of them had turned and started walking back to their respective cabins. The only one who didn't move was Ella. She had a strange look in her eyes. "I thought you were intelligent," she told Joshua.

Joshua looked worriedly at her. "That man's taking away everything we built," he said slowly.

Then Ella was in his arms, holding him as if she thought that if she didn't keep him in her arms, she'd lose him.

Chapter 34
Aftermath

Gone. Like the waves grasshoppers make
Before a boy who runs into a field of weeds,
The news raced through the island as the seeds
Of mystery began to reawake
The sense that something sinister, a snake,
Was in the emptiness that almost pleads
To hear the shouts of children, men whose deeds
Had made their days of freedom by the lake.

Where did they go? Why did they have to flee?
The island people said, "It is a mystery."

When Craw's barn burned, the chill was palpable,
And now the black community is gone.
The news was like a fire, insatiable.
They took their fishing boats and fled at dawn.

The mystery of the disappearance of seven black families, possibly runaway slaves, from Washington Island in the 1850s still persists today.

Notes on Sonnets

In the Unsettled Homeland of Dreams started out as a sonnet sequence before it was a novel. The sequence was never envisioned as a traditional sonnet sequence that creates a thematic unity based upon a single sonnet type. Rather, there was going to be a collection of sonnets that used a variety of sonnet types as it developed. Therefore, a number of different sonnet types are used for the novel's chapter headings. All of the sonnets, except for the Miltonian, are fourteen lines and use iambic pentameter. Sonnets are defined as different types by their rhyme schemes. A volta is the line in which the substance, of movement, of the sonnet's action or argument changes. The sonnet types used in the novel are as follows:

Shakespearean Sonnet
Miltonian Sonnet
Spenserian Sonnet
Italian Sonnet
French Sonnet
Terza Rima Sonnet

Additional information on these sonnet types can be found on the author's website: www.fourwindowspress.com

End Notes

- "I will strengthen thee; yea, I will help thee; yea," *King James Bible*, Isaiah 41:10.

Chapter 4, The Bridge that was a Wall

- The idea for the following fictional incident was suggested by an experience described in Bradford, Sarah Hopkins. *Harriet, the Moses of Her People*. 1886. New York: Geo. Lockwood & Son, pp. 44-45.

Chapter 5, Miracle Inside a Storm from Hell

- After the destruction of the city of Jerusalem, the prophet Jeremiah prophesied the word of the Lord, saying, "And I will be found of you, saith the Lord: and I will turn away your captivity, and I will gather you from all the nations, and from all the places whither I have driven you, saith the Lord; and I will bring you again into the place whence I caused you to be carried away captive." *King James Bible*, Jeremiah 29:14. This essentially promised exiles true to the Lord a return to a new Jerusalem.
- Stand fast therefore in the liberty wherewith Christ hath made us free, and be not entangled again with the yoke of bondage, *King James Bible*, Galatians 5:1.

Chapter 7, A Force Inside the Dream of God

- According to what Jessie Miner said in his memories of Washington Island, Preacher Bennett claimed to have served under Commodore Perry at the Battle of Put-in-Bay during the War of 1812. This has been difficult to corroborate through the historical record.

Chapter 9, Chicago on the Road to Freedom

- Information about activities of abolitionists in Chicago is largely drawn from Campbell, Tom. 2009. *Fighting Slavery in Chicago: Abolitionists, the Law of Slavery, and Lincoln*. Chicago: Ampersand, Inc.

- Gordon Burr was one of my best friends when I was young and working with Wisconsin Indian Tribes. One of the leaders of the Stockbridge-Munsee, I have named this character in honor of his memory.

Chapter 11, Emerging Into Freedom

- Frederick Douglass became the most famous ex-slave in America after William Lloyd Garrison, who had founded the abolitionist newspaper, *The Liberator*, introduced him as a powerful speaker and storyteller to eastern audiences in pre-Civil War America. Wendell Phillips was an attorney who was one of the most respected abolitionist orators of his time. He also campaigned as a powerful advocate for American Indians.

Chapter 12, Arrival of a Prophet in Washington Island's Wilderness

- Gills Rock, on the tip of the Door Peninsula, was originally known as Hedgewood Harbor, a name given to it by a Washington Island fisherman and boat builder, Amos Lovejoy.

Chapter 14, Beneath the Waves, Above the Waves, A Song of Death and Light

- The steamship Niagara sank in Death's Door in 1856 due to a fire onboard. The schooner A.P. Nichols sank a year later when fierce winds and blinding snow tore apart her rigging and drove her onto rocks. Wisconsin Sea Grant, Wisconsin Historical Society. 2018. "Shipwrecks, Shipwrecks Everywhere!"

Chapter 15, The Vagaries of Time

- Let not your heart be troubled: ye believe in God, believe also in me, *King James Bible*, John 14:1.

Chapter 16, The Metamorphosis of Zeal

- So if the Son sets you free, you will be free indeed, King James Bible, John 8:36.
- For I know that my Redeemer liveth, and that he shall stand at the latter day upon the earth; and though after my skin worms destroy this body, yet in my flesh, my black flesh! I shall see God: whom I shall see for myself, and mine eyes shall behold, and not

another, though my reins be consumed within me, *King James Bible*, Job 19:25-27.

- The Preacher's sermon in this chapter is partially taken from Albert, Mrs. Octavia V. 1890. *The House of Bondage*. New York: Hunt & Raton, accessed from docsouth.unc.albert.html#albert130, 7/20/2017.
- Irish Village eventually was abandoned on Washington Island, primarily due to disagreements between the fishermen who lived there and those who purchased James Craw's warehouse in Washington Harbor.

Chapter 20, Chicago's Gift

- For it was little which thou hadst before I came, and it is now increased unto a multitude; and the Lord hath blessed thee since my coming: and now when shall I provide for mine own house also? *King James Bible*, Genesis 30:30.
- For God hath not given us the spirit of fear; but of power, and of love, and of a sound mind, *King James Bible*, 2 Timothy 1:7.
- There is more than one version of this battle. I use the one told by Holand in this passage, although Holand is not always the most accurate of the Door County historians. His version is the most colorful of those available. Martin, Chas I. 1881. *History of Door County, Wisconsin: Together with Biographies of Nearly Seven Hundred Families, and Mention of 4,000 Persons*. Sturgeon Bay, Wisconsin: Expositor Job Print, 1881) has the battle occurring between the Potowatomi and the Chippewa.
- Stockbridge, Munsee Delaware, and Brotherton Tribes migrated, due to pressure from white populations, from New York, Pennsylvania, and New England to Wisconsin in the 1820s and 1830s. The Oneida Tribe came to Wisconsin during the same time period.
- Therefore take no thought, saying, What shall we eat? Or, What shall we drink? Or, wherewithal shall we be clothed? *King James Bible*, Matthew 6:31-32.

Chapter 21, Beyond Fear and Depression

- Thou wilt shew me the path of life. In the Lord's presence is fullness of joy, *King James Bible*, Psalms 16:11.
- Behold, how good and how pleasant it is for brethren to dwell together in unity! *King James Bible*, Psalms 133:1.
- We are troubled on every side, yet not distressed; we are

perplexed, but not in despair, *King James Bible*, 2 Corinthians 4:8.
- Now the Lord is that Spirit, and where the Spirit of the Lord is, there is liberty, *King James Bible*, 2 Corinthians 3:17.

Chapter 22, Throwing Off Old Chains

- Noah Webster in 1783 created his speller using a method to teach reading that he called synthetic phonics, which first teaches letter sounds and then builds up blending these sounds together to teach the sounding out of words. In the 1800s *The American Spelling Book* was used in North America as a primary teaching text along with one of the readers available at the time.

Chapter 23, In the Chains of Having Lost Expected Love

- Behold, How good and how pleasant it is foe brethren to dwell together in unity. It is like the precious ointment upon the head that ran down upon the beard. Even Aaron's beard: that went down to the skirts of his garments; As the dew of Hermon, and as the dew that descended upon the mountains of Zion: for there the Lord commanded the blessing, even life for evermore, *King James Bible*, Psalms:33 1-3.

Chapter 24, The Working of Hope and Dreams in Being Human

- In the beginning God created the heaven and the earth. And the earth was without form, and void; and darkness was upon the face of the deep. And the Spirit of God moved upon the face of the waters, *King James Bible*, Genesis 1 1-2.
- Information about James Jesse Strang is largely drawn from Van Noord, Roger. May 1, 1988. *King of Beaver Island, The Life and Assassination of James Jesse Strang.* Urbana Champaign, Illinois: University of Illinois Press.

Chapter 25, Washington Island Ice

- These things I have spoken unto you, that in me ye might have peace. In the world ye shall have tribulation: but be of good cheer; I have overcome the world, *King James Bible*, John 16:33.

Chapter 26, A Time of Aftermaths

- For whether we live, we live, we live unto the Lord; and whether we die, we die unto the Lord: whether we live therefore, or die, we are the Lord's. For to this end Christ both died, and rose, and revived, that he might be Lord both of the dead and living, *King James Bible*, Romans 14:8-9.

- And I heard a great voice out of heaven saying, Behold, the tabernacle of God is with men, and he will dwell with them, and they shall be his people, and God himself shall be with them, and be their God, *King James Bible*, Revelation 21:3.
- Lo, children are an heritage of the Lord, King James Bible, Psalms 127:3.
- A man can receive nothing, except it be given from heaven, King James Bible, John 3:27.

Chapter 27, The Healing Human Spirit

- Therefore shall a man leave his father and his mother, and shall cleave unto his wife: and they shall be one flesh, King James Bible, Genesis 2:24.
- God so loved the world, that he gave his only begotten Son, that whosoever believeth in him should not perish, but have everlasting life, *King James Bible*, John 3:16.
- The reasoning in the passage about marriage practices in pre-Civil War black communities owes a debt to a discussion in O'Neill, Patrick W. 2009. *Tying the Knots, The Nationalization of Wedding Rituals in Antebellum American*. Chapel Hill, University of North Carolina: A dissertation in partial fulfillment of the requirements for the degree of Doctor of Philosophy in the Department of History, pp. 186-231.

Chapter 28, An Incident on Washington Island

- There is no sure history of what happened to the Noquet. It was a small band that lived in Wisconsin during the French fur trade. General historical opinion is that the tribe was related to the Menominee. Some historians believe the tribe was absorbed into the Menominee after first contact, but working with the Stockbridge-Munsee in the late 1970s I was told by an elder that what happened was that the Noquet were all killed by a smallpox epidemic caused by infected blankets given to them by an Indian agent, not an unusual story during the early reservation period of American history. I have used that story here.
- The Menominee are indigenous to Wisconsin. I have had a long association with the Menominee, helping to found both

Menominee Indian School District and the College of the Menominee Nation. The Menominee lived near Green Bay when the French explorer Jean Nicolet arrived there in 1634. The French called the Menominee *Folles Avoines*: "the wild oats people" because of their reliance on wild rice as a food source. Prior to the coming of the French the Menominee settled village sites at the mouth of the Menominee River.

- Reverend Porter and his wife, Eliza Chappel Porter, provided a way station on the Underground Railroad in Green Bay, Wisconsin in the years surrounding 1854. A plaque in front of the church commemorates that portion of church history. The University of Wisconsin—Green Bay library archives has Eliza Porter's description of those experiences in its collections.
- For God hath not given us the spirit of fear; but of power, and of love, and of a sound mind, *King James Bible*, 2 Timothy 1:7.

Chapter 29, Remembering a Winter Sky

- After the Fugitive Slave Act was passed by Congress and signed into law by President Millard Fillmore in 1850, bounty hunters, usually called fugitive slave hunters, began trolling through northern free states, looking for any black person that could not prove they were legally free blacks and not escaped slaves.
- But be ye glad and rejoice for ever in that which I create: for, behold, I create Jerusalem a rejoicing, and her people a joy, *King James Bible*, Isaiah 65:18.
- Basically this was the compromise between Clay and Illinois Senator Stephen Douglas that led to the Civil War. It generated fugitive slave bounty hunters that only required an affidavit from a southerner who claimed to be missing his human property. Free blacks as well as ex-slaves were caught up in the hunt since the blacks could not appeal to the courts for relief through a jury or any other kind of trial from a specious arrest. Special commissioners were paid $5 if an alleged fugitive was arrested and then freed as a result of possessing proof they were not an escaped slaves, and $10 if the black was sent away with the agent of the supposed slave owner. Over 20,000 blacks fled to Canada during the ten years after the Act's passage, increasing dramatically the traffic on the Underground Railroad.
- If ye have faith as a grain of mustard seed, ye shall say unto this mountain, Remove hence to yonder place; and it shall remove; and nothing shall be impossible unto you, *King James Bible*, Matthew 17:20.

- Westbrook refers to an incident on Detroit Island in 1834. The story is told by Holand, Hjalmar R. in *History of Washington Island, Door County, Wisconsin (Part 1)*. 1917. Chicago: The S.J. Clark Publishing Company.
- When the righteous are in authority, the people rejoice: but when the wicked beareth rule, the people mourn, *King James Bible*, Proverbs 29:2.
- Trust in the Lord with all thine heart; and lean not unto thine own understanding, *King James Bible*, Proverbs 3:5.

Chapter 30, From Inside the Gates of New Jerusalem

- Fear not, little flock; for it is your Father's good pleasure to give you the kingdom, *King James Bible*, Luke 12:32.
- By the 1860s roughly 150 fugitive slaves lived in Northern Michigan. As recounted in Chandler, D.L. "Little Known Black History Fact: Michigan's Upper Peninsula". Accessed at https://blackamericaweb.com/2017/02/23/little-known-black-history-fact-michigans-upper-peninsula, 2/4/2018, "one of the area's most notable destinations is Gaines Rock. The location is a rocky plot of land that juts out to Lake Superior. William Washington Gaines, a former slave, and his wife moved to the town of Marquette after leaving Virginia. At the turn of the century and beyond, Gaines Rock served as a haven for vagabonds and others with no place to go. Like the Gaines', many of the U.P. Black families came from Virginia, Georgia and other parts of the south looking for new opportunities."
- There are several different versions of the story of the Mormons coming to Washington Island in a raid. The account in Van Noord has a different flavor from those written from the Washington Island perspective. I take the elements of the story told here from Eaton, Conan Bryant. 1972. *Washington Island, 1836-1876*. Washington Island: Jackson Harbor Press, pp. 31-32.
- The famous case of Joshua Glover led to a Wisconsin Supreme Court decision that nullified the Fugitive Slave Act of 1850 in Wisconsin. Glover escaped from a slave owner, Benammi Stone Garland, in St. Louis Missouri to Wisconsin. When slave catchers who were agents of Garland found him, they captured him in his cabin late at night and drove through a heavy fog to Milwaukee where they threw Glover into jail. Abolitionists, led by Sherman Booth, however, found out about the capture and battered down the jail door and spirited Glover away in a buggy. He was on the run on the Underground Railroad in Wisconsin for 40 days before

he was finally put on a steamer so that he could escape to Canada. His story is fully told in Baker, Robert H. 2006. *The Rescue of Joshua Glover: A Fugitive Slave, the Constitution, and the Coming of the Civil War (Law Society & Politics in the Midwest)*. Athens, Ohio: Ohio University Press.

- The description of the arrest and imprisonment of Joel Westbrook was found in Miner, Jessie. 1937. Washington Island, WI: Duo Van Amateur Press, pp. 7-8. The first edition of Vol. 4 is in the Washington Island Historical Archives.

Chapter 31

- For this cause shall a man leave his father and mother, and shall be joined unto his wife, and they two shall be one flesh, *King James Bible*, Ephesians 5:31.
- Thou shalt not commit adultery, *King James Bible*, Exodus 20:14.
- Thou shalt not covet thy neighbor's wife. We have to be true in the flesh to the joining of a man and woman, *King James Bible*, Exodus 20:17. This is a misquote by Preacher, but gets across what he is trying to say.
- Martineau, Harriet. 1817. Deerbrook, A Novel. London: Edward Moxen, Dover Street.
- Wherefore laying aside all malice and all guile, and hypocrisies, and envies, all evil speakings, as new born babes, desire the sincere milk of the word, that ye may grow thereby, *King James Bible*, 1 Peter 2:1-2. This verse was given as the passage used by a Baptist preacher for a wedding in the slave narrative by Campbell, Israel. 2001. *An Autobiography. Bond and Free: or, Yearnings for Freedom, from My Green Brier House. Being the Story of My Life in Bondage, and My Life in Freedom: Electronic Edition*. Chapel Hill, NC: University of North Carolina, accessed at http://docsouth.unc.edu/neh/campbell/campbell.html, 1/1/18.

Chapter 32, Upon the Edge of Sanity and Fear

- Most of the Stockbridge who moved from New York to Wisconsin had already converted to Christianity. John Metoxen, their leader, was a Deacon in the Stockbridge Mohican Church. The Tribe, once they had settled on the Fox River, built both a church and a school that was taught by a Stockbridge teacher. Henry Miner's father was a respected missionary to the Stockbridge, and that was one of the reason Gordon Burr in the story is so accepted on the island.

- The title of the sonnet and the book is a paraphrase from a line written by Pablo Neruda in his poem, "Ode to the Eye." This sonnet was inspired during a workshop I attended in Door County led by Ralph Murre, then the Door County Poet Laureate, who handed me this line and asked me to write a poem with Neruda's words as its theme.

About the Author

 Thomas Davis helped found the College of the Menominee Nation with Dr. Verna Fowler and has been a leader in STEM education and supercomputing in Wisconsin, nationally, and internationally. He served as President of Lac Courtes Oreilles Ojibwa Community College in Hayward, Wisconsin; Little Priest Tribal College in Winnebago, Nebraska; and Acting President/Chief Academic Officer of Fond du lac Tribal Community College in Cloquet, Minnesota. Before retirement, when he and his wife, poet and artist Ethel Mortenson Davis, moved to Sturgeon Bay, Wisconsin, he served as Provost for Navajo Technical University in Crownpoint, New Mexico. He also helped found a number of national and international organizations that have affected the lives of American Indians and indigenous peoples from around the world.

After graduating from the University of Wisconsin Oshkosh, Davis began his career teaching English for one of the first Indian Controlled Schools, the Menominee County Community School. He was a key figure in the founding of Menominee Indian School District and was named Friend to Indian Education by the Wisconsin Indian Education Association in 1998.

In the world of literature and arts he served as President of the Shawano County Arts Council and helped found three literary publications: *The Rimrock Poets Magazine, The New Quiver,* and *Wisconsin Trillium.* In Door County he participates in the Wisconsin Fellowship of Poets, Write-On literary workshops, and the Dickenson Poetry Series.

Davis has published several books, including *Sustaining the Forest, the People, and the Spirit* (State University of New York Press 2000), which describes the forestry management and sustainable development of the Menominee Indian people. *Salt Bear (2012)* is a children's story about mythical creatures from the American West. *Inside the Blowholes* (2013) is about Anglo and Pueblo adolescents who find dragons in New Mexico's El Malpais area. *The Alkali Cliffs* (2014) is about a poor family fighting against a big bank in Colorado. Bennison Books, a British publisher, published Th*e Weirding Storm, A Dragon Epic* (2017), a formal epic poem about a young girl and the dragons that help her as conflicts between humans and dragons move inexorably toward human/dragon war.

For more information, visit his website: www.fourwindowspress.com

ALL THINGS THAT MATTER PRESS

FOR MORE INFORMATION ON TITLES AVAILABLE FROM
ALL THINGS THAT MATTER PRESS, GO TO
http://allthingsthatmatterpress.com
or contact us at
allthingsthatmatterpress@gmail.com

Made in the USA
Middletown, DE
31 March 2025

73437991R00184